WITCHFEST

The Hollowbeck Paranormal Cozy Mysteries
Book 4

AMELIA ASH

KIM M. WATT

STERLING & STONE

WITCHFEST

1. Pigs do fly

The pig was flying.

In the middle of a cocktail party.

I mean, I know it was Hollowbeck, and all manner of things that shouldn't happen did happen, but somehow the flying pig felt like a step too far, and I was really struggling to reconcile it with the swanky cocktail party surrounds. Where had the pig even *come* from? I looked around surreptitiously and sniffed my drink, just in case Tanya, who was in charge of the welcome cocktails, was having an off day. Not that I'd ever ask her to her face. She'd never gone full werewolf on me, or even part-wolf, and I had no desire for that to change.

"Pig!" a man shouted, and he was answered with a resounding slap. "*Ow! No!* I mean an *actual pig!*"

Well, that answered one question, at least, even if I still wasn't sure where the thing had come from. I turned in a circle, looking for a flying pig herder, and spotted a skinny, elderly woman in a deep red cocktail dress, who was pursuing the pig at as frantic a pace as the tight confines of her dress would allow.

"*Get back here!*" she screeched, waving a cream bun frantically, and the pig did a little loop-de-loop before zooming towards one of the long wooden tables that lined the town hall's grand ballroom, bearing champagne and mulled wine and bottles of dubiously-labelled spirits, vats of coffee and trays of cakes and pastries, sizzling hot plates of seafood and meat, and, in the case of the table the pig was aiming for, half a dozen different varieties of hot chocolate. One of the men behind the table saw the pig heading for them and dropped his ladle, splashing the contents over a waiting party-goer's white suit jacket. His wail of horror was drowned by the man's shout.

"*No!*" he yelled, waving frantically. "No, dammit, Elsie, not *again!*"

"I'm trying!" the elderly woman shouted back, pushing to run faster. The pig was trailing a lead studded with diamantes, a matching collar glittering on its neck. "*Horace!*"

Hot chocolate man slammed the lid onto the nearest fat-bellied pot, then grabbed the handles and hefted it up, evidently planning to stash it under the table or something similar. He must have misjudged the weight, though, because he staggered, almost dropped it, and banged it back onto the work surface, splashing hot chocolate over his hands with a yelp. The impact jolted the table hard enough to knock a tall whipped cream canister into half a dozen pretty, insulated glasses of hot chocolate, and they tumbled like dominoes, rolling across the red tablecloth and splashing their contents everywhere. One glass took out an open tub of chocolate shavings, another knocked over a tall jar of nuts, and still others felled the marshmallows, the Flakes, and the wafer straws.

Only the festive biscuits survived. Everything else spilled across the table and onto the floor, and a cockatoo, two ferrets, and a Chihuahua in a Santa suit all lunged for them. Their owners grappled to get the creatures away from the treats, pushing and shoving among themselves, and the pig redoubled his efforts, wings whirring frantically. He wasn't a massive pig, as far as that went, but he wasn't some miniature variety, either, and there was nothing delicate or flimsy about his wings. They were great leathery bat-like things, and their downdrafts blew fascinators and elaborate hairstyles into disarray across the hall and set people scattering. A good thing, too, as the pig evidently wasn't housetrained. Or air-trained.

"Elsie, *nooo!*" the hot chocolate man wailed, giving up on moving the pots and brandishing a ladle at the oncoming pig instead. His partner seemed frozen in shock, both hands clutched to his head. The pig's mouth was open as he swooped towards them, tongue lolling out eagerly and drool descending from his chops.

"*Horace!*" Elsie tried again. "Horace, *please!*"

Horace didn't respond. Horace was intent on the hot chocolate stand, little eyes glittering in delight, and Horace wasn't stopping for anyone.

Except Horace was also still trailing his leash, and was going right past me, so I lunged for it. I'd like to say it was from the goodness of my heart, but the truth was I'd already tried the smooth Swiss milk chocolate and the thick, rich Italian one, and I was not having a pig snaffle the spiced Mexican, dark Belgian, or super-rich French varieties before I did. Everyone else was just watching the pig go, and it didn't occur to me to wonder why until I had the leash snagged in one hand and was digging my unaccustomed high heels into the hall's smooth floor, hauling Horace to a halt.

"Be careful!" Elsie shouted.

"Let go!" someone else yelled, and I hesitated, still thinking of the treats at stake.

"No, don't!" hot chocolate man yelled, pointing the ladle at me. "He ruined *all* my stock last year!"

"I paid for it!" Elsie protested.

"Sure, but what about all the good will I lost because of it?"

"You're a hot chocolate stand!"

Horace zoomed side to side at the end of the leash with surprising strength, straining to break free and almost pulling me off my feet. I grabbed the soft leather in both hands, the leash biting into my fingers and my footing feeling more precarious by the moment. I wasn't exactly at my most stable in heels at any time, and I hadn't been planning on pig wrestling when I agreed to — or, rather, was press-ganged into — coming to the opening night cocktail party of Hollowbeck's Midwinter Festival. The crowd scattered out of the way of the seesawing leash, leaving the path between me and Horace free.

"Um, help?" I said, looking around for Elsie. "Are you going to take him?"

Elsie hadn't exactly rushed to join me. She started to say something but was cut off by Starlight shouting from behind me, "Morgan, look out!"

I was suddenly aware Horace wasn't trying to pull me off my feet anymore, and I looked back at him so fast my neck twinged painfully. That small discomfort was rather overshadowed by the mouthful of furious porcine teeth heading my way, though, as Horace swooped towards me, squealing as he came. Suddenly he didn't seem compact at all, but distinctly on the wild boar size scale. I gave a squeal that at least matched his, dropped the leash, and hit the ground on my belly as the pig swooped harmlessly over me and took off across the room. Elsie kicked off her heels and ran after him, waving frantically, and I looked up just as a pair of old but well-kept boots stopped in front of me.

Ben crouched down, hands dangling between his knees. "Are you alright?" he asked.

"No," I said, pushing myself onto my knees. "I just got attacked by a *flying pig*."

"Let me rephrase that. Are you hurt?"

"I don't think so." I took his hand when he offered it and let him pull me to my feet, his fingers warm and smooth, dark against my own winter-pallid skin. "Is the hot chocolate safe?"

He grinned, dimples surfacing. "I thought you were very passionate about stopping the pig. Now it all makes sense."

"Morgan!" Starlight exclaimed, hurrying up to us with her long pale hair caught in an intricate assembly of butterfly-shaped pins. She was wearing a pretty, floaty dress in shades of blues and greens that swirled around her as excitedly as she was swirling around the party. "That was *amazing.* And so brave of you!"

"Well, I don't know—"

"It was for the hot chocolate," Ben said, and I scowled at him. He just grinned back, making it very hard to be upset at him. We'd got off to a bit of a wobbly start when I first arrived in Hollowbeck, what with him dosing me up with calming teas (he claimed it was no different to camomile, but it was *magical* calming tea, which made it seem a bit more nefarious to my mind), but just a month or so back he'd taken on a zombie horde to help me, which I felt had rather earned him some points. Plus, dimples. And some very nice forearms for a librarian. Not that Hollowbeck's library was entirely like other libraries, and it probably required a certain level of fitness to handle its books.

"It *was* brave," Starlight said. "I wouldn't mess with Horace."

"Is this a regular occurrence?" I asked.

"Well, not *regular*," she said. "But he does get away from Elsie pretty often, and all the flying makes him super-hungry. He tends to trample anything that gets between him and what he wants to eat. Or he eats it as well." She looked up at the domed ceiling, where chandeliers glimmered softly from ornate sconces and rained warm light over the room. "Poor Mr Bennet lost a leg."

"He *what?*"

"It was a wooden leg, but Horace did chew it in half."

I looked at Ben, who shrugged. "I suppose that's why Elsie was running about with that bag of cream buns. Tastier than wooden legs."

"I'd have thought it would've been better to not have the wooden-leg-eating pig running — or flying — about a cocktail party."

"True," Starlight agreed. "But it's very hard to tell someone they can't keep their familiar with them. And you stopped him, anyway."

I straightened my dress and turned to look down the length of the hall, where I could see a woman standing on one of the tables with a chef's knife in each hand, keeping Horace away from some smoked salmon platters while Elsie jumped up and down underneath him, waving a cream bun hopefully. He swung one way, then the other, then shot out the big double doors in the direction of the hall kitchen. I winced, hoping they had the pots covered in there.

"Hot chocolate?" Ben offered.

"Yes," I said immediately, and fell into step with him and Starlight as we walked towards the tables, while around us the crowd re-formed quite as if there hadn't just been a near-miss with a flying pig.

Welcome to the Hollowbeck Midwinter Festival, I suppose.

~

The Hollowbeck Midwinter Festival was *the* event of the winter calendar, apparently, and the town had certainly thrown itself into preparations. For the last month, lights had been blossoming across all the streets in town, and shops had been sprouting tinsel and holly and wreaths like a highly infectious rash. Even the local coffeeshop, Bewitching Brews, had got in on the act, and James was splashing gingerbread syrup and peppermint sprinkles about the place with blatant disregard for those of us who still believed in the sanctity of a proper cup of black coffee. Petunia, the landlady at the guesthouse where my brother Ruiner and I had been living since we arrived, had pulled out an astonishing variety of frog-themed festive decor (who knew there was such a market for lights in the shape of Santa frogs?), and there had been mince pies and marzipan-encrusted fruitcake in the kitchen every morning since the first of December.

It was enough to make me consider moving out, although *considering* was as far as it had got. I had, as it happened, unexpectedly become the proprietor of a store with accommodation above it when we arrived in Hollowbeck, but the reason I'd acquired the place was due to the previous owner being found dead in her cauldron in the kitchen. Found by me. I wasn't convinced the old witch wouldn't still be haunting the place, no matter how many times Starlight saged things. Plus, Petunia had yet to charge us any rent, and always left food out for my whiny brother, so I wasn't super-motivated to make a change.

And even if I had moved out, the Cosy Cauldron, my shop, wasn't exactly a haven from the festiveness. I'd forbidden Starlight from bringing a scrap of tinsel or any inflatable snowmen over the threshold, but fairy lights were draped over every available surface, mulled wine-scented candles burned in the windows, and there were so many pine boughs on the shelves and in the window display that I was expecting squirrels to move in at any moment. Assuming they lived in pine trees. I wasn't sure about that.

And that was only the lead-up. The Midwinter Festival was the crowning achievement, thirteen days leading up to the winter solstice, with tonight's party plunging us into the final, longest three nights before the revelry of the solstice itself. *Opening party* was a bit of a misnomer, as it was always held on the Friday before the solstice, which Starlight said was because Friday was a witch's favourite day due to being associated with both Venus and Frigg. Ben, with rather more practicality as well as a lot of town history books at his disposal, said it was because no one was ever able to work the day after, and possibly the day after that, too.

Whatever the reason for the party's timing, there had been something wild and fierce rolling about the valley all throughout the festival. Even I, questionable witch that I was, could feel the deeper thrum of Hollowbeck's magic, as if the shorter days and deeper nights were wakening old power in the land, calling it into being with candy canes and mistletoe. The arrival of the market a week ago had only served to increase the feverish sense of excitement, stalls blooming like mushrooms in the green beyond the town hall. Lights flowed above the aisles like stars come to rest, creating glittering pathways overhead, and the stalls were awash with golden lights and flickering lanterns. The scents of mulled wine and cinnamon sugar curled themselves around the breath of pine and the whisper of spiced oranges, and it seemed to wash across the whole of town, so when I walked out the front door of Petunia's guesthouse every morning, I caught the whiff of midwinter celebrations, full of mystery and promise.

Not that I'd had any time to explore the market, because Starlight had been alternating between insisting I help her prepare all the salves and tinctures needed to fend off the town's collective hangover and incidental injuries, and dragging me into the local dressmaker to get something to wear for the upcoming solstice ball. I was highly reluctant on both fronts, as clothes shopping is even worse than other types of shopping, and also my charmed remedy skills weren't up to much. I hadn't been paying as much attention to them as I should have, mostly because I was still trying to get to grips with the ancient spell book I'd acquired along with the shop. The old witch's familiar, Jackie, had somehow chosen me to take it on, and with it a whole bunch of nefarious deals that bound half the population of Hollowbeck to the book in unpleasant ways. I was doing my best to figure out how to release everyone from them, but the results so far could politely be described as *mixed*, and more accurately as *a complete balls-up*, involving the book taking nasty little revenges on anyone it deemed wasn't fulfilling their deal. I was fairly sure both Jackie and I regretted her choosing me as the new town witch.

All of that, however, was now an after-Festival problem. Right now, the book and Jackie were tucked safely into a hiding place in the walls of Petunia's guesthouse, and I was standing in the middle of the most glamorous party I'd ever seen outside of a Netflix series, wearing a slinky black dress and about to have hot chocolate with a dimpled librarian with appealing forearms. I suppose I should've opted for champagne to really stick with the theme, but I hadn't fought a flying pig for nothing. I avoided the worst of the spillage in front of the stand and smiled at Ben as he turned to ask me what variety of hot chocolate I wanted, flicking some hair over my shoulder as elegantly as I could manage. The effect was rather ruined as a large cat with long, soft grey fur leaped to the table, slid across the tablecloth, and crashed into the just-righted topping jars, sending them flying again. He braced himself against the cloth to stop his slide, bunching the whole thing up and knocking over a clutter of empty glasses.

"Gods *take* you," the hot chocolate man complained. "Don't any of you have *any* control over your damn familiars?"

"Meow," the cat offered, sounding entirely unlike a cat, and stuck his head in the jug of whipped cream.

I grabbed the cat around his middle with both hands and hefted him off the table before the hot chocolate man could take after him with a ladle, which it looked like he was highly tempted to do. I didn't blame him. I'd not only wanted to take after my brother with hard objects, I had, more than once. It never changed anything, though. And his transformation into a cat hadn't improved matters.

"Hey!" he spluttered, but luckily he had such a gob full of cream it was a more convincing cat sound than his mew had been.

The cat. My brother. The Ruiner.

"Sorry," I said to the hot chocolate men, holding Ruiner out at arm's length. "He's a menace."

"Should have a leash on the damn thing," one of them grumbled.

"That really helped with the pig, didn't it?" Starlight

said, adjusting one of her butterfly pins, which was making a break for freedom.

"At least they were trying," the man protested, and Starlight sniffed.

"They're animals, not prisoners. And familiars, at that. Would *you* like to be chained up?"

Judging from one of the men's expressions, he wasn't against the idea if she were offering, so I just said hurriedly, "I'll try the dark chocolate."

Ruiner pawed at my arms, twitching his ears towards my shoulder, so I deposited him there with a sigh. My dress, which was a temporary loan for tonight while the dressmaker created my ballgown for the end of the Festival, had reasonable coverage on the shoulders, if not the front or back. Even so, I could feel my brother's claws very easily as he shifted around, trying to find a comfy spot.

"Get me some cream," he hissed.

I kept my voice low as I muttered, "You can't have cream. I have to live with the consequences."

Starlight must've heard me, though, because she said, "They must have lactose-free," and looked expectantly at the man currently ladling hot chocolates into fresh glasses. His companion had given up on glaring at Ruiner and was back to scanning the room with his ladle clutched in both hands, braced for the return of Horace.

"I *suppose*," Ruiner said. "I mean, I'd rather a whisky."

"You definitely can't have whisky," Starlight said.

"Not even in the cream?"

"*Shut up*," I hissed, and he growled, his tail whipping against my bare back. Ruiner definitely had a better grasp on some cat things than others, and when he remembered to shut up, he made a very pretty feline, only his blue eyes giving away the fact he might not have always been four-legged and furry. Hadn't been, in fact, until earlier this year, when he'd crashed into my tatty, post-separation flat and bounced me straight into a world of flying pigs, talking cats, and threatening books. Ruiner still refused to tell me exactly how it had happened, or who was responsible (other than himself and his endless ability to talk himself into trouble), and the only thing we were sure of was that, even in Hollowbeck, cats didn't talk, so he shouldn't be running his mouth in front of strangers.

Ben handed Starlight a glass of hot chocolate minus the cream, the liquid dark as tar, then passed me one crowned with a tower of whipped cream and chocolate shavings, as well as a small tub of lactose-free cream. Then he picked up his own glass, which was decorated with a Flake and curls of candied orange. "Everyone good?" he asked.

"Yes," I said, breathing in the scent of rich, sugary goodness, then yelped as Ruiner strained to reach the cream, digging his claws into me. "*Ow!*"

"Oh, stop whinging," he said, reaching for the cup with one front paw.

"Shut *up*," I said again, and Ben grabbed Ruiner, depositing him on the floor.

"*Hey*," Ruiner protested, and Starlight shushed him, then looked at me.

"You should get a bag for him. Like I have for Howard." She opened the big patchwork bag she had hanging from one shoulder, showing me the ferret curled inside. He was wearing a rather fetching yellow and green knitted jumper and yawned at me sleepily.

"I'm not carrying my brother around in a bag," I said, although, to be fair, it couldn't be much worse than him hanging out on my shoulder and trying to remove my skin with his claws. Still, I didn't want to make things too comfortable for him. For all his whinging, he'd adapted very well to being fussed over by women who didn't realise he wasn't really a cat, and having Petunia supply him with fresh fish every day was just the sort of hand and foot service he appeared to think he deserved. Or paw and paw, I supposed. He needed to remember that we were only stuck here for as long as it took for us to figure out how to reverse his curse, after all. It wasn't like we could stay in Hollowbeck forever, with me pretending to be a witch. We'd have to go back to real life eventually, at least when Mum finally threw all her toys out and insist I bring her precious boy home for Sunday dinner (as to why she didn't question why he didn't bring himself, well, that was just how little brothers worked, in my experience). I was struggling to come up with enough decent excuses for not going to hers for Christmas this year already.

But first, hot chocolate.

2. The mask-keeper comes

I LED THE WAY TO A BAR TABLE SET UNDER THE TALL, arched windows at the far end of the hall, Ruiner trailing me and muttering under his breath. To anyone else, hopefully, it just sounded like regular cat growls, but it was pretty graphic if you listened too closely. I put his cream on the table and left him to it, turning to the windows while Ben and Starlight pulled up stools. Heavy cream and gold brocade curtains framed the glass, which stretched almost the full expanse from the floor to the high ceilings, and I could feel the chill of the night creeping in, plaintive and lonely. Outside, lights glittered in the trees and bushes, lighting the paths to the market on the green, and gleaming on the snow.

We'd had a fresh fall last night, soft and delicate, and there was currently a snow creature competition underway on the green, which was visible beyond the low stone wall which encircled the hall's garden with its dormant flowerbeds and topiary wearing caps of snow. The competition looked to be made up of local kids, and things were escalating rapidly in the absence of any sort of adult supervision that I could see (although, given most of the adults I knew around here, it would likely only have got worse if they'd been involved). A snow spider scuttled after a sprinting girl who was yelling, *"I made you!,"* some snow rabbits were doing what snow rabbits do while half a dozen kids laughed helplessly, and a dozen snowmen of various proportions were having a pitched battle, limbs and eyes flying free to roll across the ground while their creators cheered them on. There was also a snow rhino that a small girl seemed to be renting out for rides in return for baked goods, which I highly approved of.

Beyond them, mired in the green, loomed the guardian of the winter solstice, a giant wicker structure with sweeping limbs and an androgynous form, holding an unlit torch aloft. It was creepy and beautiful all at once, and I had an odd moment of sorrow at the thought that the whole thing would burn at the moment of the solstice, ensuring the days would lengthen and the warmth return.

Ben joined me at the window, and we watched the battle for a moment. "Petunia's outdone herself on the snow," he commented.

"She always makes sure it's perfect for the market," Starlight said, perched on a stool with her mug clutched in both hands. "It's *so* pretty."

Starlight was annoyingly positive about utterly everything, but I had to agree with her on this. Petunia, as well as being my landlady, was the local weather witch, and while I did wonder if the rest of the country's customarily dire weather was due to her hoarding all the good stuff for Hollowbeck, I wasn't complaining. Not right now, anyway.

Ben and I both flinched as a snow-bear tore the head off a more classical snowman and used it to pelt the kids. That seemed to mark a sudden revolt, and the kids scattered as the snow monsters turned on them, their screams inaudible through the glass.

"Should we…?" I asked, gesturing at the snow-based carnage.

"I imagine someone's got it in hand," he said, not sounding very sure, and we watched a moment longer, until a couple of teenagers appeared with flaming torches and started chasing the monsters off. "In a manner of speaking," he amended.

Since no one seemed in danger of getting eaten by a snow-bear, I joined Starlight at the table, boosting myself onto a stool and rolling my feet with a sigh. I was already wondering if there was some sort of charm to make high heels actually comfortable, and was wishing I hadn't let Starlight talk me into the pretty but pocketless black dress. It very much wasn't my normal attire, or my normal sort of evening. But, as much as I might not have been very keen on either the heels or the lack of coverage in my dress, I was hardly going to miss a Hollowbeck cocktail party. I mean, I'd never even been to an average cocktail party, and a Hollowbeck one had to be a whole other level.

And so far, it hadn't disappointed. Isabella, the hostess with the mostess, as she had delighted in describing herself as the first time I met her (although she'd actually said *ghostess* with the mostess, which I hadn't figured out until later, but both worked), swept through the crowd in her eternal outfit of long, full dark skirt and white blouse that exposed a generous expanse of bosom, her dark hair curling over her shoulders and down her back. She nodded and smiled at the crowd, clasping her hands gratefully at the people working the refreshment tables and cooing at the geese and hamsters and unfeasibly large grasshoppers that guests were carting around as familiars, checking on everyone and missing nothing.

Music played from one corner, where a trio of musicians juggled unfamiliar instruments and veered from high energy renditions of soul classics to slowed down hip-hop beats with barely a breath between the two. A small collection of groupies whooped and cheered and tried to put words to the tunes without an awful lot of luck, and an elderly couple in matching, frothy gowns danced enthusiastically with zero regard for what the music was doing. Everyone else perched at tables or drifted about in knots and circles, exchanging pleasantries and complimenting hairstyles and the familiars' outfits, sipping on everything from single malt whiskies and Tanya's welcome cocktails to what I'd discovered was highly potent sparkling apple juice made by my own landlady. I'd had one glass and decided switching to hot chocolate was advisable if I wanted to stay upright for more than half an hour.

"So this is the Midwinter Festival?" I said to Starlight. "Snow-monster battles and boozy parties?"

She smiled at me, the butterflies in her hair shivering as she shook her head. "It's more than that. I mean, tonight *is* kind of a boozy party, I suppose, but traditionally it's where we acknowledge the darkness and all it brings, because we need the dark as well as the light. Then we call in the sun with the masquerade ball on the solstice." She looked around expectantly. "Alaric should be here soon, and we'll get our masks. I can't wait to see what mine is this year!"

I frowned. "You don't have one from last year?"

"We get a new one each year, because we as people are always changing. The mask has to reflect the energy we want to carry out of the solstice."

I made a non-committal sound. "What if I don't want one?" Or couldn't afford one, more to the point. Hollowbeck ran very much on a barter system, so unless this

Alaric was happy taking honey and mint jam in payment, I was a bit stuck.

Starlight gave me a look that was really far too horrified for the question. "You *have* to have one."

"Why? And why can't I just make one or something?" Not that I was any more crafty than I was witchy, but I should be able to cobble one together out of stuff in the shop.

"It's tradition," Starlight said, in the manner of someone who didn't feel such things required any more discussion. "*Magical* tradition. Do you really want to mess with it?"

"Well…" I looked at Ben, hoping he had something in his encyclopaedia brain to counter Starlight's enthusiasm.

He grimaced. "I read up on the masks a bit. They're all about warding off evil spirits and ensuring the town rises again out of winter."

"Yes, exactly," Starlight said. "The masks both stop the evil spirits recognising you and scare them off, but it's really a form of self-actualisation, if you ask me. Every winter solstice you rise anew, and the mask you choose to wear affirms your true self for the year ahead."

"That sounds like some really clever marketing by the mask-seller," I said, and Ruiner snorted, splattering cream out of his mug. "*Ew,* Ruiner."

He licked his chops. "What about me, then? I'm doomed to be possessed by evil spirits because I'm in cat form?"

"It's not like we'll be able to tell the difference," I said, and he bared his teeth at me.

"It's fun," Starlight insisted. "I mean, leaving aside the tradition part, it's all about projecting a different version of yourself onto the world."

"If that's what you *want,*" a new voice said. "I don't like masks, myself. Make you wonder what people are hiding, don't they?"

We looked up at Grace, standing with one slim hip cocked and a champagne glass in her hand, her soft dark hair tumbling over her shoulders in such an artful way there *had* to be charms involved. She wore a much slinkier black dress than mine, with the addition of a generous split over one thigh, and she gave us an amused smile. "I've never felt the need to hide who I am."

Well, no. If I looked like that, neither would I.

We made room for Grace at the table, not necessarily willingly, but I really had no reason to dislike her. I mean, there was the small matter of her twin being cosy with the witch who'd both murdered my predecessor Norma and tried to do the same to both Starlight and I, but that wasn't Grace. I didn't think. Her sister Faith wasn't just a twin, she was a carbon copy, and it still unsettled me somewhat. Then there was the fact Ruiner had *history* with Grace from his pre-cat days. And also that Grace was far too interested in my inherited grimoire, and her constant offers to help me sometimes crept into less *help* and more *here, let me take that off your hands*.

Still, she'd never *done* anything, and I couldn't dismiss the fact that I might just be unnerved by how much more witchy than Starlight and I she was. Grace practically oozed witchiness from her pores along with modelesque poise, and I didn't need any more reminding that I wasn't exactly excelling at the town witch position.

"Did you manage to sort out the marshmallow issue?" she asked me, sipping her champagne.

"Mostly," I said, trying to surreptitiously check if I had

chocolate in the corners of my mouth. I wasn't entirely lying about the marshmallows. The town chocolatier (because of course Hollowbeck had a town chocolatier) had apparently had a deal with Norma to make sure his chocolate always tempered perfectly. When I'd tried to free him from the bargain, one of his mixing bowls had started sprouting marshmallows like mushrooms, no matter how he scrubbed it or froze it or otherwise tried to clean it. And they continued to sprout whether he used the bowl or not, spilling out of his shelves and threatening to overwhelm the kitchen. Throwing the bowl out had simply shifted the issue to a different one, and he'd basically begged me to reinstate his deal. I hadn't, but I had suggested he try making marshmallow snowmen, and he was doing quite good trade from it.

"Well done," Grace said. "I'm telling you, you're going to be an amazing witch."

See? I had *zero* reason to dislike her.

The night unravelled slowly towards midnight, the music growing more frantic and the dancers more enthusiastic. More and more food appeared on the tables, along with glass after glass of unidentifiable spirits and wines and beers, and servers circulated through the room with trays, swapping empties for full plates and glasses. Familiars got loose and were chased across the room, accompanied by uproarious laughter, and outside the snow monsters fought to a standstill, leaving the lights washing across the lonely guardian and the green, and the closed stalls of the market. The heat and laughter of the partygoers filled the room, making me as lightheaded as the champagne Grace convinced me to swap to, and I decided the only option was to eat more mini Yorkshire puddings with roast beef and gravy, and little smoked trout quiches, and even some vegan tarts crowned with a wilderness of herbs. I was just arguing with Ruiner over the fact he couldn't simply lick the caviar off the blinis and leave the rest behind when Starlight said, "*Ohhh!* Here they are!"

"Here what are?" I looked up, and she pointed excitedly across the room. Her hair had slipped from the clips a little and left the butterflies looking as if they'd been doing a little dancing of their own.

"The masks!"

Ruiner took the opportunity to snatch another blini off Ben's plate, and I examined the crowd. I hadn't really been paying attention, but at some point, masks had started appearing. At least half the revellers were wearing them, and they weren't cardboard and plastic pound shop varieties. They were delicately detailed, slim half-masks crowned with feathers and dramatic, glittering accents, or larger ones with cat ears and horns and, weirdly, a lobster tail in one case. Others looked to be made of wood inlaid with shell and bone, gleaming above low-cut gowns and sharp suits, and still others — mostly on the younger attendees, but not exclusively so — were alarmingly realistic alien or dinosaur heads. Some had headdresses attached, or plague doctor-style noses, or sweeping constructions of gauze and tulle that swept behind the wearer, glamorous and disconcerting all at once. I thought I spotted Petunia in a green mask with foliage blooming gracefully above it, scattering blossoms and scent as she moved, and Asger in an astonishing contraption of wood and iron, which looked both heavy and impractical. He seemed to be tangled up with Ruby's own towering headdress of twisting horns, and they were both laughing helplessly and doing nothing to untangle themselves.

"Wow," I said, and Ruiner looked around, licking his chops.

"Impressive," Ben agreed, not sounding much more enthusiastic than me.

"What did you have last year?" I asked him.

He shook his head. "I went home. This is my first Festival."

Well, at least I wasn't the only novice. Starlight slipped off her stool, clapping her hands excitedly, and, as if summoned, a man swept out of the crowd. His age was impossible to place, but he was tall and broad shouldered, with slim hips and the sort of lush, shiny brown hair than made my fingers itch to touch it, although his outfit was countering the effect somewhat. It consisted of black trousers that were a smidge too tight and a white shirt with the top buttons undone, the whole outfit walking a *very* fine line between the aesthetic of an Eighties romance book cover and that of a Nineties magician. He was pulling it off, though, and rather effectively judging by the flush rising on Starlight's cheeks and the excited chatter in his wake.

Sticking to theme, he took one of Starlight's hands in both of his and gazed at her with rich brown eyes, the lights dancing in them. "*Starlight,*" he breathed.

"You remember me!"

"How could I forget?" He squeezed her hand a little tighter, pulling it to his chest. "And where is your love?"

"Oh, I'm single now."

"*How* is that possible?"

She giggled, and Ruiner growled. I poked him with one finger and stole a look at Grace. She took a sip of her champagne, then unfolded herself languidly from the stool, walking off without saying a word. Ben caught my gaze and shrugged.

The man released Starlight and smiled at us. "Ah, new faces! Who is this lovely couple?"

"We're not a couple," I said hurriedly, and Ruiner snorted, arching his whiskers at Ben, who just took a sip of beer without answering. "Morgan," I added.

"Morgan! *Delighted.*" He didn't move to grab my hands, which I was *mostly* happy about, and instead pressed a hand to his chest, bowing slightly. "I am Alaric, the keeper of the masks."

"Hi," I said. That was a weird way to put it, but I suppose you could charge more as a mask-keeper than a mask-seller. Sounded more exclusive, didn't it?

Alaric introduced himself to Ben, who shook hands with him a little stiffly, then turned back to Starlight, taking hold of her arms as he examined her. "Yes," he said. "I have just the thing. Finn?"

It was only then that I noticed the man standing a couple of steps away, a large wicker basket which looked a bit like a laundry hamper clutched in front of him. He set it down, a thick mess of multihued brown-blond hair spilling over his forehead, and stepped back, tucking his hands into the back pockets of his jeans, unshowy and patient. His eyes were pale, grey where the light caught them, and I found myself watching him instead of Alaric as the mask-keeper tapped the basket lid before opening it and fishing around inside. Finn didn't watch the performance, just examined the crowd, and when his eyes slid to me, he looked faintly startled, then gave me a small smile. I smiled back, the hall suddenly warmer than it had been a moment before.

"Ah-ha!" Alaric exclaimed, producing a mask with a flourish, and Starlight squealed, bouncing up and down. I frowned, and Ruiner twitched his ears at me. That was excessive even for Starlight levels of excitement.

Alaric passed her the mask, smiling like an off-duty Santa, and Starlight spun towards us, holding it aloft, a frothy creation dripping in pale, glittering jewels and gauzy pastel swirls of lace and tulle.

"Look! Isn't it beautiful?" She held it to her face, striking a pose, and for a weird, disorienting moment, it wasn't Starlight anymore. Her dress curled and twisted like a living thing, and wings as fragile as the mask's gauze blossomed above her. I could have sworn her mouth stretched and distorted, her delighted smile grown hungry and toothed, and Ruiner hissed, backing up across the table until he was next to me. She whipped the mask away again, grinning, and then it was just Starlight once more. "Don't you love it?"

Ruiner and I looked at each other, then at Ben, but he only smiled encouragingly and said, "Very nice," while not looking at all horrified.

"Um," I started, and Starlight spun back to Alaric.

"Oh, do Morgan next! I can't wait to see hers!"

"I don't want a mask," I said immediately, and Alaric raised his eyebrows. Behind him, Finn gave me a curious look, the corners of his mouth quirking up.

"But you need one for the ball," Starlight said.

"I don't *want* one." I didn't know what I'd just seen, but I didn't like it. Plus they were basically works of art, so there was no way I could afford one unless Alaric had a bargain bin in the bottom of his basket.

"Everyone needs a mask for the ball," Alaric said. "And *Unmasked* serves all needs. We have a mask for everyone, collected from all over the world, from the finest of artisans and the smallest of producers." He swept an arm in a grand gesture that took in the entire ballroom. "One can buy *a* mask anywhere. But only *Unmasked* provides you with *the* mask, the one that allows you to be your true self."

"That seems to kind of go against the whole point of masks," I said.

"No, no. A mask allows you to bare your soul while hiding your identity," he said. "One is never so honest as when one is masked, and that is what we do. We sell freedom of self, don't we, Finn?"

"*Mmm-hmm,*" Finn said, closing the lid of the basket. His shoulders did things under his white T-shirt that were quite distracting, but not distracting enough to convince me a mask was a good idea.

"And look how lovely mine is!" Starlight insisted.

"Let's see what we can find," Alaric said, tapping the basket again, one-two-three, quick and neat.

"Is no one listening?" I demanded. "I don't *want* a mask. I don't even want to go to the damn ball!"

"I think you have to," Ben said, and I scowled at him. He spread his hands apologetically. "You know how Hollowbeck works. Some things you just have to do."

"Balls aren't my thing. I'm not sodding Cinderella," I said, holding onto my scowl for a moment longer, then sighed. Ben was the one person — other than my furry brother — who still seemed to understand just how weird Hollowbeck was. Even others who had come in from outside the valley somehow fell into the strangeness and accepted it as just the way things were. But Ben didn't. He'd buried himself in all the books and the history, though, so if he said this was one of those things that had to happen, he was probably right. He wouldn't just be blindly repeating it. It'd be one of those things like the roads to the valley simply bypassing it if someone tried to get there uninvited, refusing them entry, or mobile phones ceasing to work as soon as you were over the border. Or like deals made with old witches being bound by blood to a book, and inherited by whoever owned it, tying the deal-maker into an eternal debt.

"*Fine,*" I said, and Alaric lavished a smile on me that sent a warm current through my stomach despite myself.

"Let us see what mask the young witch will wear," he said, and the warm current turned chill and strange, twisting in the pit of my stomach as the noise of the room retreated, and the mask-keeper reached into the depths of the basket, those dark eyes never leaving mine.

I didn't want it. *I didn't want it.* The words wouldn't come out.

3. It begins

"AH-HA!" ALARIC SAID AGAIN, SWEEPING A MASK OUT OF the basket with a flair that reinforced his Nineties magician credentials, then paused, frowning at it. "No. This is not for you." He shot Finn a disgruntled look, and the other man held his hands up in an apologetic gesture, but didn't say anything. I wasn't sure if Finn was younger than Alaric, or if the dynamic was simply that of employer/employee. His age was as impossible to guess as the mask-keeper's, but the way he faded into the background made him seem younger.

Alaric rearranged his face back into the charming smile and turned to Ben, offering the mask to him with it cupped in both hands. "But it is, of course, perfect for you, man of books and knowledge. The basket never lies!"

"No?" Ben said, looking from Alaric to me. I gave a helpless shrug, and Alaric raised his well-formed eyebrows, waiting. Ben took another sip of beer, sighed, and took the mask, turning it over in both hands. It was a full-face one, wrought in some dull, worn metal, riveted and etched in decorative swirls, looking like a very fancy version of a knight's helmet.

"Thanks?" he said, not moving to put it on.

Alaric didn't push the point, just smiled and tipped me a wink before returning to the basket. Again that trio of taps, a little firmer this time, and I found my gaze fixed on his hands as he opened the top, fishing inside briefly before straightening up, his smile spreading as he turned back to me. He offered me the mask in the same way he had Ben, supported in his cupped hands. It was light and small, barely enough to cover my eyes, a deep matte black without any ornamentation at all, no feathers or sequins or paint. But the material itself was cut into a delicate filigree, curls and tendrils and feathered edges, looking more as if it had bloomed from some nighttime seed than been made.

I didn't want to touch it, as if it were an ornament in one of those shops with *you break it you buy it* signs, but Alaric nodded at me as I hesitated, his smile gentle. I met his gaze, still wanting to refuse, but there was so much warmth and understanding in his eyes that I couldn't disappoint him. It felt like I'd be slapping him in the face, and that was hardly a good look for the town witch. I took the mask, desperately fragile under my fingers, and for one moment I imagined simply crushing it to dust, but instead I lifted it to my face without meaning too, the motion automatic and natural.

It fit perfectly, as if it had been moulded to the exact lines of my cheeks, and I couldn't even glimpse it in my peripheral vision. I could barely feel it, it was so soft and light. A shiver worked its way up my spine, the ballroom bright and luminous through the eyeholes, the noise of the crowd rushing around me, music painting the night. I held the mask in place with one hand and lifted the other, examining it. Light glittered on my fingertips, as if I'd dipped them in a tank of luminescent paint, and I blinked, tapping them together and watching them spark. That was new.

Ruiner growled, a low, angry sound, and I jumped, pulling the mask away and looking at my fingers again. They were perfectly normal, no fireworks in sight, and no one else seemed to have noticed anything untoward. Starlight spun on the spot, her mask held to her face, and Ben clutched his, still looking uneasy. I looked at Finn for some reason, as if he could explain what had just happened, but his attention was on the basket, a slight frown drifting over his face.

"You're welcome," Alaric said, giving me that warm, inviting smile again. It didn't seem to have the same effect this time, and I wondered if there had been a bit of enchantment to it before, some salesman glamour.

"Sure. I mean, thank you." I glanced at Starlight, glimpsing again the shadow of wings and teeth at the edge of my vision as she twirled.

"They're *perfect*," she said, finally stopping.

Perfect for something. I just wasn't sure what.

ALARIC MOVED OFF, continuing his mask-Santa routine around the room with Finn lugging the basket after him. Well, *lugging*. It was nowhere near big enough to hold all the masks that were being handed out, and Finn carried it fairly casually, so it couldn't have been that heavy. Although, his shoulders looked like he wouldn't have had much trouble with it even if it had been full.

"Oh, *Starlight*," Isabella exclaimed, and I was pulled from a lingering assessment of Finn and his enticing shoulders as the mayor swept up to our table. She clasped both hands in front of her chest and stared at Starlight. "You look *beautiful!*"

And if I forgot the lingering unease in my belly, she really did. The mask somehow deepened all the purples and blues of her dress and turned her pale hair to silver and gold, rendering her luminous and delicate. She struck a pose, and I caught that disorienting glimpse of those half-seen wings again, the lines of her face shifting and untrustworthy.

I frowned. "Is that a bloody fairy princess mask?"

"I do feel like one," she said, pirouetting, and Isabella clapped in delight.

"I met a fairy," I said. "Well, a Fae. In Darrowdale. He wanted to steal me off for a couple of hundred years. It's not something to aspire to." I thought about it. "He did lend me his bike, though, so he wasn't all bad."

"I'm not stealing anyone away," Starlight said, and pointed at me so imperiously I thought I saw a wand in her hand, complete with a sparkly star at the tip. "Put your mask on!"

"No," I said.

"Oh, *please* show me," Isabella said. "I'm sure it's just *perfect.*"

It was basically impossible to say no to Isabella, not because she was the mayor, but because she was Isabella, and was simply that sort of person. So I sighed and put the mask on, lacing the ribbons behind my head and shivering as the thing melded to me once again. Ruiner stared up at me with his pupils wide in his blue eyes, and I said, "There. Happy?"

No one answered for a moment, the warm air of the ballroom brushing against my cheeks and curling in my hair, whispering something I couldn't quite hear. Goosebumps blossomed on my bare arms, and beyond the scents of perfume and candles and mulled wine spices I could somehow smell the snow, sharp and crisp, and a strange undercurrent of ozone. Instead of the chill I'd felt when I first tried the mask on, there was heat in my fingertips and uncurling in my belly, a fire formed from some strange, wild excitement, as if I stood on the precipice of something I couldn't quite touch. Isabella pointed behind me and I spun to face the tall windows, an unfamiliar grace blossoming in the movement, as if, for the first time, I wasn't expecting to stumble. My reflection stared back at me, the simple dress rendered suddenly exquisite, curling itself around me like mist taken form, the black cloth run through with variegated shades of grey, covering everything yet somehow sexier than anything I'd ever wriggled myself into in any of my going out days. It clung to me lovingly, and had given me some unfamiliar cleavage while also doing very nice things to my legs.

And the mask … The mask. It was made for the dress, or the dress was made for it, the dark shades echoing each other and setting off the blue of my eyes, the same as my brother's. And rather than crushing my hair, it turned it into a tumble of unruly browns, so that I touched it with a sense of bewilderment.

"I don't like it," Ruiner announced, the hair on his spine rising, and the heat was gone as quickly as it had arisen, my stomach crawling with fright. I pushed the mask up onto my forehead, and my reflection was me once again, the dress pretty but unremarkable, my hair bunching up under the mask's ribbons. I turned away from the windows.

"Me either," I said, avoiding Isabella's gaze. She was frowning faintly, brow furrowed in concern.

"But it's perfect," Starlight insisted. She had her mask

off but was bouncing gently from one foot to the other, as if desperate to be prancing around again.

"I really don't know how else to say *I'm not going to the ball.*"

Isabella made a small noise of disagreement. "Of course you're going to the ball, Morgan."

"No. I don't dance—"

"You do," Ruiner said. "I mean, *really* badly, but you do."

"After a few drinks. I'm hardly going to be good then."

"Maybe if you were drunker, you'd dance better."

I ignored him. "One big party in a week's enough for me, Isabella. It's too much."

"But it'll be a delight," she said, doing that spooky there-then-not thing, so she was suddenly standing next to me. She linked her arm through mine without actually touching me and tipped her head towards me. "And, as the town witch, you do have certain responsibilities. You need to be there, I'm afraid."

I groaned. "But I never *wanted* to be town witch."

"Yet you do such a wonderful job of it," she said, and looked at Ben. "Doesn't she, Benji?"

"Absolutely," he said, then added, without much hope in his voice. "Ben. Benjamin, even. Please."

"How about you, Isabella?" Starlight asked. "What's your mask like?"

"Unfortunately, masks aren't an option for me," Isabella said, and Starlight flushed.

"Oh! Of course. I'm sorry. They're just … they seem to have masks for *everyone*, so I thought…"

"That they'd have ghostly ones too?" Isabella chuckled. "Even Alaric hasn't come up with anything like that yet." She gave us all a little wave and swept off again, and I watched her go, vanishing into the press of revellers, more and more of whom were masked. A pack of kids in cat masks chased a dinosaur-headed man across the room without much respect for the food chain, and a teenaged boy in a tiara and a pink half-mask danced delicately in the middle of a circle of his cheering peers, half-seen swirls of ribbon and tulle snaking around him. A woman in a gorilla mask raced past, using her hands to help her along, and another woman ran after her, shouting, "Can you just *stop?* You're going to make yourself sick if you keep eating so many bananas!"

"You see this, right?" I said to Ben, since Starlight was dancing again.

"What's that?" he asked.

"The people wearing the masks. They're acting a bit weird. Plus there's … stuff." I waved vaguely, meaning the trails and shapes that surrounded the mask-wearers, half-seen and undefined, wings and horns and extra limbs.

"Stuff?" We watched an elderly man in an astronaut's helmet bounce past, taking alarmingly big strides that my head couldn't quite make sense of. "What d'you mean?"

"*That,*" I said, pointing at the bouncing man.

Ben didn't answer straight away, then he said, "Well, it is Hollowbeck. They're hardly going to be just normal masks, are they?"

Which made perfect sense, of course, as much as anything in Hollowbeck ever did, but it still seemed *off* somehow, as if the oddness had been dialled up a notch and everyone was too enamoured with their masks to notice. I leaned over the table and said to Ruiner softly, "Do *you* see anything weird?"

He looked away from the twirling Starlight and said, "Morgan, the whole town's bonkers. You should know that by now."

"More weird than normal."

There was a pause, as if he were considering it, then he said, "Yes. Those masks are super creepy. And the people wearing them..." He trailed off, and I understood that. It was hard to even be sure what I was seeing.

"Good. It's not just me, then." I wasn't sure how much better it should make me feel, that there was extra strangeness going on at the Midwinter festival, but at least I wasn't imagining it. The last thing I needed was to become the town eccentric as well as the town witch.

THE MASKS CONTINUED to spread throughout the room, and the strange, half-glimpsed visions flowed with them. It was unsettling, made more so because no one except me and Ruiner seemed to think anything at all was wrong. I'd lost my appetite for both the trays of snacks that were still circulating and the drinks, and was just wondering if I could sneak off home unnoticed when the ringing sound of a bell echoed through the room. Everyone fell silent, turning towards the door to the entry hall expectantly. Theodore, the entirety of Hollowbeck's police force, had climbed onto a chair, his dark hair slicked back and his cheekbones looking sharp enough to cut the night. A charcoal grey suit hung from him in a manner that would've made even Grace look dowdy, but it was rather offset by the colour of his skin. He'd evidently really dosed up on the fake tan for the event and was virtually luminous.

"Friends," he said, his voice clear and carrying. "It is time."

He didn't say anything else, just stepped down from the chair and vanished from view, but everyone in the room surged towards the hall doors, and I scrambled off my stool, caught by the movement. "Time for what?" I asked Ben. "What's happening?"

"For the Festival to begin," he said, and slipped his mask into place, his warm brown eyes examining me through the eyeholes of the knight's helmet. It looked to fit him just as well as mine did me, and it made him alien and strange, hiding his dimples and easy smile. He swept me a bow and offered me his arm as he straightened up. "My lady?"

"Um…" I stared at his arm, and Starlight rushed up to us.

"Come on, come *on!* It's starting!"

"Right," I said, and took Ben's arm, since he was still looking at me expectantly. He patted my hand in a weirdly paternal manner, and Ruiner leaped to my shoulder, claws digging in as he tried to balance. I winced but let him be, his weight oddly comforting as we followed the flow of the crowd, Starlight dancing ahead of us with her mask firmly in place, giving me glimpses of those swirling colours and gauzy wings. "Do you really not see that?" I asked Ben.

"I see only your beauty," he replied, inclining his head, and Ruiner spluttered laughter until I shoved him off my shoulder. He wasn't *that* comforting.

"Sure, okay," I said to Ben. "Method acting, is it?"

"Yeah," he said, and pushed the mask onto the top of his head, carefully not meeting my gaze. "Sorry. Got a bit carried away."

"No kidding," I said, but I left my hand on his arm, and he kept his own on top of it. It was warm, okay?

The revellers were oddly silent, no one chattering or laughing as we washed out of the hall, a silent mass of humanity following in the wake of the vampire police sergeant. We passed through the entrance hall and out the vast double doors that stood open onto the clean-swept steps and snowy gardens beyond. Outside, we crossed the garden and walked out onto the green, through the glittering night to the towering wicker guardian and the unlit bonfire at its base, forming a circle around Theodore where he stood next to it. He gripped a flaming torch in one hand, lighting his face in severe angles, and snow was falling, delicate as a promise. I barely felt the chill of it. The sharp, clear dark, the loom of the stars above, the golden light rolling from the hall — it all stole the breath from me, and I lifted my face to the sky, full of a sudden, wild hope, some resurgence of the heat the mask had woken in me.

Then Ruiner tried to jump to my shoulder again and just ended up clawing his way painfully into the flimsy material of my dress while I swore and grabbed him, shaking off Ben's grip at the same time. "Stop *doing* that," I hissed, settling him into my arms as well as I could. It was always a bit awkward for the both of us. We weren't a huggy family.

"I'm going to get frostbite on my paws," he whispered, and Starlight shushed us both.

Isabella stepped up next to Theodore, her hair gleaming in the light of the torch and a stray branch from the bonfire protruding from her arm. "We begin," she said, sliding a hand down over her eyes to mime putting a mask on. The crowd shuffled, a whisper of movement running through it along with the rising tide of excitement. Starlight tugged my arm, pointing at my own mask, and I reluctantly slid it into place, delight and misgiving warring with each other in my belly.

"Midnight comes," Theodore intoned, his voice deep and rolling, and the crowd shifted and sighed. "The countdown continues. The deepest shadows of winter approach.

Yet we stand firm against the night. Against the darkness. And we wait for the sun."

"*The sun,*" everyone breathed, and Ruiner and I looked at each other. I could tell he was thinking just the same as me — that Theodore was hardly looking forward to long summer days. Not a vampire's best friend, those.

"Three days," Theodore continued. "Three nights. Hold firm, my friends. The sun returns, and we *rise.*" His voice rose to a shout on the last word, and the crowd shouted it back.

"*We rise with the sun!*"

Theodore plunged the torch into the bonfire, and it caught with a hungry *whoomph*, the flames roaring into the night with an explosion of sparks. All around, the smaller green braziers burst into life without anyone going near them, and an *ooh* went up from everyone, me included. The guardian remained untouched by the bonfire, but its torch flared into sparkling green and purple flames, transforming it from a silent monolith into something trembling with secret life.

"*The Festival begins!*" Isabella shouted, her bare arms lifted to the night as she spun on the spot, skirts swirling and hair flying. "*It begins!*"

A cheer burst from the masked crowd, a raw, animal sound as hands were raised towards the sky and masked faces looked to the long winter dark, raised in defiance and delight. Everyone started moving, circling the guardian in a stomping, dancing mass, and I joined them without even thinking about it. My heart thrummed, my breath raw in my throat, and I hugged Ruiner to me without thinking about it. He didn't complain, his tail whipping and his blue eyes narrowed, and all around us ran a feverish, night-defying, winter-banishing excitement. I'd lost sight of Starlight and

Ben, swept up in the adrenaline of the wild dance, every face hidden behind their strange and treacherous masks, ridiculous and unnerving all at once. The mirages I'd glimpsed inside blossomed everywhere, ghosts in the dark, fiercer out here and charged with potential and promise, gifts from the masks to help call back the sun. Everything was darkness and dreams and wild, wild magic, and I was part of all of it, more so than I've ever been a part of anything. I *belonged,* just as every single one of us did, child and adult and familiar alike.

I don't know how long we would have spun out there in the cold, revelling in the night and forcing back the winter, if a scream hadn't gone up, holding none of the joy that surrounded us.

It was a scream of pure terror, and the crowd ground to a horrified halt, while I clutched my brother tighter and spots swam in my vision, and someone shouted, "Is she dead? *Is she dead?*"

Suddenly the dark was a lot more dangerous than it had been a moment ago, and we were nothing more than children playing dress-up, shouting pointlessly at something so much vaster and older than any of us.

4. Alcohol & magic-workers don't mix

THE CROWD PUSHED ONE WAY THEN THE OTHER, TORN between the voyeurs' desire to see what had happened and the very sensible urge of self-preservation, a need to flee before the night claimed its next victim. Ruiner and I were caught up in the tangled mass, jostled from all sides as masked faces loomed all around us, eyes shining and unreadable, mouths twisted in unfamiliar shapes, a chaos of swirling dresses and sharp suits and wailing fright. I had one moment of near-panic, where I wondered if the dead woman *(dead? Really? Again?)* had been mown down by the sheer weight of the crowd, and if I'd be next, then I put my head down and shouldered my way out of the pack, employing elbows and the sharp heels of my shoes with grim abandon.

I spilled out of the pack onto the edge of the green closest to the market. The tents and cabins were painted in cheery colours that felt strained and false, the glimmering fairy lights no more comforting than my previous experience with a Fae had been. Ruiner was growling steadily, a low, uneasy noise, and I looked back at the mass of people.

A steady stream was retreating into the hall, but a lot were still clustered in a semicircle at the base of the guardian, drawn in tight against the dark and silhouetted by the flames of the bonfire. I could only imagine what lay inside their circle.

I took a couple of unsteady breaths and watched someone hurry towards one of the market tents, a big one with double peaks and twisting patterns worked into the fabric. It looked like it should be in some fantastical bazaar, not crouching in a Cumbrian village green. As much as Hollowbeck could be said to be in Cumbria, anyway, which I wasn't sure of. Light shone off the man's thick, untidy hair, and I frowned. He pulled a panel of the tent open, evidently meaning to duck inside, then stopped and stepped back as someone else emerged. The newcomer wore black trousers and a heavy, swinging overcoat, and seeing them together, I was sure it had to be Finn and Alaric. They conferred briefly, then turned to look at the hall. It felt as if they were looking directly at me, and I took an involuntary step back, unsettled by the scrutiny. But of course they were looking this way. There had been screams. It'd be weirder if they *weren't* looking.

Ruiner's growl hiked into a snarl, and I looked down at him, startled. His tail thrashed, and his ears were back as his eyes flicked over the crowd.

"What?" I almost whispered.

"The *masks*," he hissed, and I stared at the gathering. Everyone was still wearing them, true, and I had the sudden sense of seeing things on two levels, like paper in the rain, some previous truth bleeding through from underneath the current one. But it didn't seem dangerous. Just as strange as before. Even so, I pushed my own mask up hurriedly, flinching at the cold, as if I'd just thrown back a duvet in an under-heated bedroom. The night was suddenly starker and more unfriendly, the heat in my belly gone.

"What do you mean?" I asked. "They look the same as before."

Ruiner just snarled again, his whole body vibrating, and I gave him a very small shake.

"Stop it. You're not *actually* a cat, you know."

He stopped growling, narrowing his eyes at me, then said, "I *know.*" That sounded more like the usual Ruiner, at least.

"So what's with the noises?"

"I don't know. Instinct, whatever. But all this — the shouting at the dark, and evil spirits, and masks, and now someone's dead? Something's off."

"Yes, that was kind of indicated by the someone being dead bit."

"Tell me you don't feel it, Morgs."

I looked away, seeing Finn and Alaric still at the tent, apparently in heated conversation. Or Alaric looked heated, anyway, but that might be just how he talked. He'd certainly been given to a lot of waving and flourishing earlier.

"Morgan?" Ruiner insisted, and I pulled my attention reluctantly back to the crowd. I'd thought it, hadn't I? That the wild dance was full of raw, hungry energy, something dangerous and not to be trusted. But that wasn't Hollowbeck. Hollowbeck was organic honey, and *this milk came from our cow Bessie,* and *Bob grew this apple,* and locally brewed beers in the pubs (well, other than the one dodgy pub. The other two, though). It was kids on bikes and people chatting on the pavement and old ladies with shopping trolleys and alligators. It wasn't murder by dance mob.

"We don't know what's happened," I said aloud. "It was probably an accident. The cold or something."

"I told you, Morgan. I *told* you this place isn't all tea parties and enchanted bird houses."

"Yet you still brought me here," I shot back, then tipped him unceremoniously to the ground, not waiting for an answer as I straightened my back and strode into the crowd. I was the town witch, and I was going to find out what the hell was going on.

My striding only lasted a couple of paces before it turned into a sideways shuffle and a lot of 'excuse me's and 'coming through's. The crowd had thinned out, but there was still a press of fifty or so people huddled together like a flock of anxious sheep, with a space at their centre. I elbowed my way to its edge, shivering steadily and my feet painfully cold, but I forgot about that entirely as the last onlooker stepped aside and I saw Theodore and Isabella, their backs to the bonfire. The mayor was standing, one hand pressed to her chest and her head bowed sorrowfully, while Theodore knelt in the trampled snow next to the prone body of a woman. She was face-down, the skirts of her dark dress spread out like the petals of a flower, brown hair flowing over her shoulders and spilling onto the snow, obscuring her face. I froze, looking at the slim line of her back and the pale skin of her half-exposed legs, searching for injury or meaning, but the whole tableau was like some hideous still-life, cast in black and white. I looked at Theodore, his skin luminously orange in the light of the bonfire, the only colour in the piece.

"Who is it?" I asked, my throat so tight I had to force the words out.

He looked up sharply, his eyes dark pools that reflected the stars, hungry and endless, and stared at me for a long moment before he said, "I thought it was you."

I took a step closer, staring down at the woman on the ground. Her dress was the same colour as mine, but half the people who favoured dresses were wearing black. "Not me," I said, both wishing I could see her face and desperate not to.

"Grace?" someone said, and the crowd twitched and gasped as one. James pushed his way to the front, his mask pushed up on his forehead, tangled in his blond hair. *"Grace?"*

I looked from him to the body again, staring at the woman's exposed calf. It was so pale and shapely that it could have been modelled from clay, all but flawless, and her hair was rich with lustrous browns. I took a step forward, and Theodore rose to meet me, hands raised gently.

"Stay back, Morgan," he said, his tone gentle but brooking no argument.

I stared at him but stopped where I was. He was right, of course. It was a crime scene, and no one wanted a civilian poking around in it, even if I was the town witch. I watched Theodore and Isabella bend over the body, conferring in low voices. All around them was churned-up snow, any evidence well-trampled by the dance. How were they ever going to find anything in this?

"Morgan?" James caught my arm, his face tight and pale. "Is that *Grace?*"

"I—" I started, and Starlight interrupted me, pushing out of the crowd with Ben just a step behind her.

"What's happened? What's going on?"

I shook my head, looking back at Theodore and Isabella. "I'm not sure."

"Is it Grace?" James asked again, and I looked at him properly. Our local barista had only been on one date with her that I knew of, but this was Grace. Half a date was probably plenty to have men — or anyone — hopelessly besotted with her.

"I don't know. I'm sorry." It couldn't be, could it? She was a proper witch, not an accidental one like me, or a wannabe like Starlight. If anyone could look after herself, she could.

"Is she *dead?*" Starlight asked, then scrunched her face up. "Sorry, James."

"It's fine. We're not — it's fine." He ran both hands into his hair, catching the mask as he knocked it off and staring at it with something like bewilderment. Ben put a hand on his shoulder. Then we were silent along with the rest of the crowd, everyone waiting to be told this wasn't really happening, that the world was still continuing on as it should. I didn't think it was, though.

I hugged my arms around myself against the cold, trying to catch a glimpse of the market again, and Finn and Alaric lingering at the tent. Wouldn't they come to investigate what all the fuss was about? They'd been keen enough to be in the middle of things when they'd been handing out the masks. Although Finn had looked as if he'd been coming from the hall, so maybe they already knew what had happened. I wondered what they'd been arguing about, aware I was trying to distract myself but unwilling to stop. Stopping meant looking back at the body, that could be someone I knew. That could be *Grace*.

My attention was unwillingly pulled to Theodore as he stood, brushing his hands off. The firelight slid off his cheekbones, and the snow nestled into his dark hair, turning him into a sculpture, marred only slightly by the mask he was wearing. I hadn't noticed it before because it had the same unnaturally orange colour as his skin. It flowed in flames across his cheeks, his eyes dark holes in its centre.

"Everyone please disperse," he said, his voice clear and carrying. The crowd shuffled about a little but made no move to leave until Isabella stepped forward, her hands held out, palms up.

"Come along," she said, her voice soft. "Some privacy, please."

As if shamed into it, people slowly turned away, whispering to one another, but I stayed where I was, looking the motionless woman on the ground. The motionless *body*, I supposed. I swallowed hard, my throat constricting, and shot a glance at Ruiner, who had crept closer to the woman, his long grey fur turning him into a shadow in the night. He edged around the body, trying to get a look at her face, and Theodore spotted him.

The police sergeant clicked his tongue. "Please don't shed on my crime scene."

"I'm not shedding," Ruiner said.

"We must allow Theodore to do his work," Isabella said. There was only our little group left now, Ben still with that one steadying hand on James' shoulder, Starlight and I shivering in our dresses. Starlight was clutching Howard, who didn't look too pleased about being out of her bag in the cold, little jumper or not.

"*Is* it Grace?" I asked Isabella, because now James had put the idea in my head I couldn't get rid of it. I had to know.

"Is what Grace?" someone asked, her voice all warm curves, and we spun around to see the witch herself standing at the edge of the hall gardens, a large white coat hanging elegantly from her shoulders. It couldn't be actual fur, but it certainly looked like it, frothy and sleek. She looked from us to Isabella and raised an eyebrow. "You're all terribly serious."

"We thought that was you!" Starlight exclaimed, pointing at the body, and Grace's other eyebrow joined the first.

"Oh, I see. Sorry to disappoint." She prowled forward to join us. "I went inside to get my coat. It's a bit cold out here without it."

Theodore finally pushed his mask up, frowning as he looked from Grace to me, then turned his attention back to the body, with its tumble of long brown hair and black dress. "Is this a theme?"

"Is what a theme?" I asked.

"The dresses," he said, waving at Grace and I, then at the body.

"I've had this for ages," Grace said, which seemed likely. She was exactly the sort of person who'd have a wardrobe full of cocktail dresses, and the places to wear them.

"I borrowed mine," I said. "Against my will, I might add."

"*Hmm.*" Theodore crouched down, rolling the body gently over. I guess disturbing the scene of a crime isn't much of a thing when there's only one police officer in the entire town, and I had an idea that Hollowbeck police were as disconnected with the police outside the valley as everything else was. Just as we had our own brands of biscuits and laundry soap, unheard of outside, so we had our own brand of laws.

"Huh," Grace said, and we looked at each other. The woman on the ground was no more our twin than we were each other's, but her build wasn't dissimilar, and her hair was somewhere between Grace's long locks and my still regrowing jumble of curls. In the dark, with her black dress and the mask I could see lying near her outstretched hand, it could've been either of us.

"Huh," I echoed, and the night wrapped its chill around us, the hall's golden lights suddenly desperately distant.

THEODORE PACKED US OFF, and we retreated to the hall. I would've liked to go home, the night feeling long and hostile, but that felt vaguely like running away, and no one else in our little group seemed inclined to move. Most people seemed to have lingered; in fact, the ballroom was still full of whispering knots of masked revellers while the musicians conferred among themselves anxiously, as if wondering what a suitable soundtrack for unexpected death might be. At least it was warm inside, and we collected some mulled wine before reclaiming the table by the window, where we could see the still-burning bonfire and looming guardian outside. Theodore had already vanished with the body, and I wondered suddenly what he'd do with it. Hollowbeck didn't even have cells, so I doubted there was a morgue. Then again, a vampire probably knew all sorts of ways to dispose of a body. I shuddered and sipped my wine as the band kicked into a jazz rendition of *Knocking on Heaven's Door*, which seemed a bit on the nose.

Ruiner jumped to the table, fur still pouffed out and ears twitching, and looked at Grace, who raised an eyebrow at him. "Did you recognise that woman?" he asked.

She shook her head. "No. She must be visiting, or one of the stallholders, perhaps."

"She had a mask," Ruiner said.

"So?" I said. "Everyone has a mask. It's the rules, right?"

"I don't like them," he said.

"You're right not to. They're very unnecessary," Grace said, trailing a finger around the rim of her champagne glass. Mulled wine evidently wasn't her style.

"You don't wear one?" I asked her.

"Never."

Starlight huffed. "You're just being difficult, Grace. There's no reason not to wear one."

Grace shrugged languidly. "As I say, they're unnecessary. One doesn't need to hide behind a mask if one is comfortable with oneself. And as witches, that's what we should all be." She looked from Starlight to me, and my cheeks felt hotter than the wine demanded.

"*Pffft,*" Starlight said, demonstrating this wasn't her first mug of wine. "It's tradition, and it's *fun*. Not everything has to be serious and witchy, Grace."

"Masks are serious business," Grace replied, not looking at all bothered. "One should always take it seriously when others are so eager to hide their faces while they let their so-called true selves out to play."

"*One* should just enjoy it for what it is," Starlight replied, getting up. "I'm having more wine. *In* my mask." She pulled it down pointedly and danced off, wobbling a bit.

"She's going to fall in a punchbowl," James said, pushing off the table. "Ben, give me a hand."

"With *Starlight?* She's not *my* ex."

Apparently, I was the only witch in the group who *hadn't* dated James, but I was okay with that. I was more interested in his coffee than I was in anything else he had to offer, despite him being very easy on the eye. It just made the coffee taste better, though.

James scowled at Ben. "Give me a hand getting more wine, I meant. But we should also make sure she doesn't turn anyone into a shrew if they tell her she's had enough."

Ben sighed. "I knew a cocktail party was a bad idea. Alcohol and magic-workers don't mix."

But he followed James, and Ruiner said, "*Anyway*. The

thing with the masks is, it's pretty hard to tell who anyone is in the bloody things."

"Kind of the point," I said.

"Quite," Grace said, draining her glass.

"So they could've been after either of you," Ruiner persisted.

He had to say it. I puffed air over my lip and looked at Grace. "What do you think?"

Grace shrugged. "Witches have mixed reputations, Morgan. Plenty of people only like us if they have use for us. But we're hardly the only witches in the country."

We weren't even the only witches in town. There was Petunia, for a start, and any number of kitchen witches and nature witches and other types. A witch was just a magic-worker, after all, and there were plenty of them, often not particularly powerful, but able to do simple spells and charms. Most witches specialised in one discipline or another, and I still didn't know what my speciality was meant to be. Starlight said it would become obvious, that my natural talents would surface (she was convinced she was destined to be a healer, but I wasn't. She'd tried to get rid of a small spot on my chin a couple of weeks ago and I'd ended up with an abscess I'd had to go to the doctor to clear up), but so far nothing was appealing to me particularly.

Of course, I'd never intended to become a witch in the first place. I hadn't even thought that was thing, other than middle-aged women in tie-dyed skirts saging houses and calling themselves pagans. Until Ruiner had turned up with four paws and a tail, I'd assumed magic was as mythical as unicorns, but now I was too nervous to ask anyone if unicorns actually existed, because I was still clinging to a small hope that I'd be able to go back to the regular world at some stage, and knowing unicorns existed felt like it would be the final thread that unravelled everything I knew to be real. Or thought I knew, anyway.

"What sort of witch are you?" I asked Grace, realising I'd never thought to ask before.

"A good one," she said, then amended, "Or skilled, shall we say?"

"Yes, but—"

"What're we going to do about this, then?" Ruiner demanded, interrupting me.

"What d'you mean?" I asked him. "Theodore and Isabella are dealing with it."

He snorted. "Sure, and meanwhile you two are waltzing around being witchy all about the place, with masked bloody strangers everywhere. Seems like being proactive might be in order. Made any enemies recently?" The question was directed at Grace, and she smiled.

"Only you, Ruiner. Although I think that was the other way around, don't you?"

"I have said sorry."

"You burned down my shop."

"I didn't," he protested. "That was Norma's curses."

"That *you* planted. Plus you ghosted me. *You* ghosted *me.*" She sounded more horrified by that than by the small issue of arson, but I couldn't blame her. People like Grace don't get ghosted.

Ruiner twitched his ears and looked down at himself. "I mean, you do see the problem here, right? I'm not saying I couldn't work around it—"

"*Ew, no,*" I said, jumping up from the stool. "No, I do *not* want to hear this."

"Me either," Grace said, getting up as well. "There's openminded, and then there's being hit on by a cat."

"Cat-*shaped,*" Ruiner protested.

"I need more champagne," Grace said, tipping her glass at me. "Coming?"

"Um." I looked across the hall, to where Starlight was dancing with a small girl in a unicorn onesie. The band had evidently decided that upbeat tunes were called for and were leaning into it furiously. Most people were back in their masks, and the whole hall fizzed with excitement again, quite as if we hadn't just walked away from a body on the snow. I spotted James with a jug of mulled wine clutched protectively to his chest, a half-eaten sausage roll in his free hand, while Ben placated an irate woman who was pointing alternately at the empty table and the jug. "I might stay." Just in case anyone needed bandaging.

"Suit yourself," Grace said. "But if that woman was killed because she looked like us, you're going to need more … knowledgeable help." She smiled at me, then swept away, her back straight and her white coat gleaming in the night.

"Don't take any Turkish Delight from her," Ruiner said.

"Why, is that what you did?" I asked. "That's how you ended up cat-shaped?"

"I told you it wasn't her."

"It'd help if you told me who it *was*."

He didn't answer right away, but when he did, all he said was, "Are you worried?"

"About you and your bloody curse? *Yes*. At some point Mum's going to want to see us, and what do we do then?"

"Not what I was talking about."

"No," I said with a sigh, and found a smile somewhere as James slid the jug triumphantly onto the table, still clutching his sausage roll.

"Drinks delivery."

"Thanks," I said, watching him top up our mugs.

Maybe I should have gone with Grace. She was right. She knew more about magic and Hollowbeck and basically *everything* than I did. And the dead woman *had* looked like me, a little, which was just as worrying as Ruiner was suggesting. Not everyone thought I should be the town witch, after all. I even received lovely little threats on a regular basis, written on high-quality stock card and popping up in mysterious places, which informed me that I wasn't destined to be *any* sort of witch for long. Certain people were definitely against me holding the grimoire and the deals that bound half the town in debt to it.

But I also knew — or thought I knew — that one of those people was Grace. Which meant the Turkish Delight might be a real concern.

5. A friendly stalking

I'M NOT SAYING THERE'S AN EXPECTED WAY TO BEHAVE when you're loaded up on free drinks, wearing masks of questionable provenance, and have just taken part in some ancient ceremony in the darkness of the long winter night which culminated in the discovery of a body, but continuing the party seemed to be at least slightly in poor taste. No one else seemed to share those concerns, though, and the band was still playing enthusiastically when I pulled my coat on, leaving Starlight dancing with a handful of kids, all of them doing some sort of pony prance around the hall. My eyes were gritty with weariness, and I suppose I wasn't seeing as clearly as usual, but the bloom of those half-seen wings seemed brighter than earlier, more concrete. The kids were a muddle of luminous light and colour, unicorns and bears and sharks, their outlines indistinct, but no one seemed to be biting each other, so that was something.

Ben and James were having some sort of male bonding moment, both of them in their masks. James' mask was distinctly dragonish, and he and Ben had got into an arm-wrestling duel which had progressed into some sort of multi-discipline competition as to who could sprint the hall faster, or do more push-ups, or burpees, or whatever else they could come up with. They were both sweaty and panting, but no one was paying any attention to them at all. Given the amount of mulled wine, whisky, and everything else of which there seemed to be endless supplies, there was reason enough for people to be distracted, but I didn't think that was the main cause.

The main cause was likely to do with the fact that neither Starlight's prancing nor the two men's wrestling was the most unusual thing going on. Mask-wearers were dancing on tables, leaping from chairs, having drinking competitions, climbing the curtains, throwing confetti at each other, starting food fights, and generally behaving like the world's worst cocktail party guests. Or maybe this was normal cocktail party behaviour. I didn't know. Like I say, it was the first one I'd been to.

Whatever it was, I was too tired to deal with it. The masks were still making me uneasy, and I could feel the strange, lingering buzz of inviting warmth and creeping excitement mine had set into me when I'd put it on. Even if Ruiner hadn't snarled and gone full cat mode every time I touched mine, batting my face and arms or whatever he could reach, I didn't like it. It felt like holding a high voltage wire, knowing it was insulated but suspecting there was a gap somewhere. Or expecting there to be. *Wanting* there to be, even.

So, with the others distracted and Grace not returned from her search for more champagne, I took the chance to slip to the front door, taking my coat from the racks set up in the entrance hall. Hollowbeck ran on honesty just as much as it did barter, and there was no one to check the coats in or out. I pulled mine on, an old puffer jacket that didn't go with my dress at all, and ventured out into the thin hours of the early morning, my breath curling into the dark ahead of me.

I circled the hall, heading to the main street and the short walk back to Petunia's, my feet cold and toes pinched, wishing Ubers — or even regular taxis — were a thing in Hollowbeck. The paths that ran through the hall's front garden and past the library were softly lit and swept mostly clear of snow, and I crunched over the gravel with Ruiner padding next to me, silent for once. The stars were high, the night still and breathless, the snow collecting on twigs and branches. We made our way towards the street without talking, and I was just stepping onto the gritted pavement when I caught the clatter of stone on stone, footsteps on the path behind me, approaching fast. I spun around, my heart surging, Ruiner darting behind my legs with customary bravery. I staggered in the unfamiliar heels as one slid on the treacherous surface, and warm hands caught my arms, steadying me. I yelped, jerking away, and my attacker took a hurried step back.

"Sorry, sorry! I didn't mean to scare you."

"Bloody *hell*," I complained, both hands pressed to my chest like I was looking for some pearls to clutch. "What're you doing sneaking up on people?"

Taking another step back, Finn raised his hands in apology, the snow settling softly in his tangled hair. He had a heavy flannel jacket on that made me wonder if there were lumberjacks in his family tree. He definitely had the upper body for it.

"I'm really sorry," he said again. "I saw you out here on your own, and—"

"And you thought *hey, I know, I'll go and scare her half to death?*" I winced at my own choice of words. "I mean…"

"Well, that's why you shouldn't be walking on your own," he said. "I heard what happened."

I thought he would've seen it, but maybe he hadn't been coming from the hall when I saw him earlier at all. I pulled my coat a little tighter around me. "I'm going home."

"I can walk you," he said. "Just to be safe."

I squinted at him. "Pretty sure walking home with a strange man who's just accosted me on the street is in the *Beginner's Guide to Not Getting Murdered*." Murdered, or anything else.

He nodded. "Fair enough. Let me get one of your friends, then."

"They seem a bit distracted. Also drunk. Not sure how much help they'll be."

He grinned, laugh lines appearing at the corners of his eyes. "Then can I call someone? Find you a lift? A large stick and a big dog?"

Ruiner hissed at the mention of a dog, and Finn looked at him.

"Oh, I see you've already got protection."

I laughed at that, unable to help it. "Yes, he's vicious."

Ruiner huffed and strutted off down the road, his ears back.

Finn watched him go, then looked at me. "Now do you want a dog?"

If he was a serial killer, he was an entertaining one, at least. "No. But you can walk with me, if you want. I should point out that my landlady'll turn you into a frog if you misbehave, though."

"I get to meet your landlady? Wow. I've got better game than I thought."

I tried to splutter out an answer, and he just laughed,

waving at the road. Light caught on a bracelet of tarnished metal on his wrist, a heavy, thick band of beaten silver.

"After you," he said.

We followed Ruiner down the street, the houses sleeping nestled into their snow-mounded gardens, fairy lights and candles burning in windows and lanterns hung in trees and at gates. It was all but silent other than the crunch of our footsteps, and I sneaked a glance at Finn as we walked. He was looking at me and gave me a small smile when I caught his gaze. Someone with shoulders like that shouldn't have a smile that edged into shy, but he pulled it off somehow.

"So were you just hanging around in the hall garden looking for women to stalk?" I asked him.

"No. I *might* have been keeping an eye out for you leaving, though."

"Oh, so it was a specific stalking then." It should have made me more nervous than it did, but it was hard to be scared of him. I wasn't sure if the thought of lumberjack shoulders was distracting me from frantically waving red flags, though. It was possible.

His smile faded, and he looked at Ruiner, still padding resolutely on ahead. My brother's ears were twitching, so I was sure he was listening to us.

"Not a stalking, exactly," Finn said. "Or not a *bad* stalking."

"A friendly stalking?"

"Sort of. I wanted to talk to you anyway, and when the … when *that* happened, I decided to hang around and make sure I caught you."

Dammit, that sounded a lot less romantic than initial impressions had suggested. Not that I needed romantic complications with mysterious lumberjack-slash-mask salesmen, anyway. That was a terrible idea. "Why did you want to talk to me? Is it the masks?"

"The masks?" He was trying for startled, or possibly bemused, but neither were working.

"Yes, the masks that…" I didn't know how to describe what I'd been seeing, so I just waved vaguely, twiddling my fingers in an *ooh, magic* manner. "You know."

He imitated my wave, attempting another smile, but I just looked at him, trying to channel a Grace-level raised eyebrow and discovering I could only do both at once. It worked, though, and he looked away again, twisting the bracelet restlessly. His skin looked chafed underneath it.

"What do they do?" I asked. "How does Alaric choose them?"

"He just … knows."

"Magic-like?"

"Magic-like," he said, and his smile resurfaced. It vanished again pretty quickly when I repeated my question.

"So what do they do? And what did you want to tell me about them?"

He took a deep breath, coming to a halt and looking around as he ran one hand back over his shaggy hair. "They allow people to be their true selves. They give freedom."

I'd stopped walking too, my hands deep in my coat pockets as I looked at him. "It's a great sales pitch."

He huffed a half-laugh. "It's true."

"And Alaric already spieled it at me."

We were silent, watching each other as the snow drifted gently around us, and the lights glimmered in the trees, soft and peaceful. There was no sound, no cars passing on distant streets or dogs barking in yards, and it felt like we were existing in a pocket cut out of time and out of the world, the moment elastic and unreal. Ruiner had paused up ahead, watching us, snowflakes melting softly on his grey fur.

"It's not…" Finn trailed off, looking as if he were struggling for the words, and before he could find them, footsteps cut through the stillness and the world started moving again.

"Finn! There you are." Alaric swept towards us, his boots gleaming and the heavy black overcoat swinging from his shoulders. "And the delightful Morgan." He smiled at me widely. "I did wonder where Finn had run off to when we were still setting up."

"We're mostly finished," Finn protested, but without much heat. He didn't look at Alaric, his eyes on the ground.

"And we re-open later this very morning to provide for those who weren't at the party. *Mostly* isn't going to cut it. But I see you're making sure Morgan gets home safely. I can hardly object to that."

"I won't be much longer," Finn said, stealing a glance at me. "Right?"

"It's just up here," I said, nodding along the street.

"Then I shall accompany you," Alaric said, offering me his arm. "I need Finn to take his expertise back to the tent, I'm afraid. Some jobs are just beyond me!"

"It's really close," I said. "I'll be fine." Whatever Finn had been going to tell me, I wasn't getting it out of him now. And I didn't want Alaric knowing where I lived. I had no more reason to distrust him than I did to trust Finn, but there it was. Call it witchy instinct. Or an affection for lumberjacks.

"Nonsense, I insist," Alaric said. "It's not the night to be out walking alone, and I would cherish a little chat with the town witch." He took my elbow, propelling me along the pavement. "Finn, you need to get the displays finished. I'll be right back."

"Alright," Finn said, mostly to the ground. "See you, Morgan."

I shook Alaric off. "I said I'm fine."

"But—"

"*I'm fine.* The only people I've seen out are you two, who I don't know *at all,* so excuse me if I'm not convinced I'm safer with you than I am alone." I turned and marched up the street, yelling as I went, "If either of you follow me, I'll turn you into hamsters."

Neither of them replied, and as I passed Ruiner, he stayed where he was, watching the two men for a little before trotting to catch up.

"Are they still there?" I asked him, my voice low.

"Yes. Not following, though."

I wasn't sure if that was creepier or not, the idea that both of them were just standing there in the middle of the deserted street, watching me walk away. It made the skin on the back of my neck crawl, and I found my fingers stroking the soft fabric of the mask where it was still pushed up on my head, drawing some slim comfort from it. I didn't look back, though, just kept walking, turning into the next street. It wasn't my usual route back to Petunia's, and I'd have to turn back on myself through one of the snickets that ran here and there between the houses, but it felt better to have the men's gazes off me. Felt better to be laying a false trail, too, even if they seemed not to be following.

"Any sign?" I asked Ruiner.

"No," he said, and I looked around. The street was empty, and he huffed a breath out. "I *said* they weren't there."

"I know." I still had to see for myself, though. "Where the hell did Alaric come from? Did you see?"

"No. Popped up like David sodding Copperfield."

"Well, I suppose he must be a magician. Or a witch or something."

"He's something, alright." Ruiner trotted after me as I ducked into a pathway, slowing my pace in the dim light. "What d'you think Sideshow Sid was going to tell you about the masks?"

"No idea." I was going to find out, though. But not tonight, out in the ghostly streets. Tonight, I just wanted to be home.

A WELCOMING COMMITTEE of a dozen frogs was sitting in the middle of the hall when I opened Petunia's front door, a single, dusky rose lying in front of them. They goggled at me and Ruiner, and the biggest one put a webbed foot on the flower's stem protectively.

"I'm sure she'll be home soon," I told them, then stepped carefully over the little group to creep upstairs. The house was still, and while I rarely saw the guesthouse's other residents, I was usually aware of their presence, the creaks and groans of old floorboards and age-warped doors and the simple sense of other life in the place. But everyone was evidently still out, not lightweights like me. We climbed the stairs in silence, and I let us into the attic room with a sigh of relief, wrestling my shoes off as soon as I was in the door. I groaned, wriggling my toes into the rug, then stumbled to the bed and face-planted onto it. An enraged chitter greeted me, and I lifted my head to see Jackie poking her nose out from among the pillows.

"Hi," I said to her, and the rat slipped out to nose my cheek, her whiskers tickling. "All good here?"

She reared back, baring her teeth, and I sat up fast, staring at her.

"Easy!"

Jackie hissed, her gaze fixed on the mask.

"She's got a brain in there after all, doesn't she?" Ruiner asked, jumping to the bed.

I had a feeling Jackie was smarter than both of us, which made it even stranger that she'd somehow decided I was the best person to hold the grimoire. I had a sneaking suspicion it had been a terrible lapse of judgement on her part. Right now, though, she was snarling persistently at the mask, and I got to my feet with a groan, taking it to the big old wardrobe at the other end of the long room and stashing it in one of the drawers in its base. I shut it in firmly and turned around to face the cat and the rat, who were both watching from the bed.

"Happy?"

Jackie glared at me for a moment longer, clearly needing to make sure I understood my transgression, then set to cleaning her whiskers.

"Apparently," Ruiner said. "Told you that thing's trouble."

"*Mmm.*" I felt vaguely bereft without it, as if in simply carrying it I'd been absorbing some of its true self power, whatever that was. But no one was hissing at me or nagging me now, so I just hung up my coat and went to brush my teeth.

Ten minutes later I was back in the room, reaching into a hidden gap in the walls. Inside, a bag was hung well out of sight from anyone who managed to get past the frogs and find the loose board that gave access to the cavity. I unhooked the bag and carried it to the bed, wriggling my legs under the duvet and pulling the grimoire out. It wasn't a big book, not some massive, impressive thing of the sort that springs to mind when one hears the word *grimoire*, but it was a grimoire nevertheless. It pretty much shouted the word, in the heavy leather cover that was always unsettlingly warm to the touch, and in the thick old pages and strange collection of notes inside, recipes and anecdotes and acerbic diary entries and questionable charms all jumbled up together in half a dozen different hands. There was a *want* to it, a hunger, and these days I could never handle it without being aware of both all the people who were bound to it by their deals, and also the fact that plenty — if not all — of those people had sealed their deal with a drop of blood to the cover. Which I was certain was a health hazard as well as being desperately creepy.

Everything about it was creepy, though. The deals particularly. Norma, the previous book-keeper, had bound people to it in such a way that there was no end to their debts. She could demand favour after favour, and did, using them to play the people of the town off against each other, for profit or to fulfil other deals, or simply for her own amusement. And whoever held the book held the debts, making it both dangerous and valuable. So I did my best to keep it secure, even though technically no one could just *take* it, since I'd claimed it, and even if they somehow got around that, Jackie, as the familiar, still had to grant it to any new keeper. Which meant it wasn't like anyone could simply bump me off and snatch the book and its deals, but there were ways around it, for those who craved its power. I'd very nearly had firsthand experience with one of those ways, and I didn't fancy a repeat.

Here, though, in Petunia's house, under the watchful eye of the frogs, the grimoire seemed reasonably safe. I opened it carefully, running my fingers across the paper. I felt like I should've read every page a hundred times over by now, the amount I'd been through it searching for ways to release the deals, or looking for recipes for salves and tinctures with Starlight. But I wasn't at all sure the contents always stayed the same.

"Masks," I told it. "I need to know about masks."

The book didn't respond, and nor did anyone else. I looked up. Ruiner was sprawled out, half rolled onto his back with one front paw curled in the air. Jackie was tucked into a neat little bundle on one of the pillows, and they were both snoring softly. I looked at the bedside table, where a frog peered out from behind a potted plant, then vanished again.

"Right," I said to the sleeping room. "Thanks for the help."

I turned back to the book, the paper thick under my fingertips, gouged with pen strokes and stained with spills and nibbled at the corners by long-gone familiars. Somewhere there had to be answers. Answers to everything, not only the masks. I just had to find the right place to look, didn't I?

6. The morning after the night before

I WOKE UP WITH MY HEAD PILLOWED ON THE GRIMOIRE AND a sticky taste in my mouth that was either the mulled wine or some serious snoring. I hoped I hadn't drooled on the damn book. Not because I might damage it, but because I didn't know what it might do with my saliva. Something unpleasant, undoubtedly. I rolled to sitting with a groan, swinging my legs off the side of the bed, and grabbed my water bottle. I hadn't discovered anything in the grimoire last night, no explanations of the masks or even a reference to the festival itself. I haven't read the entire thing, of course, but I wasn't holding out much hope. I had the impression the masks were basically a force of nature, as much a part of the festival as mince pies were a part of winter celebrations in the world beyond Hollowbeck's borders. There was no explanation for them, they just *were*. Although mince pies didn't have you seeing sparks shooting from your fingertips. Or none of the ones I'd encountered did, anyway. Presumably there were certain homemade additions that might have a similar effect.

But the point was, I was no further forward, and in the clear light of day — well, in the pale winter sun ambling through the attic windows to puddle on the floor with no great enthusiasm — I wasn't sure it even mattered. They were *masks*. What did I think, they were made from poison cloth or something? That would hardly be great for Alaric's business, would it? Everyone had just been caught up in the excitement of the whole night, myself included, and then the death had put a horrible spin on things. No wonder I'd been looking for reasons behind it, motive wrapped in cloth and papier-mâché. The idea it had been a random act was too awful to simply accept.

Also, the possibility that *I* was the intended target, and the woman had paid the price, was a doubly hideous thing to contemplate. So the masks had been a pretty tidy scapegoat, but now I'd lost the terrible certainty of the night before. I needed to get up, get into town, and find Isabella, to see what progress Theodore had made before sunrise. Probably he'd have some perfectly sensible explanation that didn't have anything to do with me *or* the masks, such as the poor woman had had a heart attack from all the excitement, or had bought some bad mushrooms (it happened, magical towns were not exempt from such things), and then I could go back to enjoying the winter festival and not dribbling on grimoires.

Decision made, I got up and ventured downstairs, knocking on the bathroom door gingerly. A splash greeted me, and someone shouted "what?" in a voice fuzzed on the edges with sleep.

"It's morning," I called. "It's my time slot."

"Really?" the unseen bather said, and there was more enthusiastic splashing. "Oh, damn. I fell asleep. Give me a minute."

I couldn't wait a minute, so I ran down to the downstairs loo in my pyjamas, encountering no one else, not even a frog. By the time I came back up, the bathroom door was ajar, and I let myself in cautiously. I didn't know who the nighttime bather was, and, like the rest of the guesthouse's residents, I'd never seen them. The only people I ever saw, other than Petunia, were Gus and Art, refugees from the fallen carnival. They were conspicuous by their absence this morning, since they could usually be spotted doing some sort of calisthenics in the garden, and kept suggesting I join them, but it was far too much exertion for pre-coffee (or ever, to be honest). For everyone else, mutual avoidance seemed to be the way the house worked, and some things weren't to be questioned. Plus, it was better than having to act like some big extended family simply because you shared a bathroom.

I checked the bath for scales, then started it filling. I mean, I hadn't seen scales so far, but you started to wonder.

HALF AN HOUR LATER, I was trotting down the couple of steps at the guesthouse's front door, feeling distinctly more comfortable than I had last night in a pair of winter boots and jeans. I headed for the street, then paused just inside the gate, looking around uneasily. The day was clear and bright, the sky a thin, scraped blue and the low sun tickling the naked branches of the trees. I had my bag slung crossways over my body, the grimoire heavy against my hip, and Jackie was curled into the folds of my scarf between my shoulder and hood. She snuffled my neck curiously as I looked each way down the street. It was empty other than a snooty-looking white cat stalking across the frosty tarmac. She paused to look at us, one paw raised out of the snow, then dismissed us and kept on her own little mission, vanishing into the garden of a bungalow with a wonky roof.

I looked at Ruiner, who was examining the street with the same wariness I was. "Friend of yours?" I asked, and he narrowed his eyes at me.

"That's a *cat.*"

I waved at him, the gesture encompassing his general cat-ness.

"Ha. See your boyfriends out there?"

"I don't see anyone," I said but still didn't venture past the gate. There was a safety behind the frog-topped gateposts, or I had the feeling there was. Perhaps it was just Petunia's presence, her strange wild essence sunk into the ground, her connection to the seasons and the world deep and elemental. Hollowbeck had never felt hostile, but my certainty that I'd misjudged the masks was fading, and the world beyond the gates seemed unfamiliar. The way Alaric had simply *appeared* last night was tugging at my mind, and while he and Finn hadn't done anything, the whole situation unsettled me. I was half-tempted to go back to bed and ignore the world for a day. It wasn't like there were going to be many people out after last night. Well, not unless they were looking for our stockpile of hangover cures. But the Cosy Cauldron didn't have opening hours, so no one would be surprised to find us closed. I wavered for a moment, and my stomach rumbled.

Ruiner looked up at me. "Elegant. I should've said not-boyfriends. No one's going near that."

"Sorry, who whinged all the way down the stairs about their poor little belly?"

"Exactly. I have a very small belly and it's very empty, and I want breakfast."

"So do I," I said, and let us out the sagging gates. "Bewitching Brews it is."

"James only ever has cat biscuits," he complained. "Where's my fish?"

"I can take you down to the river. See what you can find."

He grumbled, trotting along next to me as we headed for town. We usually didn't see Petunia in the mornings, but there was always breakfast laid on, homemade muesli and yoghurt in glass pots, or fresh crusty bread and jars of jam with handwritten labels, and always fish or chicken or scraps of liver chopped and waiting in the fridge with a little heart-decorated note for Ruiner. This morning, though, there had been nothing. I hoped Petunia was just sleeping off the night before, and it wasn't a recurrence of her strange carnival affliction. But she hadn't been holed up in the lounge, turning it into a frog-infested sauna, so I was fairly sure she'd resurface at some stage. That didn't help with breakfast, though.

It wasn't a long walk to Hollowbeck's main street, just a few meandering, uneven blocks, but usually we'd see people out walking geese or miniature ponies or even dogs, smoke puffing from chimneys and people shovelling snow off paths, muttering complaints about Petunia's picturesque but impractical weather. Today, though, the streets remained quiet, and even when we got into the heart of town, foot traffic was scarce.

Hollowbeck was home to a strange mix of architecture, graceful wooden Queenslanders rubbing shoulders with thick-walled thatched cottages and glossy glass and metal towers, as if someone had done a lucky dip through a bunch of architecture magazines. The shops were just as eclectic, sporting very non-Lake District style awnings and overhangs and bifold doors along with more typical stone fronts and display windows. It wasn't big, but there was everything here, whether you wanted to buy fishing lures or spinning tops or hiking boots or fascinators. Or a handy pocket charm for fending off pixies. The only thing it didn't sell was any brand I'd ever heard of, meaning I was currently in withdrawal over Penguins and Ribena, although Ben usually brought me some back from his monthly shopping trips. My old car hadn't been up for unnecessary trips initially, and after some mysterious recent repairs, it *seemed* to be running better than it ever had, but I didn't quite trust it. I suspected the repairs of not being entirely mechanical in nature.

Quiet as town was, Bewitching Brews was open, and I pushed through the door into the coffee-scented interior. It was empty other than James, sitting on one of the stools on the customer side of the counter with both hands around a mug and his hair sticking up in strange directions.

"Morning," I said.

"No," he replied.

"Sorry?"

"What?"

"This almost makes me miss having a hangover," Ruiner said. "I'd like to be able to get that drunk."

"You talk too much," James said. "Also too loud."

"No morning?" I asked. "Or no coffee, did you mean?" Please, no.

"I thought you said *good* morning. I was saying no to that."

"Right." I looked longingly at the coffee machine, but James didn't seem inclined to move. "Um … are you open?"

"You're in here." But he pushed himself off the stool with a groan and stumbled around the counter. "I think I cracked a rib. Or Ben did."

"*Ben* cracked your rib?"

Ruiner huffed feline laughter. "The *librarian?* How soft are you?"

James scowled at him, but his heart clearly wasn't in it. "We might've broken a table or two."

I shook my head, unzipping my jacket as I sat down. "What were you *doing?* I'm pretty sure it was a cocktail party, not the WWE."

James flinched away from the racket of the coffee grinder, letting out an audible sigh as it stopped. "I don't really know," he said, tamping down the grounds. "It just … felt right, somehow? It made sense to have a bit of a competition."

"You couldn't have stuck to cards or something?"

He shrugged, setting my mug on the coffee machine and rubbing a hand over his face. "Too much whisky, I suppose."

"I suppose," I echoed, and looked at the empty cake domes. "No muffins this morning?"

He looked at the domes blankly. "I took some brownies out of the freezer."

"Breakfast of champions."

James managed to get my coffee made, and a clutter of half-defrosted brownies on a plate, then told me to help myself to the cat biscuits. He vanished out the back and hadn't come back when an imposing woman with sturdy legs in purple trousers came in, followed by three others, all of them of a certain age and dressed in practical footwear. I nodded at them in as friendly a manner as I could manage. The Upstanding Ladies weren't to be trifled with. They firmly and vocally opposed any sort of magic, which was a very odd stance for people who lived in a town which didn't exist on any maps, and where the ghostly mayor and vampire police officer were among the least strange residents. I had yet to figure out if the Upstanding Ladies possessed some sort of anti-magic, or if it was simply their resolute disapproval of basically the entire population of Hollowbeck that rendered them so intimidating, but either way I wasn't going to cross them. Besides which, one of them had already helped me out a couple of times, once intervening right here when James' aunt had me immobilised, and another time giving me a book that had helped me defeat a necromancer. Sort of.

The ladies sat down rather noisily at one of the cafe's tables, scraping chairs and coughing pointedly, but James didn't emerge. I didn't look at the little group, but I could feel them staring at the counter, their impatience rolling over me like a heatwave. Ruiner twitched his ears at me, and I slid off the stool.

"James?" I called, but there was no reply. I gave the Upstanding Ladies an apologetic look. "He was just here. He must be out the back."

"Evidently," the purple-trousered woman said. She was the one who'd given me the book, which had been called *Miss Edna's Guide to Proper Comportment for Young Witches*, so in my head she'd become Miss Edna. I didn't know if that was actually her name or not. "Unless he's lying on the floor behind the counter, he can hardly be anywhere else, can he?"

"Um, no," I admitted, and wondered if I should offer to make them coffee. But that seemed like a really good way to upset both the ladies and James, so I just ate the last bite of my brownie and pulled my jacket back on. I really wanted another coffee, but I'd settle for tea at the shop instead.

"*Honestly,*" one of the other women said, loosening her scarf. "The whole town goes to pot every festival."

"Debauchery," a third sniffed. "It's an utter disgrace, even for Hollowbeck."

"And we all know how low its standards are already," the fourth woman said, nodding sagely. The others murmured agreement, and I hesitated. As much as they were terrifying, they also knew *everything*.

"Um," I said carefully, and all four women looked at me. I tugged at the front of my jumper under the weight of their gaze, suddenly sure I'd spilt coffee all down myself.

"Yes?" Miss Edna asked, her tone imperious.

"Stand up *straight*," one of the others said. "What's wrong with people these days? Terrible posture."

I was suddenly sure I'd been given the book to practise walking around with it on my head, like a debutante in the Sixties, and I pulled my shoulders back so hard I felt a twinge in my spine. "Sorry."

"Don't apologise for everything," a woman with large round glasses said. "What are you apologising for?"

"I don't know?" I offered a little desperately, deeply regretting not leaving as soon as they arrived.

"Of *course* you don't," Glasses scoffed.

"What did you want to ask?" Miss Edna said. "Spit it out!"

"Yes, right. Um … you didn't go to the cocktail party, then?"

"Absolutely *not*," Posture Police said. "The whole thing with the masks fending off evil spirits is just so *distasteful*."

"That's not a real thing, then?" I asked.

"I didn't say that."

"So it is real?"

The fourth woman waved dismissively, her hand heavy with old gold rings. "That's irrelevant. It's the principle."

I felt it was fairly relevant. If there were evil spirits

wandering about the place, it seemed like it should be something to be worried about.

"It's the *masks*," Glasses said. "Exposing oneself like that." She said it with such disgust, she might've been talking about everyone getting naked and making like the snow rabbits. Maybe they did. The party had still been going after I left, after all.

"The mask-seller said something about the masks exposing the true self. Is that what you mean?"

"In a way." Miss Edna examined me. "Where's yours?"

I touched the pocket of my jacket automatically. I didn't know why I'd taken it out of the drawer this morning, and I hadn't actually thought of it until she mentioned it, but now I suddenly wanted the smooth feel of its surface, the whisper of sparks on my fingertips, real or imagined.

"I thought so. You'd be better to throw it away," she said, crossing her arms over her substantial bosom. "Do it now, before it gets its claws into you. Starts making you do strange things."

Like have brawls in cocktail parties, I thought. *Or murder someone.* "They always do that?" I asked.

"Not officially," Gold Rings said. "The official line is that people are just *blowing off steam* after the year." She sniffed. "In my day, that meant getting drunk and skinny-dipping in Windermere."

My brain glitched at the idea of the Upstanding Ladies being drunk, young, *or* skinny-dipping, and I just stared at them.

"*Where* is James?" Posture Police demanded. "Honestly, we should have gone to Mystic Munchies. We'll probably get magic mushrooms in the tea, but at least we'll *get* some tea."

"And the mind-broadening aspects are occasionally

helpful," Glasses said, nodding sagely. "Good for creative thinking."

Yep, I was out. This was too much for one morning. I hurried through the open archway into the kitchen and found James standing just around the corner with his head and as much of his shoulders as he could fit in the fridge, his cheek resting on an empty shelf. I grabbed the back of his hoodie and pulled him out.

"Customers," I said.

He groaned, but I didn't wait to see if he was going to cope. I just grabbed another piece of brownie on my way past the plate and headed for the door, Ruiner jumping from his stool to follow me.

"Morgan," Miss Edna said, and I spun around, startled. I hadn't even realised she knew my name. "The masks aren't safe. Nothing about this festival is safe."

"Right," I said.

She held my gaze for a moment, then looked away as James emerged. He'd evidently stuck his head under the kitchen tap and his hair was dripping on his hoody. "*Finally.* This is an appalling level of service, young man."

He gave his customary, charming smile a valiant effort, and I left before I could take pity on him and offer to help. It was all self-inflicted, after all.

THE COSY CAULDRON WAS LOCKED, so evidently Starlight hadn't surfaced yet. I'd suggested more than once that we should have actual opening hours, but given that certain portions of Hollowbeck's population only came out at night, there were never going to be regular shop hours anyway. Plus I wasn't sure Starlight was designed for a schedule.

I unlocked the door and flipped the sign to open, flicking on the lights and washing the packed shelves in warm colour. Crystals and voodoo dolls rubbed shoulders with tacky snow domes and fridge magnets, dreamcatchers and imp repellents twisted gently from the ceiling along with wind chimes and mobiles formed from twigs and pinecones and bird skulls. It was endlessly dusty and disorganised and comfortingly familiar, and I was abruptly glad to close the rest of Hollowbeck out. Things were *off,* from the Upstanding Ladies who had barely acknowledged me before other than as someone to glare at disapprovingly, to James and his cracked ribs, and the missing Petunia and the silent streets. And that was still resolutely not thinking about the poor mystery woman from the night before.

"Well?" Ruiner asked.

"Well what?"

"Throwing out the mask yet?"

"I'm putting the kettle on first," I said. "I'll worry about the mask later."

"Not sure about your priorities there," Ruiner started, but before he could start lecturing me, a young man with an impressive beard and a pretty sweater dress stumbled in the door.

"Thank the gods, you're open," he said. His eyes were bloodshot behind well-applied makeup, his cheeks glaringly pale.

"Hangover tincture?" I asked him.

"I will *marry* you if you have one handy."

I ducked behind the counter and pulled out the crate of cures Starlight and I had made up the day before. "Want a glass of water?"

"You are the best witch ever," he said, snatching the little tube of herbal infusion off me. "Set the date."

I snorted and went to get a jug of water and a stack of

glasses. I could see three more people marching towards the shop through the windows, two with dark glasses on and the other sucking desperately on one of the local juice shop's mysterious energy drinks, which I knew from experience tasted like the inside of a compost bin. Starlight had been right. We were going to do excellent trade.

And it meant I didn't have to think about anything else for a while.

7. To market, to market

THE FLOW OF CUSTOMERS WAS STEADY BUT NOT overwhelming, one person after another staggering through the door wearing dark glasses and clutching juice or off-brand energy drinks or coffee. There were quite a few who hadn't made it out of cocktail dresses and evening finery, and a handful still swigging from near-empty bottles of homemade damson gin and jugs of mulled wine, and I handed out the tinctures without comment or any demand for payment. Nearly everyone was already indebted to the grimoire anyway, so I didn't feel much like adding to their tab.

In return, though, I had a steadily increasing stash of honey, eggs, clumsily knitted scarves and beanies, and assorted baked goods building up behind the counter. I didn't even need to go digging out the back to find something for breakfast, but rather snacked my way steadily though a batch of bran muffins, only taking the time to make a cup of tea in between the hungover clientele. Even Ruiner stopped complaining after someone turned up with a tub of potted shrimp that I was pretty sure had been liberated from last night's tables. I tried to tell him it was bad for his cat stomach, given all the butter, but he listened about as well as he usually did. Plus, seeing as I was eating muffins and brownies for breakfast, I wasn't exactly arguing from the moral high ground.

There weren't too many masks in evidence, which was at least a little reassuring. Surely if they'd been *that* bad, everyone would still be wearing them, right? Instead, all I saw were a lot of people deeply regretting making such liberal use of the free bar last night. Or deeply regretting the side effects, anyway. Although I did see the usual pack of kids on bikes go tearing past at one point, all of them in feathery masks, and I could've sworn they left flaming tyre tracks behind them that didn't quite touch the road. I also spotted a woman in a clown mask somersaulting into the little shop that passed as our local supermarket, which set me shuddering. Even if clowns hadn't been inherently creepy, the carnival would've put me off them for life.

But they were outside, not in here, and only isolated cases, so I could mostly ignore them. There were always going to be *some* people more deeply invested in acting out their true selves, or whatever the masks promised. Everyone else just needed some hydration and a greasy fry-up, basically.

Things eased off around lunchtime, and I carted the last of the bartered goods through to the big kitchen and living area out the back, Ruiner trailing after me and complaining his stomach hurt. A huge stone hearth occupied by a cauldron big enough to swim in (not the cauldron I'd discovered Norma's body in, but a new one of a similar size) took up the majority of the back wall, with an old-fashioned but well-equipped kitchen to the right and a couple of sagging sofas and a large TV to the left. Starlight was face-down on one of the sofas, a clutter of ingredients abandoned on the big, scrubbed wood table that filled the centre of the room.

Ruiner jumped to the arm of the sofa next to her head and yowled, "*Morning!*"

Starlight shot up to sitting with a yelp, and Ruiner snickered.

"Hello," I said. "Didn't hear you come in."

"*Urgh.* Your brother sucks."

"I'm right here," Ruiner said.

"Fine, you suck."

I snorted. She really was in a bad way. I don't think I'd ever heard Starlight say anything negative about anyone, other than me when I kind of accused her of cursing my car and trying to kill me. "Good night?" I asked her.

She squinted at me, her hair looking as if Howard had been nesting in it. "Why didn't you tell me you were leaving?"

"You were having a dance-off with a bunch of ten-year-olds. I didn't want to interrupt."

"I think I lost," she said, getting up and investigating the latest haul of goods. She picked out a ruddy-cheeked apple, which was the sort of hangover food only someone like Starlight could favour. "I was starting another batch of the tincture, but it's really hot in here."

It wasn't, but I didn't bother contradicting her. "We've still got about half of the last lot left."

"We'll need more," she said around a mouthful of apple.

"Tell people to bring better fish," Ruiner put in, and we both ignored him.

"Every night can't be like that, can it?" I said.

"Not quite like that. But we'll still need a good stock."

No wonder half the town shut down. But I just said,

"Well, we've got enough for tomorrow. Don't worry about making more now."

"Really?" She sat down at the table with a sigh. "Good." Her mask was lying next to her bag as if she'd taken it off as she came in, and she picked it up, stroking it absently, like she might a small pet. Or a ferret. Howard wasn't in her hair, but I spotted him belly up on the sofa, wearing a red herringbone jumper.

"Put that thing down," Ruiner said, jumping to the table and glaring at Starlight.

"What?" she asked, looking blankly at the mask as if unsure where it had come from. "It's just my mask."

"Those masks are as creepy as back-alley Botox."

Starlight frowned at him. "They're works of art."

That was true, but it didn't make Ruiner wrong. "Does everyone get their masks from Alaric?" I asked. "There's no other supplier?"

Starlight shook her head. "It wouldn't be the same. He always has the perfect mask for everyone."

"How does he get paid? He didn't ask for anything last night."

She shrugged. "I suppose Isabella sorts it out. At least for anyone at the opening party. He has his stall at the market, though, so maybe he makes the money there."

I didn't know where Hollowbeck town hall got its money from, and I wondered for the first time what the taxes and business license fees were going to be like for a magic shop. Should I have insurance? I wasn't sure AXA was going to cover risk of exploding cauldrons and infestations of ferrets.

"Did Theodore or Isabella come back last night?" I asked. "After the … you know."

She took a bite of apple and looked at me quizzically. "The what?"

"The dead woman? You haven't *forgotten?*"

"Oh." She still looked puzzled. "Weird. Now you say it, *of course* I remember. That was awful. And she looked like you."

"Bet it's those bloody masks making you forget," Ruiner said. "You'll all be running around with a pig's head on a stick before long."

"It's a *mask*," Starlight said, looking confused. "What's a pig got to do with it?"

I wanted to agree with her, but hadn't I thought how weird it was last night, that the party had just carried on as if a corpse hadn't popped up right in the middle of the opening ceremony? I looked at my coat, hanging from a hook by the back door. I should've left the mask at home.

"So did they come back after I left?" I asked, deciding to leave the question of the masks alone for now.

"I didn't see them." She twisted in her seat, looking at the clock over the kitchen cooker. "We should go to the market. Isabella will probably be there, and we can have a look around, too. It's always *so* fun the day after the party!" Apparently I should be looking to apples for my next hangover cure, because she sounded almost as perky as usual.

"Alright," I said, putting the rest of the potted shrimp in the fridge before Ruiner could make himself any sicker. "Let's do it."

Starlight bounced up, clapping her hands excitedly. "Yay! Come on, Howard." She scooped the ferret up off the sofa, ignoring him baring his teeth and trying to bite her fingers. "Hot chocolates on me!" She vanished into the hall, heading for the shop, and Ruiner and I looked at each other.

"How can you even stomach a hot chocolate after all those muffins?" he asked.

"It's better than you and your potted shrimp," I said,

pulling my coat on. "Do you really think the masks made everyone just forget about the body?"

"Don't you?"

I didn't answer, chewing on the inside of my lip as I followed Starlight down the hall. It should sound ridiculous. It was giving them way too much importance. But at the same time, it felt deeply possible.

THE SHOP WAS EMPTY, so we simply flipped the sign to closed and left, abandoning the barrow of used books and rack of faded postcards outside. No one was likely to steal them (no one had even bought any in the time I'd been there), and we'd be back later anyway. The sun was already on the way down, laying long rich shadows along the main street. There were more people out now, wandering around with a desultory, Sunday afternoon energy, and mostly tending in the direction of the hall and the green. We headed that way too, the snow still resting smooth and luminous on the verges and gardens. The library crouched low between the leafless trees, warm gold light glimmering inside, and for a moment I considered dropping in for a cuppa with Ben and seeing if he was feeling as rough as James. And also if *he* remembered the dead woman. Surely he would?

But Starlight was intent on the market, and I found myself not wanting to know if Ben didn't remember the woman. He was meant to be my other touchstone to normality, him and my brother, and a more reliable one than Ruiner. I didn't feel like having that illusion shattered.

We skirted the library and the hall, heading further down the road towards where a gently rutted lane led between the low stone wall that enclosed the hall's garden and a worn wooden fence to the other side, beyond which the market had blossomed into musical, sweet-scented life. Someone was making waffles, the sugary scent hanging in the air, and onions fried somewhere else, and the pungent scent of mulled wine bulldozed through everything, asserting its festive notes. The aisles of tents and cabins and trailers overflowed with stands of clothes and hats and ornaments, wooden statues and stone birdbaths and metal sculptures tiptoed out of the confines of the stalls, and extension cables ran everywhere, lifted overhead or trapped under trip guards, feeding lights and heaters and chargers. Families dragged kids past toy displays and tried to keep sticky fingers away from clothes racks, teenagers ate sausages in buns washed down with vats of bubble tea, and shoppers rushed from stall to stall, encumbered with scarves and hats and bags and familiars, faces bright with delight.

The aisles radiated out from a central space formed by the main food and drink trucks. Large, upended wooden barrels served as bar tables, men in flat caps and women in well-used wellies leaning on them with pints in hand. Wooden picnic benches held feasting groups, paper parcels of fish'n'chips and bamboo bowls of curry and rice fighting for space among cardboard cartons of noodles and paella. More barrels were cut out and padded with cushions to form deep, soft chairs, gathered around fire pits along with folding canvas seats, and I spotted at least a few of my customers from earlier dozing in front of the flames or working on their new hangovers. There were games laid on too, giant Jenga and hoop toss and lawn darts. That one seemed highly risky given the crowded grounds and the oversupply of mulled wine.

I spotted a coffee stall and went straight to it, despite Starlight's promise of hot chocolate. That could come later. I had to pay actual money, which made me more sure than ever I needed to find a way to move at least a tiny bit of the Cosy Cauldron's trade out of the vegetable section, but the scent of the coffee shifted the last of the day's odd, disjointed mood from me. I breathed deeply, settling my shoulders and scanning the market. It was just a market. A really *nice* market, but just a market. I had to stop thinking everything had teeth.

Of course, it still had a Hollowbeck twist. There was more on offer than the usual personalised novelty socks and glitzy ornaments that looked great by candlelight but fell apart as soon as you got them home. There were those, of course, and food stalls selling venison sausages, or crêpes, or potato spirals on sticks, but there was also a very small ice palace at the far end of the central area which appeared to have a Viking pub inside it and a glitzy oyster and champagne bar like we were on the French Riviera somewhere. As we ambled slowly through the stalls, I discovered I could also buy everything from fairy circle banishments to flying carpets (very unreliable, apparently, and liable to flip you over at inconvenient moments, according to Starlight), to carnivorous ivy that promised to devour any intruders (even I could see that was a bad idea — how did the plants know who was an intruder?). Still, it was all very within the normal realms of Hollowbeck weirdness, and I was almost starting to relax when Ruiner did his normal scramble to my shoulder.

Jackie and I both hissed, and I snapped, "Stop doing that!"

"What? You've got a coat on."

"It's the principle."

"Whatever. You noticed how many people are still wearing their masks?"

"I—" I stopped. I *had*, but I also hadn't. Starlight had

put hers back on at some point while I was examining the plants, and now she spun gently ahead of us, her takeaway mug of herbal tea clutched in one hand. And she wasn't the only one. It might not have been the majority of the shoppers, but a good half of them were wearing masks, scaled and feathered and sequinned and horned and bedecked with ribbons and gauze. No one was acting too oddly, other than two small girls in lion masks who were stalking an increasingly alarmed-looking teenaged boy. "They're just masks," I said to Ruiner quietly.

"That induce amnesia?"

"Everyone was pretty drunk."

"Keep telling yourself that."

"Morgan!" Starlight called, wheeling around with her long skirts swirling around her legs. "Isabella's just up there!"

"Oh, grab her," I said, breaking into a jog to catch up while Ruiner complained and Jackie cuddled closer to my neck, the grimoire banging against my hip. Starlight ran on ahead, and I was just in time to see her duck into the large, ornate tent I'd seen Finn and Alaric at last night. It was constructed of heavy, tapestry-like cloth with curling patterns running across it, and the broad front had two doors, the flaps pinned back to reveal a shadowy interior. Lining the exterior walls like blank-eyed sentries were masks, a little bedraggled by wear and weather, but full of scowling presence anyway. They watched with empty eye sockets as I slowed, coming to a stop before I reached the entrance, the hair on the back of my neck prickling with their scrutiny.

"Starlight?" I said, hearing the uncertainty in my own voice.

There was no answer, and I stepped a little closer, trying to see into the dimness beyond. Jackie chittered softly, the noise comforting. I still harboured suspicions she was merely putting up with me until someone more suitable came along, someone witchier who knew what they were doing, but there was something reassuring about her presence even so.

I couldn't see far past the threshold. The interior was turned into narrow aisles by more masks in hanging columns, stacked so closely together they almost hid the worn tapestries that supported them, forming impenetrable walls. Sequins and beads dripped from the heavily lined eye holes of masquerade masks, and feathers sprouted and flowed from their tops. Jumbled in with them were full-face animal masks that ranged from the highly stylised to the alarmingly realistic, as if someone had taxidermied foxes and leopards to make them. For all I knew, they had. Wooden masks glittering with shell and bone rubbed cheeks with half collapsed latex masks of celebrities and aliens and creepy doll faces, and I stayed where I was.

"Starlight?" I tried again.

"Nope," Ruiner said. "Don't like it."

"We can't just leave her in there."

"She's a grown woman. She can look after herself."

"It's just masks," I said, trying to find some conviction somewhere. "And no one's even wearing them. They can't do much on their own, can they?"

"Maybe that's what they want you to think."

Even if the masks weren't *just* masks, I doubted they were capable of such depths of deception. There was no sign of Starlight, though. The tent seemed to have swallowed her. I couldn't see any movement inside at all, and somehow, despite the crowds washing through the rest of the market, there was no one nearby. Just me, a cat, and a rat.

Plus one missing witch.

"Dammit," I said, and headed in, trying not to make eye contact with the masks. "*Starlight!*"

There was still no response.

The stall swallowed us. That was the impression I had, and the breath caught in my throat. On my shoulder, my brother hissed, "Feels like the bloody carnival."

"It's not that bad," I whispered back, but I knew what he meant. The press of the tent was giving me flashbacks to the carnival's big top, that semi-sentient, hungry beast of canvas that had almost devoured us both back at the end of the summer. This was different, the roof low above us and formed of more heavy tapestries that trapped a lingering warmth inside, along with the scent of musk and sawdust. It didn't feel like it was waiting for us to let our guard down to pounce. It felt like what it was, a well-travelled and crowded tent, more at home in a Marrakech marketplace than a (possibly) Cumbrian village green, in itself offering no threat.

Its contents were a different matter, though. Everywhere I looked were more masks, row upon row of them, filling every spare scrap of space, pinning the tent to the world with overdrawn fangs and blank eyes and horns and antennae and lolling, mocking tongues. It felt like they were moving on the edge of my vision, jostling each other gleefully but freezing again as soon as I looked around.

I swallowed hard, and Ruiner whispered, "Still think it's not that bad?"

I hesitated, not quite able to answer, and spotted a flash of movement deeper in the stall. "Starlight!" I shouted, and hurried after the glimpse of colour, setting Jackie grumbling and scuttling about on my shoulder, until she scrambled down my arm and perched on top of the bag, her teeth bared. "Starlight, stop messing about."

"That wasn't Starlight," Ruiner hissed, and I stopped,

my heart going too fast and spots swimming in my vision, as if I'd been climbing hills instead of simply stepping into some market stall.

"Are you sure?" I asked.

"No," he admitted. "But are you sure it *was?*"

I didn't answer, wavering for a moment and trying to ignore Jackie's complaints. I glanced down at her, then opened the bag so she could dive on top of the grimoire, baring her teeth at me. I should listen to her. Should listen to them both. But Starlight was in here somewhere, and I couldn't just leave her. Someone would ask her to be the winter's ritual sacrifice and she'd say yes just to help out. I started walking again, albeit a little more carefully.

"Morgs," Ruiner started, and I pushed him off my shoulder. I didn't need him complaining at me. He tumbled away with a yelp, and I spotted a narrow gap in the tapestries, between the columns of masks. I slipped through it into another aisle, just as crowded and shadowed as the first. Soft low lights crawled through the masks, the source uncertain, and rendered them Halloween-ish. As the tapestries moved in the wake of my passage, everything seemed to shift and creep, setting my skin crawling even more.

"Starlight?" My voice came out a lot more wobbly than I'd have liked, and I cleared my throat before trying again. "Starlight, are you there?"

Silence came back to me, not even a murmur from Ruiner, and I looked around for my nuisance of a brother. He wasn't in sight. I was alone.

8. Something rotten

BEHIND ME, THE GAP I'D COME THROUGH SEEMED TO HAVE sealed itself off, leaving behind a tapestry of masks indistinguishable from all the others. I hesitantly prodded a large plastic Godzilla head, and it wobbled, but the cloth it hung from didn't move. It had swung aside just fine when I'd pushed through from the other side. I looked around, frowning. It *had* been that panel, hadn't it? Suddenly I wasn't sure. They all looked the same, just mask after glaring mask, and I was abruptly unsure as to which direction we'd even come into the tent from. My left? Maybe? I took a couple of steps in that direction, whispering, "Ruiner?"

He didn't reply, and I licked my lips, the coffee stale on my tongue. Movement caught my eye and I spun toward it, confronting a figure in skinny jeans and a long, black puffer jacket, the face white and strained under a green hat dragged down by the weight of a frog-shaped pompom. The hat was unmistakable (a gift from Petunia, who had taken to crocheting recently), but I still flinched so violently that Jackie pulled herself half out of the bag, glaring at me.

"Sorry," I whispered, and examined myself in the mirror, tucking some stray hair under the hat. "Get it together," I told my reflection. "You're the town witch."

Jackie gave a squeak which seemed to throw some doubt on that statement, and I didn't blame her. I didn't feel like the town witch. I felt like a kid who'd lost their mum in a supermarket. I started to turn away from the mirror, and as I did so, I saw a hand emerging from the wall behind me in the reflection, reaching for my bag. I spun to look at the wall, almost expecting the hand would only exist in the reflection, some mirror monster that would grab mirror-me and gobble them up (I realise it was a hand, but this was mirror logic, and besides, it was likely attached to *something*). But the hand was there in real life too, reaching out blindly, so I snatched up the nearest wooden mask, tearing it from its hook, and smashed it straight down on the disembodied limb. A yelp went up behind the tapestry, and the arm tried to pull back, but I dropped the mask and grabbed the rogue limb with both hands, relieved to find it was definitely attached to someone, the sleeve of their fleece soft under my fingers.

"*Ow!*" the arm's owner howled, trying to twist out of my grip.

"Where's Starlight?" I demanded, digging my fingers in deeper. "What have you done with her?"

"*What?*"

I hauled on the arm, and the mask-cluttered tapestry bellied out as someone stumbled behind it then pitched forward, evidently tripping on the folds of cloth. Too late, I realised I was right in their path and tried to jump back, but masks were tumbling all around me as the tapestry ripped somewhere near the ceiling and went into a slow-motion collapse. I stumbled on the fallen masks and the arm's owner crashed into me, both of us crying out as we were swallowed by the folds of fabric and carried to the ground. I thrashed wildly, trying to fight free from both the cloth and the uneasy feel of the masks sliding past me, eye sockets and horns and teeth. One of my flailing arms connected with someone's nose.

"Ow! Bloody hell!"

"Get off me!" I yelled, paddling madly at the cloth as if I could swim my way free.

"You're on *me!"* The arm's owner was thrashing about themself now, and I took an elbow to the belly.

"Oof!"

"Sorry!"

Someone else was shouting beyond the cloth, and one of my arms found open air. I scrabbled towards it, but my attacker was doing the same, and for a moment all was a confusion of cracking, sliding masks and ripping cloth, then I managed to get one good knee into somewhere soft, more by accident than design. I was rewarded with a pained yelp, and finally rolled free of the mess, flopping onto the floor of the tent and finding Ruiner staring at me with wide eyes and a puffed tail.

"Where the hell did you go?" he demanded.

"Shut up," I panted, in case the owner of the arm emerged to see him talking. I struggled to my knees, and checked the bag. The book was still there, Jackie curled next to it and glaring up at me as if this was all my fault. Which, to be fair, it kind of was.

The tapestry heaved violently, like some great sea beast beached in the confines of the aisle, scattering masks across the heavy rugs of the floor, then a tangled head of streaky blond hair emerged, and Finn looked at me with watering eyes. "Morgan? What the *hell?*" he complained. "Needed to get out some frustrations, did you?"

"Sorry," I started, then shook my head. "Wait, you *attacked* me!"

"Did not," he said, collapsing back to the floor and bracing his hands on his bent knees as he stared at the low ceiling. His face was pale, freckles standing out starkly across the bridge of his nose even in the low light. "Oh, that was a low blow."

I winced, realising what the soft area I'd hit likely was. "You did grab me."

"I never *touched* you," he said, taking a shaky breath. I could see the heavy bracelet on his left wrist now. If he'd just used that instead of the right, I'd have known who it was straight away, and we wouldn't be in this situation. "*Ow,*" he said, with deep feeling.

"Brutal," Ruiner said in a low voice, peering around me. "You do go for the throat, Morgs. Or other bits." He sounded approving, which wasn't great. Anything my little brother approved of was something I needed to be doing less of.

"Sorry," I said to Finn. "I didn't realise it was you. I thought you were attacking me."

"*How?*"

"Well, you just reached through the wall and grabbed me. Or tried to. What was I supposed to think?"

"Oh, I don't know. That I was adjusting tapestries, maybe? In the shop I work in? How about that?" He looked at me finally, his eyes pale in the dim light. He looked more bewildered than angry, and I scratched the back of my head, dislodging the bobble hat then pulling it back down.

"It was an instinctive reaction. Also an accident."

"Great. I feel so much better." He took a couple of shaky breaths, and I puffed air over my lip.

"Have you seen Starlight?" I tried. "My friend with the fairy mask?"

"Not in the time between you hauling me through a wall and kneeing me in the bits," he said, and Ruiner snickered. Finn looked at him, then at me.

"I realise I'm in rather a lot of pain, but did your cat just laugh?"

"No," I said, and Ruiner gave another of his unconvincing *meows*. He really needed to work on that.

Finn nodded, closing his eyes, and I settled my bag in place then picked my way carefully through the mess, wincing at some nasty (and potentially expensive) cracks from underfoot. I crouched down next to Finn and he opened his eyes warily. Close up, they were a soft grey-green, and currently a little watery.

"Are you going to hit me again?"

"Only if you jump out at me again." I offered him a hand. He took it, and I awkwardly pulled him to a sitting position. There was a little more colour in his face now, and he wiped his mouth, looking from me to Ruiner, sitting in the aisle with his tail twitching and his ears back.

"Ah … who were you looking for again?" Finn asked.

"Starlight. Fairy mask, long blonde hair, insufferably cheerful. And a ferret."

He nodded, as if the ferret was to be expected. It was hardly the most unusual familiar in town. In fact, ferrets had become pretty standard ever since one of the book's deals had resulted in us being overrun. We'd been giving them away to anyone who'd take them. Buy one salve, get a free ferret type thing.

Finn started to get to his feet, and I scrambled up first, helping him. He let me, straightening up with a groan.

Close up, he was taller than he'd seemed the night before — but then, I didn't have the heels on anymore — and his arm was roped with muscle under my hands. It made the red, chafed skin under the bracelet seem like even more of an insult, somehow.

"Doesn't that hurt?" I asked, touching his wrist, and he looked down at my hand, still on his forearm.

"A bit," he said, his voice low and warm. "Wasn't really thinking about it."

I met his gaze, and he smiled, that same oddly shy, hesitant expression, so out of place on someone who looked like he should be chucking trees about the place. I dropped his arm hurriedly and said, "Alright then?" in a cheery voice, cringing inwardly even as I did. I sounded like I was channelling some bloke in a sleeveless T-shirt down at the local pub.

He cleared his throat. "Sure. You know, other than the possibly permanent injuries." But his smile widened to a grin, giving me a flash of white teeth, so I didn't think he could be *that* injured. "What's your cat called?"

"Ruiner."

"Interesting. Ruiner, who doesn't laugh."

"Cats generally don't." Maybe he'd heard Ruiner talking the night before, or maybe my brother's reputation was already spreading — he was hardly good at being subtle — but I wasn't about to admit to a stranger that the cat was anything more than a cat. Not even a stranger with nice eyes.

"Of course." Finn rubbed a hand through his hair as he examined the collapsed tapestry and broken masks. "Ugh."

"I'll help you pick it up," I said. "But I need to find Starlight first."

"She won't have gone far. It's not that big a tent."

I made a doubtful noise, looking at Ruiner, who twitched his ears. I took that to mean he wasn't so sure either. After all, we'd lost each other in the space of two aisles. "I'd really rather find her."

Finn moved a couple of masks aside with his foot, then looked at me. "You think someone might jump out of a wall at her, too?"

"Well, you did."

He grinned at that. "I was meaning you're the problem."

Ruiner snickered again, and I nudged him with my foot urgently. "Ha," I said, but Finn talked over me.

"That cat definitely laughed."

"He just has a very weird meow," I said. "Can you help me find her?"

"Find who?" a new voice asked, and I spun around so fast I tripped over Ruiner, who yowled in outrage and fled a ways down the aisle before stopping, staring around with his tail lashing. "Oh, *sorry*," Alaric said, catching my arm and steadying me before I could fall through another wall. "Didn't meant to sneak up on you."

I had no idea where he'd come from, and given the way both Finn and I had stumbled through the tapestries I supposed he could've just stepped out anywhere. I looked around warily, wondering if there were any other annoyingly attractive men waiting to pop out of the walls and grab me. I wasn't *exactly* complaining, but I wasn't sure I could take too much more. I was starting to feel the effects of my extended bout of singleness.

Alaric pressed his free hand to his chest, giving me that warm smile which did strange things to my stomach. It had to be an enchantment of some sort. I hadn't been single *that* long. "Apologies, Morgan. I didn't mean to scare you. The half-destroyed shop distracted me somewhat."

I flushed, looking at the broken masks at my feet. "Sorry. Small misunderstanding."

He laughed softly. "Quite alright. The stall can be somewhat disorientating. Finn was meant to be correcting a few of the more confusing routes." There was a touch of reproof in his voice, nothing too severe, but Finn cleared his throat, looking down the aisle and twisting his bracelet restlessly. I wanted to reach out and stop him, before he made the skin underneath any worse.

Instead I just said, "It was my fault. I was looking for—"

"Morgan!" Starlight peered around Alaric, her face flushed and excited under the pale purples and greens of her mask. "Morgan, there you are! I found Isabella!"

"Where did you go?" I demanded. "I was shouting for you!"

"Sorry, I didn't hear."

"The acoustics can be tricky," Alaric said. "The tapestries misdirect things."

"I suppose," I said, although Starlight hadn't been *that* far ahead of me. "Where's—"

"Hello, Morgan, dear," Isabella said, stepping straight through the tapestry next to me and making me give a very undignified squawk. I shouldn't have wished away the annoyingly attractive men. Not that Isabella was unattractive in the slightest, just that she was really working the ghostly thing, and had currently paused with a large alligator mask protruding from her belly, which was hard to look away from. "And Ruiner." She wriggled her fingertips at my brother, who purred roughly.

"Show her!" Starlight said, quite literally bouncing on her toes. "Show Morgan!"

I was starting to wonder what Starlight had been eating

other than the apple, because she'd recovered far too well. "Show me what?"

"*Unmasked* meets the needs of all," Alaric said, smiling broadly.

"*Mrrow*," Isabella said, sounding more like a cat than my brother usually did, and I looked back at her, startled. She still had the alligator emerging from her torso, but she also had a mask on, a floating, smoky creation that didn't seem to quite have a fixed shape. It sported ears and whiskers though, plus sweeps of eyeliner that bewildered me for a moment. I knew she had large brown eyes, but suddenly they were bright green, the pupils not quite right, then she whipped the mask away again with a delighted laugh. "My first mask! Isn't it *wonderful?*"

"Um," I said. Her eyes were back to normal, but the lingering impression unsettled me. "How does that even work?"

"A master craftsman doesn't give away the secrets of his trade, Morgan," Alaric said, and Finn gave a small *huh*. Alaric shot him a sharp look, and Finn held up two pieces of a porcelain mask.

"I think I can fix this," he said.

"See? All sorted," Alaric said, giving me another lavish smile.

"Great. Sorry again." Most of my attention was on Isabella, who had put the mask back on and was tiptoeing up to Ruiner, half bent over. Ruiner watched her come with his ears flat, leaning further and further back as she got closer, then fled to hide behind my legs.

"Oh," the mayor said, straightening up. "I'm sorry, Ruiner."

He peered at her from around my boots, and I stole a look at Finn, but he was still picking up bits of broken mask, not looking at any of us. He seemed to have shrunk away, fading into the background, as if Alaric cast too deep a shadow.

"Isn't it amazing?" Starlight demanded, hurrying to Isabella's side and pointing at Isabella's mask urgently, as if I couldn't see it. "Alaric's a *genius*."

"Oh, well. I wouldn't go *that* far," Alaric said with a wink, and Finn dropped a handful of broken masks with a clatter. "*Finn*."

"Sorry."

Isabella touched the ears of her mask and stretching languidly. "I'd go that far," she all but purred.

"We should go," I said aloud. I wanted to tell her to take the mask off, but I couldn't do that here.

Alaric made a regretful noise. "Are you sure? Perhaps we could take a little tea—"

"No," I said, seeing Starlight already nodding eagerly. "I mean, thanks, but no."

"I'll see you out," Finn said, piling the scraps of broken mask to one side of the aisle.

"Is there a rush?" Alaric asked, giving me that smile again, and I tried to ignore the flare of heat in my belly. "I had hoped to speak with you, Morgan."

"We're not in a hurry, are we?" Starlight asked.

Isabella ignored us, poking a feathery mask with one finger. I thought I could see it moving, which was odd. Maybe she could go a bit poltergeist when she fancied it.

"We do have a shop to run," I said, my tone curter than I intended. The tent was feeling too hot and too enclosed, and the air was tight with some old, unspoken tension.

"Come on," Finn said, indicating the general direction I'd thought the market was.

"You've got cleaning up to do," Alaric said. "I shall see the ladies out. Come, come!" He turned away with a sweeping motion that looked as if he should have had a cloak swirling from his shoulders, then strode down the aisle, one hand drifting along the tapestries. He didn't seem to really touch them, the masks barely moving in his wake, but suddenly where I was sure there had been only walls before a clear path appeared, running straight to the market outside and inviting in a curl of cold air and the whiff of hot sugar.

"Let's go." I waved Starlight ahead of me. "Isabella?"

"*Mrrrow?*" She blinked at me lazily.

"Isabella?"

She ignored me, batting a ribbon descending from a mask. Great. Apparently ghost masks were even worse than human ones. I looked at my brother. "Ruiner? A little help?"

He looked at me blankly for a moment, then gave a lazy "*Maow*" that almost sounded authentic.

Isabella looked around immediately, and Ruiner headed after Starlight. Isabella followed, and I turned to Finn.

"What the hell's going on with the masks?" I asked, my voice low, and he shook his head.

"I don't know."

"You *do*. You were going to tell me something last night."

He licked his lips, plucking at his bracelet again as he checked down the aisle, but Alaric was standing at the entrance, adjusting Starlight's mask. In the low sunlight, she glittered and shone, fragile wings shimmering in and out of existence behind her.

"This isn't usual," I said to Finn. "You can't tell me it is, even for here."

"*Shhh.*" He glanced around, and I shivered, the weight of all those empty eyes heavy on my neck. "Later. I have to be careful."

"*When?*"

"Morgan?" Isabella called, sounding almost like herself. "Are you coming?"

"Be right there," I called back, then raised my eyebrows at Finn.

"I'll find you, soon as I can," he said. "Go on." There were strained lines around his mouth, and I hesitated a moment longer, but the walls felt as if they were beginning to close up again, the light from outside growing fainter, so I just nodded. I jogged for the entrance, feeling like a free diver struggling for the surface on the last dregs of their breath, and suddenly sure the walls would slam shut before I got there, trapping me inside and swallowing me up.

But I emerged breathless onto the frozen grass of the green, market-goers washing past in either direction, and Alaric smiled at me almost indulgently.

"Terribly sorry if you were a little unnerved in there, Morgan," he said. "The masks can be unsettling for some people, especially in the low light."

"I'm not unnerved," Starlight said. "I *love* them."

"Me too," Isabella said, running her hands through her hair and reaching for the sky, wriggling in a manner that made a passing woman stop and stare with open admiration. "All these years, and I've missed out on it *all!*"

"And I am so glad to be able to make it up to you," Alaric said, pressing his hands together in front of his chest and bowing slightly. "Everyone deserves the freedom of a mask." He looked at me. "Are you not happy with yours, Morgan?"

I wished he wouldn't say my name so much. It had

such a salesman-y feel, overly friendly and falsely intimate. "It's fine," I said.

"*Fine?* My masks have never been described as just *fine.*"

"Great, then. Wonderful," I said impatiently.

Alaric hesitated, and for a moment the salesman smile slipped, revealing something paler and more honest beneath. "I am finding they're requiring a little adjustment this year. If yours is not ideal…"

"I said it's fine," I replied. There was no way I was putting it on in front of him and letting him *adjust* it. I'd wind up crawling about with Isabella. "I really need to get back to the shop."

"Already?" Starlight asked. She was standing on her toes, looking as if she might float away at any moment. Howard hung half out of her bag, teeth bared.

"Yes. Howard looks hungry," I said, and she immediately looked down at him.

"Oh, *Howard.* I'm so sorry, sweetie." She pushed her mask up and plucked the ferret out of her bag, fussing over him. I stole a peek at Alaric, seeing a muscle tic in his jaw as that moment of vulnerability passed, but his smile widened and he swept his arms wide.

"Ladies, it is *wonderful* to pass a moment with you. We shall do more later, yes?"

"Yes," Isabella said immediately. Starlight made an agreeable noise, but she was mostly concerned with the ferret now.

"Morgan? I really would like to talk with you." He examined me with those warm, dark eyes, and I nodded.

"Sure. We can do that." I turned away from the tent before he could ask when, avoiding eye contact with the masks, my breath still sticking in my chest a little. Ruiner trotted next to me, giving another unconvincing mew, and Starlight and Isabella followed.

The masks were never going to be normal masks, but this was something more. And *still* no one was talking about the dead woman.

Something was very, very rotten at the heart of this festival, and everyone was too busy playing dress-up to see it.

9. Deadly & disastrous

Ruiner and I led Isabella and Starlight away from *Unmasked*, Starlight still fussing over Howard, and Isabella darting from one side of the aisle of stalls to the other, inspecting softly moving flags and glittering crystal beads hanging from mobiles and wind chimes with her head cocked, or rubbing her face on woollen shawls and running her fingers through dangling scarves.

"Sorry," I said to a bemused stallholder who had paused his knitting to watch, heavy eyebrows pulled down in puzzlement. "She's very tactile."

"Sure," he said, not sounding very sure at all.

I wasn't either. Isabella's skirts were still sweeping through tent posts and passersby with impunity, but when she tried to touch things, they seemed to move. Not as much as they might if I did it, but more than I'd seen happen before. Not that it meant anything, of course. Maybe it just took a lot of energy and she preferred not to bother.

"Come on," I said to her as she worked her fingers into a bobbly pink jumper, squeezing and stroking it.

"*Hmm?*"

"Let's go." I tried to sound bright and cheerful, as if it was *completely normal* to be dragging a ghost mayor cosplaying as a cat through the market, hoping she didn't try to catch a bird in her teeth. I made an encouraging *pspspsps* noise, as if I really was calling a cat, and she abandoned the jumper, following me.

"What the *hell* is going on?" Ruiner hissed. He'd taken the pause at the stall as an opportunity to scramble to my shoulder again.

"It's the masks," I mumbled, grabbing Starlight's elbow and leading her away from a display of crystals. She'd put her mask back on while I'd been concentrating on Isabella and was dancing about on her tiptoes again.

"Yeah, that bit I got," Ruiner said. "But why? And how come Isabella's gone straight to kitty-land without passing go or collecting a hundred pounds?"

That wasn't a question I could answer, especially not now, as I herded the two women into the market's centre, depositing Starlight at one of the big barrel tables. "Take that off," I ordered, pointing at her mask.

She blinked at me but pushed it onto her forehead. "Why?"

"Because it's making you act weird."

She snorted. "It's a *mask*. I'm just having fun. You need to relax."

I put my hands on my hips, then immediately felt like everyone's least favourite schoolteacher so I dropped them again, trying for a casual stance instead. "I'm fine. It's just—"

"Morgan!" Ruiner hissed, and I turned around to see Isabella at the next table, concentrating hard on a half-full pint glass as she pushed it towards the edge. The man it belonged to had his back to her as he watched two little girls, one in a woolly mammoth mask and the other in a dinosaur one, hitting each other enthusiastically with inflatable caveman bats. I supposed it was better than them trying to stomp on each other.

Isabella pushed the glass a little closer to the edge, tipping her head to one side.

"Isabella!" I almost grabbed her arm, but stopped myself in time, instead picking up the glass and moving it back to the man. He caught the movement and jumped, staring from it to me.

"Hey, what are you doing with my drink?"

"Nothing. It was going to fall off."

"It wasn't. Did you put something in it?" He straightened up, peering into the glass.

"What? No!"

"Bloody witches," he muttered, lifting the glass to inspect the bottom. "Going about spiking drinks with love charms and so on."

"I would *never*," I started, then commotion broke out behind me and I spun around.

"*No! Stewie!*" someone wailed, and I spotted a hamster scuttling across the grass as fast as its fuzzy little legs would take it, Isabella running in pursuit, hunched over with her hands hooked into claws like a cartoon witch.

"Ruiner, *go*," I said, turfing him off my shoulder and breaking into a run in pursuit of the mayor. "Isabella! Isabella, *stop!*"

My brother shot ahead of me, a low-slung shadow with his long fur flying, weaving between legs and chairs and tables. I followed, not sure what either of us were going to do — I could hardly tackle a ghost — but also not wanting someone's traumatised familiar (or, worse, family pet) on my conscience.

"*Isabella!*" I swerved around the small dinosaur girl,

who roared at me, and was just in time to see Ruiner pounce on the hamster, rolling over twice then coming up with the creature pinned in his paws. So much for not traumatising it. Ruiner sat there, tail flicking furiously, and growled at Isabella as she came to a stop next to him, dropping to her knees with her eyes on the rodent.

"Isabella," I said again, putting as much authority into my voice as I could. "Take your mask off."

She didn't look at me, and we were rapidly becoming the centre of a circle of interested onlookers, holding beers and mulled wine and potato spirals on sticks. A young man with a shaved head and half a dozen earrings in one ear pushed through the crowd, his eyes wide and panicked.

"Stewie? Where's Stewie?"

"He's okay," I said. "My cat's got him."

"*What?*"

"In one piece! He's in one piece!" I hurried over to Ruiner, skirting Isabella carefully, and took the hamster from my brother. "Thanks," I whispered, and he gagged.

"I *licked* a rodent," he said. "I don't even know why."

I ignored him and turned back to Stewie's anxious owner. "See? He's fine."

The young man almost snatched the hamster off me, examining him anxiously. "If your cat hurt him…"

"He didn't. He didn't like the taste."

Both Stewie and his human gave me matching horrified looks, then the young man hurried off, still crooning over the hamster. I looked at the crowd, none of whom seemed too impressed.

"Done," I said, as cheerfully as I could. "All okay."

"That's the town witch," the big man from earlier said. "She spiked my drink. Bet it was a love spell." A murmur went through the crowd.

"I didn't spike your drink."

He folded his arms over his chest, scowling at me, the little dinosaur and mammoth flanking him in matching poses, their own conflict forgotten. "What, you saying I'm not worth a love spell?"

The murmurs were louder this time, and a woman in a fox mask said, "*Honestly.* How rude."

I glared at her, then back at the man. "You *wanted* me to spike your drink?"

"No," he said. "But you don't have to sound like you wouldn't do it."

"But I *wouldn't!*"

"Just because he's hefty," Foxy said, crossing her arms. "So superficial!"

"I'm *burly,*" the big man protested.

"And it's beside the point," I said. "I'd never spike *anyone's* drink."

"Because you can't?" Foxy suggested. "I heard you were a bit of a rubbish witch."

I wasn't happy with the level of agreement in the murmur this time, although I had to admit it was pretty justified. "Because it would be a *terrible* thing to do," I said.

"Some excuse that is."

I just stared at her, bewildered and not sure which accusation to defend myself against first, the charge of being a useless witch or a love-charm-spiking one. The big man looked faintly confused as well, and the little dinosaur tugged his arm. "Daddy, I need a goat."

"You already have a guinea pig."

"No, to eat."

He stared at her, then patted her on the head. "You'll need to eat your veggies first."

I rubbed a hand over my face, the weight of everyone's regard scratching my nerves and making me wish I really was a decent witch, that I could feel the spark and slide of power on my fingers the way I had the night before. I touched the pocket of my coat where the mask was without thinking about it, and Jackie leaned out of the bag, hissing at me. "Oh, shut up," I muttered, and she bared her teeth.

"Look at the way she treats her familiar," Foxy said. "Abusive, that is."

I was tempted to show her just how abusive my language could get, but that wasn't going to help my case. Instead, I ignored her and turned to Isabella, who was still crouched on the ground, engaged in a staring match with Ruiner. "Come on," I said to the mayor. She didn't look around, just crept a little closer to my brother, who scuttled to me. I grabbed him before he could try climbing to my shoulder, lifting him up and setting him in place instead. "*Come on,*" I repeated, beckoning to Isabella urgently. Hollowbeck was hardly your average town, but it still felt like having the mayor chasing hamsters across the market-place was a bad look.

"Now she's treating our mayor like a *dog,*" Foxy announced.

"That does seem a bit off," the big man agreed.

"Have some respect," a stooped woman in a tiara and a pink mask said.

"What sort of witch *are* you?" a young woman with a tray of drinks asked. "What've you done to Isabella?"

"I bet she put a spell on her," Foxy said, and there was a collective gasp.

"You just said I couldn't do spells," I protested.

"That's what you want us to think," she said, giving me a slow grin.

I stared at her, my face hot and my eyes prickling, and my hand strayed to my pocket again.

"Just walk," Ruiner hissed. "You're not going to talk any sense into them."

I wanted to help Isabella, of course I did, but, on the other hand, she wasn't in any danger, and unless she gave a hamster a heart attack, she couldn't do too much damage. And I couldn't stand the weight of the crowd's scrutiny. I really couldn't. I retreated, hurrying past the big man, and headed out of the circle of tables and food stalls, clutching my bag close. It felt like everyone was watching me, their gazes critical and unforgiving, and I could barely breathe for it.

"Morgan? Morgan!"

I ignored Starlight's shout, wanting nothing more than the silence of my attic room at Petunia's, populated only by reticent frogs, or at least the shelter of the shop, where I could leave the sign on closed and shut the world out. I'd had enough.

I marched towards the gate, my eyes on the ground, and I almost ran straight into someone as they stepped in front of me.

"Sorry," I mumbled, trying to go around them, and they caught my arm.

"Morgan? Are you alright?"

I looked up at Ben almost reluctantly, sure he'd be in the bloody stupid knight's mask, dimples hidden and eyes shadowed in the metal sockets, even his stance stiff and unfamiliar. Instead, he looked back at me with his forehead creased in concerned lines, his gaze warm and brown and entirely himself. I could've hugged him. But I didn't, obviously, because that would've been weird.

So I said, "Yes," the word coming out curter than intended.

"Really?" he asked, raising his eyebrows.

I hesitated, and he looked over my shoulder.

"Morgan?" Starlight called, and I turned with a sigh. She'd pushed her mask up on her forehead and had Howard clutched in both arms. He was nibbling on a chunk of apple but looked distinctly disgruntled. "What happened?"

I looked from her to Isabella, who had followed as well, her eyes fixed on Ruiner.

"Isabella?" Ben asked. "Have you got a *mask?*"

Her gaze shifted to him, and she raised a hand to her face, a hesitant little gesture.

"Please take it off," I said, and she lingered a moment longer, then did, pushing it up.

She blinked at us, then said, "Oh, hello, Ben," in bright tones.

Ben frowned slightly. "Are you alright?"

"Yes." She looked around, touching the long coils of her hair. "Ah … I was doing something."

"You were *chasing a hamster*," I said.

"No, I don't think that was it," she replied, and started to drift off.

"*Isabella*," I said, and she stopped, giving me a puzzled look. "I don't think you should wear the mask."

She touched it. "But I've never had one before."

"Maybe that's a good thing."

"But I like it."

"*But you were chasing a hamster.*"

"I…" She looked uncharacteristically uncertain. "That doesn't sound like something I'd do."

"You did," Ruiner said. "I had to catch it first."

She *hmm*ed, then looked away.

"The masks are doing something to people," I said, looking from Isabella to Ben and Starlight. "I don't think they're safe."

"It's just freeing people to be their true selves," Starlight said. "It's like this every year."

I didn't have an argument for that, considering it was my first festival, but this was more than people just letting loose a bit, I was sure of it. I rubbed my face and looked at Ben. "You've read up on this whole thing. What does it say about the masks?"

"Just what Starlight said," he replied. "They're just masks. They don't change anyone's personality."

"Ghost masks too?" I asked, pointing at Isabella, who frowned and crossed her arms.

"We're people too, you know."

"I'm not arguing that. I'm just saying, you're chasing hamsters, which doesn't seem too true self-y. That's not *just a mask*." I barely stopped myself making air quotes around the last few words. Just because I was frustrated was no reason to be unbearable. "And what about the dead woman?"

My words silenced them. Starlight covered her mouth with one hand, and Isabella looked at the mask in her hand, then shoved it into the folds of her skirt (it evidently had pockets — how did an ancient ghost have pockets in her skirt, and I still couldn't get decent ones in my jeans?). Around us, the market surged and chattered, shouts of excitement and happiness drifting through the aisles, people rushing from stall to bar to stall again, and we looked at each other without speaking.

"Come on," Ben said finally. "We all need a drink."

"I think that was half last night's problem," I pointed out.

"Well, I need a drink," he said, and put his hand lightly in the small of my back to get me moving towards the little ice palace. "And you look like you need a sit down. No tea, I promise."

I let him guide me around the edge of the market's centre, comforting myself with the fact that at least four people in the place didn't seem to think I was both the worst witch in the world, and the most dangerous. It was something.

INSIDE THE ICE palace was warmer than I'd expected, the chill radiating off the walls cut by the animal skins and thick rugs on the floor, as well as the braziers holding fires dotted about the place. Rather than one big room, it was a rabbit warren of low-ceilinged nooks and crannies, all blossoming out from one central bar like the petals of a flower, dimly lit and secretive. Laughter and whispers rustled along the walls, dampened by the rugs and the ice, and we tucked ourselves into a remote corner, out of sight of the entrance. We collected a jug of beer and some glasses on the way past the bar, where the bartender nodded at me and noted it down in a book, then said, "I'll come by next week to settle up. I need something … personal." I gave him a thumbs up and hoped no one told him what a crappy, dangerous witch I was in the meantime. Wooden benches with woollen blankets and worn cushions served as chairs, and we settled into place, Ruiner complaining until the bartender turned up with a bowl of peanuts for the rest of us and some cat biscuits for him. My brother glared at it furiously, then at me.

"What?"

"*Biscuits?*"

"It's food," I told him. "You can't expect Tanya-level treats everywhere."

"I can," he snapped, but then fished a couple of biscuits out of the bowl with one paw. "Ugh. So *dry*."

I ignored him and looked at Isabella, who was reclining among the throws on one of the wooden benches that lined the nook, her mask on her knee. She stroked it gently, frowning.

"So?" I said to her. "What did Theodore find out? Who was the woman?"

She straightened up, lifting her hair over one shoulder gently. "I don't know," she admitted.

"You don't know?" I didn't mean it to sound as accusing as it did, but she was the *mayor*. She and Theodore were Hollowbeck's law and order. If she didn't know…

"She isn't local, and Theodore hadn't identified her by the end of the night," she said, her voice quiet. "And I am ashamed to admit that I was rather distracted by general festival duties, and then Alaric's offer of a mask. I have not devoted the time to it that I should have."

"So you don't have any suspects?" I asked.

"Without an identification, it makes it somewhat difficult to form any theories."

"I suppose everyone at the party could be a suspect," Ben said. "It happened during the opening ceremony, didn't it? She wasn't there before?"

"Definitely not," Isabella said, sounding much more sure of herself.

I took a mouthful of beer, bracing myself. "Theodore thought she looked a little like me, or Grace. Were we the targets?"

Isabella spread her fingers gently. "It's impossible to say. She was dressed in black, with a mask. That's all we know." She paused. "*Oh.* And she's not dead."

We all stared at her. "Possibly could've led with that," Ben said.

"Well, *sorry*," Isabella said, in such a sniffy tone I

wondered if the mask's cat influence was still in play. "Such differentiations aren't as vital for those of us no longer living."

"That seems *super* for the town's only form of law enforcement," Ruiner said, and I flicked his ear. He hissed.

"So she's okay?" I asked Isabella.

Isabella grimaced. "We can't wake her. She seems to be in a coma. I…" She trailed off, touching her hair with insubstantial fingers, and when she continued, her voice was quiet. "I was meant to come and find you last night, Morgan, to see if you could help. But then Alaric came with the mask, and I simply *forgot*. It's quite unforgivable."

I started to say I thought it was the mask's fault, not hers, but we were interrupted by the bartender ducking into the alcove, a tray tucked under his arm. We looked up at him, Isabella smiling questioningly.

"Ah…" His gaze fell on me. "I need some help."

"With the personal issue?" I asked.

"No." He rubbed the back of his head. "More of a medical thing."

Starlight and I looked at each other, then I got up. "Let's see, then," I said, and hoped he wasn't going to show me an ingrown toenail or something.

The bartender led me through the convoluted folds of the ice palace, like chambers in a seashell, past the bar itself and towards another quiet little alcove.

"No mask?" I asked him, and he touched his head as if searching for it.

"Not while I'm working," he said. "Gets a bit distracting." He stopped in front of a small wooden table, framed on one side by a bench and on the other by a high-backed chair. A woman of about my age was in it, her head tipped back and her eyes closed behind a simple, pale mask with gentle flourishes of yellow and green paint on it, bright against her dark skin. I vaguely recognised her, one of those people I'd passed on the road but never met.

"Mella?" Starlight said from behind me, but the woman didn't move.

I looked at Starlight. "You know her?"

"She has bees," Starlight said, and looked at the bartender accusingly. "How much have you served her?"

"One mulled wine," he said, pointing at the half-empty mug on the table. "I came over to see if it was okay, and…" He trailed off, rubbing one hand over his face, and I saw a tremor in his hand. "She won't wake up."

I frowned at him, and Starlight skirted the table, putting a hand on Mella's shoulder. "Mella?" She gave the woman a little shake. She didn't respond, but her head tipped forward. The rest of her body started to follow, and Starlight grabbed her shoulders, pushing her back into place. "Morgan, help me!"

I joined her hurriedly, and we got Mella settled back in the seat again. I picked up the mug and sniffed it, not sure what I was looking for. The gently herbal scent of whisper-wind, perhaps. It just smelled of cinnamon and alcohol, and I looked at the bartender. "Was she on her own the whole time?"

"I don't know," he said, looking around anxiously. "Is she okay?"

"Well, she's unconscious," I pointed out, then froze, and set the mug down carefully, looking at Starlight. "She's unconscious, right?"

"I don't know," Starlight whispered, and I stared from the woman's dark dress to her mask, and swallowed so hard I heard my ears click.

10. Sir Books-a-lot & PC Chomp

Starlight and I stared at each other, neither of us moving. I knew I needed to check for a pulse, but the last time I'd done that … well, the last time I'd done that I'd ended up with a shop, a rat, and a spell book, as well as a near-death experience. I wasn't sure I was ready to try again.

"Check her pulse," I whispered to Starlight.

She looked at the body. "I don't think I remember how."

"Just feel her wrist."

Starlight picked up one of Mella's hands gingerly, and the woman started to slide down the chair, the rugs rucking up under her feet. We both yelped and grabbed her, and the bartender hissed, "*Shh!*"

"Don't shush us," Starlight snapped, straightening up and leaving me struggling to push Mella back up the chair. "This is your problem!"

"Okay, okay, but can we keep it quiet? I don't want anyone thinking it was the wine. I just made a fresh batch."

"*Was* it the wine?" Starlight demanded.

"Of course it wasn't!"

"A little help, Starlight," I said. I had both hands braced on Mella's abdomen, but she was surprisingly heavy and seemingly had no intention of staying in the chair. Plus, a couple of bees had appeared from some-where, and were far too interested in what I was doing.

"Oh! Sorry." She grabbed the woman's legs, trying to slide them back into place, which was of precisely no use whatsoever.

"We need to lie her down," I said.

"No!" the bartender exclaimed. "Someone will see."

"Well, what d'you want us to do? Tie her to the damn chair?"

"I mean, if it'll work—"

"*No*," Starlight and I said together, and he raised his hands.

"Sorry, sorry."

Starlight lifted Mella's feet, and the woman immedi-ately slid the rest of the way down the chair, heading for the floor. I threw my weight against her torso, trying to trap her in place, and her chin dropped onto my shoulder. The bees swooped at me, and I gave an involuntary little wail of alarm. The bartender shushed me again.

"Don't you *dare*," Starlight spat at him.

"Never mind *that*," I complained, sinking onto my knees with my arms still around Mella, desperate to let go but not wanting her to just flop to the floor. It seemed an awful thing to allow anyone to do, and I had an idea the bees might object, too. "Help me!"

Between the two of us, we managed to get Mella on the ground, kneeling on either side of her and examining her anxiously. I rubbed one hand over my face and looked at Starlight, and the bartender said, "Well?"

I looked up at him. "Get Isabella."

He nodded and hurried off, leaving us alone.

"Poor Mella," Starlight said mournfully.

"She's alive," I said. I'd felt her breath when she'd fallen over my shoulder, whispering against my ear. It had been creepy as anything, but it was also reassuring. Now I pinched her nose shut gently, and after one anxious moment where I wondered uncomfortably if had just been the last of her breath leaving her body, forced out by the fall, her mouth dropped softly open, and I felt the tickle of air against my other hand when I hovered it close.

"Oh, thank the goddess," Starlight whispered. "The bees would've been so upset. It would've been a disaster."

I looked at her. "Why, because she didn't collect their honey or something?"

"No. She doesn't *keep* bees. She's a nature witch. All the bees answer to her."

Well, that didn't sound creepy at all. I looked down at Mella, seeing a bee tattoo behind one of her ears as I pinched the lobe between my fingernails, tight enough to be a sting itself. She didn't flinch. Her breath didn't even hitch, still shallow and barely detectable. The two bees had settled into her hair, antennae twitching fretfully, and a couple of others came darting out of the shadows to join them.

"Morgan?" Isabella crouched next to me, her skirts swirling through the table. "Oh, dear. What's happened?"

"She's alive," I said. "But I can't wake her up."

"It's not my fault," the bartender said. "That's good mulled wine, that is."

"Oh, do shut up," Starlight said.

Ben had followed Isabella, and he rubbed the back of his neck as he frowned down at us. "Another witch?" he said. "That doesn't seem good."

No, it didn't. It seemed like a pattern, if you asked me.

WE WERE STILL WORKING out how to move Mella out of the bar, the bartender getting increasingly flustered and attracting ever more attention in his attempts to divert the same, when someone pushed past him.

"'Ello, 'ello, 'ello. What do we 'ave 'ere, then?" they asked, in the round English tones of an Eighties sitcom.

We stared up at Theodore, who was wearing a domed bobby's hat and his flaming mask over a tightly buttoned tweed suit. In the mellow light of the bar, his orange shade had deepened to something alarmingly close to red, and he was smoking slightly. By which I mean smoke was rising from him. He hadn't suddenly taken up a pipe.

"Ah," I said, pointing at the thin plumes rising from his cheeks.

"What is it?" Theodore asked, turning to look behind him.

"Theodore, dear, are you feeling alright?" Isabella asked. The unconscious Mella seemed to have distracted her from her mask, but I noticed her hand kept straying to her side, where she'd tucked it into her hidden pocket.

"Of course. Why?" He sounded more like himself, his smooth, unplaceable accent resurfacing.

We looked at each other. I wasn't sure how rude it might be to say to a vampire, *I think you're burning up.*

So Ruiner said it, of course, his voice pitched low enough that the bartender, still guarding the alcove like a goalkeeper, didn't hear. "Did you forget you're among the undead and head out for a bit of sunbathing or something?"

Theodore straightened his already flawless posture. "One does not allow such small things as sun sensitivity to place limits on one's abilities."

Ben frowned at him. "That's a nice thought, but you are … um, smoking."

Theodore gave a sudden, massive yawn, exposing some truly horrifying fangs, and covered his mouth quickly. "My apologies. As I said, one must not allow such artificial constraints as sunset times to stand in the way of one's life."

"Yes, but…" I pointed at the base of his neck, where his usually smooth, dark hair was looking distinctly melted and clumpy in places.

He touched it lightly, frowning. "It's of no matter." He cleared his throat, swept his bobby hat off, and boomed in the same clunky accent as before, "What's all this, then?"

We looked at each other uncertainly, and Starlight said, "It's Mella?"

"Somebody's done a blinder!"

I rocked back on my heels where I crouched next to Mella, pressing my fingertips into my forehead and looking at the bees. They seemed the most sensible creatures in attendance right now.

"Someone's lost the plot," Ruiner announced, and Theodore pointed an old-fashioned truncheon at him. It looked like he'd stolen it from a Punch and Judy show.

"'Ere, wot's your problem, then, lad?"

"Theodore," I tried, "What happened to the woman from last night? Do you know who she was yet?"

"I'll ask the questions here, lass."

Ruiner snickered, and I looked at Isabella. "I think it's the mask. He has to take the mask off."

She nodded gravely and turned to the sergeant. "Theodore, dear—"

"Quiet down, love. I'm going to examine the scene." He clasped his hands behind his back, rocking on his heels, and started to pace the small area.

Isabella crossed her arms, her eyebrows almost comically high. "Theodore Ianculescu—"

"*Shh.*"

Isabella looked so unimpressed I almost joined Ruiner when he snickered again, but I didn't fancy offending the only member of the town's authority who seemed to be currently in possession of her senses. She looked at me. "Take it off him."

Any desire to laugh vanished instantly. "I'm not taking it off him."

"Someone has to."

"He's a *vampire.*"

"Don't be judgemental."

"I'm not," I protested. "But he's not himself. What if…" I couldn't bring myself to say it with him right there, so I just hooked my forefingers into fangs and mimed a bite. Isabella huffed, putting her hands on her hips, and looked at Ben.

He raised his hands. "I'm just the librarian."

"I'll do it," Starlight said in a long-suffering tone, and bounced to her feet. She tiptoed up to Theodore from behind, as he hemmed and hawed his way around the seats, and reached for the mask's strap, just visible under his helmet. Theodore spun, so quickly my eye couldn't make out the movement, and Starlight stumbled back, a small cry cut off as her own mask slipped into place. Her stumble turned into a pirouette, and she twirled away gently.

Theodore pointed at us. "Now then," he said. "I think we best get you all down to the station."

"Theodore, *no,*" Isabella said, as if he were a dog trying to get on the new sofa. "Stop this nonsense."

"I shall be getting to the bottom of this! Masks on, all of you."

"Why?" I demanded.

"So I can see the guises you wear. Hurry up!"

Isabella already had her mask out of her pocket, as if she'd just been itching for a chance to put it back on. "If we must."

"No, *don't*," I said, but she raised it to her face, and it simply sank onto her features, not needing straps or ties. She gave a little purr of happiness.

"Come on," Theodore said, giving me a *hurry up* gesture.

"Take yours off," I said.

"You are not in charge here," he replied, his voice sharp.

"Theodore," Ben started, and the sergeant turned on him.

"Where's yours? You of all people should know of their importance for the festival."

"I do," Ben said. "But—"

"*Masks on!*" Theodore roared, and it really was a roar, something vicious and toothed, the night coming down at its edges. His face shifted under the mask, and those teeth sprouted again, even longer and more vicious, plus more besides, crowding his mouth and cutting into his lips. Someone dropped a glass in one of the other alcoves, and a scream went up, and I snatched my mask from my coat, jamming it on clumsily and snagging my hair in the ribbon ties, struggling for breath.

There was one spinning moment where the fright seemed to send the world off kilter, as if the ice palace had turned into the multi-chambered heart of some unknown creature, pulsing and shivering around us, then everything settled, becoming clear-cut and vivid. The light was sharper, the colours brighter, and Starlight glittered as she danced across the room. Ben stood tall in his knight's mask, half-seen armour shimmering around him, and Theodore turned to him, his tweed jacket taking on navy tones.

"What do we have here, then?" Theodore asked, looking Ben up and down. "What do you know about this?"

Ben hung his head. "I was not present to protect the lady."

Theodore poked him in the chest. "I should book you, lad."

"But is it not your duty to protect the town? Where were *you?*"

"I'll ask the questions here!"

I was having trouble focusing on the conversation, because everyone seemed to have grown an aura. Theodore's was a shimmering silver, giving to flashing lights at the edges, while Ben's was a mellow blue under a coating of cold steel. Isabella was impossible to make out, and Starlight was a glimmer of greens and golds. Everywhere were smudges of colour, like footprints left by those who had walked past before, and when I looked at Mella, she had soft amber all around her, other than the purple seal of the mask. The bees were embers, clinging to her shimmering hair as if born from it.

"Morgan," Ruiner said, and I blinked at him. Pale chains wrapped my brother, binding his fluffy form, and I reached out a finger curiously, trying to touch one. "*Morgan!* Sort yourself out!"

"What?"

"Take the sodding mask off while PC Chomp's busy."

"I shouldn't." More to the point, I didn't want to. I'd caught sight of my own hand, and it was outlined in orange light, flecked with red and gold. I was on fire, in the best possible way, as if the sparks I'd seen the night before were just the beginning. I *glowed,* and I could feel the power moving in my belly. *A terrible witch.* They didn't know *anything.* I hadn't even got started yet. I was going to be the best damn witch—

My thoughts were rudely cut off by Ruiner launching himself at my face, claws out and teeth bared. I squawked, falling backwards onto the floor with the chill of the ice radiating through the rugs and into my spine. My brother's claws raked my cheeks as he tried to drag the mask off, and I had a flash of fury so intensely white-hot that the entire bar blurred out of existence, as if I'd stared at the sun to the point of blindness. I came to my feet with a completely unfamiliar grace, my hands raising from my sides as I imagined bringing the world down around us, burning it from the inside out.

I'm not saying I *could* have done it, but I was ready to try. As I stood, though, the mask fell away. I'd put it on hastily, and Ruiner's attack had been enough to dislodge it. It slipped off my nose and slithered to the floor, where Ruiner belted it with one paw, trying to send it spinning out of reach. It didn't go far on the rugs, but it didn't matter. It was enough that it was off.

I stared around the little alcove, panting like I'd just been running for the last bus home. The auras had mostly gone, but they still lingered as glimmering smudges, and the half-seen armour and uniform on Ben and Theodore were still just visible, mirages in the corner of my eye, just like Starlight's wings. Only Isabella looked much the same, but she was rubbing one balled fist over her hair absently as she crouched next to Mella, ignoring everyone.

"You back?" my brother demanded, pulling my attention to him.

"Yes," I said, not even bothering to try denying what

had just happened. My chest and belly were still twisting with fire, and I swallowed hard.

"Let's go," he said, nodding at the entrance. "We can get out while Sir Books-a-lot and Constable Fang are still squabbling."

They really were squabbling too, each accusing the other of not protecting the town properly. Ben put one hand on Theodore's chest, pushing him back, while his free hand drew a sword I saw more in my imagination than in reality. Theodore raised his truncheon in response, and I scrambled to my feet, running towards them.

"Oh, *come on*," Ruiner complained, but I ignored him.

"*Stop*," I ordered the men, grabbing their arms and pulling them away from each other like a couple of arguing toddlers.

"*Stand down, woman*," Theodore snapped.

"Do not address the lady like that," Ben said, trying to push me behind him with one hand.

"Stop it, both of you," I insisted, twisting away from Ben.

"This is obstructing an investigation," Theodore started, and someone knocked his mask off from behind. He stumbled, grabbing for it, but I kicked it, sending it under the table. He paused, then straightened up, touching his cheek, where the skin was red and blistered. I turned to Ben, grabbing his mask before he could react and pulling it off, then dropped it hurriedly. It was hot and sticky-feeling, and I wiped my fingers on my coat as I looked past Theodore. Grace stood there, both hands back in the pockets of a heavyweight red wool coat, frowning faintly as she examined us.

"Looks like I've missed all the fun," she said.

Theodore cleared his throat. "I seem to have risen

slightly early. How embarrassing. Please excuse my appearance."

"Your *appearance?*" I demanded. "You called me *woman*. And *lass*. And got all…" I waved at my face, managing not to say *bitey*, but evidently communicating it, because he pressed a hand to his chest and bowed his head.

"Morgan, I'm dreadfully sorry. I beg your forgiveness. I don't know what happened."

"The masks happened," Grace said, her voice level.

"I'm sure that's not the case," Theodore said.

"You went out in *daylight*," I pointed out.

"One makes these misjudgements from time to time."

I managed not to shake him, mostly because I could still picture all those teeth. "Fine. But can you look at Mella, at least?"

"Mella?" Grace asked, and looked past us, to where Mella was still stretched out on the floor. "Oh, *dammit*." She didn't wait for Theodore, just pushed past him and went to crouch beside the prone woman, touching her face with gentle fingers. The bees darted at her, but she ignored them, pulling the mask away.

Or, she tried to. It didn't move, and she tugged harder, only succeeding in lifting Mella's head clear of the floor. She looked at me, her face unreadable, and I dropped to my knees next to her, trying myself. The mask was soft and slick under my fingers, unpleasantly warm, and entirely immovable. I let go, wiping my fingers on my jeans, and Grace and I stared at each other.

"That's not right," I said softly, and she quirked one eyebrow in a very clear, *well, genius,* expression. My cheeks went hot, and I looked back at Mella and her bees.

"What's happening?" Ben asked.

"The mask won't come off," I said.

Grace made a small *hmm* sound. "What have you tried?" she asked me.

"Pinching her earlobe."

She gave me a blank look. "Right. No tinctures? Spells?"

"Ah, no."

To her credit, she didn't roll her eyes. "I need rosemary and—"

"Can you not do this in here?" the bartender asked, reappearing. "You're starting to draw attention now. All the yelling is really bad for business."

"It's a *Viking bar*," I snapped. "Yelling's basically your brand."

"Stereotyping," he sniffed but walked away again.

"He's right, though," Grace said. "This isn't the place for it. She's going to get cold." She stood up, brushing her hands off. "We'll take her to your shop."

"My shop?" I asked.

"There's still accommodation upstairs, right?"

"Yes." I'd barely touched anything since I'd acquired it, other than getting rid of the worst of Norma's clutter. The beds were still made up and undisturbed.

"Then we'll have all the supplies we need downstairs, plus the grimoire."

I placed a hand over my bag protectively. "I mean, I suppose…"

"Come on. This is what being a witch is, Morgan. Let's go." She pointed at Mella. "Theodore, you'll carry her." It wasn't a question.

"Of course." He picked Mella up easily, cradling her against his chest. The blisters still stood out brightly on his cheeks, and the faint scent of melted hair and burned flesh rose from him as he started for the doors.

"Ben," I said quietly, "Is the sun down yet?"

He checked his watch. "Just about."

I wasn't sure if *just about* was close enough for a vampire, but we were going to find out. I turned to follow Theodore, and Ben caught my arm.

"I'm sorry," he said. "Those masks … I haven't put it on since last night. I got in a whole fight with James. It was awful."

"Yeah, I know," I said. "But can we talk about it after I've dealt with the comatose woman?"

"Right, yes."

"Come on, Morgan," Grace called, halfway to the door. "We need the town witch."

"See if you can get Starlight's mask off her and bring her to the shop," I said to Ben. "And Isabella, too."

"On it." He sounded relieved, as if he'd found a way to redeem himself, and I hurried after Grace and Theodore.

Outside, the sky was bleached of colour, the last of the sun running away with the day, so at least we wouldn't have a melting vampire to deal with. The lights softened the dusk, and the band had appeared in the centre of the market's heart, launching into a frenzied medley of soft rock mashed up with some noughties hip-hop. Somehow, it worked, and I found my head bopping to it as I caught up to the witch and the vampire.

"Where's the other witch, Theodore?" I asked, and he glanced at me, his dark eyes deep and reassuringly familiar.

"At the hall," he said. "We have a cot for anyone who needs to overnight there."

"You can bring her to the shop, too," Grace said. "May as well do this all in one place."

Whatever *this* was. I checked the crowd for Alaric, or Finn, but there was no sign of the mask-sellers, and I thought of Alaric and his *adjustments,* Finn and his chafing bracelet and furtive promise that he had something to tell me. I needed to find out what it was. It might be the key to everything.

11. A pantry prisoner

I DIDN'T GET BACK TO THE MARKET THAT NIGHT. I DIDN'T even get to Petunia's. I'd never spent a full night in the shop before, the kitchen still haunted in my mind by the spectre of Norma, her lifeless arm hanging out of the cauldron and her hair spilling down the side. But I barely thought about her, to be honest. Theodore carried Mella upstairs and laid her on one of the beds in the twin room, then went to collect the other woman. He was back before Ben and Starlight reappeared with Isabella, and everyone spent the next hour getting in the way as Grace demanded rosemary and citrus and lemongrass and the chrysalids of nocturnal snub-nosed caterpillars, or whatever. Starlight was better with that side of things than I was.

I mostly kept close to the grimoire and did what Grace told me. Jackie looked on with sharp dark eyes, but didn't stop Grace leaning over the book next to me. She didn't even hiss when Grace flipped the pages with one elegant finger. In fact, I wasn't sure if Jackie was baring her teeth more at me than Grace by the time midnight rolled around. Not that I could blame her. Grace seemed to know just where to look to find the charms she needed, and when she read the incantations aloud, she didn't stumble on the syllables. I finally demoted myself to chopping herbs and boiling water, and Jackie barely looked my way when I left the room. I tried not to feel slighted by a rat. It was the most efficient division of labour, was all.

Theodore and Isabella left before it got too late, heading to the market to make sure everything stayed in some sort of order (relatively, anyway, it being Hollowbeck), and Ben vanished to the library to search through the old tomes of town records and books of magic to see if there was anything to be found on masks and sleeping curses. Starlight fell asleep on one of the sofas with Howard curled up on her belly, and Ruiner offered up useless suggestions until Grace threatened to turn him into a hairless cat. He took himself off in a huff to sleep in the shop, and then there was just Grace and me left.

I was paging through one of Norma's other old books, searching for any references to the festival, when Grace came downstairs from checking on the sleeping women. The sleeves of her jumper were pushed up, her hair pulled back into a bun, and she sat down across the table from me, setting a jar and an eyedropper down in front of her and resting both forearms on the table. There were tight lines around her mouth.

"Nothing?" I asked.

"No change." She rubbed her face. "I can't think of anything else to try. Have you found anything?"

"No. Perhaps we're trying too many things at once? You know, they're cancelling each other out or something?"

"It's not like mixing medications. We're not going to overdose them on lemon water and charms."

"Just asking."

Grace sighed. "No, it's a fair question. Sorry. This is just so frustrating."

"I know." I got up and took a couple of tumblers from the cupboard over the sink, then found some whisky above the fridge. I sat back down and slopped a generous measure into each glass, sliding one across the table to her. She raised it to me before taking a mouthful, and we were both silent for a while.

"Do you know who the first woman is?" I asked eventually, and she shook her head.

"She's a witch, that's all I'm sure of."

"How can you tell?"

She tipped her head to one side. "You can't tell when's someone's a witch?"

"No," I admitted. "No one's given me a manual, you know."

She took another sip of whisky. "I told you I'd help you learn, but all you do is call me when you've got a plague of bunnies or something."

I looked at my glass, my cheeks hot. "I know. And thank you for helping."

"I'm your friend, Morgan. No matter what your brother says."

"He hasn't said anything."

"No? Nothing about not trusting the scary witch?" She was smiling.

"Well, he might've mentioned that."

"Coming from the man who set curses on my shop."

"Cat."

"That too." She drained her glass and picked up the bottle, topping up both our tumblers. I didn't protest.

"So, two witches doing the Sleeping Beauty act," I said. "That can't be a coincidence."

"Unlikely."

"I take it this isn't usual festival stuff either."

"I think you'd be hard-pressed to get many attendees if there was a potluck going on for if you ended up in a coma or not. Even here."

"Fair point." I took a mouthful of whisky, grimacing slightly. It wasn't my usual drink, but Norma had left so much behind I seemed to be developing a taste for it. I investigated the takeaway containers still on the table, a selection Ben had collected from the market, and discovered half a Scotch egg in one. I offered it to Grace and she shook her head, so I took a large bite while I considered the situation.

"So, the masks," I said finally. "Something's gone wrong with them, do you think?"

Grace let her hair down, combing her fingers through it and somehow doing a better job than any hairdresser had ever done with mine. I really needed to get her to teach me any charms that gave you hair that gorgeous. "Or they're doing exactly what they're meant to," she said. "I told you they're no good. You should get rid of yours."

I made a small noise, meaning I agreed. But at the same time, I could still feel the simmering heat when I'd worn it, the sense of power. Of *competence*. The feeling that I really was a witch, that I wasn't just muddling along like some misguided, knackered pony thinking it could be a racehorse. I pushed that aside and said, "Do they always send everyone bonkers?"

Grace frowned. "Not bonkers, but people do get a bit weird. People will do all sorts of things when they think no one can tell it's them."

"But Theodore never walked out into the sun before?"

"Theodore never had a mask before."

I stared at her over the rim of my glass. "Like Isabella?"

"Exactly. Apparently, Alaric's branching out this year. He'll have kitty masks by the end of the week, so watch out for Ruiner."

"It's got to be Alaric then, doesn't it? Sabotaging Theodore and Isabella, and bumping off witches?"

She made a doubtful noise. "Firstly, he hasn't bumped anyone off. Secondly, what would he gain from it?"

"I don't know," I admitted. "But why don't you like the masks, then, if they're not usually an issue?"

"Because people should be themselves, not some caricature. His whole thing about the true self is rubbish. We're not our unfiltered selves, our untempered urges and impulses. We're who we create ourselves to be. Our choices mean more than our base reactions." She finished her glass and stretched. "I need sleep. Are you staying here?"

"Yes?" It hadn't sounded like a question.

"Let me know if anything changes." She grabbed her coat from the back of her chair and left, striding out with loose-limbed elegance and leaving me holding a bite of Scotch egg and a whole lot of questions.

I DIDN'T THINK I'd sleep, curled into a gently sagging armchair in the big back room of the Cosy Cauldron, not with the unconscious women upstairs and the memory of Norma still planted firmly in the hearth. But evidently festivals and suspicious masks were more tiring to deal with than I'd realised, because I woke up with pale morning light washing through the windows to paint patches on the floor, and someone banging insistently on the shop door.

I tried to roll out of the chair, but my legs had gone to sleep from my awkward position, and I collapsed to the floor instead. Ruiner appeared in the hall doorway with his ears back.

"We've got company," he announced.

"I can hear that," I said, staggering to my feet and limping towards him. "Who is it?"

"I'm not your secretary."

I stepped over him and hurried down the hall in my socks, skirting the counter and going to the front door of the shop. Blond hair was visible through the glass, and as I flipped the latch, James turned towards me, frowning.

"There you are! I was knocking for ages."

I looked at the closed sign on the door, then back at him pointedly.

"I know. But I saw Ben last night, and he said you were staying in the shop."

"You're friends again, then."

"Of course. The other night was just … the other night was weird."

I examined him. He wasn't wearing his mask, and looked a lot better than he had the day before, so evidently he'd been sticking to coffee. Which is something I'd really like right now. "What's up?"

"Something weird's happened."

"Oh good. How unusual."

"No, this is weird even for here."

I rubbed a hand over my face. "Is the coffee machine on?"

"As always."

"Get me one while I wash my face?"

"You need to come to the shop anyway."

Suddenly I was very awake indeed. "There's a problem at the shop?"

He seesawed his hand. "Sort of. Just hurry up, okay?"

He turned and hustled back across the road, and I watched him go with a steadily rising tide of alarm in my belly. There was no smoke rising from the roof or water washing out the door, though, so I had to assume the coffee was okay. The alternative didn't bear thinking about.

I didn't take long to get ready. I had a toothbrush at the shop for when Starlight got a little too enthusiastic with the garlic in the hummus, so I scrubbed my teeth and splashed some water on my face, and that was as much as I could do. I supposed I could shower upstairs, in Norma's old bathroom, but the idea made me feel uneasy, as if her presence still lingered in the half-finished shampoo bottles and decorative soaps. And I definitely wasn't borrowing any of her clothes. I had a quick sniff test of my jumper, and all I could smell was a little lingering smoke and rosemary, which seemed alright.

Jackie was curled up on the grimoire, and I hesitated for a moment, wondering if I needed it, and also wondering if it was really any safer with me than it was in the shop. Starlight was still asleep, so she wasn't going to be much help if someone did come in and nab it. I dithered for a moment longer, but the need for coffee was insistent, so finally I picked up both Jackie and the book and carried them through to the office. I locked the book in the top drawer of the desk, dropped the key back in the jar of pens, and gave Jackie a piece of apple that I'd tried to convince myself to eat at some point last night. She sighed so deeply her whole body heaved, but accepted the apple, and snuffled my hand in a way that wasn't entirely lacking in affection. I was increasingly convinced she regarded me as some sort of charity case she still hoped to shape into something worthwhile, but that hope was slimming by the day.

"Back soon," I told her and let myself out of the shop, heading across the road with Ruiner trotting next to me, his ears twitching.

"He didn't say what the issue was?" he asked me.

"No." The little bistro tables outside Bewitching Brews were empty, and the street was quiet. A woman in large dark glasses headed for the tiny supermarket, clutching a green juice and a squirrel, and an elderly man was sitting outside Mystic Munchies, whispering to a trio of bemused chickens. There was no one else in sight, and none of the other shops seemed to be open. I paused as we reached the pavement, looking each way. "Does it seem really quiet to you?"

Ruiner squinted down the road. "I suppose. What time is it?"

"No idea." I really needed to get a watch. Hollowbeck didn't have mobile signal at all, so I'd got out of the habit of carrying my phone. It usually lived in my bag with the grimoire, but half the time when I thought to check it, the battery was dead anyway.

I pushed open the door to Bewitching Brews, unleashing a current of coffee-laden air. Inside was as empty as outside, and James hurried through from the kitchen, his hair looking as if he'd been pulling it in half a dozen directions. Something was banging behind him.

"Took you long enough," he said, and tried for a smile. His heart wasn't in it, though.

"What's going on?" I asked.

"And who've you got locked in the loo?" Ruiner demanded.

James winced. "Not the loo. The pantry."

"You've locked someone in the pantry?" I checked for his mask again, but he still wasn't wearing it, which was something, I suppose. Maybe the whole fight with Ben had put him off.

"I had to. He wasn't listening."

"Who?"

"Theodore."

"You've got *Theodore* locked in the pantry?"

James nodded. "I was counting the coffee beans and saw him walk past outside. The sun wasn't on him yet, so he was just sort of smoldering. But he didn't want to come inside. I had to tell him I had a coffee thief in the kitchen. Then I shoved him in and put a bunch of stuff in front of the door to make sure he couldn't get out."

"And he hasn't calmed down?"

James waved at the kitchen pointedly, where the banging continued.

"Have you talked to him, at least?"

"I came to find you," James said. "I didn't want to mess about too much, really. I don't fancy him breaking out. He sounds a bit…" He hesitated, then gave up. "Vampiric."

I looked at Ruiner, who put his ears back. "You're on your own. I'd barely be a snack, anyway."

I slumped against the counter, looking at the kitchen as if Theodore might come bursting though the wall at any moment. For all I knew, he might. "Don't vampires have like super-strength or something?"

James shrugged. "Maybe not in the daylight?"

"Or he's baked it out of himself," Ruiner said.

"He can heal from that, though, right?" I asked. He'd had blisters the evening before, so obviously it wasn't instant, but you couldn't live that long and *not* heal up. Vampires would be nothing but a mess of scar tissue otherwise.

"I suppose so," James said. "I'm not a vampire expert."

The banging in the kitchen went up a notch, and we waited for the sound of splintering wood. It didn't come, though, and my brother said. "Bet he's hungry. You know, from healing himself up. Must take a lot of energy."

We both looked at him. "Thanks," I said. "Helpful."

He licked his shoulder and said, somewhat indistinctly, "Someone's got to think of these things."

"Great," James said. "I've got a hungry, injured vampire in the pantry."

"Can I have a coffee?" I asked. "I can't deal with this without a coffee."

"I suppose." He sounded deeply unenthusiastic, but I suppose he had other things on his mind. He clattered about with the grinder, and Ruiner and I looked at each other.

"Well?" Ruiner asked.

"Well what?"

"What're you going to do about Sergeant Sizzle?"

"Stop making up names for him. You're not as clever as you think."

"I'm a talking cat. I'm *incredibly* clever."

"You're a full-grown man who's got himself stuck in a cat's body. How clever can you really be?"

He narrowed his eyes at me, and I pushed off the counter, heading for the kitchen. It had a swinging door, and I eased it open gingerly, peering into the room beyond. The worktops were mostly clear, just some butter set out to soften and a mixing bowl waiting to be put to work. A set of big double sinks were empty and shining, and the old flooring was clean and well-swept. The only clutter was a stack of six big sacks of unroasted coffee beans, all piled up in front of the pantry door. There was a chair too, the back wedged under the door handle and held in place by the sacks.

The door shivered under more blows, and I eyed it warily. It seemed pretty secure, though, so I took a few steps closer and called, "Theodore?"

The banging stopped, and a slightly ragged voice said, "Morgan?"

"Yes. Are you alright?"

"I'm *locked in a pantry*."

"Sorry about that. How're you feeling?"

"That I'd rather not be locked in a pantry."

Well, he sounded fairly normal, at least. "It's light out."

"And?"

"You don't want to get burnt."

"Why would I get burnt?"

Right. So much for normality. "Sun sensitivity?"

There was silence for a moment, then that irritating, *now-then now-then* voice resurfaced. "Whatever you're playing at, lass, you're for it! I'll throw the book at you!"

I sighed. "Do you have your mask on?"

"I'm the law here! I'll ask the questions!"

"Theodore," I tried again. "You really need to take the mask off. It's messing up your thinking."

He didn't answer straight away, and a little bit of hope jumped in my chest, then he said, "I'll lock the lot of you up and throw away the key. Let me out!"

I retreated without saying anything else, ignoring him shouting my name, and went back into the shop. Ruiner was lapping from a bowl of milk, and he looked up at me with it dripping from his chin.

"He still off his head?"

"We definitely can't let him out. He asked why he'd get burnt."

"That's a yes, then." He went back to his milk, splattering drops on the counter.

"Here." James slid my mug across the counter.

I took a sip, then wrinkled my nose. "How many shots is that?"

"Two," he said.

I peered at the mug. It was definitely more tea shade than coffee. "Are you sure?"

He huffed and took the mug back, and I tried to figure out what to do about Theodore. We needed help if we were going to try and get him out of there, someone who could persuade him to keep out of the sun. Or else we needed to leave him in there until dark. Mostly, though, we needed someone who knew about vampires, and could tell us if he was going to get all bitey if we let him out. Which meant we needed a ghost.

"Can I use the phone?" I asked James, and he nodded, taking a cordless handset from under the counter and passing it to me along with the topped-up mug. I took a mouthful of coffee and nodded. "Better."

He made a displeased sound and tapped the hopper of beans, inspecting it. I wondered if it was jamming or something, and that was why the first round had been so weak. I looked at the handset and realised I didn't know the number I needed.

"Do you have the library number?"

"Sure." He pulled a slim phone directory from behind the counter, handed it to me, and turned back to the hopper.

I watched him for a moment, spotting the dragon mask hanging from the back pocket of his jeans. The other night I'd assumed it was some sort of latex, a full-face construction of plasticky scales, but where it spilled out of his pocket it was luminous, and as liquid as fine chainmail. "James," I said, "did you say you were *counting the coffee beans* when you saw Theodore?"

"Yes," he said without turning around, as if that were perfectly reasonable.

I looked at Ruiner, my eyebrows raised. He ignored me, his ears twitching as he watched the kitchen door. Well. A little coffee bean hoarding was hardly the worst problem we'd seen. I opened the phone book.

12. Injuries & incidents

BEN DIDN'T TAKE LONG TO GET THERE, PULLING UP TO THE kerb in his little Micra and swinging out hurriedly. He was wearing a waxed jacket over faded jeans and a Nordic-y jumper that made him look like he was just off the slopes and about to recline in a leather chair in some upmarket ski lodge somewhere, book in hand. I went to meet him, pulling the door open as he reached it, and his smile of greeting was more warming than the watery coffee had been.

Don't forget the calming tea, I reminded myself. *Can't trust anyone who gives you calming tea.*

"Are you alright?" he asked, reaching out as if to touch my arm but thinking better of it.

"Fine," I said. "But Theodore's about to chew his way out of the pantry."

Ben looked towards the kitchen, where the banging still hadn't let up. "Right. He's okay, though?"

"He's secure as he can be," James said. "Considering it's a pantry, not a vampire prison." We'd added a few more sacks while we'd waited for Ben, just in case, and the fortifications appeared to be holding. One of the sacks had turned out to have a hole in it, though, and had left a little trail of beans behind as I dragged it to the kitchen. James had got very huffy about that and was still trying to find all the strays.

"Where's Isabella?" I asked. I'd wanted Ben to bring her, as if anyone could get through to Theodore, she'd be able to.

Ben grimaced. "She's in the hall."

"She wouldn't come?" That didn't sound like Isabella. I'd never known a mayor — or anyone — to be so keen to be involved in absolutely everything that occurred in her town.

"Ah — she's found a patch of sunshine and a box."

"A box?" I stared at him, and he shrugged helplessly.

"She really loves that mask. It seems to let her interact with the world, at least a little. She can touch things."

I tried to imagine what it must be like, to pass all those years and decades — centuries, I supposed — without ever being able to touch *anything*. Could she even feel the sun? She certainly didn't seem to notice the cold, so probably not. No wonder she liked the mask, if it gave her that back. It must be like being alive again, at least a little. So I couldn't blame her for that.

On the other hand, we now had a vampire who'd forgotten he was a vampire to deal with, and no ghost to help us out.

"What do we do about Theodore, then?" I asked.

"I don't know," Ben admitted. "If we can get him in the boot of my car, I can take him to the hall."

"And how're you going to do that without getting bitten?" Ruiner asked.

"Or him getting more burnt," James put in. "The sun's on the street now."

We all looked out the front windows. It was still quiet, but the hesitant winter sun was painting the tarmac and the pavements with soft light.

"We could just talk to him," Ben said. "We explain the situation, then maybe he'll let us wrap him in a blanket or something. He's still *Theodore*, not some monster."

James waved at the kitchen. "Knock yourself out."

Ben looked at me uncertainly, and I shrugged. "He wouldn't listen to me, but you two had your fellowship of town protectors thing going on, so maybe you'll do better."

"Alright." Ben straightened up, tugging at the front of his coat, and looked at James. "Any chance of a coffee?"

James shot a look at the coffee grinder. "Well…"

"I'll have another, too," I said, sliding off the stool. "Thanks, James."

James made a plaintive little whining sound, but I ignored him, following Ben to the kitchen door. Ruiner came with us, presumably to make sure he didn't miss any entertainment, and a moment later we were gathered at the pantry door while the coffee machine hissed in the shop.

"Theodore?" Ben called.

"Ben? Is that you?" Theodore had slipped back into his usual, almost musical tones again, and a little hope flowered in my chest that this might work, that Ben might get through to him.

"It's me. Are you alright?"

"Other than the fact James has shut me in a cupboard?"

"Well, yes."

"Then I am. Now open the door."

Ben looked at me, and I shrugged.

"The sun's out," Ben said to the pantry. "We'll have to

figure out a way to get you to my car, then I can get you back to the hall."

There was a pause, then Theodore replied, an edge in his voice. "I suppose you think you'll bundle me up like a sack of grain again?"

"Again?" Ben asked, frowning.

"Yes! Shoving me in the boot like you did in Darrowdale!"

"I didn't shove you anywhere," Ben protested.

"You did! It was undignified and unacceptable. You're no protector of this town!"

Okay. We were off again. I spoke up. "It wasn't in Darrowdale, and you *wanted* to get in the boot. It was to stop you—" I broke off. *Munching on anyone* was how I'd been going to finish the sentence, but that didn't seem very diplomatic.

"*Let me out!*" Theodore shouted. "This town *needs* me!"

"It needs you *whole*," I shouted back. "Not as over-cooked bacon!"

"Don't define me by my limitations!"

"Your *limitations* are going to kill you, and what use will you be then?"

There was a pause, and I felt the words coming before I heard them, like heat advancing before a firestorm.

"*Don your masks now!*" Theodore roared, and in my mind I saw him as he was last night, all teeth and ancient, ravenous fury. Primal fright leaped in my chest, forcing the breath from me, and I grabbed for my coat pocket, where the mask still lurked. I didn't even have a chance to touch it, though, because Ruiner threw himself at my hand, latching on with teeth and claws and zero concern for the resulting bloodshed.

"*Ow! Dammit*, Ruiner!" I tried to shake him off, my heart still too fast.

"Are you in distress?" Ben demanded, grabbing my brother and pulling him away. Ruiner snarled, twisting in Ben's grip, and attacked him furiously. The wax coat went some way to protecting his arm, but Ruiner tore into his hand, and Ben swallowed a curse.

"Put him down," I said sharply.

"But he has injured you—"

"*Open the door,*" Theodore snarled from inside the pantry. "Open the door and I won't lock you up and throw away the key." His tones veered from something vicious and guttural, setting the hairs on my neck lifting, to that weirdly chipper *now then now then* fake copper's voice, the one that promised he wouldn't just throw away the key, he'd get a few sneaky kicks in at the same time, when no one could see and you couldn't fight back. I couldn't tell which voice was worse, but neither of them were the Theodore I knew. Or thought I knew. It was as if the mask was stripping away everything that made him himself and was leaving behind nothing but his ugliest urges.

Ben turned to the door, driven to obey, perhaps by some ridiculous bloody knight's code, or simply the weight of the vampire's voice on his mask-addled brain, and I said, "*Ruiner.*"

My brother growled, but he stopped trying to fight his way free and instead bit down, hard, into the webbing between Ben's thumb and forefinger.

"*Oh you—*" Ben let go of Ruiner, who clung on, snarling furiously, and I lunged forward, smacking the mask off Ben's face. I also managed to smack him *in* the face, and he yelped, staggering away from the door as he tried to shake Ruiner off. "Bloody *hell,* Morgan!"

"Sorry! Ruiner, let go."

He did, dropping lightly to the floor and gagging violently. "*Gross.* I've got librarian in my teeth."

Ben stared at his hand in dismay, blood dripping off the fingers, his other hand pressed to his face. Either the mask had caught his lip on the way past, or I'd hit him harder than I thought, because that was bleeding too. I ran to the sink, wetting a cloth and hurrying back to him. Theodore was still shouting in the pantry, but the words seemed to have lost their power in the face of our small crisis outside.

"Here." I took his bleeding hand, intending to wrap it in the cloth, and he pulled away.

"Are you trying to give me gangrene on top of the toxoplasmosis?" he demanded, and I looked at the cloth. It did have some bits of egg or something caught in it.

"I'll get another one." I hurried back to the sink area, clattering through the cupboards as I looked for clean cloths.

"*Me* give *you* something?" Ruiner demanded. "You'll have given me sodding bookworms or booklice or whatever." He gagged again.

I hurried back to Ben with a clean tea towel, and this time he let me wrap his hand in it. "Sorry," I said to him. "I couldn't let you open the door."

"Sure." He didn't sound entirely convinced, and I left him to look after his hand while I dug into the freezer to find ice for his lip.

"*Masks!*" Theodore roared behind the door, and I spun to check on Ben. Ruiner had his ears back and was glaring up at the librarian, who looked as if he was about to bolt out of the kitchen.

"*I'm not touching it!*" Ben said to Ruiner. "Don't bite me again!"

I relaxed slightly. I hadn't made a grab for my mask, either, so evidently if you were prepared for Theodore's orders, you could resist them. That, or being bitten was a good deterrent. My hand was both bleeding and smarting, so the theory held up.

Even so, it didn't seem to be a great idea to hang around with Theodore shouting. The sacks of beans hadn't budged, so I handed Ben the ice and headed for the door to the shop, wondering why James hadn't turned up in all the commotion. "Come on," I said.

Ben followed me out, holding the ice to his lip with his roughly bandaged hand, and Ruiner trotted after, still licking his chops with his ears back.

"James, do you have a first aid—" I stopped. He wasn't behind the counter, although two mugs of coffee waited under the machine.

I started towards them, and Ben said, "Morgan."

I looked at him, and he nodded towards the coffee roaster. It lived on the other side of the shop to the counter and handful of indoor tables, looming up in sage green paint and gleaming stainless, and casting the distinctive, toasted-bread scent of roasting beans over the whole place. Hessian sacks of green beans were stacked to the far side of it, and the exhaust climbed in stainless pipes up to the ceiling and across it to a vent in the wall. There weren't any guards around it to stop careless customers falling in or burning themselves, but given the fact that no one paid any attention to the various familiars sitting at restaurant tables and cleaning their paws at cafe counters, that was hardly surprising.

What was surprising was the sight of James, huddled on the far side of the machine with his back to the sacks, arms spread to protect them as much as he could. He saw us looking and hissed, his mask moving with his face far too naturally, scaly eyebrow ridges pulling down and long teeth exposed, glossy with drool.

"Oh, for—"

"*Nope,*" Ruiner said. "I'm not biting dragon-boy. His teeth are bigger than mine."

"I didn't ask you to," I snapped, although I had been thinking it. My brother gave me a look that indicated he knew perfectly well that I had, too.

"James," Ben said, starting forward, and I grabbed his arm as James' hiss transformed into a snarl that made the hair rise on the back of my neck.

"Not you," I said. "You're a knight. We need a princess."

Ben stared at me, then said, "I need a drink."

"It's … I don't know. Morning. I think, anyway."

"Your point being?"

"Fair." I retreated to the counter as he went behind it and checked the coffees. James gave a rumbling roar, and we both jumped. "Leave those," I said, and Ben sighed.

"No coffee. Your brother bit me. You slapped me. Theodore's in a cupboard and Isabella's in a box. What more can go wrong?"

"Please don't say that," I said, just as people loomed beyond the door. "See? You *had* to say it."

The Upstanding Ladies pushed the door open, led by Miss Ethel, who looked from Ben with his busted lip and bandaged hand to me, with my unbrushed hair and yesterday's clothes still on. I mean, there was no way she could really tell they were yesterday's clothes, but I was sure she knew anyway.

"Where's James?" she asked. "Mystic Munchies is closed, the juice shop's overrun with geckos, and the tea shop—"

"We won't talk about the tea shop," one of the women behind her said. Posture Police, I think. She was supporting a third woman, who smiled around dreamily with her head rested on the other's shoulder. "People can't just *serve* that sort of thing without asking!"

James scuffled around, trying to extend his lean body over more of the sacks of beans, and the women looked at him.

Miss Edna sighed heavily. "Another one." She took a deep breath and shouted across the shop in a voice that boomed loud enough to shudder the glasses on the shelves (or it seemed like it should, anyway), "James Allen, you take that mask off right now!"

I staggered back a step, as if her voice had come in on a howling gust of wind, and Ben gave a little yelp. Ruiner's ears went flat to his head, and he scooted behind me.

James vanished behind the coffee roaster, dropping to his belly on the floor, and a moment later his head emerged over the cooling tray, his mask off.

I stared at Miss Edna. "How did you do that?"

"One just has to establish one's authority," she said, and waved imperiously at James. "Four cappuccinos and whatever today's cake is." She led the way to one of the tables, and the ladies sat down with a clamour of scraping chairs and muttered imprecations against festivals and masks.

James crept up to me and whispered, "I haven't made any cake. I was too busy dealing with Theodore. And, well, stuff. *What do I do?*"

"Buy some from the supermarket," I whispered back.

"Right." He looked at the Ladies, then at me.

"I'll get it," Ben said, heading for the door. "Too many things in here want to bite me."

James watched him go, then said to me, "Theodore?"

"Still in the pantry."

He sighed deeply. "Alright."

He busied himself with the coffee machine, and I did

my best to comb my fingers through my hair before approaching the Upstanding Ladies' table. I felt like I was heading into the head's office at school.

Miss Edna looked up at me, her lips tight. "Yes?"

"I was wondering if you could help me," I said, pushing my hands into the pockets of my coat to stop myself twisting my fingers together.

"Help the town witch?" Gold Rings said. "What do you want, our *souls?*"

"No, I've already got plenty. Thanks anyway." The words were out before I could help myself, and Ruiner snorted.

Gold Rings pressed a hand to her chest, narrowing her eyes at me, and Miss Edna raised her eyebrows. "That's not the way to go about it, is it?"

"No," I agreed. "Sorry. But we have a bit of a crisis."

"Just the sort of thing you witches specialise in," Posture Police said, adjusting a helmet of fine blonde hair. Next to her, Glasses, the one who'd evidently had some dodgy tea, was playing with the sugar bowl, pushing it across the table and whispering, "*zooooom,*" under her breath.

I looked at Miss Edna. She'd seemed at least a little helpful before. "Theodore won't take his mask off, and he thinks he can go out in the sun. Will you tell him to take it off, so I can talk some sense into him?"

She crossed her arms over her chest. "I'm not in the habit of cleaning up the messes of amateur witches. Why don't you ask Grace?"

"Because she's not here, and I'm scared Theodore will break out before I can find her. Can't you do it for his sake?" I was surprised to find my voice catching on the last words, and I swallowed hard. It was awful, the idea that Theodore with his snazzy dress sense and terrible fake tan habit, his old-fashioned courtesy and occasional toothiness, could just go stumbling out into the sun and crumble to ash, all because of some horrible *mask*. And all I could seem to do was trap him in a cupboard, which wasn't going to hold him forever.

Miss Edna examined me, and Posture Police said, "So we need to help a witch to help a monster? If you can't manage your own problems, that's your issue."

"The masks are kicking things up, though," Gold Rings said, catching the sugar bowl before it fell off the table. Glasses made a sad noise. I really needed to find out what their names were, but asking that felt even more terrifying than asking for help, for some reason.

"Where is he?" Miss Edna asked.

"In the pantry. You can hear—" I broke off as I turned towards the kitchen door. No, I *couldn't* hear him. I bolted across the shop, swinging around the counter with James shouting at me to stop, and shoved through into the kitchen. The pantry door hung open, the chair pushed away and the sacks of coffee beans toppled. The back door was open, and I ran towards it, racing out into the narrow alley behind the cafe. One direction held nothing but a blank brick wall, two big commercial rubbish bins pushed up against it, but the other ran towards the street, and Theodore was striding across the cobbles, his head up.

"*Theodore!*" I shouted, and he glanced back at me, the bobby hat on his head and the truncheon in his hand. The flaming curves of the mask shimmered and glowed, and he dismissed me, turning back to the road, neither slowing nor picking up his pace. Smoke rose softly from his shoulders, as if he were steaming in his skin before he even got to the sun.

I sprinted after him, ignoring Ruiner yowling my name behind me. The alley wasn't long, and I caught Theodore just before he reached the pavement, grabbing his arm. "Theodore—" I was cut off as he spun, snarling, one hand clutching my throat and lifting me effortlessly off the ground, pinning me to the brick wall. His eyes were invisible even this close, hidden behind a twisting gauze of the same oranges and golds as the mask. I clawed at his hand, trying to pry his fingers away, but it was like trying to shift a statue.

"Well, well, well," he said, his mouth dropping open, suddenly crowded with teeth and distorting his words until I could barely understand him. "What 'ave we 'ere, then?"

One dead witch, unless things changed fast.

13. Questionable techniques

I BARELY HAD TIME TO REGISTER WHAT WAS HAPPENING. I couldn't even recognise Theodore, not with that awful mask swallowing his face, and his teeth looming huge and ravenous. He was a stranger, something monstrous and lethal, and he was going to devour me.

But even as I thought that, Miss Ethel's voice snapped across the alley, full of an irresistible authority.

"Theodore Ianculescu, put that woman down!"

Theodore's hand snapped open instantly and he dropped me, turning to look at Miss Edna with his face shifting and changing under his mask, his teeth not retreating yet, but the urgency fading. I collapsed to the hard, frost-rimed ground, banging my knee on a loose piece of two-by-four, my legs not wanting to hold me. It wasn't lack of air. It was simple shock.

"Take your mask off," Miss Edna said, pointing at him imperiously. "You *silly* man."

He lifted one hand to his face, uncertain, and I knew he wasn't going to do it. Who knew how long he'd been wearing it without taking it off? How deep it had set its nasty roots? But he was still looking at Miss Edna, whose face had gone quite an astonishing shade of red.

"Are you ignoring me? How *dare* you?"

He tried for his customary, elegantly charming smile, but he still had too many teeth, rows and rows of them like a shark, and they weren't built for polite expressions. I could almost see the turmoil going on behind the mask, three different natures all vying for supremacy, Theodore the vampire and Theodore the lawmaker and then simply Theodore, who held doors for people and treated rats with no less respect than humans, who liked pocket squares and well-cut suits and fake tan. So that was the Theodore I said a silent apology to as I came to my feet and smacked him over the head with the lump of two-by-four.

Well, less smacked him over the head than belted his bobby's helmet and sent it flying, the mask going with it, the two of them tangled together. He cried out, stumbling forwards and trying to catch them, but Ruiner made himself unusually useful. He shot across the alley, snatched up the mask, swerved past Theodore's clutching hands, and vanished behind the bins. Theodore plunged after him, grabbing the first bin and spinning it out of the way while Ruiner fled to the next.

"*Theodore!*" I shouted, and he paused, his hands still tight on the next bin. I could see my brother with the mask still in his teeth, his blue eyes all pupil as he stared out from behind the remaining bin. "Theodore," I said again, my voice calmer. "The sun's out. You need to get inside."

He remained half-crouched for a moment, then straightened up, looking at his hands. They were smoking at the fingertips and the fake tan had vanished under an angry red shade, as if he'd been holding his hands above a steaming kettle.

"Oh dear," he said, sounding almost like himself. The

tone was right, at least, but he was still having a bit of difficulty talking. "How embarrething."

"It's going to be more than that if you don't get over here *this instant*," Miss Edna said, and I almost ran towards her myself. She had that sort of voice.

"I rather think I need to get back to the hall," he said, his voice a little clearer. He still wasn't turning around, though.

"You're already burning," I said. "There's no time. You can do one day in James' pantry, can't you?"

"I can't lie down," he pointed out.

"You're also not going to spontaneously combust."

"In. *Now.*" Miss Edna stepped out of the door and pointed inside, like we were a bunch of misbehaving dogs.

I joined Theodore warily, touching his arm and prepared to bolt if he turned around with a mouthful of fangs again. Instead he gave me a small smile, his cheekbones revealed in all their usual glory with the mask gone. It had made his face round and pink and unfamiliar, and he said, "I'm terribly sorry, Morgan."

"It's fine," I said. "It's the masks." I nodded at the shop's back door. "Let's just go in, though, alright? I don't want to have to explain to Isabella that I let you melt behind Bewitching Brews."

"I'd also rather not have to clean that up," James said, leaning around Miss Edna. "I can put a chair in the pantry."

"I suppose that shall have to do," Theodore said, and let me lead him back to the shop. I didn't miss the way he looked back at Ruiner though. My brother hadn't emerged from under the bins, which seemed like a sensible option. It wasn't as though I'd be able to hold Theodore back if he decided to go for the mask.

But he didn't. He came inside docilely enough,

yawning hugely and exposing fangs that hadn't quite retreated entirely. James put a chair in the pantry, which had just enough floorspace to fit it in, and added a soft blanket and a throw cushion from the outside seating.

"Is that okay?" he asked Theodore, who was already slumped in the chair, his eyelids at half-mast.

"I have slept in much worse places," he said, and I leaned into the pantry to pull the blanket up over his chest. He yawned again, making me snatch my hand back, and he grimaced, covering his mouth with one hand. "I really am terribly sorry."

"Do you need anything else?" I asked, rather than acknowledge the fact that my heart had just about turned inside out when I'd seen his teeth from that close.

"No," he said, his voice slow and drowsy and his eyes already closed. "Thank you, Morgan. You are a delightful witch." His chin dropped to his chest, and a moment later a small and inelegant snore drifted from him.

I stepped back and closed the door, looking at James. "We need to block it up again."

"Even without the mask?"

"Even so. Just until it's dark, anyway."

I left him to redo his barricades and went through to the shop, looking for Miss Edna, but the tables were empty. All that had been left behind was a note on floral paper, written in a neat, rounded hand.

We waited for our coffees for fifteen minutes, and you didn't come back!!

Terrible service!!!

I went to the door and looked each way down the street, but there was no sign of the Upstanding Ladies. Town was still quiet, although I could see the sign on my own shop across the road had been flipped to *Open*, so

Starlight was up at least. A scraping noise accompanied by some disgruntled muttering caught my attention, and I spotted my brother backing out of the alley, dragging Theodore's helmet with him. He'd managed to wedge the mask inside and had the helmet's chinstrap in his teeth. His ears were back, his eyes squinted closed, and he took one step backwards, braced himself, pulled, then repeated, working his way onto the street.

"Filthy sodding vampires and creepy bloody masks, and does anyone ask how I'm doing?" he mumbled indistinctly. "No. Do they *bollocks*. Ruiner, run! Ruiner, jump! Ruiner, kiss my damn—"

"You alright there?" I asked him.

He dropped the strap and glared at me. "You *shut the door* on me!"

"I didn't want Theodore seeing the mask and getting tempted." Not *entirely* true. I'd just been more concerned about getting the vampire out of the sun. I definitely remembered being very concerned by the possibility of spontaneous combustion when I was a kid, but that had rather faded with the years. I didn't fancy having my fears reawakened by way of Theodore's extreme version of sun sensitivity.

"Well, he's not here now. Take the bloody mask."

I ambled over and picked up the helmet gingerly by the strap, keeping the mask caught in its bowl. The helmet wasn't as unpleasant to touch as the masks had been before, but I still didn't like it. It didn't feel entirely inanimate. Of course, that could be my imagination, but it was hard to convince myself of that.

"What do I do with it?" I asked Ruiner.

"Exorcise it," he suggested.

"Super. Got an instruction manual for that?"

"You've got a spellbook. Use it."

I sighed. He wasn't wrong, of course. There probably was something in the grimoire about exorcisms. Whether it would work on masks or not was another question, but I supposed I could try. Neither my confidence nor my enthusiasm were exactly high, though. So far, the only times I'd been able to make the book *work*, as far as that went, was when things got very dire, and the end results had been not entirely predictable. With my luck I'd incinerate all the masks at once and inflict third degree burns on half the town.

"Morgan?" someone called. "Are you leaving?"

I turned to see Ben coming down the road from the little supermarket, carrying a selection of wrapped cakes, with a box of muffins perched on top of them. My stomach rumbled, reminding me I'd been up most of the night and that coffee might be essential, but it wasn't actually a food group.

"We got the mask off Theodore," I said, lifting the helmet to show him.

"*We*," Ruiner sniffed, and I scowled at him.

"Yes, *we*. I'm the one that hit him."

"You *hit* him?" Ben asked. "Is this your mask control technique then, just going around hitting people?"

"*No*," I said. "It's just … well, it was heat of the moment, and it works, alright?"

"You may want to refine it a little," he said, but he was smiling. He nodded at the mask. "What're you going to do with it?"

"Don't know," I said, opening the cafe door to let him in. He set the cakes on the counter, and I opened the muffin box, selecting two and wrapping them in napkins. "Where's your mask?"

He touched his coat pocket. "Here."

"Give it to me." I held my hand out, and he frowned.

"Why?"

"Because you call me *my lady* and want to have sword fights with Theodore when you wear it."

"I'm not going to wear it."

"No, you're not, because you're going to give it to me." I beckoned to him impatiently. "Come *on.*"

He still didn't move to hand it to me. "What're you going to do?"

"Get rid of them."

"Is that a good idea?"

"Bloody *hell,*" Ruiner said. "Do you actually think you're Sir Paperback of Library-land, watching over Hollowbeck with a book and a quill?"

"No," Ben said. "But the masks are part of the festival tradition."

"And traditionally people burn books they don't agree with," my brother said. "As well as the people who read them. What's your point?"

Ben crossed his arms, scowling at my brother. "My *point* is that we're not in bloody Manchester anymore, are we? How do we know we don't actually need the masks? That it's not a necessary part of the winter solstice ritual? That there isn't a reason behind them, even if it's not literally evil spirits?"

Ruiner looked like he wanted to say something smart, then just sat down and cleaned a paw.

"Really?" I said, thinking of the Upstanding Ladies and the way they hadn't denied there were evil spirits, just that the masks weren't necessary to deal with them. "Is this from your research? What do the records say?"

Ben shrugged. "It's not entirely clear. The masks are an integral part of the festival, for sure. But it's hard to say how much is legend and how much is fact."

The door to the kitchen creaked open, and James peered out. "Are they gone?" he asked.

"The ladies?" I said.

"Yeah."

"They have. They left you a rude note about the service, though."

"That's alright. Just as long as no one shouts at me." He pulled his mask out of his back pocket, working it in his fingers anxiously as he went to the main door and checked the street each way, as if someone might be lurking about, just waiting for the chance to shout at him.

I looked at Ben. "Can you keep your mask off? Honestly?"

"I think so. I did before, until Theodore yelled at me."

I tapped my fingers on the counter. I didn't like it, but Ben was probably right. Research was his thing, after all, and there was no point freeing everyone from the masks' influence if they just ended up possessed by evil spirits. Which was a ridiculous thing to even think about, but Hollowbeck was teaching me that ridiculous didn't mean impossible. "Fine," I said. "Don't put yours on, and try to keep James away from his. I'll stash Theodore's somewhere safe. Apparently he doesn't usually have one, so it can't be vital for him, and I can always get it if needed. Just don't put the bloody things on, okay?"

"Okay," he said, and touched my arm, letting his fingers linger. "What happened to your neck?"

"Call it a mask side effect," I said, scowling, and headed for the door with Ruiner trotting close behind me. I really wanted another coffee, but Bewitching Brews was hardly an oasis of calm this morning. The Cosy Cauldron felt like a much better option, even with the unconscious women upstairs. At least they seemed unlikely to try to bite me.

~

I PUSHED through the door into the Cosy Cauldron, setting the bell jangling, and shouted, "It's only me. I've got muffins!"

There was no answering shout from Starlight, but maybe she was upstairs with our guests. The shop was empty, the air warm and dusty with old incense and wax, and mobiles built of feathers, twigs, and the odd small bone spun gently overhead. I ambled down the hallway to the kitchen, Ruiner padding after me, and dropped the muffins on the table. There was no one in the big room, but Starlight's bag was still puddled on the coffee table in front of the sofa, and a half-eaten apple had been abandoned on top of it.

I filled the kettle then left it to boil as I trotted up the stairs, not worrying about trying to stay quiet. If I managed to wake up Mella and the other woman, it was all for the better. I went straight to the twin bedroom, which had been designated our makeshift infirmary, already saying, "Starlight…"

My voice trailed off. Starlight wasn't in the room. Grace was, sitting on the edge of one of the beds with her long legs crossed at the ankles. But that wasn't what made me stop. No, that was because she was holding the grimoire, and Jackie, rather than trying to bite Grace's hands off, was sitting on her shoulder, snout twitching as she stared down at the book.

"Oh, hello, Morgan," Grace said. "I wondered where you were."

"What're you doing?" I asked, not sure if I was directing the question to her or Jackie.

"Seeing if I can find anything useful," she said, not moving to get up.

I walked into the room and took the grimoire from her, almost expecting Jackie to attack me. She didn't, though, just watched me with sharp little eyes. "You can't just take it like that."

Grace shrugged, making her hair ripple softly. "I was trying to help. And Jackie didn't seem to mind." She took the rat from her shoulder and handed her over to me. "She knows it's safe with me."

Safe, or Jackie really was about to trade me in for a better witch. I could hardly blame her, but this wasn't the time for it. Unless it was. Maybe I should be handing everything over to Grace, hoping she could sort out the whole mask situation. I hesitated, looking down at the rat cradled in my cupped hand. She put one paw on my thumb, looking back at Grace. Traitor. Had Jackie showed her where to find the book, too? Or had Grace gone hunting for it? I supposed it didn't make that much difference, but… "Did you find anything?" I asked aloud.

"So far, no," Grace said, getting up. "And no change in these two."

I looked at them. They were both on their backs, blankets pulled up to their chins, Mella's darker skin still looking reasonably healthy. The other woman looked deathly pale, but maybe she was like that all the time. "How long can they survive like this?"

Grace shrugged. "No idea. But they need fluids, if nothing else. They'll be getting dehydrated."

"How do we do that?"

"Doctor and an IV?" she said.

"Oh." I'd somehow imagined there'd be a charm for it, but I was starting to realise that magic seemed to be fairly inextricably linked to everyday life, rather than existing separate from it. You couldn't replace antibiotics with a tincture. I lifted Jackie onto my shoulder and hugged the book to me in both arms, still looking at the women. There were bees resting in Mella's hair, and more buzzing dully at the window.

Finally, I turned my gaze back to Grace. Her face was freshly scrubbed, one of those no-makeup looks that took more skill than my full makeup looks did. She was back in jeans and boots, and she folded her arms over her chest as she looked at the two witches.

"Can you contact the doctor?" I asked her. Hollowbeck had one, and while he'd admittedly given me an herbal salve instead of medication when I'd had a car accident, he seemed to be an actual GP. He had a licence on the wall, at least.

"Of course. What're you going to do?"

"Try and find out about our mystery guest," I said, nodding at her.

"Are you sure you don't want help? With two of us, we could canvas the market faster."

It was tempting, but we couldn't leave the women here alone. What if they woke up? Or got worse? "You should probably stay," I said. "You're better with this sort of thing." I waved at our patients.

"Starlight's better," Grace said, and I gave her a surprised look. "She is. She's got a talent for healing. That's not my strength at all."

"Her tinctures do always seem to work," I agreed. "The ones that don't blow up, anyway." There had been the whole abscess thing, but I had an idea my fiddling might've messed that up, so I couldn't blame Starlight entirely. "To be fair, the explosions are usually when I'm involved. I don't think healing's my strength, either."

"You have other strengths."

"I doubt it," I said with a sigh, looking at the grimoire.

I really should just hand the bloody thing over. And Jackie, for that matter.

"You have plenty of strengths," Grace repeated. "And your main one will come clear in time. The rest of us have been working on being witches for years. You've been here a few months. Stop thinking you should be sodding Glinda already."

I couldn't help smiling at that. "Thanks."

"Sure." She stretched, languid as a cat. "Where is Starlight?"

I frowned. "She didn't open up the shop?"

"No, I did. Thought I might as well, since I was here anyway."

That wasn't good. "Her bag's still there, but I didn't see Howard. Or her mask."

Grace sighed deeply. "I hope you've got rid of yours?"

"No," I admitted. "But I've got Theodore's."

"It's a start. He wasn't himself yesterday at all."

"Should've seen him today." I lifted my chin, pointing at my neck, and her face tightened. She touched the skin gently, her fingers warm and soft.

"Bloody hell, Morgan. And you got the mask off him?" There was an admiring note in her voice, and she left her hand on my neck, soothing as any tincture.

"Well, I had help."

"Oh, stop it. Come on." She took one of my hands, pulling me towards the door. "We all have *help*. It doesn't mean we don't accomplish things ourselves. Let's get something on that to stop the swelling, and I'll call the GP."

I let her tow me downstairs, still unsettled by how easily Jackie seemed to have come around to her, but wanting to trust her. I didn't *really* have a reason not to.

Just that niggling sense in my stomach that Grace

didn't need a mask because she was already wearing one. Her and her twin Faith.

FOURTEEN

14. A risk of pre-emptive charming

DOWNSTAIRS, RUINER WAS CHOWING DOWN ON ONE OF THE muffins, having apparently taken a bite out of the other before dismissing it.

"Oh, bloody *hell*," I complained. "Ruiner, if you throw up again I'm *not* cleaning it."

"No one's giving me any decent food," my brother complained. "It's not like I can open a bloody tin, is it?"

I slapped the grimoire down next to him and grabbed the muffin off him. "You could *wait*."

"Eh."

"There's always something with animals," Grace said, and my brother bared his teeth at her.

"I'm *not* an animal."

"Animal-shaped."

Jackie jumped to the table and put a paw on the grimoire, giving me a look I couldn't quite read. "Not *always* something," I said, despite feeling the loyalty was a bit one-way at the moment.

Grace made an unconvinced noise. "Almost always."

"Is that why you have a bird for a familiar?"

"Birds," she corrected me. "And they're not my familiars. I just work with them."

I frowned. "So not every magic-worker has a familiar?"

"No. Some do, some disdain the whole idea as beneath them, some work with certain creatures, like I do with birds, others have inanimate talismans that amplify their power."

"Like the grimoire."

She shook her head. "No, grimoires are different. They *hold* power, and it can be passed on. They're almost animate, really, and their own entities. Talismans are more about directing and focusing your own abilities." She thought about it for a moment, then grinned, impossibly charming with her slightly crooked teeth. "Like a magic wand, I guess. Although I've never seen anyone with an actual wand. They'd get laughed out of the first town they walked into."

I was too focused on the idea of the book as an animate entity to really get the humour in the wand thing, but I took her word for it. "How do you work with the birds, exactly, then? What's your speciality?"

"Nature-based." She picked up Starlight's bag from the sofa and checked inside it. "I don't see her mask."

"Great," I said, although it wasn't exactly a surprise. Starlight might have her ditzy moments, but she never took our responsibility to the village lightly. Most villages have a pharmacy. Hollowbeck had the Cosy Cauldron — although both the supermarket and the shop-that-sells-everything did have small sections dedicated to Dettol and plasters, which were vital for anyone dealing with familiars. But we supplied everything from creams for arthritis to charms to repel pixies, along with infusions for soothing water sprites, tinctures for congestion, and tea for insomnia (which, Starlight had confided in me, was often just camomile. For some people she added moonshade, a gentle sedative, and the odd person did get more heavy-duty mixes, but for the majority camomile was enough. The ritual of brewing it, and their belief in its power, was all the magic needed). "I need to find her," I said. "I don't want her running about with a mask on."

"No," Grace agreed. "Until we can figure out if these are isolated incidents or not, no one's safe."

I shivered and looked around. "I'll have to shut the shop."

"Leave it open. I can't do any more than I have with Mella and the other one, so I'll run across to James' to call the doctor, then come back and keep an eye on things down here."

"Are you sure?"

"I think I can manage," she said, giving me an amused look.

"Alright." I watched her pick up the decimated muffins, giving a chunk of the apple and cinnamon one to Jackie before dropping the rest in the bin and flicking the kettle back on. She didn't *look* like she was actively trying to steal the town witch position out from under me, but maybe she didn't need to. Maybe she was just going to step into it as elegantly as she did everything else. And why was I worried, anyway? I'd never asked to be town witch. I should just let her take over if she wanted to. Whatever her *nature-based* speciality was, she was just overall better at things than I was.

"So Ratface McGee gets breakfast and I don't?" Ruiner demanded, looking at me. Jackie hissed, and he bared his teeth at her.

"We'll get something at the market."

"The market? It's *cold*."

"You've got a fur coat." Our produce haul from the

day before looked depressingly healthy, so I checked the cupboards. There was nothing edible other than some cheese and onion rice cakes that I knew, with great disappointment, tasted like neither cheese nor onion. I slammed the cupboard and straightened up, pulling my coat and scarf on instead. "Come on."

"Are you taking that?" Grace asked, nodding at the grimoire. It was still sitting on the table, fat and brooding, and Jackie looked from one of us to the other, her scrap of muffin still clutched in her paws and her cheeks full.

"I don't know," I admitted. "I should take it back to Petunia's."

"Should you? She was wearing a mask the other night."

"Well, yes. But it's *Petunia*." I couldn't imagine anyone less likely to steal the grimoire. Petunia loved frogs, midnight skinny-dipping, and day-drinking. She was hardly a power-hungry monster. "Plus I have a hiding place. She doesn't know about it."

"What about the frogs?"

"You think the *frogs* are going to nick off with it?"

"I have birds. She has frogs."

That was a fair point. And one of the reasons the grimoire always felt safe at Petunia's was *because* of the frogs. They'd conspired with Jackie to keep it hidden when it had first fallen into my hands, after all, before she'd decided to allow me to keep it. If Petunia was so addled by the mask that she wanted it, the odds were she could persuade the frogs to show her where it was.

"I'll take it with me, then," I said aloud.

"Into a market full of magic workers in masks?"

"So you expect her just to hand it over to you?" Ruiner asked Grace. He still hadn't moved from the fridge. "Her new bestie?"

Grace gave him a very small smile. "I've not touched a mask, and I won't. And *you* might not trust me, Ruiner, but this is your sister's decision."

They both looked at me, and I ran both hands back over my hair, snagging in the knots. I was weary, and the decision seemed harder than it should have. I closed my eyes for a moment, briefly wistful for a job where I actually got a salary, and made boring decisions about what category to put tea supplies in when balancing books, rather than how best to protect magical ones. But I'd also had a pointless husband, never went to cocktail parties featuring hot chocolate stands and flying pigs, and didn't have friends to worry about, thanks to the pointless husband. I opened my eyes again and looked at Jackie. She stared back at me, her ears perked.

"You kept it safe here before," I said to her. "Before Ruiner stole it, anyway."

She twitched her whiskers at me.

"And you managed to stash it somewhere after you got it back, too. So that's what we're going to do again. Alright?"

She didn't respond for a moment, then she went back to the remains of the muffin. I had a brief flash of embarrassment, because she was just a *rat*, even if she was a familiar, then she held half a walnut out to me. I took it.

"Ah, thanks?"

She patted the book and jumped to a chair then the floor, looking back at me.

"Well," Grace said. "I suppose they do have their uses."

I didn't answer, just picked up the book and followed Jackie to the hall door, glancing at Ruiner as I went and raising my eyebrows at him slightly. He lifted his chin. He could hardly stop Grace following, but he'd yowl his furry little heart out if she did. Or that was what my raised eyebrows meant. Hopefully his lifted chin meant the same thing.

Either Grace had no intention of following, or Ruiner's presence was enough to dissuade her, because Jackie and I were undisturbed as she led me into the shop. She scrambled up the shelves, sleek and agile despite the grey hairs flecking her little muzzle, and made a leap to the heavy old beams, hanging for a moment with her back legs pedalling, and making me rush towards her, ready to catch her if she fell. But she wriggled her way up and peered at me from a narrow gap that led into the cavity between the plastered ceiling and the floorboards above it.

"Clever girl," I said, and checked for anyone outside the windows before dragging the stool from the counter over and climbing up on it. "How did you get it up here on your own? Is that what you did?"

She just looked at me. I supposed I should be grateful she couldn't talk. Her looks said volumes.

I slid the book into the gap next to her, managing not to dislodge too much of the old plaster as I did so, and she twitched her nose at me, then vanished out of sight.

"Right. Thanks," I said. "Do you need anything?" I waited a moment, but she didn't re-emerge, so I climbed back down. The book was as safe as it was going to be, and with Theodore and Isabella out of action, we had work to do.

Also breakfast to find. My stomach was still mourning the muffins.

~

RUINER and I headed straight for the market, armed with a tote bag that had *This is my Resting Witch Face* printed on it.

I was pretty sure it was some of Norma's old stock, and the sort of thing Starlight didn't approve of. I thought it was funny enough, but, as has been observed, I was hardly a proper witch. Either way, it was big enough to shove some masks into. I'd left Theodore's in the freezer compartment of the fridge at the shop, next to a bottle of vodka I hadn't known was in there and an open box of ancient fish fingers. It was hardly the safest place in the world, but I wasn't putting it anywhere near the grimoire, even if I thought Jackie would let me. Hopefully it was safe enough.

"Where's your mask?" Ruiner asked, trotting next to me with his fluffy tail waving gently.

"In my pocket."

"You should burn the bloody thing."

"I'm not going to put it on."

He didn't say anything, just looked up at me with narrowed eyes. I didn't say the rest of what I was thinking. That I might need it, if the place filled up with evil spirits. Every time I thought that was a bit far-fetched, I remembered flying pigs, and I wasn't sure anymore.

The market was even busier than it had been the day before, and I went straight to the food area in the centre, all but elbowing my way to the front of the queue at the coffee truck. I swapped some of our limited funds for a large Americano, then headed to another truck that was making nothing but toasties, with a wild variety of breads and fillings. I went simple with cheese and ham on fat slabs of softly toasted bread, oozing butter and cheddar, and moved on to a stall selling chicken in various guises, getting some plain bits for my brother. We found a couple of empty chairs and settled down to scoff our very late breakfast, watching the crowd.

There were more masks in evidence today, those without them becoming outliers. I kept my head down, trying not to attract attention, and watched for any sign of Starlight. By the time I'd finished my sandwich I hadn't seen anything, and I wiped my greasy fingers on a napkin, taking my phone from my coat pocket. It might be no use for what it was designed for around here, but that didn't stop the camera being handy. I'd taken a photo of our mystery woman before I left the shop, because my other reason for coming to the market was to try and figure out who she was. I could do that at the same time as look for Starlight.

"Come on," I said to Ruiner.

"I'm not done," he complained indistinctly. "Just coz you scoff your food."

I had scoffed it, to be fair, but in my defence, I'd been starving. "Catch me up," I said and headed for the emptiest of the food stalls, my camera open to the photo of the unknown witch. *Someone* had to know her.

Three stalls later, Ruiner had caught me up and I was rethinking my whole plan. I'd been unable to get anyone to so much as look at the picture, waving me away as soon as they realised I wasn't buying anything. Every stall was busy to some degree, and I evidently wasn't the only one who'd missed breakfast or was after an early lunch.

Ruiner hooked his claws into my jeans, tugging insistently, and I crouched down with a sigh, so he could jump to my shoulder. "I should get you one of those fancy cat carriers," I said, my voice low. "The ones that look like a goldfish bowl in a backpack."

"Try it and see how many fingers you'd have left."

"What about a baby-carrier type thing? I've seen cats in those, too."

"I will remove your face."

I grinned and headed for the aisles of non-food stalls. If everyone was eating, maybe they wouldn't be shopping.

There were still a surprising amount of people drifting from stall to stall, more than seemed possible given the size of Hollowbeck, and the fact that it wasn't possible to get into the valley unless one were invited. Although, I supposed that only applied to non-magical types, such as I'd once been. And given the number of familiars among the attendees, and their entire lack of surprise at the fact there were entire stalls devoted to charms, or organic potion ingredients, or cauldrons, they had to be part of the more esoteric world. I knew there were other towns out there like ours, plus it wasn't as though magical folk *had* to live in such places. For all I knew, the guy who ran the corner shop near my old house had been a werewolf. He'd been hairy enough.

I tried a crystal stall first, a quiet place run by a rotund woman in a bright pink ski jacket and lime-green fleecy trousers. Crystals hung from the frame of her tent, twisting gently on the ends of almost invisible threads, and more glowed on the counter under soft lights, craggy things like miniature, otherworldly mountains in pinks and purples and oranges.

I gave the woman my friendliest smile, which seemed to work. She looked more receptive than the food stall people had been, anyway. "I'm looking for someone. Can you take a look at a photo for me?"

"Of course, dear." She took a pair of reading glasses from her pocket and popped them on, leaning forward, but as soon as I held my phone out to her, she recoiled rapidly.

"This is hideous!"

I looked at the photo, startled, and suddenly realised what was wrong. "No! No, she's not dead. She's uncon-scious, is all. I'm trying to find someone who knows her." She did *look* dead, though. We'd thought she was, after all.

The woman picked up a small blue crystal and rubbed

it rapidly between her hands, then against her cheeks. "No, no, no," she muttered. "No, no, no."

"No, you haven't seen her?"

"*No*, what're you doing showing me such a dreadful thing? It's quite thrown off my magnetic field!"

Ruiner made a noise like the chicken was coming back up.

"Sorry," I said. "I didn't think about what the photo looked like."

"Not the photo! Your infernal device!" She grabbed a milky white crystal and brandished it at me like a spray bottle at a cat. "Get it away before it ruins all my stock."

"It's not—"

"*Get away!*"

I retreated before she started flinging the damn crystals at me.

"That went well," Ruiner observed.

"Shut up."

The next stall was crowded with crocheted blankets and macrame plant holders and knitted scarves, as well as some rather interesting forays into home-crafted fashion that went far beyond the usual socks and jumpers. I stared at a macrame bikini for a moment, trying to figure out if you wore another one under it or if the gaps were a style choice, then dared approach the stallholder with my phone. She didn't run screaming from it, but she didn't recognise the woman, either. Not that she looked that closely, as she was mostly concentrating on trying to sell me the bikini.

The man at the jewellery stall thought the woman looked familiar but couldn't tell me anything else. The woman at the woodworking stand didn't know her, but asked if she could have a copy of the photo to carve her likeness, which seemed a little creepy. The couple at the soap shop conferred in sweet-scented whispers, and finally one said to me, "You should ask at Bits and Bats."

"Bits and Bats?"

"It's the witchcraft supply store," the other half of the couple said, pointing down the line of stalls. The two of them were wearing matching sage green fleeces, their hair dyed pale lilac. "Everyone goes there."

"Alright. Thanks."

"Would you like some soap? Sexy Siren might be a helpful choice."

I scowled at them. "I'm fine."

"Are you sure?" They both stared at me, taking in my slept-in clothes and tangled hair.

"Probably not," I said with a sigh. "But no thanks anyway."

I headed straight for Bits and Bats, Ruiner still balanced on my shoulder. "Making great progress here," he said.

"What else do you suggest? We need to find out who she is if we're going to have a chance of figuring out what connection she and Mella have."

"They're both witches."

"So's half the bloody town."

"Alright, then, they're both young witches, like you and Grace. Well, young-ish."

I ignored the dig, the worm of unease back in my gut. "It's not really a pattern."

"We'll just wait for the next one to get bumped off then, shall we?"

I hushed him as I entered Bits and Bats. It wasn't an open stall like many of the others, but a large, enclosed white tent, with free-standing shelves all around the perimeter as well as in the centre. Large containers of herbs and spices were stacked everywhere, and fresh ones sprouted from jugs or grew in decorative pots, labelled with little wooden signs stuck in the soil. Dried insects and clutters of shells filled glass jars, and a man looked up from filling a brown paper bag with dried flower petals as we came in.

"Welcome! I'll be right with you," he said, and folded the bag over, sealing it with a bat-shaped sticker. He handed it to a bent old man wearing a red puffer jacket about three sizes too big and a yellow and black striped beanie. "There we go. Anything else?"

"Three tins of pickled herring and a pot of dried shrimp."

"Coming right up." He busied himself with the last of the man's shopping, while I looked around curiously. The place was like the Cosy Cauldron minus the tat and dust, and with the addition of a whole lot more things that looked actually useful. There were recipe books and spellbooks, vials and flasks and sickles and mortar and pestles. This was what a *proper* witchy supply shop should look like.

"There we are," the man said, coming out from behind the counter and smiling at me broadly as his customer tottered away. He had close-cropped grey hair, an appealingly crooked nose, and skin tanned in a way that suggested far too many long hikes and outdoor sports for sensible people. "How can I help?"

"I'm looking for someone," I said. "I've got her photo, but it's on my phone. Would it be okay to show it to you?"

His grin widened. "Did you try to show it to Cathy up at the crystal shop?"

"I did," I admitted.

"Too much crystal dust, if you ask me." He held out his hand. "Show me."

I found the photo quickly and handed it over. "She's not dead. We think she was attacked, though."

He was silent for a moment, looking at the picture with his smile fading to nothing. "Well, I'm glad she's alive, at least," he said, and handed the phone back.

"Do you know her?" I asked, when he didn't say anything else.

"I do," he said, rubbing a hand over his short hair.

"And?" I prompted. "What's her name? What was she doing in Hollowbeck?"

He looked towards the door of the tent, as if to check we weren't going to be overheard. "Her name's Ariel, but I don't know her last name, I'm sorry. She buys a few things from me, and she has a business selling charms and light spells. I wondered why I hadn't seen her about."

"She's a regular at the Festival?"

"Not here, but at other markets I attend. I was surprised she came to Hollowbeck, but then I heard your town witch had witched her last."

I frowned at him. "She had a problem with Norma?"

"*Everyone* had a problem with Norma," he said. "Or rather, she had a problem with anyone coming in selling things. She liked her monopoly. Her and her little deals. She made things pretty unpleasant for people." He looked around his stall. "It's been nice not to have to put protections all over the place to stop her cursing my stock. Although maybe I should, if someone's going around bumping off the competition."

"I'm sure it's not that," I said, and he gave me a thoughtful look.

"Maybe. But I can't see why else anyone would be after Ariel. Unless she got one of her charms wrong. That's unlikely, though. She's an excellent witch."

"Right," I said, then wouldn't think of anything else to ask. "Um … do you know where she was staying?"

"Her camper van. It'll be around somewhere." He

waved vaguely. "Old black and purple VW. It's pretty distinctive. You can't miss it." He headed back to the counter. "Now if you'll excuse me, I'm going to get some protective charms up. Could be the new witch is as bad as the old one."

I didn't defend myself. He might try to throw some sort of pre-emptive charm on me, and I already had enough to deal with. Instead, I went in search of the camper van.

15. No offence, but...

WE WOVE OUR WAY THROUGH THE SHOPPERS IN THEIR heavy coats and fanciful masks, adults and children alike sporting woolly hats and flat caps and horns and antlers. No one in the stalls seemed to have masks, and the market-goers without them were all strangers to me. Which didn't mean much, as it wasn't like I'd been here long enough to know everyone, but it still niggled at me, the idea that it might be only Hollowbeck residents who were falling for the masks.

"What'd'you think you're going to find at the camper van?" Ruiner asked. "A note saying *Call this number to find Doctor Sleep*?"

"No, but maybe there'll be something that'll tell us why her. Or an idea who to contact, next of kin type thing. And she didn't have a familiar with her, so we should check for that. It might be hungry."

"We're not becoming a home for stray familiars. Bloody bee swarms and rabid ferrets."

"Howard's not rabid. Or a stray."

"Can we change that?"

"What, you want him to be rabid?"

"Oh, ha." Ruiner shifted on my shoulder, scanning the market. "These bloody masks are no good. Can't tell who's behind them."

"Kind of the point."

"And that's not worrying you? Given the sleeping beauties at the shop?"

I didn't answer. Of course it was worrying me, as was the not entirely unexpected news that Norma had evidently been as unpopular with the stallholders as she had with the townsfolk. Was that what this was about? A pre-emptive strike, as I'd been thinking in Bits and Bats, in case the new witch was intending to continue Norma's favourite activities of extortion and coercion? It wasn't like anyone outside Hollowbeck knew who I was, after all. Someone could be targeting any witches in the hope of hitting the right one.

Worrying wasn't getting me anywhere, though. I needed to *do* something, and while I didn't know what I was really going to be able to figure out on my own, the camper van could hold a clue. It was worth trying, anyway, while we kept an eye out for Starlight.

There wasn't a dedicated area for the visiting stallholders to park up their caravans and motorhomes, and plenty of them were likely staying at the village's B&Bs and guesthouses (because Petunia's wasn't the only guesthouse — she was just the cheapest, and best suited for long stays as long as one didn't mind shared bathrooms and frogs). Those who had brought accommodation with them seemed to have simply parked behind their stalls, and in many cases they were one and the same, so I just circled the market, looking for an old VW with a *distinctive* paint job, whatever that was when it was at home.

"Hello," Ruiner said, his tail tickling my neck.

"What?"

"Five o'clock. Not loving my distance vision these days — or colour, for that matter, cat vision sucks — but there's a freaky-looking old VW back there."

"At least you've got night vision," I said as I turned to look for the van. There was definitely an old, purple and black VW half-hidden behind a stall selling various animal skins and horns wrought into musical instruments (which seemed like it should be a really niche market, but there were five separate people in there, blowing on stuff and banging things and generally making about as much good music as a toddler with a drum kit), and another, very quiet one that was all hanging plants. It didn't have prices on anything, and as I watched, a leafy vine lashed out and grabbed a budgie from a man's shoulder. The bird squawked, the man screamed, and a woman leaned over the counter, brandishing a spray bottle of weedkiller. The plant released the budgie and collapsed dramatically into a puddle of wilted leaves, and both man and budgie fled. Ruiner scrambled around to my opposite shoulder, furthest from the plant stall.

I shaded my eyes against the low sun, peering at the van. "What's freaky about it?"

"You can't see that?"

"See what?"

"It's…" He hesitated, apparently thinking how to say it. "It's not just a van. There's another shape to it, hiding behind the van shape. And it keeps shifting, like it's alive."

"Well, that's creepy."

"Definitely. It looks like it bites."

"That seems about right." I started slowly towards the van, thinking of Grace's questioning look when I said I couldn't tell a witch just by looking at them. This was probably more of my sub-standard witchiness, not being able to see charms. Except with the mask. I touched my pocket. I shouldn't just walk in there without seeing what was actually there. And Ruiner's description wasn't exactly helpful.

I paused as I took the mask out, the fabric slippery under my fingers, smooth and warm. Ruiner was still glaring at the plant stall, where a couple of grabby-looking blooms had inclined their heads towards him.

"Can we move?" he demanded. "I'm going to lose some whiskers if we're not careful."

I didn't answer, just held the mask to my face, not quite daring to let it touch the skin, as if it might do an Alien impression and latch on. It felt like I was having to fight it, to keep it from pressing to my cheeks like a second skin, and wanted to believe that was just my imagination. I stared at the van, the edges of the eyeholes creating a black frame, and caught a glimmer of *something*. Not another shape, as Ruiner had said, but maybe some sort of vapour or steam rising from the van. Old charms, perhaps? It was hard to tell, what with not being able to see through the mask properly. I relaxed my arm a little, letting the fabric rest naturally against my face, soothing my cold-stung skin. I wasn't using the straps, after all. It wasn't on *properly*.

And now I could see.

See the curling shadows of the plants, unfurling towards the sun, scenting the air, curious and thoughtful, and maybe a little hungry as well. See the woman walking past with a goose on a leash, trailing purple sparks from her fingertips. See the shadowy forms of lithe, well-shaped men leaning out of a tent selling truly tacky T-shirts, whispering in people's ears and trailing fingers down their spines, tempting them in. See blossoming auras and stalking, ghostly familiars, and people with more than one form to them, superimposed over each other like tracings.

I forgot all about the van as I stared around, wondering

if this was how witches saw the world, or if it was something beyond even that. My fingers sparked and shone when I lifted my free hand in front of me, and I could hear static electricity hissing through my hair, as well as a wild heat rising in my belly, something that belonged to empty moors and ice-girt lakes and—

Ruiner slapped my cheek, claws out, and the edge of the mask tore off, sharp and violent as one of those pore-cleaning strips that take about three layers of skin off along with the blackheads. I yelped, jumping, and the movement whipped the mask off entirely, leaving my face raw and tender.

"*Ow!*"

"What're you *playing* at? You want to end up snoozing above the shop for all eternity?"

"No," I said, touching my face gingerly. That had really hurt, both the mask and Ruiner's claws. "I just wanted to see the van. I'm not walking in there with no idea what it is."

"You're not. I *told* you what it is."

"It's not the same, though, is it? And I didn't put it on properly. I was just holding it in place, and it helped. There's so much stuff I just don't notice, and I'm meant to. I'm meant to be the sodding *town witch,* and I can't even tell another witch on sight."

"I said your name half a dozen times. You notice that?"

I huffed, but shoved the mask back in my pocket, that sense of power dissipating. He was right. I *hated* my brother being right, but he was. Maybe if it had just been that intoxicating, addictive sense of power I'd have been able to ignore it, but my face still stung. The mask had all but fused to me, some hungry entity, and I didn't know what it was taking from me, because there had to be something, some exchange of power. Maybe whatever it took was how I'd ended up with two witches in the beds above my shop.

"*Fine,*" I said aloud. "Let's check the van. Since you're so clever, you can tell me if anything's going to eat me, can't you?"

"That mask is. I'll tell you that for free."

"Sure it is." I marched towards the van, still seeing smudges of movement in the corners of my eyes and wishing there was another way to get that witchy sight.

The van didn't lash out with clasping tentacles, or open a yawning maw to snaffle me up. It just sat there, painted a flawless, glossy black below the windows and purple above. The curtains were open, and inside I could see it had been fitted out with a modern interior, minimalist and tidy. There was a small table, with a rock'n'roll sofa to one side and on the other a small workspace with a cover over it, probably hiding a little sink and a burner. A collection of folders was lined up neatly on top of it, held upright by a silver skull and a cut glass vase holding six deep orange tulips, their heads bending sadly. The table was clean and empty, and the sofa held a couple of throw cushions. It was all very tasteful, very tidy, and looked utterly bereft of clues.

I tried one of the double side doors, not expecting much, and the handle turned under my hand. I paused, glancing behind me, and said to Ruiner, "What's the van doing?"

"Nothing, so far. I think it's watching you, but it doesn't have eyes, so that's just a feeling."

"Awesome." No one was looking at us, so I opened the door and climbed in, ducking my head and pulling the door shut behind me. It smelled of coffee and fresh lemons, bright and sharp, and I pulled one of the folders out of the row, opening it. Inside were plastic sleeves, each split into four, and each of these held a small envelope, fat with whatever was inside. "Lost love," I read off the first one, the printing neat and firm on the paper. "Near-miss romance. Forced proximity. Enemies to lovers— wait, these are tropes."

"Dopes to pay for them," Ruiner said, looking around uneasily. "Put them back. The van doesn't like it."

I shut the folder hurriedly and slid it back into place. "*Tropes,*" I said. "Like, for stories."

"People like stories in their lives," said my brother, the philosopher. "Bet there's a rags to riches charm in there somewhere too. Probably a *lot* of them."

"I wouldn't mind one of those," I muttered but left the folders where they were, checking the compartments under the sofa cushions instead. "Look — dog food. She has got a familiar somewhere."

"Really?" Ruiner snuffled audibly. "This place smells too nice for a dog."

"She's just got high standards," I said, pocketing some dog chews in case we came across the familiar and thinking a little guiltily of the shop. Starlight and I kept *trying* to clean, but the dust was faster than we were. How did anyone keep a place this spotless? "Where d'you think her familiar is, then?"

"Oddly enough, I don't go looking for mutts."

The other cupboards held no surprises. A bag of clothes and one of toiletries, some cans of soup, and a cool box with milk and cheese in it. There was storage in the doors, holding mugs and plates, and a fold-down seat by the sink, but unless I wanted to take notes on how to be a roving witch with excellent style, there was nothing. I did find a tattoo gun, along with what looked like homemade inks, which I could only assume were for more lasting charms.

I leaned into the front, intending to have a dig around in the glovebox, and someone knocked smartly on one of the windows. I jumped so violently Ruiner fell off my shoulder and I bumped my head on the roof, then spun to face the side door and banged my leg painfully on the table. I swore, rubbing the injured spot vigorously, and Finn pulled the door open.

"Sorry," he said. "I thought the knocking would count as not creeping up on you like a stalker, but I may have misjudged."

Ruiner shook himself off and narrowed his eyes at Finn, showing a fang.

"It's fine," I said, surprised my voice wasn't shaking. I'd thought for a moment the van had decided to pounce on the intruders in its belly. "Just surprised me."

"So I saw." He looked around the van. "Is this yours?"

"No, it's Ariel's. The woman who was found at the cocktail party."

"Oh." He grimaced. "What're you doing?"

Looking for clues wasn't exactly a justifiable reason for the town witch to be poking around a comatose woman's van, so I floundered for a moment, then said, "Checking if she had a familiar that needed feeding or something. I found dog food, but no dog."

"That's no good." He was still frowning, but he stepped back to look along the outside of the van. "Yeah, there's a dog bowl out here."

"Where's the dog, then?" I took a final glance around, then paused. A single envelope lay on the little worktop, just like the ones holding the trope-y charms in the folders. It hadn't been there before. It wasn't like I could've missed it, either.

"I don't know," Finn said, his voice fading as he peered under the van.

I snatched the envelope up and shoved it in my coat pocket, deliberately keeping it away from the mask, as if it might get infected. I climbed out of the van, Ruiner leaping after me, and Finn straightened up.

"No bed under there or anything."

"I suppose I'd better keep asking around, then," I said.

Fin ran a hand back through his thick hair, his shoulders doing the lumberjack thing again. I wished he wouldn't. It was really denting my motivation to get on with my search. "Do you think you should?"

"Why?"

"It could be dangerous."

The shoulders weren't so distracting now. "Why would it be dangerous?" I asked.

He hesitated. "I heard there was another one. Another witch. And you're a witch, so, you know. You should leave it to the police."

"The police are currently indisposed," I said. "But you were going to find me. Was it to do with the masks?"

He rocked on his heels, looking around. "Sort of." He hesitated, then said, "Alaric's too interested in you."

"In *me*? Why me?"

"New town witch. And no offence, but—"

"Anything that comes after someone says *no offence, but* is always offensive. It's like *I'm not racist, but*, and then they say something horrendous."

He grinned, holding both hands up. "Alright, but don't hit me anywhere delicate again. I'm repeating the gossip is all, okay? *I* think you're fantastic." He immediately went luminously red, and from the feel of my face I was about the same shade. Ruiner made a noise that suggested he was hoicking up a hairball, and I nudged him with my foot. He huffed and trotted off towards the main thoroughfare, his head tipped as if hearing something.

"Right," I said to Finn, trying to ignore my hot cheeks. "Well, what's this gossip, then?"

Finn flushed even more deeply, if that were possible. He just about matched his red flannel jacket. "That you're not … you haven't quite … you're…"

"I'm a crappy witch?"

He shrugged helplessly, spreading his hands. "It's just gossip."

"It's right," I said with a sigh. "I didn't even think actual witches existed until a few months ago."

"What? But how … where did you think the stories came from, if nothing else?"

"Fairy tales? Traditional dislike of women with power?"

"Eh. Fair point. But still — you had *no idea?*"

"No."

"And now you're the town witch?"

"It's been a busy few months."

"Wow." He looked back at the market. "Okay. I mean, I'd heard you were the new witch — Alaric wouldn't stop going on about that. But you're actually a *new* witch."

"Yes," I said, a little curtly. "So is that why Alaric's interested? Or just in the fact of there being a new town witch in general?"

"I suppose it's the fact Norma's gone. Things have changed."

"How, exactly?"

"Can I buy you a coffee or something?" he asked. "I feel this would be easier with coffee."

I crossed my arms. "It's not that difficult. And if you can't tell me anything about the masks or the witches, just say so and I can get on."

His face tightened, a shadow of displeasure. "Fine. I'm just trying to help, you know."

"Alaric wants to talk to me too. If you can't tell me anything useful about the masks, I'm sure he can."

Finn's scowl deepened. "You can't trust him. You could get trapped."

"What does that mean?" I demanded, and he shook his head, looking away and twisting the bracelet on his wrist restlessly. There were shadows under his eyes, noticeable when he wasn't wearing his smile. I softened my tone without thinking about it. "Finn, are you trapped somehow?"

He shook his head, the movement violent, more a refusal of the question than a denial, and he never stopped fiddling with the bracelet, even as it gnawed more deeply at his skin. I reached out to stop him, and he caught my hand quickly, moving it away from the metal band. He twisted his fingers through mine without speaking, and I examined his face. He didn't meet my eyes.

"Finn?" I said again, my voice low. "Is it the bracelet? Is it a charm?"

He shushed me, his fingers tightening on mine almost painfully, and when he spoke, his words were fast and low. "Don't worry about me. You need to stay safe. Please, Morgan. Don't meet with Alaric."

"But—"

His hand tightened enough to make me wince. "*Listen*—"

A yowl cut him off, and Ruiner came bolting past the plant stall, ears back. He leaped for me, and I wrenched my hand away from Finn, catching my brother and lifting him high enough to hear his hiss of, "*Starlight.*"

I stared at him, and he twitched his ears desperately, tipping his head towards the hall. "I have to go," I said, setting him on the ground.

"What?" Finn asked. "But—"

I was already hurrying off, Ruiner sprinting into the aisle of stalls ahead of me. Why hadn't I gone looking for her straight away? I should've been doing that, not hunting out strangers. I should've found her and got the bloody mask off her. What if she was … what if …

My stomach rolled, and when Finn caught up to me and grabbed my arm, I pulled away, hard. "Let me go!"

He held up both hands. "I'm trying to help," he said, his voice pitched low.

"All you're doing is dropping hints and dancing around things." I looked for Ruiner, but he was gone.

"There's only so much I can do."

"Because of being trapped?" I looked at his wrist pointedly, and he pulled the cuff of his jacket down, an odd, vulnerable movement.

"Please don't talk to Alaric," he said. "It's not safe."

I examined him. "Are the masks dangerous?"

"I don't know," he said, the words slow. I started to turn away and he touched my arm again, stopping me without restraining me. "Morgan, I really don't know. Before, Alaric always dealt with Norma. He had an arrangement so that he could sell his masks here. Now there's other witches around, who weren't here when she was. I know she wasn't a good person, but she had a lot of power. A lot of influence."

I frowned. "Are you saying she kept the festival safe?" That didn't sound like the Norma I'd been learning about, but if it kept her hold over Hollowbeck intact, maybe she would protect it. Like a predator protecting its hunting grounds.

"Maybe."

I took a slow breath. "And the masks?"

"I'm not sure. They're Alaric's thing. But I can show you where he sets the enchantments. You might be able to find something out from there." He lifted his hand, the bracelet invisible under his sleeve but the redness of his wrist obvious. "I can't."

I didn't know if I could trust him, didn't know what was truth and what wasn't. But the masks *were* Alaric's, and if Alaric had had an *arrangement* with Norma, that likely meant he had a deal. Again with the bloody grimoire. Maybe he was after it, to break his deal or steal *all* the deals, maybe he was just making sure the new witch didn't try to cash in on his deal, or maybe this was nothing but conjecture, something fanciful made up by Finn, a plea to help him escape whatever the bracelet was shackling him to.

I was abruptly desperate for Theodore or Isabella or *anyone* who actually knew what they were doing to step in and take over, but there was only me. I took a breath, looking at Finn with his face drawn in anxious lines, but before I could think what I could ask to make things even remotely clearer, Ruiner came belting back through the crowd, his teeth bared. He skidded to a stop in front of me and snarled, urgent and furious.

"I'm coming. Go," I said, and he took off. This time Finn did grab me before I could run after him.

"I *can* help," he said. "Come and find me."

I pulled away without answering and sprinted after my brother. The questions would have to wait. I needed to find Starlight.

16. Old deals & new dangers

THE MARKET HAD GROWN EVEN BUSIER WHILE I'D BEEN exploring Ariel's van, and I bumped into people as I ran after my brother, shouting 'sorry!' as I went, but not pausing. Everyone had a meandering, thoughtless pace on, taking up every scrap of available walking space as they perused the stalls, assuming everyone else was as unhurried as they were, and it lit an almost incoherent rage in me. I needed to get to Starlight, and my path was filled with *idiots*. I all but shoulder-barged past a couple in matching, furry-looking coats and fluffy masks with teddy bear ears, the two of them clutching each other in a tangle of warmth and outrage as I ran on, one hand clenched around my own mask for no reason I could explain. In the absence of the grimoire and Jackie, it was *something*, and I needed it.

Ruiner raced ahead of me, long grey fur flying, and we burst out of the market's crowds, aiming for the hall gardens. They were open as always, but as it wasn't the most direct way to the market from town, there weren't a lot of people in sight. My brother vanished into the old, well-established flowerbeds, with their neat gravel paths and elegant topiary, and I stumbled to the gate, panting.

"Ruiner!" I managed between gasps for air. "Ruiner, dammit — where the hell are you?"

"Did your familiar get away on you, dear?" a small woman in a floor-length, wildly fluffy purple coat and matching hat asked, peering at me through the eyeholes of a glittering purple mask. "The pretty cat?"

"Um, yeah," I said.

"He went that-a-way," she said, flinging a hand out and raining glitter down over me, the gate, and the flowerbeds. She giggled. "Oops. Don't worry, it's biodegradable." She toddled off towards the market, and I forced myself into a run again, wondering if it was a mask thing, or if she just carried pocketfuls of biodegradable glitter around with her just for the fun of it. Either option was possible.

I rounded the corner of the hall and almost tripped on Ruiner as he leaped out of a snow-choked flowerbed in my path, then bounded up with his front paws raised to attack my legs.

"Don't *do* that!"

"Sorry. It's—"

"If you say instinct again, I'll throw you in a snowdrift. You're *not a cat*."

"Fine, fine. Just come on!" He spun, bouncing back through the dormant plants, and I skirted around the bed as fast as I could, finding another path and chasing my brother to where it ended on a small square, like a minia-ture courtyard. There was a bench on each side, and a circular mound in the centre, the plantings buried under snow. The top of the mound was off-centre, and an elegant statue rose from it, a woman with wings and softly folded robes, holding a willow switch. The switch's shadow painted itself neatly across the snow, and I knew that when it melted, a variety of different flowers would be planted in clearly delineated sections, turning it into a huge and very pretty sundial. Also rather ineffective at this time of year, given the plants being both buried under the snow and dormant.

But I wasn't concerned with the logistics of a winter sundial. I was concerned with Starlight, who was reclining comfortably at the feet of the statue, her mask in place and a crown of loosely woven ivy on her head. She wasn't wearing a coat, and she had to be freezing. I kicked through the snow to reach her, dropping to my knees and grabbing her shoulder. Howard popped up from behind her, but he didn't even hiss, just looked at Ruiner with his ears twitching.

"Starlight! *Starlight!*" Her skin was chilled when I touched her face, and I stripped my jacket off hurriedly, tucking it around her and trying to lift her off the ground. For someone so slight she was ridiculously heavy. "Ruiner, we need help. I can't carry her."

"I can help," someone said.

I almost fell back into the snow, trying to spin around in a crouch. "Would everyone stop *doing* that!"

Alaric had stopped at the edge of the mound, his heavy woollen coat accentuating his shoulders and his hair bare in the snow. He raised his hands apologetically. "Sorry. I saw you run past, and something was obviously wrong. I followed to see if I could help."

I didn't want to trust him. I *didn't* trust him, not with Finn's hints of being trapped and mysterious deals with Norma. But Starlight was getting colder and colder, and I could hardly send him away and hope someone better came along, or that I could find a wheelbarrow, because that was the only way I was getting Starlight out of here.

"Alright," I said aloud. "I need to get her to the shop. Can you carry her?"

"Hopefully I'm not that decrepit yet," he said, winking at me, and I moved back a little as he came to crouch next to Starlight. He smelled of soap and open skies and the faintest whiff of some musky cologne, warm and appealing, and I wondered if that was his salesman enchantment, or just him. He worked his hands under Starlight's knees and shoulders, then lifted her, the movement awkward and setting him wobbling as he tried to get to his feet. Howard raised himself on his hindquarters to watch, and I grabbed Alaric's waist to steady him. He adjusted his stance, then nodded at me. "She's not too heavy. Let's go."

I released him but kept one hand on his back as we headed for the path, still lulled by that warm scent and the simple relief of having *help*. Plus I wanted to be handy in case he slipped. It was a safety thing. He wasn't built like a gym-goer.

It soon became clear I was right to be worried. Starlight might not have been heavy, but whatever else Alaric was, he wasn't a vampire. Theodore didn't seem to have any problem carting damsels casually about the place, but by the time we reached the road in front of the library, Alaric had had to stop twice to adjust his grip, and I pointed him to a bench that sat in the shade of a skeletal tree.

"Put her down," I said, shivering in my jumper. "We need transport."

He staggered to the bench obediently, setting Starlight down with a sigh. "Okay, so I am a bit decrepit."

Howard leaped up onto Starlight's chest, trying to scratch her mask off with his paws.

"Steady on, little one," Alaric said, and tried tugging the mask himself. It didn't move, and he frowned, then muttered something under his breath and made a couple of passes over the mask with one hand.

"*Hey*," I snapped. "What're you doing?"

"Trying to get it off," he said, giving me a confused look. "What else would I be doing?"

"More of whatever got it stuck in the first place."

He shook his head. "My masks don't get *stuck*. This is why I wanted to talk to you. Something's wrong."

"You've had plenty of chances to talk to me."

"With people around," he pointed out. "That'd be terribly bad for business."

I scowled at him, crossing my arms over my chest, and he shrugged out of his coat, holding it out to me. "No," I said.

He sighed, took my coat from around Starlight, handed it to me, and wrapped her in his instead. He tapped her mask. "I don't understand what's wrong."

He sounded honestly bewildered, and I hesitated, then said, "It's the same with the other two witches. The masks won't come off."

"This has *never* happened, Morgan. They must've been tampered with." His face was drawn in serious lines, but I could still see the chafed skin on Finn's wrist as he pulled his sleeve down.

"Let's just get her to the shop," I said aloud. "I know someone with a car." I hurried for the library door as Ruiner jumped up next to Howard. They could keep an eye on Alaric.

But the library was locked, and no amount of knocking roused anyone. Evidently Ben hadn't returned from Bewitching Brews. The only person likely to be in the town hall was Isabella, and that wouldn't have helped even if she hadn't been convinced she was a cat. Ghosts didn't have much need of cars. So I needed to find Ben, or go back to the market and try to get a lift from someone, or maybe Starlight's bike would be at the shop, since she rode in almost every day. But all of that was going to take time, and it meant leaving Alaric with Starlight for a lot longer, which didn't seem like a great idea, even with Ruiner and Howard to keep watch.

It didn't look like I had much choice, though, so I turned to head back to the bench, and as I did so, the cart of second-hand books caught my eye. They lived outside the door during library opening hours, inviting people to pay at the desk, and were usually rolled back into shelter at night. Ben had evidently left in too much of a rush to bother putting them away. I shook the cart with one hand experimentally. It wasn't a *terrible* idea.

"THIS IS A TERRIBLE IDEA," Alaric said, staring from Starlight to the cart. "If I can just get her in a fireman's carry…"

"And drop her head-first on the road when we're halfway there? No, this'll work."

He made a doubtful noise but picked Starlight up and lowered her carefully onto the top of the cart, pausing in an awkward, bent position with her bum just touching the surface. "This thing's too short. Her legs and her head are going to be off the ends."

"I know. Put her down like she's sitting."

"What?" He sounded irritable, the smooth salesman veneer fading. "She *can't* sit up."

"*Like* she's sitting, I said."

He mumbled something under his breath that I doubted was complimentary, then lifted Starlight up again. "You owe me a salve for my back."

"I'm still not convinced it's not your masks doing this." We scowled at each other, then Ruiner growled, pulling us both back to the job at hand. I adjusted the cart so it was in the right position. "Put her down."

Alaric lowered Starlight obediently, and I adjusted her position so her knees were at the edge of the cart, her lower legs dangling comfortably off as if she'd just perched herself on it for a rest. Then I went back to where Alaric was crouched in what did, admittedly, look like a pretty uncomfortable position for his spine. I slid one of my arms around Starlight's back to give her body something to flop against and gripped the side of the cart with my other hand.

"You do the same," I said to him, and he adjusted his stance, our arms crossing over each other behind Starlight and our heads close enough to touch. I met his dark eyes, which were crinkling in the corners with barely restrained laughter. They were warm and distinctly un-sales-y, and my stomach did a not-unpleasant swoop that I didn't think I could blame on any enchantments.

"Morgan," he said, his voice low, and he was using that warming smile again.

"Yes?" I managed, my own voice far too squeaky.

"She's going to slip off."

"What?" I forced myself to look away from him and at Starlight instead, who was easing slowly away from us. "Oh, *bollocks*." I let go of the cart and grabbed her waist instead, pushing her back into place. "Okay, you keep her upright and I'll stop her sliding. Let's go."

We stumbled away, almost losing Starlight entirely as we bumped off the kerb into the road ("should've done that first," Alaric observed, but *he* hadn't thought of it either), then veered wildly from one side to the other as we trundled towards town. Luckily we didn't have far to go, and Hollowbeck's traffic was both sparse and used to the myriad hazards posed by kids on bikes, rambling livestock, and fleeing would-be familiars. The cart had developed an alarming squeak in at least one wheel by the time we made it to the Cosy Cauldron, where we had another scuffle as Alaric tried to pick Starlight up without her flopping onto the road. The shop door was locked, the sign turned to closed, so I led the way around the back and found the spare key under the flowerpot to let us in.

"High security," Alaric puffed, jouncing Starlight as he adjusted his grip.

"Witchy alarms," I said, going for a mystic wave. He didn't laugh, so maybe he believed me. I'd hide the key somewhere else later, anyway. Starlight and I were the only ones who used it, and she definitely didn't need it right now. That thought brought a bubble of grief to my chest, taking me by surprise and squeezing my breath out, and I couldn't manage to find words as I waved Alaric to the sofa. He deposited Starlight gently on the cushions, straightening up with a groan as Howard leaped up next to her. I turned away, my vision blurring. "Cheers for the help," I said to the kitchen.

He didn't answer, and I heard him fussing around on the sofa. What was he *doing?* I risked a glance back, seeing him tucking a throw over Starlight, and touching her cheeks, frowning slightly. "She's cold," he said.

I looked at the kitchen ceiling. "Yeah, lying in frozen flowerbeds will do that to you."

Another silence, then he said, "Morgan?"

He was right behind me, and I lurched away, smacking my hip painfully into the big table, which didn't so much as shudder. I kicked it, which likely wasn't the wisest move, but at least I had boots on so it only hurt a bit rather than a lot. "*Stop doing that!*" I shouted at him, and Howard, who was perched on Starlight's chest once more, hissed and lashed out at Ruiner, sending him scooting backwards along the cushions with an answering snarl. I looked at them both rather than at Alaric, everything indistinct and too far away.

"Sorry," he said quietly, not moving towards me. "Are you okay?"

"Great, just great. Theodore and Isabella are useless, witches are dropping like flies, Starlight just about froze to death, and I'm town witch and meant to know how to fix this. I'm *fantastic*." I took a deep breath. That had been a little more information than I intended to give to the possible enemy. I would've been a *terrible* spy. I bit back a giggle.

Alaric lifted his hands and dropped them, as if wanting to reach out to me but not daring. "You're not on your own," he said after a moment. "I want to get to the bottom of this, too. This is my business at stake."

I looked at the ceiling. "You said something's wrong with the masks. How?"

"I wish I knew. But they seem to be *exaggerated*, if that makes sense. The effects are more intense than usual. And now this." He nodded at Starlight.

"And nothing's changed?" I asked him. "You didn't use a new charm or something?"

He shook his head. "Everything's the same. The masks are acquired from around the world, and we caretake them until they find their wearer. It's less charms and more an introduction service."

Great. A dating service for masks. I pinched the bridge of my nose. "We? You and Finn?"

"Yes. He's been my apprentice for many years. I trust him implicitly."

"How many years?" I asked, and a flicker of something

crossed Alaric's face, too quick for me to be sure what it was.

"Enough that he is as well-versed in the masks as I am. This can't be an accident. And I would greatly appreciate you coming to the stall to take a look at things. Maybe you can see something I cannot."

And maybe he could *trap* me, like Finn. "You used to work with Norma," I said.

He inclined his head, his tone dry. "Norma demanded a certain payment from anyone in her territory. Call it a tax."

"Must be nice not having to worry about that."

He smiled faintly. "I won't say it's not a relief. One never knew what she'd ask for."

There had definitely been a deal. I was suddenly very aware we were alone in the shop except for three unconscious witches. I rubbed a hand over my face, unable to think of what to ask next. That charmed smile of his wasn't to be trusted, and I had to be careful. He couldn't know Finn had offered to help me.

"Is there anything I can do here, Morgan?" Alaric asked.

I had no answer, and if he used that soft tone on me one more time, I might actually cry, looking at Starlight unmoving on the sofa. Turning into a snotty, red-eyed mess wasn't going to help anything, including my sense of dignity.

"I'll let you know if I come up with anything," I said, walking around him to get to the door. "Thanks again for the help."

He didn't move for a moment, and a worm of fright jumped into my chest as I wondered what I'd do if he didn't leave, then he nodded and followed me, pausing on the threshold.

"I really am here to help, Morgan," he said, and touched my cheek with one hand, his fingertips barely grazing my skin but leaving lines of heat like scorch marks behind. "You know where I am if you need me." Then he headed off into the last of the afternoon light, adjusting the collar of his coat against the cold, and I pulled the door shut, slumping against it and closing my eyes. They felt swollen, and as hot as the trail of his touch, but in an entirely different way.

I STAYED AT THE DOOR, the wood smooth and cool against my cheek and my legs feeling like they were barely keeping me upright, until Ruiner said, "You broken, Morgs?" His tone was light, but when I looked at him, he was sitting on the back of the sofa with his ears up and his tail flicking, ignoring Howard tracking its tip with his teeth bared.

"A little," I said. "How'm I going to fix this? I need help."

He didn't answer straight away, just looked around the room with those bright blue eyes, his ears twitching gently. Finally he said, "Do you, though?"

"Well, yes. Three comatose witches, and no idea what from? I can't reverse it. I can't even figure out how it happened, other than it's got to do with the masks."

"Just like you couldn't figure out who killed Norma, or how to get me out of the carnival, or how to stop a bloody undead army?"

My eyes were hot again. I didn't need my *brother* being encouraging at me. I'd start thinking he'd fallen prey to the masks as well. "I had help for all of those," I said aloud. "And the only help I've got here is the sodding mask that seems to be like a witchy power-up."

"And which you *cannot* put on, because we have exhibits A, B, and C in the house already."

"And which I cannot put on," I agreed. "Unless you've suddenly decided to come clean about all your magical knowledge?"

He sighed. "I've done that already. I am not witchy, Morgan, as much as it'd come in handy. I'm not even human-y anymore. I am of no use whatsoever here."

"You found Starlight."

"Howard found *me*."

We both looked at him, and he bared his teeth at us. I sighed. "Which leaves Grace."

He bared his teeth. "You can't trust her."

"She's been nothing but helpful. And she hasn't worn the masks."

"Exactly. You don't think it's weird that she just *happens* not to believe in masks? And is being so super bloody helpful, getting her paws on your grimoire and being all sweet at Jackie?"

"She's been telling me not to wear my mask," I protested, but without a lot of heat. It wasn't like I hadn't been thinking the same thing.

"Being helpful seems to be working for her, doesn't it?"

We looked at each other for a moment, then I shrugged. "Well, we're screwed, then." I pushed off the door and went to crouch next to Starlight, pressing the back of my hands to her cheeks. She was still cold, but not excessively so, and I adjusted the blanket over her, then went to put the kettle on. Norma had some hot water bottles in the linen cupboard, and this looked like the best possible use for them.

And it was something I could do, at least. Unlike all the other things that felt entirely beyond me right then.

17. Pagan nonsense

FIFTEEN MINUTES LATER, I HAD STARLIGHT COCOONED with a couple more blankets and the hot water bottle, and I'd filled two more and taken them upstairs to tuck in with the women in the spare room. The bees were still bumbling around Mella, and I had to move the blankets gingerly to get the hot water bottle in next to her. I wished I knew how the insects had got in. I supposed it didn't matter, since they didn't seem to be interested in anything except staying close to their witch, and I wouldn't have wanted them to freeze outside, but Starlight's comment about the bees not being happy without her wasn't far from my mind. I didn't fancy the village's bees going on a rampage, so I said to them, "I'll figure this out."

They just buzzed sleepily at me, and I went downstairs, frowning around the kitchen. "I thought Grace would've left a note," I said to Ruiner.

"You're lucky she left the shop," he said. I blinked at him, then turned on my heel and hurried down the hall, grabbing the stool from behind the counter and swinging it into place below the exposed beam with its little gap.

Which ... didn't it look a little bigger? Like someone had been pulling at the edges? I looked at the floor, but it was clean-swept. I hadn't done that.

"Jackie?" I called, but no little head reared itself. "*Jackie!*"

I scrambled onto the stool, wobbling dangerously in my rush, and tried to peer into the space between the ceiling and the floor, but it was impossible to see anything. I jumped back down and dug around under the counter until I found the torch we kept handy for Hollowbeck's somewhat regular power cuts, then ran back to the stool, ignoring Ruiner wandering through from the kitchen to watch me.

"You're kidding me," he said. "*Again?* You need one of those briefcases with a handcuff on it. Or an AirTag, at least."

"Shut up," I said, almost falling off the stool. The torch lit the space up better, but I couldn't see in, so I scrabbled my phone out of my pocket, shoving it into the gap and clicking off a series of photos. I scrolled through them without moving from the stool. Nothing. There was *nothing*. I looked at Ruiner. "It's gone."

"AirTag," he said again. "I'm serious."

I couldn't say he was wrong, but I was about to ask what help he thought it was at this point when there was a scraping from above. We both looked up, and there was another scrape, the sound of something heavy being pushed across the old plaster, and dust drifted down over us. More scraping, moving towards the gap, and I said, "Jackie?" again.

There was no immediate answer, just that laboured, persistent movement, until finally the corner of the grimoire appeared at the edge of the gap.

"Oh, Jackie," I said. "You are the *best* of rats."

A squeak answered me as I took the book down, touching it with trembling fingers, then lifted Jackie down as well, stroking her head. She had cobwebs in her whiskers and her little heart was going fast, sides heaving after the effort of dragging the book. She leaned against me, and my chest tightened at the sight of the grey on her muzzle. She shouldn't have to do all this work. She should be having a nice little rat retirement, with heated beds and sliced apples and peanuts, or whatever rats preferred as treats.

"Do you like peanuts?" I asked her, and she looked at me quizzically.

I still had a missing and potentially treacherous Grace and no help, but at least I had the book and Jackie. It felt like something. And it was enough to get me moving again. If I could deal with near-retirement office workers still putting their liquid lunches in as expenses, I could deal with this.

I CHECKED on the women again, making sure they were all warm and wondering if Grace had called the GP. There was definitely no IV in evidence, but maybe she'd gone to get him and that was where she was? Yet another downside to the lack of mobile phone coverage in Hollowbeck. I'd be able to just message her and find out if I was anywhere else. Or call, if things got desperate.

Then again, I wasn't sure I wanted to. The shop had been locked up, and my keys were gone from the table where I'd left them, and that maybe, possibly slightly larger gap in the ceiling worried me. Had she been trying to reach the grimoire? At least Jackie, for all she seemed perfectly happy with Grace using the book earlier, hadn't thrown me over entirely. It was thin encouragement, but exactly what I needed as I headed out into the night, locking the back door and pocketing the spare key. The grimoire was back in its bag on my hip. I wasn't letting it out of my sight again. Maybe taking it out into an uneasy town was a bad idea, but so was abandoning it in the walls of the shop.

"What's the plan?" Ruiner asked as I headed around the shop.

"I'm not sure it's as well-developed as a plan," I admitted. "But I want to talk to Miss Edna. She and the Upstanding Ladies are the only ones other than Grace not using masks, and I want to know why, and how she made Theodore listen to her."

"And what about Bloodsucking Bobby himself? Are you just leaving him in James' pantry?"

"We can't do that," I said, looking up the fading sky. Afternoon sun still lay in luminous shafts along the street, but it wasn't going to hang around for long. "Without his mask, he should be okay, though."

Ruiner made a grumbling little noise at the back of his throat that seemed to indicate a certain scepticism, and I couldn't blame him for that. I wasn't at all sure Theodore would be fine, either. I didn't know how long since he'd eaten, or how much energy healing up might've taken him, or what lingering hold the mask might have. We could be letting our familiar, calm sergeant out, or some sort of ravening monster. I picked up the pace.

James was eating a sandwich when we came in, his hair looking even more dishevelled than usual, and he pointed at the coffee machine, which was decorated with a sheet of paper, *out of order* scrawled on it in black pen. "No coffee," he said.

I examined him. "Out of order, or you don't want to use the beans?"

He hesitated, taking another bite of sandwich, then said a little indistinctly, "I might've thrown a spoon at Ruby when she asked for an extra shot. And told Daniel from the hardware store that hot chocolate helped male pattern baldness. Trying to get out of serving coffee seems bad for business."

I sighed. "Where's your mask?"

"Ben took it. When can I get it back?" His voice was a little plaintive, but that was good to hear. Ben must still be himself. Unless taking the mask was part of his village protector thing, but not much I could do about that if so.

"Soon as we can," I said aloud. "Where does Miss Edna live?"

He frowned. "Who?"

"Ah, the Upstanding Lady. Purple trousers today." I really did need to learn their names.

"Oh. Right. I think in one of those bungalows with the fussy flowerbeds on Whistlebeck Close. I have an idea they all live along there."

"Good." I started to turn away, then looked back at him. "I'll be back before dark. You know, for Theodore."

"Alright." He kept munching his sandwich, running his fingers disconsolately through a saucer of coffee beans, and Ruiner and I went back out into the chill afternoon.

I headed straight back to the shop and Starlight's bike, and my brother groaned as I took it from where it leaned against the wall.

"You have a car, Morgan. It even works now. Can't we use it?"

"I'm not wasting time going back to Petunia's to get it," I said, swinging a leg over the bike and pumping the brakes experimentally. Only one set worked, and I couldn't remember if it was the back or front. Front, I thought. The ones that wanted to throw you off, anyway.

"It's too cold for the bike," Ruiner complained, but he jumped into the little basket on the front anyway, which was wound about with pretty white flowers (fake, obviously, or they'd have been frozen flowers). He hissed at them, and batted one with his paw.

It *was* too cold for the bike, and even though I tucked my fingers inside my sleeves as much as I could to try and protect them, they were icy blocks of pain by the time I coasted to a stop outside one of the bungalows on Whistle-beck Close. It wasn't far from the centre of town, only five minutes on the bike, but it was far enough that my lips were numb and my nose was dripping as I examined the houses. I had no idea which one was Miss Edna's, as there were four perfectly square, red-brick bungalows crouched in a row, bedecked with net curtains at the windows and porcelain ducks on the walls, concrete gnomes and furi-ously tidy bird feeders in the gardens. Ruler-straight flowerbeds ran inside the low brick walls that enclosed the properties, and the lawns were smooth expanses of snow that dared the slightest imperfection to make its presence felt.

The bungalows glowered across the narrow street at the houses on the opposite side, which, in true Hollow-beck fashion included what appeared to be a concrete above-ground bunker with round porthole windows, a periscope, and a moat in which something that sounded very large was splashing lazily. Next to it was a building made of a conglomeration of towers, all drifting at slightly different angles, with patchy tile roofs, too many chimneys, and a garden that even in winter was over-grown and neglected. I thought I could see a bulldozer abandoned halfway between the road and the house, and wondered if that was a style choice or a neighbourhood attack gone wrong. A terracotta-hued house that should've been in the Spanish hinterlands flanked it, and next to that was a detached bungalow which was structurally no different to those of the Upstanding Ladies, but which had murals of whales diving through fractured rainbows and drifting dandelions covering every scrap of wall, and a grass-covered roof currently sporting a grazing goat. I stared at the buildings, fascinated. It was as if every possible Hollowbeck extreme had heard where the Upstanding Ladies were living and had parked themselves across the road, just for the hell of it. For all I knew, maybe they had.

Ruiner jumped from the basket to the gritted pavement, and I leaned the bike against the first bungalow's stolid, square-edged garden wall. Or, rather, I started to, because before the bike could even touch the brick, one of the big bay windows in the bungalow popped open, and from behind the net curtains a strident voice shouted, "Don't you *dare* put that *contraption* there and leave grease spots on my wall!"

I jerked the bike upright again. "Sorry! I'm looking for Miss Edna?" Only that wasn't her name, and I should've asked James what it actually was.

But maybe it *was* her name, or the unseen woman guessed who I wanted, because she snapped, "Next door. Don't mess up the pavement!" The window slammed shut again, violently enough to send the curtains billowing, and Ruiner and I looked at each other.

"Got the right place, at least," he said, and we walked to the next house. There was a lamp post over the road, so I took the bike across and leaned it there, then walked up the snow-free path to the bungalow's front door. The edge of the path had been done in a perfectly straight line, as if someone had taken a hot iron to it rather than shovelling or sweeping. It was unnerving.

I had my hand raised to knock when the door opened, and Miss Edna glowered down at me. "Yes?" she demanded. The scent of lavender drawer sachets and boiled meat drifted out to me, and I glimpsed a well-polished standing clock and a wooden side table in the hall. The carpet had a plastic runner on it, protection from her pale pink slippers.

"Hi," I said. "We haven't really met properly. I'm Morgan."

"I don't need to meet you any more than I have already."

Ouch. Okay. "Right, well, I wanted to ask you something."

"Then do it quickly. I'm letting all the heat out."

No chance of being asked in to defrost my fingers, then. Ruiner peered into the depths of the house, a low rumble starting in the back of his throat. I nudged him, and he quieted. "Why don't you wear the masks? Or come to the festival at all?"

She huffed, a great breath that heaved her considerable bosom, and looked down the street as if worried her neighbours might be watching. "It's a bunch of pagan nonsense."

I nodded, scratching my neck and making Jackie shift and burrow deeper into my scarf. "Okay. But, well, it is a magical town. Pagan is kind of baked into the brand."

"It doesn't mean civilised people have to have anything to do with it. The Upstanding Ladies boycott *all* festivals, and *we've* never been attacked by evil spirits." She paused, then amended, "Not successfully, anyway."

Now that last bit didn't surprise me. "How did you stop them? Was it like the voice thing with the masks?"

"The *voice thing*, as you call it, isn't some magic trick, Morgan."

She used my name. We were practically besties. "It worked really well on Theodore, though. How did you do that?"

She checked the street again. There was a curious growling coming from behind her, and I wondered if she had a dog. "I'm not in the habit of helping witches."

"Of course. I get that. But I want to get the town back to normal, too. Get rid of the, uh, pagan masks. Back to no one dosing the tea, and James not trying to bite anyone who orders a coffee. And get him making cake again. The shop stuff's nowhere near as good."

She dragged her gaze back to me, and I tried to read her expression. It was impossible, her lips tight and her eyebrows drawn together, but she could've been worried or angry or scared, or any of the above. Except probably the scared bit. She didn't strike me as someone who was ever scared. "Use your voice," she said.

"Use … what?"

"*Your voice*. Just like you're not doing now, turning up on my doorstep squeaking about how lost you are."

Wow. Okay, not besties after all. "So I just shout at them? And you think that'll work?"

"It does for me," she said, and started to close the door.

"Wait!"

She paused, examining me with her mouth tighter than ever. She was going to get a cramp if she kept that up.

"There's no trick to it? You just tell people to do something, and they do it?"

"You haven't read the book I gave you, have you?"

"It … it got a little singed during a small altercation with a necromancer and bunch of zombies," I admitted, and she shook her head, looking at the ceiling.

"Young folk these days." She started to close the door again, but before she could, a bundle of long ginger fur came barrelling out, claws scrabbling on the plastic runner as it gave voice to a furious yowl. Ruiner rose on his hind legs to meet the charging cat, snarling, and Miss Edna bellowed, "*Stop that right now!*"

The cats — or the cat and my brother — ignored her entirely, tumbling down the path in a flurry of grey and ginger fur.

"*Well?*" Miss Edna demanded, glaring at me. "Stop them! Mr Fontainebleau's going to get snow in his fur!"

"Right." I ran after the brawling cats, who were off the path and crashing through the snow, still entangled, leaving tufts of fur behind them. "*Ruiner!* Get your fluffy bum out of it!"

Ruiner said something unrepeatable that might've been aimed at me or at Mr Fontainebleau, then exploded out of the scrap, the ginger cat right on his tail. My brother bounced off my outstretched arms and landed on my shoulder, then launched himself down my back and onto the lawn again. As the other cat tried to take the same route, I seized him around the middle, holding him out in front of me. He thrashed in my hands, setting me swearing as I tried to keep hold of him, and just as I thought I was going to have to drop him if I wanted to avoid stitches, Jackie popped her head out of my hood, hissing. Mr Fontainebleau froze, his teeth and claws still bared but his eyes on Jackie. I turned back to Miss Edna, the ginger cat held out in front of me, and carted him to the door.

"Here," I said, and she took him from me, clicking her tongue.

"Don't bleed on my path," she said and shut the door. I looked from it to my lacerated hands, then turned around and headed back to the bike, flicking as much blood off of my fingers and onto the snow as I could manage, Ruiner chuckling his little cat laugh behind me.

It made me feel better, but it hadn't got us very far forward.

I HAD one more option to find help. Maybe I wouldn't even *need* the help, and Theodore would be just fine when he woke up, and he could go straight to the market and demand Alaric recall all the masks. Get them off *everyone*, and then we just had to worry about waking up our three sleeping beauties. It sounded possible, but not only did I not trust Alaric to actually help, I could still feel the tender skin on my throat from that morning. I didn't want to face that without a little more backup, so I looped around the centre of Hollowbeck, taking the shortest route to Petunia's. I dumped Starlight's bike at the gate and ran up the path, dusk already rising under the trees. I banged through the front door, not worrying about any other guests, and yelled, *"Petunia!* Where are you? Petunia!"

Ruiner ran upstairs, vanishing into the unlit curves of the staircase, and I hurried through the downstairs. It was as empty as it had been when I'd left the day before — had it only been the day before? It felt like *forever.* There was no one in any of the rooms, the fire out in both the living room and the lounge I'd taken to calling the frog room. That was living up to its name, anyway, the frogs diving into a slightly deflated paddling pool and goggling at me from just beneath the surface.

"Petunia?" I asked them, but they were as communicative as ever. I headed for the kitchen, discovering a plate on the table holding a half-eaten sandwich and a half-full mug of tea next to it. I frowned and touched the mug. It was still warm.

Ruiner appeared in the doorway. "No Petunia upstairs that I can see. The whole place feels empty."

"It's like the bloody Marie Celeste," I said, nodding at the table, and he put his paws up on one of the chairs so he could see better.

"That's probably just Gareth," he said.

"*Who?*"

"He doesn't like people. He'll be in the cleaning cupboard, waiting till we leave."

I stared at the tall cupboard in the corner of the kitchen. The door snicked shut with a click of alarm. "Gareth?" I called, but there was no reply. I started across the kitchen, and Ruiner hooked my jeans with his claws.

"What part of *doesn't like people* are you not getting?"

"We need to find Petunia."

"Well, sod off outside and I'll ask him."

I scowled. "You're people."

"I'm a cat. It doesn't count."

"*Fine.*" I stomped out of the kitchen and into the hall, then stopped. I really wanted to know what the mysterious Gareth looked like. What he *was*, even, because there wasn't exactly a lot of space in the cleaning cupboard. I didn't think even I could fit in it, between the mops and buckets and hoover and hanging baskets of pegs and ancient bags.

"*Out!*" Ruiner yowled. "As in properly out!"

"*Okay!*" I yelled back and retreated out the front door, leaving it ajar. Jackie snuffled my ear. "I know," I told her. "But it makes sense, I suppose. I'm not sure my brother was ever people, even before he was a cat."

It didn't take long for Ruiner to join us, slipping around the front door. "He doesn't know," he said. "No fresh bread or anything this morning either, and the frogs are restless, apparently. He did say he saw someone skinny-dipping in the town pond last night, but he's not sure it was her. There's a few people hanging about thinking they're sirens, and he didn't want to get close enough to figure out who it was."

The idea of anyone skinny-dipping — or swimming in any degree of dressed or undressed in this weather, to be honest — made me pull my scarf up over my nose. "Fine," I said and checked the sky. "We're just going to have to deal with Theodore ourselves. I doubt he'll eat us."

"He definitely won't eat me," Ruiner said. "The fur'll get in his teeth."

"Reassuring." I returned to the bike with him trailing after me, and a moment later we were heading back into town, the chill locking down as the last of the sun vanished, lights blooming brighter and brighter in gardens and windows, and the streets dotted with people heading in the direction of the market. There was no wind, and I fancied I could hear music winding its way through the streets, tempting the revellers out, pulling them into its grip.

Not that the market itself was the problem. But I didn't see anyone without a mask, and by the time I leaned the bike against the wall of Bewitching Brews, the anxiety was a tight, ugly knot in my belly. I pushed through the door into an empty shop and stopped in the middle of the floor.

"James?" I called.

He didn't reply, and I walked hesitantly around the counter, placing my fingertips on the door to the kitchen while I tried to hear any movement beyond. Nothing. I looked at Ruiner, and he twitched his ears, his pupils wide in the low light of the shop. I took a deep breath and eased the door open, just a tiny crack at first, then when all I could see was a sliver of floor and cabinets I kept going, ready to jump back at any moment. But no one wrenched the door out of my hands and hauled me through, or tackled me to the floor. I simply opened it onto a kitchen that was as empty as the shop, with the exception of the toppled chair and sacks of coffee beans strewn across the floor.

"Oh," I said, and edged over to the pantry door. It was open a sliver, and I carefully pulled it wide, still poised to run. But it was empty, and I turned slowly on my heel, taking in the silence. "*Oh.*"

"On the upside," my brother said, "no exsanguinated baristas."

There was that.

18. Unacceptable in modern policing

WE DIDN'T HAVE AN EXSANGUINATED BARISTA, IT WAS TRUE, but we did have a missing one, as well as a missing vampire police officer who might or might not be in biting mode. I didn't like the combo, and I wasn't entirely sure what to do, so I did the only thing I could think of. I went back into the shop and made a cup of coffee. If nothing else, that'd flush James out.

It didn't, and my barista skills weren't up to his, but it was hot, caffeinated, and drinkable, so I stood at the counter doing just that while Ruiner gobbled down some of the cat biscuits James kept in a jar behind the counter, and Jackie helped herself to some chopped fruit I found in the fridge. It looked like it was destined for a smoothie, but I'd put it on my tab.

"Now what?" Ruiner asked, licking crumbs off one paw.

I took another mouthful of coffee before I answered. "The market."

His ears went back. "Is that a good idea?"

"Probably not. But we have three unconscious witches, Alaric claiming someone's sabotaging the masks, Finn hinting Alaric's the one doing it, and *everyone* wearing the damn things. We have to fix this, or half the town'll be down by the solstice."

"So, you're just going to march in there and use your outdoor voice?"

"No, I'm going to ask Alaric nicely to recall them, and if that doesn't work, I'll find our vampire copper and hope he's still in sensible Theodore mode."

"What about all the stuff Finn said? Do you believe him? Because you probably shouldn't be messing with Alaric if you think there's any truth in it."

I hesitated. I'd told Ruiner about Finn referring to being trapped, and my suspicions that Alaric might have designs on the grimoire. "I know, but something doesn't add up. Why wreck his own business?"

"Because the grimoire would let him run a whole new and entirely more profitable business?"

"Maybe. But he'd have to get Jackie to agree." We both looked at Jackie, who peered back at us over a piece of melon clutched in her front paws.

"There's ways around that," Ruiner said. "I still think you need to be careful of him."

"I'm going to be. But he did seem really worried about the masks, so … I don't know. Maybe Finn meant trapped in a monetary sense or something? Anyway, it's not like I'm going to let Alaric drag me into the tent and steal the book away."

Ruiner made a doubtful noise. "So it's nothing to do with you going all giggly whenever the dashing mask-salesman rides around the corner? Like half the rest of the town?"

"*No.*" I gulped the last of my coffee and made a face. I'd somehow got about half the grounds in the cup instead of the machine, but it'd give me a kick anyway. "Come on."

I left Bewitching Brews unlocked behind us, because I had no idea where the keys were, or if James might come back at some point and find himself having to break into his own shop. Besides, Hollowbeck was hardly crime central. I'd never heard of any robberies, and the only reason we locked the Cosy Cauldron was to stop people wandering in and leaving courgettes as payment. We'd tried out an honesty box once, which had made sense, given the way Hollowbeck's population lived on all sorts of internal time zones. We'd just left everyone's tinctures and tonics in bags with their names on them and trusted them to leave a reasonably proportional payment.

But the tricky part of working with a barter system is that payment varies depending on what people have to hand, and at that time of year what *everyone* had to hand was courgettes. We'd only made that mistake once, and I had no intentions of ever eating another one of the bloody vegetables. There'd been so many cluttering up the shop, we'd had to climb over them to get to the counter, and Starlight had been frantically searching every potion book in the place for things to do with them. It turns out courgettes have zero magical properties, and now we were more specific about what payments we accepted. You can only eat so much courgette soup, courgette curry, courgette noodles, and courgette cake, after all.

We joined the procession of people headed for the market. The town was empty, Mystic Munchies and The Witching Hour shuttered and dark, the shops closed and large signs in the windows reading, *At the market!* No one was fussing around looking to be allowed in, so I supposed it was just accepted. Life in Hollowbeck stopped when the festival started, and once we'd all escaped the evil spirits, it'd start up again. Hopefully.

I detoured to the library to try banging on the door again, but there was still no answer, so I could add Ben to my list of missing people. Ruiner stayed close to my legs as I headed on towards the market, and Jackie burrowed deep into my scarf, supported by my hood. I could barely feel her there, except when she shifted around a little. The bag was heavy against my hip, the grimoire a reassuring if slightly uncomfortable presence. Not that I knew what to do with it. The only times I'd been able to use it for anything had been in dire circumstances that I had no desire to repeat, and the last time, I'd almost razed a town to the ground because a guy was being a bit of a numpty. Well, a colossal, murderous numpty, and there had been a lot of stress leading up to that moment, as well as an army of the undead, and my useless ex-husband (also a numpty, but not a murderous one) had been involved, but still. I was at least as scared of using the grimoire as I was of someone else getting their hands on it.

But there was no reason I'd have to use it. I wound my way through the masked crowds, people clutching bottles of craft beer and tumblers of wine, kebabs and ice cream tubs and cardboard boxes of fish'n'chips. Kids ran through the tangle of adults, trailing shouts and wings and tails, and I caught a glimpse of the snow-monster battles back in full swing. A tight knot of people huddled together in one corner of the battleground, all waving their money at a woman in a frock coat and a top hat, who was tucking it into her pocket and handing out tickets, so evidently there was more riding on the monsters than just kudos.

In the dark, the market was truly alive, the lights glowing warm and inviting, the scents of mulled wine and hot chocolate and spiced oranges wafting from tents and stalls. Despite the masks — or maybe because of them — the whole place had the fizzing excitement of the start of summer holidays, full of the potential for delight, and I wondered briefly if I was overreacting. But the simple lack of anyone around me, no Starlight, no Ben, no Theodore or Isabella or James, was enough to remind me that nothing was right. Everyone might be having fun now, but any one of them could be the next person laid up in my shop.

I didn't walk straight up to *Unmasked* but lingered in the cover of a stall selling knitted blankets, petting one absently while watching the open front of the mask tent. Finn was outside, holding a mirror for a slim woman in an expensive-looking coat as she tried to decide between two wooden masks. His smile looked strained and tired.

"Oh, I just don't know," she said to him. "It's for my foyer. Which one would you choose?"

"You could take both," he said without a lot of enthusiasm. "Frame a doorway, or pick a third and make a real feature out of it."

"I do like that idea," she said, looking at the masks pensively.

"And here is the ideal third," Alaric said, emerging from the depths of the stall with his hair gleaming and his smile wide, holding out another wooden mask. I blinked at it — for a moment, it had seemed to twist in his hands, but then it was just smooth, simple wood again. "Although, you might prefer to wear this one. I think it's for you. You weren't here on the cocktail night?"

"No, I had to be out of town," she said, shoving the

other masks at Finn and reaching for the one Alaric was holding. "Oh, it's *perfect!*"

"Indeed," he said, placing a hand on her shoulder. "Let me show you in a mirror."

Finn's shoulders slumped as he watched Alaric guide the woman away, then he looked at the masks in his hands and turned to take them back into the tent. I didn't move, a slow anger in the pit of my belly. Alaric was still handing masks out, just as if he hadn't been talking about the possibility of them being tampered with. Just as if he had no concerns whatsoever other than getting the whole town wearing the damn things.

"Told you," Ruiner murmured. "Humans just can't see past all that greasy charm."

"Try to remember you're human too," I whispered back.

"Sure, but I'm not that silly," he said, then followed me as I slipped across the frozen grass and into the tent while Alaric was out of sight. Finn was hanging the masks back on the wall, squeezing them into a crowded row.

"Hello, welcome to *Unmasked,*" he said, not looking around but evidently hearing me walk in. "What takes your fancy today?"

"Stopping these masks getting sold," I said, keeping my voice low, and he spun around, almost knocking a Venetian masquerade mask flying. He grabbed it, fixing it back in place, then caught my hand, pulling me further into the tent. He didn't stop until we were deep in the winding walls, watched by the empty eyes of the masks.

"What're you doing here?" he whispered, looking past me, back towards the entrance.

"I was going to talk to Alaric," I said, matching my voice to his. "Ask him to recall the masks. But he's still selling them, isn't he?"

Finn nodded, rusty blond hair tumbling softly into his face. He pushed it back with his free hand. "He won't stop. And you can't ask him to. He can't know you suspect him."

"I have to do *something*. Starlight's down."

"Your friend? The one with the fairy mask?"

"That's her. I found her in the hall garden."

His hand tightened on mine. "I'm *so* sorry, Morgan. But you mustn't confront Alaric."

"I thought maybe it wasn't him," I admitted. "He really seemed worried about the masks."

"That's because he knows you're suspicious. He wants you to think he's on your side." He hesitated, then added, "He uses charms, you know. To get people to trust him."

"I wondered."

"He's *dangerous*. I told you." He let me go to scratch his arm anxiously, above the bracelet. The chafe marks seemed worse, and I touched his hand gently, stilling him.

"Did he put that on you? Is this what you meant about being trapped?"

He glanced at the bracelet, then caught my hand in his again, his fingers warm and smooth. "That's my problem. You need to protect yourself. And watch out for the other one. The witch who won't wear a mask."

"*Grace?*"

"I don't know. She was at the cocktail party."

And at the ice palace, and the last one to see Starlight. She was also conspicuously absent when Norma had been in town, but had returned as soon as she was gone. I looked at Ruiner, who stared back at me, his blue eyes wide and his tail twitching. His gaze gave away nothing, but I knew his feelings on Grace anyway. "You think they're working together?" I asked Finn.

He shrugged, his face twisted with uncertainty. "I don't know. But she's been around, talking to Alaric."

"Alright," I said. "I'm going to sort this out. And I'm going to get you out, too."

"You've got a plan? What is it? Maybe I can help."

"Um … it's more a concept at the moment, but I'll let you know. You could keep an eye on Alaric, though. And help me get out without him seeing me?"

"Sure." He laced his fingers through mine with an easy intimacy that seemed at odds with his nerves, then pulled me after him, leading me through a tangle of masks and tapestries, popping from one aisle to another, pausing at corners and turning around on himself, until I had no idea where we'd come in or where we were going. But finally he stopped at a wall which seemed identical to any others and squeezed my hand one more time before releasing me. "Be careful," he said, raising a hand as if to touch my face, then letting it drop. "And … I don't know, get a message to me. Send your familiar or something if you need me. I'll come straight away."

He didn't wait for me to answer, just lifted some unseen corner of the canvas and ushered me through it. I emerged into heavy dusk, the blank back of the tent behind me and the featureless panels of the side of a white van in front of me, with barely enough room for me to wriggle along it to open space.

"That was helpful," Ruiner said as we picked our way around the van. "What's this concept, then?"

"Find Theodore. There's no point talking to Alaric."

"Simple, anyway."

"All the best plans are." We emerged into the crowded lanes of the market, and I added, "Where would a vampire be hanging out, then?"

"If he's hungry, hopefully someone's doing a Tanya special."

I made a face. At The Witching Hour, Tanya created

bespoke cocktails for everyone who came through the door. You never ordered anything, you just got what she felt was the best match for your mood or your scent or whatever werewolf mixologist sense she had going on. For most people it was different all the time, but not for Theodore. Or not visually different, anyway. It was always thick, red, and warm, but maybe it *was* always different. Maybe some were B+ and others were O-, or some were vegans and others were pescatarians. I didn't really want to know the details.

But Ruiner was right. It was a good place to start, so I headed for the foodie part of the market, keeping a wary eye out for Grace or Alaric. Not that the masks made it easy to tell who anyone was.

THE CENTRE of the market was even more packed than the previous night, the ice bar already full despite the relatively early hour and people overflowing to the tables outside, clutching beers and mulled wine. The rest of the food and drink stalls were no less busy, the pop of champagne corks ringing regularly from the oyster bar, bottles clattering and ringing at the craft beer stalls, a steady stream of waffles and crêpes and venison sausages washing past us. People jostled for room at the tables, and shared chairs and stools, and the band were playing with frantic energy, half a dozen dancers already throwing themselves into the music. It was a sea of faces, and every single one of them was masked. My own bare face felt exposed and raw, and I crouched down next to Ruiner, pulling my hood up.

"I'm never going to find anyone in here," I whispered to him. "See if you can find Theodore for me. Or Ben. Anyone, really."

To my surprise, he didn't argue. He just said, "Keep your head down," and slipped away into the crowd, a sleek grey shadow. I kept to the edges, working my way slowly around the circle and trying to keep my face hidden. A few people threw curious glances my way, but everyone seemed more interested in their food and drinks. I spotted the elegant woman Alaric had sold the wooden mask to bounding over a table like a gymnast, whooping as she went, and had a stab of anger that he'd lied to me so easily, invited my trust with his warm scent and charming words. Not just invited it, *won* it. I had to fix this. But what did I do?

I was still wondering that when I saw Grace. I almost didn't recognise her, a small white mask with pink detailing held up to her face, but something about her posture and the tumble of enviable hair caught my eye. She turned, a champagne glass in one hand, and there was no mistaking the curve of her smile as she scanned the crowd. I ducked behind a large man in a onesie and a tiger mask, who purred and tried to rub his head on me.

"*Gah.* Good cat," I said, petting his bald head gingerly. Apparently it was the right thing to do, as he purred again and prowled on, and I stole another peek at Grace. She was looking straight at me, and I cursed, ducking behind a table. A pair of women with leaves tangled in their hair and masks of lichen and moss looked at me with interest, wriggling long fingers in my general direction in an unnec-essarily creepy manner, but they didn't say anything. I started to duckwalk through the crowd, heading for the tents, still with my head down, but I'd only gone a few metres when Ruiner reappeared, staring at me.

"What're you doing?"

"I think Grace saw me."

"Bollocks. Well, I found Theodore."

"Where is he?"

"Batman-ing on the top of the ice palace."

"*Bollocks,*" I said, with even more feeling than my brother had. I didn't feel that was going to be an improvement on him being some sort of ultimate bobby. "Does he look like he's eaten?"

"I'm going to say no," Ruiner said, then someone screamed. I shot upright, turning towards the sound, and saw Theodore drop from the roof onto the middle of a picnic table, landing lightly. The people crowded onto its benches threw themselves backwards, scrambling to get away, and more screams went up as he turned on the spot, his grin a toothy, ravenous caricature of his normal charming smile.

"Einey, teeny, money, mo," he said, his voice low and carrying in a sudden silence, the music stilled and everyone frozen in fright. "Someone's going to lose their soul."

There was a long, shocked silence, then he started laughing, a terrible, hungry sound, and the market exploded into panicked movement. People fled in every direction, pushing and shoving, dragging kids and familiars and fighting to get out. I was almost knocked over by the first wave, and I grabbed Ruiner, dumping him on my shoulder as I fought against the wash of the revellers.

"We're going the wrong way!" he yowled at me.

"We can't let him eat anyone!" I shouted back, as Theodore leaped off the table and into the crowd. I lost sight of him for a moment, but I just followed the loudest of the screams, and as the circle drained of people, I found myself quite abruptly in the centre of an empty space, populated by dropped plates and glasses, abandoned hats and scarves and half-eaten ice creams. Theodore was loping lazily after the fleeing market-goers, running up to one and plucking the back of their jacket, setting them screaming before darting to someone else and knocking their hat off with a casual, amused cruelty. The screams were getting more and more panicked, and the stalls were empty, everyone hiding or fled. I had no idea if anyone was selling any vampire-approved treats, but I couldn't just leave him to it. I'd been the one who locked him up and left him hungry, after all.

"Theodore!" I shouted, and his head snapped towards me. I waved weakly. "Hi?"

He was beside me so quickly I staggered, biting down on my own scream, and he leaned over me, clamping one hand down on the top of my head to hold me in place as he inhaled deeply. "Hello, Morgan," he said, his voice low and smooth. "What an *interesting* scent you have. I always wondered how you'd taste."

"*Gross,*" I said, trying to wriggle out from under his hand. "I'm going to pretend you didn't say that, or our friendship'll be ruined forever." It would be anyway if he tore my throat out, but if I treated him as normal Theodore, maybe he'd act like it.

"*Friendship,*" he mused, although it came out more like *fwenthip* with his teeth getting in the way. "No, I don't think so. Predators aren't friends with prey. That gets rather awkward, wouldn't you say?"

"But we are friends," I insisted. "We have been since I got here. We have drinks together, and … and we went to the carnival together, and…" I seemed to be drawing a blank on anything else, but it was a bit more than an acquaintanceship.

"True," he said, and shifted his grip suddenly, hooking me around the shoulders with one arm and pulling my back against the hard plane of his chest, lowering his head to sniff my neck. "But you really do smell so tasty. Maybe I'll keep you."

"What, like a pet?" I demanded, tugging at his arm. "*Stop it*, Theodore! This is just the sort of behaviour that's unacceptable in modern policing!" Probably vampirism in general was, too, but I wasn't sure on that.

"I'm not always convinced by modernity," he replied, his lips brushing my neck.

This was definitely not part of the concept *or* the plan.

19. Very pretty but very bad

He'd started it, with his *you smell tasty* and grabbing me, not to mention the fact that he wanted to *keep* me, and currently had his fangs far too close to some vital blood vessels for any level of friendship. Even so, I felt a stab of guilt as I grabbed the grimoire in one hand and the mask in the other, thinking *power up the witchiness* with a kind of giddy horror. I let my knees give out and dropped straight down into a clumsy squat, snapping my chin painfully against his forearm. It felt carved, something belonging to a hungry statue. He reacted fast, latching a hand under my jaw to pull me back up, but I'd avoided his bite, and he didn't have as good a hold of me as before. I twisted and swung the grimoire into his face as hard as I could, catching him on the chin. He swore, losing his grip and staggering back a step, and I slapped the mask to my face even as I heard Ruiner yowl my name.

The world exploded into colour, painted wild across the night. The stars left trails of luminous dust, the stalls blossomed clouds and streamers of charms and flowing magic, and the crowd that had lingered, drawn back to the edges of the makeshift square to leave us in a gladiator's area, exhaled a tangle of auras or spirit or *something*, and I would've been stuck just staring at it all in blind awe if the vampire directly in front of me wasn't taking all my attention. He was a man-shaped black hole cut out of the world, equipped with a beating silver heart and outlines in glittering tones, beautiful and terrible all at once.

I didn't have much time to admire him, though, because he struck out at me, shark-fast. I *knew* it was terribly fast and it should be impossible to react in time, but still I slapped his hand away with the grimoire almost casually.

"No," I said, my voice firm. "Stop that."

He growled, the sound echoing at the edges of my brain, setting fright into all the lizardy bits that were in control of making sure I ran rather than doing ridiculous things like face down vampires. But he didn't move towards me again, and I could feel him weighing up the risk of it, the grimoire alight in my hand. The leather curled and twisted under my fingers, flexing like an animal eager to run, feeding from the mask, perhaps, or the mask feeding into it. The sparks weren't just in my fingertips but under my skin, and I thought, with a certain detachment, that if I asked the book to give me a vampire-flattening spell, it just would. And I'd know exactly what to do with it, and would have no need of Grace or Alaric or anyone else to bloody well help me. I could just *deal* with things.

Theodore took a step back, as if aware of my thoughts.

"Stop," I said to him. "You need to sit down and get yourself together. Put those bloody teeth away." I giggled, a wave of light-headedness throwing me off. "*Bloody*."

Theodore didn't answer. He spun and sprinted away across our gladiator's ring, hurdling chairs and vaulting over tables effortlessly.

"*Theodore Ian—*" I started, the words thundering off the tents, suddenly understanding what *use your voice* meant, even if this felt rather like a stolen voice, and not mine at all. Theodore faltered, catching his foot on a barrel mid-leap, and crashed to the ground, and suddenly this was *all wrong.* I was on fire, and not in a good way. My whole body surged, power passing from the grimoire to the mask and back, and in some remote corner of my head I was aware of Jackie biting my fingers and Ruiner with his claws in my jeans, and I tried to drop the grimoire. My fingers seemed to be melded to it, though, sunk deep into the strangely organic cover, and I ripped my scarf off with my free hand, using it as a glove. I was panting, my ears ringing and the colours so bright and so intense I could barely see past them, but I grabbed the grimoire with my scarf-covered hand and wrenched it free of my other. For a moment I thought it wasn't going to come, my grip cramped into something far too close to a claw, then I tore the book away, yelping as I lost what felt like a few layers of skin.

The result was immediate, everything going down from a ten to a five in intensity, the colours still running over the tents and the crowd, but fainter and gentler, no longer an assault on the senses. The ringing had left my ears, and now I could hear Ruiner, screeching at the top of his feline lungs as Jackie scrambled for my shoulder, evidently intent on nipping some sense into me.

"And the mask! *And the sodding mask, Morgan!*"

I grabbed for it, both hating the undertow of power I could still feel washing around me, and hating that I was about to lose it. But the light-headedness hadn't gone, and I staggered, hooking my fingers under the edge of the mask. A yell caught my attention, and I spun to see Ben with his arms wide, in a crouch with the flicker of a half-seen sword in one hand. Next to him, James threw his head back and roared, translucent flame filling the night. They had Theodore cornered, the sausage van at his back, and he snarled back at them, the sound vicious and ragged.

"*Ben!*" I shouted, abandoning my efforts to dislodge the mask, and ran towards the men.

Theodore rushed forward, and Ben swung his sword, the movement oddly graceful. Theodore grabbed Ben's sword arm, pulling him forward and sending him stumbling into James, then kept running, racing toward one of the lanes of stalls. The onlookers in that area scuffled frantically to get out of the way, and I sprinted to intercept him. His path passed close enough to me that I had a least a slim chance I might catch him. Not that I knew what I'd do when I did.

"Theodore!" I yelled, trying for Upstanding Lady tones and falling woefully short even to my own ears. "Theodore, *stop!*"

He didn't falter, and I ran straight at him. He probably thought I'd stop, and if *I'd* thought about it, I probably would have, but instead I simply charged into him, doing my best impression of a rugby forward. He gave a very human yelp as I hit him, and I wrapped both arms around his waist, carrying both of us to the ground. I had a moment when I realised I was being as optimistic as a kitten tackling a Rottweiler, but even a Rottweiler can be taken by surprise, and we crashed into a clutter of abandoned folding chairs, dropped bottles and plastic cups scattering under us.

Theodore rose again with a roar, throwing me off. I rolled twice, squawking as I bounced over the litter of collapsed chairs, then fetched up against a barrel table.

"I will *devour you!*" he bellowed, his arms flung wide and

his fists clenched. "I will use your skulls as cups when I drink your fluids, and I will arrest you *all!*"

"You might want to reverse that order," Ruiner said from the top of the table above me. "Also, fluids? *Ew.*"

Theodore stared at him, his mouth still open, and Alaric reared up behind the vampire, hefting a large, fluffy white mask in both hands. Theodore must have sensed something, because he started to turn, and Alaric slammed the mask over his head. It was a full head deal, slotting into place like a helmet, and Theodore froze, his arms still outstretched like he'd been caught out in the middle of a game of Statues. Alaric put a hand on top of the mask, muttering something, and I caught a whiff of ozone.

"What're you doing?" I demanded, trying to untangle myself from the chairs. "What *is* that?"

"He's fine, he's not hurt," Alaric said hastily, taking Theodore by the shoulders and turning him to face me. "Look."

An oversized, chubby-cheeked rabbit's head looked back at me, and through my own mask I could see fluffy pastel chicks and what looked suspiciously like decorative eggs drifting over the thing's ears. Theodore reached for one, the movement placid and gentle.

"You've turned him into the *Easter bunny?*"

"*An* Easter bunny. Not—"

"Take it off!" I demanded, finally making it to my feet and kicking a chair with rather more enthusiasm than was needed. "You can't turn our police sergeant into a sodding bunny rabbit!"

"I haven't," Alaric said, his voice still calm. "I've just stopped him biting anyone, you might've noticed."

"We were doing that," Ben said, joining us. James prowled next to him, shaking his dragon head and puffing smoke.

"*You,*" I said, jabbing a finger at Ben. "You weren't meant to put the mask back on!"

"But the town needed protecting," he protested. "With Theodore unavailable in the day—"

"*He's always unavailable in the day!*" I yelled at him, and the world shifted around me, things twitching and blooming with colour.

"*Mask!*" Ruiner hissed, ignoring the fact that Alaric was right there, and staring at him with an unreadable expression.

I ignored my brother, turning back to the mask-seller. "Get that sodding bunny head off Theodore."

"You need a plan, then," Alaric said. "He's going to be very unhappy *and* very hungry."

"We shall manage that," Ben said, and James growled agreement. Apparently, any instinctive enmity had been put aside in the face of this new threat.

"There we go," I said to Alaric, although I was putting more faith in my rugby technique than I was in Tweedle-Sword and Tweedle-Puff, which might or might not have been wise. "*Take it off.*"

"If you insist." He laid a hand on the bunny's head, whispering something inaudible, and I caught that ozone whiff again, then he buried his hand in the fluff and pulled.

Theodore staggered, but the mask didn't budge.

Alaric frowned. "Oh."

"I *knew* you were behind this," I spat at him. "Reverse it right now!"

"Yes! Or I shall run you through," Ben announced, waving his mostly invisible sword.

"I'm not behind anything," Alaric said, sounding genuinely hurt. He did the touch and mutter thing again, then tried pulling it off once more. "This has never happened. I did say to you, Morgan. Someone's tampered with *everything*. This is a brand-new mask. No one's had a chance to touch it, but it seems to have the same problem as your friend's. And it's *not* my doing."

"I'm oddly unconvinced by that," I said, as he pushed down on Theodore's shoulders. The vampire sank obligingly to his knees, and Alaric grabbed the bunny's ears, pulling up hard. Theodore rose back to his feet again, uncomplaining.

"Bloody hell," Ruiner muttered. "What is this, amateur hour?"

I grabbed Theodore's shoulders, persuading him back to the ground then holding him in place. "Do it properly, or I'll let the librarian have at you."

"With pleasure," Ben said.

"I am doing it properly!" Alaric tried his incantation again and pulled hard enough on the mask that Theodore drifted upright, even with all my weight on him. "I'm sorry," he started, and Ben interrupted.

"Let me try holding him, my lady. This is not a job for—"

"Ben, if you call me a lady one more time, I'll slap that helmet off you. *Again.*" He subsided, and I looked back at Alaric. "*Fix this.*"

"*I can't.* I don't know what's happened. The masks can't just get *stuck.*" He shook his head, looking around in apparent bewilderment. "You have to believe me. I'm not doing this."

"Fine. *I'll* fix it." I reached for the grimoire, but my hand closed on an empty bag. Oh. *Oh, no.* I must've dropped it in my rush to stop Theodore. I spun, panicking squeezing my throat, and Jackie gave a little, distressed squeak, but didn't move from inside my hood. *Grace.* Where was she? What if she'd seen me drop it? I scanned the little stretch of field, cluttered with chairs and tables, but no people. Everyone had fled, and for now it was empty. The crowd were beginning to filter back in though, drawn by the commotion, a mass of masked, unknowable humanity. Or humanity-shaped people.

"Morgan?" Alaric said.

I couldn't let him know I'd lost the book. *No one* could know. I glanced at Ruiner, touching the bag and lifting my chin, and he narrowed his eyes but leaped off the table, vanishing into the shadows. He'd find it, and faster than I could.

I turned back to Alaric. "I'd better not just rip it off, on second thoughts. Could do all sorts of damage. Are you sure you can't do it?"

He shook his head. "I've tried twice. I mean, I did use a fastening spell, but I reversed it. The bloody thing should just pop off."

We both looked at Theodore, who had sat back down of his own accord, finding scraps of lingering snow to shape into eggs.

"I suppose it's better than him wanting to devour us," I said.

"Or use our skulls for mugs," Alaric agreed, and gave me that wide, infectious smile.

I scowled at him, because otherwise I was going to smile too. His charm didn't seem as effective now I was ready for it, but it was definitely still there. "This is unacceptable."

"Of course. The mask will come off of its own accord at the solstice, but I'm going to fix it now. Tonight. If we take him to the tent, we can work this out."

"I'm not sure I trust this sorcerer," Ben said, pointing at Alaric with his sword. "James, what do you think?"

James growled and spat a little smoke.

"I'm a mask-keeper, not a sorcerer," Alaric protested. "I mean, there's some crossover, but…"

"Ben, take your mask off," I said. I didn't like his *conviction*, or James'. The way they'd sunk so deep into character. And I was scared to touch my own mask. I'd never tied the ribbons, yet it was so firmly in place, so flawlessly a part of me, that I kept forgetting it was there.

"Yes, my — Morgan," Ben said immediately, and tucked his fingers under the edge of his helmet. He tugged, then paused, feeling along the underneath as if looking for straps or clips. "Ah. I may be in need of assistance."

I hurried to him, grabbing the helmet to wrench it off, but all it got was a squawk of surprise from Ben, and we staggered back and forth together for a moment, both trying to keep our balance.

"Sit down," I snapped.

"Yes," he said, cutting the rest of the words off, and knelt in front of me like he was expecting me to knight him — a second time, I supposed, given that he already thought he was a knight. I grabbed his helmet, trying to lever it off, Ben making strangled noises that suggested he was in a lot more discomfort than he wanted to admit, but the ridiculous thing wouldn't budge.

I turned to James. "If I try and take your mask off, are you going to flame me?"

He shook his head, and I had a go at peeling the soft latex off his face, with as much luck as I'd had with the helmet and the bunny head. Finally I stopped, my fingers drifting to my own mask, too scared to try, because what if it didn't come? What then?

"Morgan," Alaric said, his voice quiet, and I turned back to him.

"What do you *want?*" I asked him, unable to hold back a tremor of horror. "Why would you do this? Is it everyone?" I looked at the stalls, the workers back inside and handing out drinks again, the crowd filling the space like the tide returning, giving us a certain wary space for now, although that wouldn't last long. Eventually curiosity would win out.

"I didn't do anything," Alaric said. "And we're going to work out exactly what's going on, but there's no point starting a panic. At the moment, everyone *wants* to still be wearing their masks. Let's just leave it that way for now. Come and help me fix this. Please."

I wanted to argue with him, wanted to demand that he come clean, confess his sins in front of everyone, but he was right. Especially with Theodore and Isabella out of action, we had no way of controlling the crowd. Not unless I could persuade Miss Edna out here, anyway, and I think after Ruiner's spat with Mr Fontainebleau, we were more out of favour than ever. What I needed right now was Alaric out of his tent, and thinking I believed him. Then I could find Finn and see what we could do about reversing the enchantment.

"Alright," I said, my throat tight on the words. "Theodore needs to be taken to the hall."

"If we take him to my tent—"

"I'm not putting him in your mask-y house of horror," I snapped, and turned to Ben, pulling him to his feet. "Can you and James take Theodore to the town hall? Put him somewhere safe, where he's not going to wander out into the sun in the morning."

"Of course," he said, hurrying past me to the bunny, who was now lying flat on his stomach on the ground, making miniature snow chickens. "James, help me."

James growled and loped past me. Between them, they got Theodore to his feet, and Ben looked at me. "Are you alright? Is there anything you need?"

"No," I said, feeling inordinately tired. "Just get him safe and keep on with the … interspecies alliance, or whatever."

Ben bowed deeply, then he and James headed off in the direction of the hall.

"How do you want to proceed?" Alaric asked. "Tell me what you need from me. I'm at your disposal."

I huffed air, looking for Ruiner. I couldn't see him, far too much foot traffic around to catch sight of one small cat, but I glimpsed a familiar, straight-backed form, long hair swinging, and I froze.

"Morgan?"

There he went using my name too much again. "I need to get something from the shop," I said. "I'll meet you at the town hall, and we'll see what we can do about Theodore. *And* Isabella. I need them both back to normal."

"As far as that goes," Alaric said, and I glanced at him quickly, but he wasn't smiling. Not quite, anyway.

"Sure." I headed off, trying to run but hampered by the crowd and the debris. Even though most of the furniture was being righted as people returned, there were still plenty of bottles and cups scattering the ground, and I kept slipping on them, everything apparently keen to trip me up. I checked behind me as I reached the edge of the circled food stalls, but I couldn't see Alaric. Hopefully he'd gone to get his spellbook or anti-mask kit, or whatever he used. I still hadn't spotted Ruiner, but maybe he was in pursuit of Grace too, if she had the book. Or maybe she had both the book *and* my brother. Bile rose in the back of my throat at the thought, and I pressed my hand to my chest, trying to soothe it. Jackie nuzzled my neck.

"It's alright," I mumbled to her, although I wasn't sure it was. "It'll be fine."

I made it into the clearer ground of the aisle of shopping stalls, breaking into a jog, trying to check every gap between the tents and the inside of every shadowed stand as I went. The cold air slapped me, fresher out here, making my head spin and odd colours swim across my vision, but I kept going, my gait a little wobbly. I staggered at one point, bumping into an elderly man who laughed as he steadied me and said, "Easy on the mulled wine, pet!"

I laughed dutifully and carried on, my legs heavy. I thought I glimpsed Grace again — in fact, I was sure of it, and she looked around, that little mask still held elegantly to her face but not touching it. *Not touching it.* Finn had been right. Grace was working with Alaric. She had to be.

Somehow I'd stopped running, holding onto the side of a van for support. It was selling fudge, the sweet scent of sugar and vanilla wafting over me, comforting and cloying all at once. I took a deep breath and pushed off it, trying to run but unable to get past a plodding walk, and found myself at the end of market. The solstice guardian loomed above the snow, its torch still burning and unlit wood for the next fire gathered at its base. Beyond it, the unused part of the green stretched out, hemmed by trees, houses beyond them on my left, nothing but fields ahead and to the right. No Grace. I made it to a bench set strategically at the end of the lane of stalls, facing out so people could sit and watch the snow monster battles. There were none on right now, and no one on the bench, so I plopped down, taking a couple of deep breaths with my elbows on my knees. Jackie chittered something distantly, and I said, "Yes. In a moment."

The green was impossibly beautiful, a wash of white snow glimmering with the reflected light of the moon, and above it the sky was ocean-deep, stars as magical and unknown as phosphorescence in the waters. It was nice to look at.

I wondered vaguely how I was looking at the stars when I'd definitely just been looking at the green and the snow between my feet, then everything got very, very distant, and the sky ate up reality, turning my entire world to velvet, star-studded night.

Oh, I thought. *This is very pretty, but very bad.*

And then I didn't think anything at all.

20. Ghost Dog & the rat

I woke to silence. That was the first thing I noticed, the weight of the quiet on my ears, like they were stuffed with cottonwool. All I could hear was the strange, low-level buzzing that always seemed to surface when things were truly quiet, like hearing the sea whispering in the confines of a shell. I lay there considering the depth of the silence for a while, because it really was *silence*, not just a quiet room, not simply an absence of traffic noises or conversation or bird song. It was a vast and all-encompassing silence, as if the … room? Chamber? I hadn't opened my eyes yet, so I wasn't sure. Space, for want of another term. As if that space had never encountered sound before, and it made me want to remain as still and quiet as whatever surrounded me.

The second thing that dawned on me, after I'd listened to the silence for long enough to begin to wonder if I still knew what sound was, was that I was alive. Or conscious. Or I *had* consciousness. The massive weight of silence confused me, setting me wondering if I was in fact dead, and if this was some sort of purgatory. It had better not be the afterlife. I wouldn't be able to cope with an eternity of that silence. I'd read an article about the most silent place in the world — some soundproofed chamber in the US somewhere — and how it sent your balance off kilter and had you hearing the blood moving in your own veins. I didn't fancy that. I'd be climbing the walls if this quiet continued much longer, assuming there were walls, and that I still had a body to climb them with.

Having decided that, alive or not, I needed to find a way out of the silence, I opened my eyes.

I immediately shut them again, much tighter, and resolved to stay like that until the silence drove me out of my mind.

I wasn't in a tidy little soundproof room, and I wasn't in some desolate, empty wasteland where sound had ceased to exist. If my little peek had told me anything, it was that I was evidently in the one of the creepier reaches of purgatory, or some version of hell. It was not a good place, anyway, and it wasn't empty. All I'd been able to see was figure after figure, shadowy and patient, all staring down at me with hungry eyes. Was I about to be dissected? *Wait.* Alien abduction? Maybe that was what had actually happened all those months ago, and my brother had never been a cat at all, and there was no Hollowbeck. It was just a really weird dream brought on by the horrors of alien surgery.

I risked another peek, to check the alien theory, but there were no bright lights or smooth, glossy metal, or (thankfully) large needles and brain drills. The figures were still there, though, appearing and disappearing, drifting into view and out again, gauzy, ill-defined forms anchored to—

"Oh come *on*," I said, and sat up. The words dropped into the silence, dull and clumsy, but no aliens rushed over with restraints or anaesthetics, and no ghouls or demons set upon me with pitchforks. Instead, the soft forms kept up their ceaseless roaming, merging briefly with each other as they passed, swirling with dull, tired colours and drifting off again, aimless yet stoic. The only concrete thing about them were the sodding masks.

None of them looked at me, if they were even capable of that. They seemed empty, less beings in and of themselves and more shells waiting to be inhabited. The masks offered bright and luscious promise, but the things behind them were mere shades, gossamer ideas yet to be born. I touched my face, feeling the outline of my own mask, and tugged at it experimentally. No good. It was as stuck as before. Well, if I was surrounded by masks, I had to be in bloody Alaric's stall, didn't I? He'd got to me, activated the mask or whatever and thrown me in here. I'd evidently been less subtle than I'd hoped with my suggestion of meeting at the hall.

I got up, dusting my hands off, the feeling odd and distant, as if I had pins and needles, likely from lying on the floor for so long. Lucky I didn't have hypothermia, although it didn't feel cold in here, or warm.

"Alaric!" I yelled, and the word fell flat again, as if the mask spirits deadened all sound. "Finn?" I tried, without quite as much enthusiasm, but it was no good. No one would hear that. It must be some sort of enchantment. I looked around, wondering if I was in a back storage area, if tents could have such things. It was dark, the lane between the tapestry walls narrow, and it looked like it went on forever in both directions. With the deep shadows obscuring the ceiling and the shifting trails of the mask creatures — I still wasn't sure how to refer to them, or what they *were* — everything was uncertain and bewildering, and I turned one way then the other, wondering what

was going to be the quickest way out. Nothing gave me any indication.

Well, standing here wasn't getting me anywhere. And wasn't there something about if you were in a maze, you just kept turning left and you'd get out? I didn't know if that was an actual thing or not, but I turned left anyway. One direction was as good as the other.

I walked steadily, not rushing. The ground seemed level enough, but the light was diffuse and murky, and I didn't want to trip myself up on a fallen mask or something. The masked creatures wafted mournfully around, chilling my shoulders where they touched me, passing in either direction and vanishing straight through the tapestry. I tried following a couple of times, looking for panels like the ones in the main part of the shop that Finn had used, but I couldn't find anything. The cloth just bent under my touch, and set a few more masks gliding off, as if they were moths come to rest on the walls briefly. They weren't frightening, exactly, but they were hardly reassuring, either. It was like swimming through swarms of jellyfish, never sure if their trailing skirts were going to simply brush past, a little slimy but innocuous, or deliver a vicious sting.

At some point, I stopped walking. I didn't know how far I'd gone, or how long it had been, but it seemed like *ages*. I didn't have my bag, or my coat, so no phone to check the time on. The grimoire, obviously, was still missing, and until I got out of here, there wasn't much I could do. I looked back the way I'd come, wondering where Jackie was. She'd still been with me when I'd lost consciousness on the bench. I pressed a hand to my chest, trying to breathe down an ugly tightness. She must still be with the bag, or my coat. Or she'd run off when I collapsed and found a warm place to hide. She had to have. It was too cold out for old rats. And what about my brother? Still in pursuit of the grimoire, hopefully.

The walls were too tight, too tall. Why couldn't I see the ceiling? I fanned my face, not even managing to stir the air.

"Alaric!" I shouted again. "Finn! Let me *out!*"

No one materialised, and I took a step back the way I'd come, then paused. No, that was no good, I'd *been* that way. I stopped again, and started in the other direction, then paused once more, suddenly confused. I'd turned left when I started out, but what wall had I been facing when I did so?

"It was this way," I muttered. "I'm sure it was this way." I set off again, faster this time, my chest so tight I was having trouble breathing, the tapestries seeming to billow towards me, the intestines of some vast beast dragging me to its belly. I stumbled into a run, raising my voice again. "*Alaric! Finn! Anyone!*"

No answer, the words swallowed along with me. I picked up the pace, not caring if I tripped or fell, just needing to be *out*, but this place just went on and on and on and *on*, and I should've been out ten times over already, surely, this was *impossible*. I was in a *tent*, not the bloody Eurotunnel.

I ran harder, my breath whistling in my ears, the tapestries billowing, the mask creatures swirling around me, more and more of them, as if my headlong flight was attracting them, drawing them to my panic or presence like fish turning towards the ripples of a dying insect in a pond. I waved a hand wildly above my head, trying to fend off their wispy skirts, then both hands, plunging on and on into the darkness, yelling and waving and wheezing and sinking ever deeper into the horrifying thought that my first impression might've been right. I really was in some sort of purgatory, and this was going to continue forever.

But I wasn't giving into that just yet. I pressed on, yelling even louder, running even faster, screaming my fury at Alaric and Grace and unhelpful Ladies and the masks and anyone else I could think of, and I was in such a rampage of movement and noise that when something appeared in front of me, I had no chance of stopping. It simply loomed out of the shadows in my path, about the height of someone down on their hands and knees, indistinct but clearly more concrete than the masks. Eyes glittered, and I tried to stop, my shouts giving way to a squawk of alarm. I stumbled, tripping on the tapestries or the ground or my own feet, and whacked whatever it was with one knee. It yelped and dived into the wall, and I tumbled to the ground, hitting at an awkward angle and rolling sideways into the tapestry.

I flailed in fright, trying to stop myself before the whole wall collapsed on me, but to my astonishment, I simply popped through a gap at its base and rolled into a new corridor, this one a little brighter. It was still lined with tapestries, but the masks here were attached to the cloth, and there were actually ends to the aisle I was in. I stared around. No floating mask-ghosts, no cottonwool silence. I could even hear music somewhere, and voices, dim and distant but real. I scrambled to my feet, putting a hand out to the wall as my head swam and I swayed slightly.

I didn't feel the tapestry, and I looked down, puzzled. My fingers had vanished into the cloth. I froze, staring at them. No, I hadn't made a mistake. My hand was missing everything below the knuckles. I drew it back warily, and it emerged from the tapestry intact.

"Oh, no," I whispered, and reached out again. This time I vanished up to the wrist, and I pulled away hurriedly. "*Oh no.*" I mean, Hollowbeck had a pretty open-minded attitude to ghosts, but that didn't mean I wanted to be one.

A whine caught my attention, and I looked around. A dog sat in front of me, tail moving gently on the rug. He was skinny and lean, nondescript in a way that suggested any pedigree in his family tree was well lost in the mists of time. He had a narrow head and graceful, greyhound-skinny legs, and he tipped his head to one side, pricking his ears.

"Hi," I said, and realised his tail kept vanishing into the wall. "Ghost dog, huh?"

He whined again. At least I had some company. I tried petting his head, and found I could feel the short hair under my fingers, coarse and comforting. I pulled my hand back suddenly.

"Wait — you're not Anubis or something, are you?" I probably shouldn't be scratching my guide to the underworld behind the ears.

Ghost Dog gave me a look that suggested he was unimpressed with such a question, then got up and padded a few steps away before stopping and looking back at me.

I looked around. There didn't seem to be much else to do, at least not until I got to the bottom of my ghostliness and found out if it were permanent or not. "Coming."

Ghost Dog led the way through the alleys and corridors of tapestries, veering into walls and taking turns seemingly at random. Sometimes we seemed to be closer to the outside world, the rumble of voices and music clearer and brighter, and once I glimpsed someone moving past us into another corridor, maybe Alaric or Finn, but when I started towards them, Ghost Dog barked once, brusque and pointed. Apparently, he did not approve of detours.

Whoever it had been didn't come back to investigate the dog in the tent, and I didn't go to find them. The idea that I might try and they wouldn't be able to hear me was too much to cope with right now. Plus, if it was Alaric, I wanted to be corporeal enough to hit him with something heavy next time I saw him.

We meandered in so many different directions that I was starting to suspect Ghost Dog didn't know where he was going at all. I was actively checking the walls to try and figure out if we were walking past the same masks over and over again, when he stepped through one final panel and stopped. I emerged through the tapestry next to him, looking around, then froze. I reached out to him, an automatic clutching for comfort, and he put his head obligingly under my hand, moving closer so he could lean against me, something real in this state of unreality.

We'd emerged into a small cubicle formed of tapestry walls. A very small lamp, one of those rechargeable ones, spilled weak light from the corner. It didn't illuminate much, but with my ghost eyes, it was enough to see a camp bed took up almost all the space. We stood at its foot, and there was just room to shuffle along one side of it, where an upended crate held a half-full bottle of water and the lantern.

Which was all creepy enough, the little hidden bedroom in the depths of the stall, but the really creepy bit was that *I* was in the bed, my coat still zipped to my chin and the bloody mask sending curling, glossy threads down my cheeks to my jaws and neck, like a spreading fungus. I took a step backwards, the tapestry swallowing me, and Ghost Dog whined. He took my hand in his mouth gently and pulled me back.

"Is that … is that my *corpse?*" I demanded, and he

tugged my hand again, bringing me closer to the bed, then leaped onto it, snuffling my coat. He gave a little yap, and the chest of my coat bulged abruptly. I swallowed a scream, wondering wildly if the mask was growing extra limbs for me or something, and the bulge travelled up to my neck. There was some scuffling and an outraged squeak, then Jackie's sleek grey muzzle emerged. She glared at me.

"*Jackie.*" I rushed forward, trying to pet her, but my fingers just passed through her back and she shook herself off irritably, hissing. "Sorry." I looked down and realised I was also standing in the middle of my own thigh, which was more than a little disorienting. "*Ugh.*" I moved back a step, and looked from the rat to the dog. "So, am I dead?"

Jackie ignored me, scuttling to one of my jacket's big pockets and working her way into it. She emerged with one of the dog treats I'd picked up from Ariel's camper, and offered it to Ghost Dog. He snuffled it appreciatively and licked through it a few times while Jackie went back into my pocket. She came out again with the little envelope that had appeared just as I'd left the camper. I blinked at it, then at the dog.

"Did you do that?"

He wagged his tail, his tongue lolling.

"So you *can* move things."

No response, but maybe it was like Isabella. He could, but it took energy. Which meant I could too, in theory at least. I reached out, concentrating hard on the envelope, and tried to poke it with a finger. I went straight through it, poking Jackie instead. She squeaked.

"Sorry. But what do I do if I can't touch it?"

She gave me her patented *you suck as a witch* look and busied herself with gnawing the packet open. I leaned over her, watching as she tipped the contents onto my chest. There was a cinnamon stick, some cloves, a circle of dried orange, some cardamon, a dried rose bud, and a couple of other things I didn't recognise.

"Are we making mulled wine here?"

Jackie clawed at the envelope some more, struggling with something caught inside, and finally managed to pull a little card out. It was about the size of a recipe card, and read like one too, with an ingredients list followed by instructions. I tipped my head so I could read it.

"*For night wandering. Infuse with purified water and drink before sleep while reciting the couplets to ensure a safe return.*" A little further down the card was printed, "*Though I wander halls of sleep, I trust the world my space to keep. I shall return with light of day, mine own breath will guide my way.*" I looked at Ghost Dog. "I think we're a bit late for preventative treatments here."

He just wagged his tail, and I looked at the bottle of water sitting on the crate. It was open, so hardly purified, and we weren't going to be hanging about for infusions and so on, but one thing I had figured out in my time as a novice witch was that charms were a lot more practical and hardheaded than the stories they were wrapped in. You needed a little mystery to sell things, after all.

"Can you get the bottle open?" I asked Jackie, but she was already pawing it, and it tumbled onto the bed. Which was a great start, but the lid evidently wasn't on properly, and it promptly started tipping water all over the thin fabric of the camp bed, spilling uselessly to the floor below. "No!" I yelped and grabbed for the bottle. My fingers passed through it, but there was a hitch of resistance, just enough to flip it onto my corporeal chest. Jackie bounded after it, pushing it with her tidy little paws until it was spilling over the herbs, emptying rapidly.

"*Though I wander halls of sleep, I trust the world my space to keep*," I gabbled, squinting at the card, its ink blurring in the water. "*I shall return with light of day, mine own breath will guide my way.*" Nothing was happening, and I started again, panic curling in my belly, because we had one chance, then the water was gone and the herbs were lost, and I didn't know how to get help, because I was a *ghost*. "*Though I wander halls of sleep, I trust the world my space to keep. I shall—* ack!"

The *ack* was because my body opened its eyes, grabbed me somewhere around the bellybutton, and jerked me straight into it. I thought I was going to fall right through and to the ground beneath the camp bed, but instead I *bounced*, shuddering like a bungee cord coming to rest, vibrating back into my body. I sat up with a gasp, my chest wet where the water had seeped through the zip of my coat, Jackie sliding into my lap with an irritated chitter. My arms and legs were suddenly heavy, and my face hurt where I'd tried to pull the mask off earlier, and I had a mysterious pain in my hip, and it was *glorious*.

I picked up Jackie, kissed the top of her head (much to her disapproval), and looked at Ghost Dog, who I could still see. I supposed it was the mask. He tipped his head to the side, watching me.

"Are there Ghost Dog treats?" I asked him. "Ectoplasm chews? Because I will buy you *all* of them. Anything you want, it's yours."

He just whined and drooped his ears, and I nodded.

"You need your witch. I'm on it. You two are categorically the best animals, living or dead, to ever exist." I kissed Jackie again, tucked her into my hood, then swung my legs off the cot and stood up cautiously. Wow, I felt *really* heavy after being bodiless. I loved it. "Get us out without anyone seeing us?" I said to Ghost Dog. "Then we need more of those charms."

He *whuff*ed, ears perked, and melted through the tapestry. I followed with a lot more thrashing, but I was up. I was alive. And I was going to get witchy on these bloody masks and their maker.

21. Waking beauties

Ghost Dog got us out of the tent much more quickly than he'd managed to get me to my body, leaving me more convinced than ever that there had been some unknown dimensions involved previously. There had to be, really, given my marathon running in the shadowy corridors. They already felt remote and distant, imagined rather than lived, but I had a feeling they'd come creeping back in three a.m. dreams, the ones that swallow you whole.

But we didn't have to venture back into them in real life. Ghost Dog wound his way through the tent, shoving his nose into tapestries to check the way was clear before showing me where a human-suitable gap was, using the same method but from the other side. It was slightly unnerving to see a snout simply appear out of the fabric, and I found myself booping his intangible nose each time, trying to muffle my giggles with the sleeve of my coat. Jackie sighed audibly, but being back in my body had me too happy to be bothered by a little rodent disapproval.

We only had one near-miss, when I emerged into a corridor only for Ghost Dog to give a panicked whine and rush me, evidently trying to push me back the way I'd come. I went, the pup huddling behind me as we waited for someone to pass by on the other side of the tapestry. I heard measured steps and the soft breath of someone sighing out, and once they'd passed, I plucked the tapestry aside to peer after them. Finn's lean form was just rounding the next corner, and I opened my mouth, intending to call out to him. If he really did know how the masks worked, and could show me, we might be able to get this whole mess sorted without any further out of body experiences or vampire attacks. But Ghost Dog snarled, a proper, no messing about snarl, and I let the tapestry drop back into place, staring at him. He gave me an apologetic whine and a wag of the tail, then pointed his nose in a new direction and trotted off with great determination. Evidently detours were not permissible right now, and considering how he'd helped me, I didn't feel I could argue. I'd come back to Finn. By that stage I should have another three witches for backup, too. Well, two witches plus me and Starlight.

After that, Ghost Dog seemed to decide that all actual routes out of the tent were too risky (or he'd forgotten that doors were preferably for those who were no longer ghosts), because the final step of my escape involved slipping into a gap between the inner tapestry wall and the outer, heavy-duty canvas. There was barely room to stand between them, the gap intended to be just enough to provide some insulation and protection from the rain, and as I wedged myself into it, I heard voices inside the tent. I dropped to the ground, where the gap was widest, but the fabric was still tight against me on both sides, outlining me like the imprint of a cartoon witch running into a wall. The voices came closer, and I couldn't make out the words, but the louder one had to be Alaric's well-rounded tones. I slid to a prone position, belly flat to the groundsheet, all my previous good humour forgotten as I wriggled frantically to get under the exterior wall.

The tent was pegged down so securely I found myself wondering if they'd used a jackhammer in the frozen ground, but not even the best tent pegs can resist a panicking witch. I clawed my way out, rolling onto the green, and lay there for a moment in the snow, panting at the sky until its paleness registered. It was *light*. The stars had been out when I'd lost consciousness on the bench. I sat up, a sudden sickness swirling in my belly. Music rolled towards me from the centre of the market, along with voices raised in happy shouts, but on this side there was nothing but the empty green and the backs of more stalls. I climbed to my feet, looking around, and saw a woman smoking a long, slim pipe, leaning against the back of a truck with mushrooms painted on its side and watching me with a mellow sort of interest.

I straightened my coat, dusting off the worst of the snow, and nodded at her. She half raised her pipe, tipping her head in acknowledgment, and watched us pass. Or me, I suppose, as Ghost Dog was so shadowy out here that even I was having trouble seeing him, his paws leaving no prints in the snow as he trotted on ahead.

We went straight to Ariel's camper van, Ghost Dog vanishing inside while I checked around warily before letting myself in. It didn't take long to find the charms, filed alphabetically in a folder marked *Self Care & Sleep*. It said something for having decent organisation. If anyone had to find a spell in my shop without Starlight to locate it for them, it'd take them three days and a compass. I knew, because I'd tried.

The other thing I discovered in the camper was that Ariel had an analogue clock stuck to a bulkhead. It read twelve o'clock, so either it was very much out, or I'd been wandering the mask-infested corridors for almost twenty-four hours. If it *was* right, it meant the solstice was only a few hours away. I couldn't remember exactly what Starlight had said, but it had been close enough to three p.m. The only thing I was sure of was that it couldn't have come and gone, because Hollowbeck was still standing. Or, if I was in a slightly less apocalyptic frame of mind, there was the fact the market was meant to finish the evening of the solstice, before the closing ball, and it was still in full swing.

So I wasn't out of time yet, but it wasn't far off. I needed to wake the witches currently sleeping in the shop, before they fell any deeper under the masks' spell, then get all of them — and myself — out of the masks, and *then* I had to either figure out how to break the masks' hold, or somehow convince the whole town to get rid of them, if that was even possible at this point. Mine felt fused to my face, so I doubted it.

That was a lot, and for a moment I just sat there in Ariel's camper, breathless and shaky, wondering how the hell I was going to do *any* of it, what possible reason I had to even think I could, and at what point my own awful mask was going to leap into action and drag me back to the endless corridors of floating mask-beasts, abandoning me there forever. I closed my eyes against the impossibility of it, the *enormity* of it, and reminded myself I had a rat, a ghost dog, and burning desire to smash some masks up.

That was going to have to be enough, and there *was* time, even if I didn't have the slightest glimmer of a plan. I'd start with rousing some witches, anyway. I shoved the charms in my pocket and pulled my hood up as I left the camper, Jackie still curled next to my neck and Ghost Dog ambling happily next to me. We'd figure it out. We had to.

I MADE it to the Cosy Cauldron without being chased by infuriated mask-sellers or pounced on by the bloodthirsty undead. I still had the spare key, and I let myself in the back door, into silence and stillness, other than the ticking of the radiators and the gentle creaks of the old building. Starlight was still on the sofa, just as I'd left her, and there was no sign anyone else had been here. I'd hoped Ruiner would be lurking about with the grimoire, but he'd vanished as thoroughly as I must have. For once I didn't think my brother was skiving off, but it didn't make me feel any better. He'd been chasing after Grace, after all, and if he'd got between her and the grimoire … Well, there was no point thinking about it. I needed more witchy brains, and a way to get the bloody mask off. I was getting sick of everything having little glows and auras. It was like living in a comic strip, swirls and exclamation marks coming off everything. I was getting tempted to bop someone on the head just to see if bluebirds started tweeting over the bump.

But bopping someone on the head would have to wait. I shed my coat hurriedly and put the kettle on, then set up three mugs and emptied the packets of charms into them. I peered at the contents cautiously, checking they all looked the same as the one I'd used in the tent. They did, as far as I could tell. Not that I'd really know, but it made me feel like I was being at least a little thorough. Jackie scuttled around the kitchen floor, pausing to exchange hisses with Howard, then came back to clamber up my jeans and jumper, back to my shoulder. She clawed at the corner of my mask as I tipped boiling water into the mugs, releasing a waft of fragrant steam, and I sighed.

"I know," I said. "Maybe when Ariel wakes up, she'll

have an idea what to do." Assuming the mask didn't have her thinking she was a badger or something.

I gave the herbs a few moments to brew, finding some unfeasibly healthy digestive biscuits in the cupboard and splitting one with Jackie while we waited. They tasted of stale oats and disappointment, but my stomach was rumbling, and they took the edge off. Finally, I stuck a teaspoon in one of the mugs and walked over to the sofa with it in one hand and the card from the envelope in the other, and sat on the edge of the heavy old coffee table. I took a deep breath. If this didn't work, I was out of options. I had no idea what my next move could or should be. I needed help. I might be almost ready to accept I was a witch, but I was *such* a novice that the idea of everything I didn't know made me want to lie down in a darkened room. And I didn't even have the grimoire.

But it had worked before. It'd work again.

"Here goes," I said to Jackie, and wafted the mug as close to Starlight's nose as I could, given the fact she was on her back, then blew some of the steam into her face. Not a flicker of response, so I filled the teaspoon, blowing on the liquid to cool it, and tried to put a few drops on her forehead. I managed to dollop the whole lot on, of course, sending it running down inside her mask, but it wasn't going to drown her. I grabbed the card.

"Though I wander halls of sleep, I trust the world my space to keep. I shall return with light of day, mine own breath will guide my way."

I looked at Starlight expectantly, but she was utterly motionless, a waxwork hippie princess. I splashed another teaspoon on her, a little less circumspectly this time, putting it higher up so it ran into her hair, in case the mask was interfering.

"Though I wander halls of sleep, I trust the world my space to

keep. I shall return with light of day, mine own breath will guide my way."

Still nothing, although I thought maybe her breath hitched just slightly. Bollocks to it. I stood up and set to with the teaspoon, flicking infusion all over her as I repeated the charm over and over, getting the mix in her hair and on the mask, splattering over her dress and arms, my voice getting louder all the time.

"Though I wander halls of sleep, I trust the world my space to keep. I shall return with light of day, mine own breath will guide my way, dammit, Starlight! *Wake up!"* I grabbed her jaw, forcing the last of the infusion into her mouth, and backing away with a groan of frustration as it just dribbled straight out again. "Oh, come *on—*"

Starlight sat bolt upright with a gasp, then burst out coughing, clutching her throat.

"Starlight!" I dropped to my knees next to her, patting her back as she spluttered and wheezed. "Are you alright? Are you here?"

"I'm here," she managed, wheezing. "You just about drowned me!"

"Sorry. I might've panicked a *tiny* bit."

She coughed again and waved desperately. I ran to the sink and got a glass of water, rushing back and helping her hold it as she gulped a few mouthfuls.

"*Urgh,*" she said, wiping her mouth. "I did hear you. It just took a bit to get back."

"Get back? From where?"

"The…" She waved vaguely. "There were corridors. Or one long corridor, anyway."

"With the mask creatures?"

She shook her head. "Fairies. But not proper ones. Little Tinkerbell ones. They were creepy, but they didn't *do* anything. I was scared I'd be there forever and become one of them, though. Like I'd shrink and shrink until that was all that was left, a little glittery ghost fairy."

I shivered. "I had ghosts in masks. But I know what you mean about being caught there forever."

She threw her arms around me and hugged me. "But I'm here! I heard you shouting and just started running towards you. You got me back!"

I returned the hug clumsily, then straightened up. "Well, I've got two more witches to get back, and then we've got to figure out how the hell to get the masks off everyone." I frowned at her suddenly. "You're not still feeling all fairy-ish? You're not bouncing about as much."

Starlight touched the mask. "Not as much as before. I think the ghost fairies put me off."

"Well, that's something." I grabbed the other two mugs and headed for the hall. Two things learned, then. Keep talking, and don't drown anyone.

Upstairs, Ghost Dog was lying next to Ariel, his translucent head pillowed on her shoulder and his front paws pulled up like a kangaroo's. He raised his head to look at me, tail thumping through the covers silently. I leaned over to stroke his head, but I couldn't feel him anymore. He didn't seem to mind, though, his eyes following me as I checked on Mella. She was as unchanged as Ariel, bees circling her like she was a new bloom, rare and fragrant. The floor creaked behind me, and I looked at Starlight as she came in, Howard cradled in the crook of her arm.

She held her free hand out. "Give me one."

I handed one of the mugs over and showed her the card. "I just splashed the infusion about, then read this until you woke up."

"Alright," she said, and shifted Howard to her shoulder. "That seems pretty straightforward."

I went to Mella's bed, eyeing the bees. "If I get any of this on you, it's not deliberate," I told them.

"Good boy," Starlight crooned, and I looked around to see her petting Ghost Dog without quite touching him.

"You can see him?"

"Mostly. He's a bit here and not."

I nodded and looked at her. "Ready?"

"Ready," she agreed, and we started, flicking the infusion on the sleeping witches like a benediction, our words falling into rhythm with each other, a steady cadence that circled the room and curled around us with the feel of something watchful and physical, stronger than what I'd felt when I'd had to do this alone. The bees rose and fell, following the words, swooping around Mella insistently, and Ghost Dog whined, the sound thin and distant, on the edge of hearing.

"I'm out," Starlight said, shaking her cup out. I nodded, waving one hand in a *carry on* gesture. She'd heard me after all. With any luck the others would too, but they didn't know our voices. They might not be as quick to join us.

My own mug was empty now, but still we kept going, repeating the words, the bees' buzzing seeming almost to be taking up the chorus too. And still the women didn't move, just lying there with the infusion spattering their hair and clothes, and Ghost Dog stood up and yapped, sharp, insistent sounds, a regular, unrelenting staccato. Sound swirled around us, human and insect and animal, rising and rising, until I was about to shout I couldn't stand listening to it for a moment longer. But even as I thought that, Ariel sat up with a gasp, reaching for Ghost Dog, and pulled his insubstantial form close as his yaps turned into a volley of excited barking.

At the same moment Mella surged up to sitting and

yelled, "*Dammit, stop cutting the wildflowers!*" The bees swarmed her, alighting on her hair and face and hands and taking off again instantly, zooming over her head at the sort of pace that would've made me expect an attack was imminent if their buzzing wasn't so unmistakably joyful. Mella drew a shuddering breath and looked blearily at Starlight and I. "Wildflowers?" she asked weakly.

"Yes?" I offered, not sure what she was asking, but she just nodded and swung her legs off the bed, then looked around blearily.

"Hang about. I was in some corridor, and there were dead bees, and the walls were woven of dead wildflowers, and—" She looked at me suspiciously. "You said yes!"

I shrugged helplessly. "I had a fifty percent chance of being right."

She touched her face, feeling the mask. "What the hell happened? And where am I? Who did this?" The bees were still zooming about, but now the tone seemed to be turning more agitated.

"Mella?" Starlight said. "You're at the shop. We found you at the ice palace."

"Did someone spike my drink? I'll bloody well spike them!"

"It wasn't a drink," I started, and Ariel spoke over me, her voice deep and a little hoarse, the sort of voice that could sell out late night radio shows.

"It was that shoddy bloody mask-seller," she said.

"That's what I thought," I said, with a mix of relief and fury. "But I wasn't sure. You were the first one down, though. What happened?"

She scratched Ghost Dog's belly as he rolled ecstatically over the bed and halfway through it. Somehow her fingers were mussing his short hair. "Booper has a nose," she started, and Mella interrupted her.

"*Booper?* What sort of name's that?"

Ariel gave her a magnificently disdainful glance, of the sort I immediately wanted to practise myself, and I noticed Starlight's mouth twisting in an imitation of it as well.

"The name a seven-year-old gives her very first pet," she said. "You know, one that's an actual pet and not a *swarm.*"

"They're not a swarm. They're individuals, and that's very hurtful, lumping them together like that." The bees seemed to agree, spreading out behind Mella. More had appeared from somewhere, and I hoped none had taken up residence in the walls.

"What's *hurtful* is making fun of my dog's name."

"He's *dead.*"

"He's still got feelings."

"Okay, okay," I said, raising my hands. "Everyone's just woken up, we've all been stuck in some nasty limbo, right?" There was a murmur of agreement at that. "So we're understandably a bit wound up, and we need some food, some caffeine, and a bit of a regroup."

"A regroup?" Mella said. "What, d'you want a status report?"

"Or will we circle back to that later?" Ariel asked, and they both snickered. Well, at least they weren't about to have a bees versus Ghost Dog throw-down in the shop's spare room. Now as long as they didn't team up against me and Jackie, who was snoring softly on my shoulder. She wasn't going to be a lot of help.

"I have vodka in the freezer and whisky in the cupboard?" I offered.

"Why didn't you say so?" Ariel asked, getting up. She wobbled slightly, and Starlight steadied her. "Oof. How long was I out?"

"A few days," I said. "You're probably dehydrated."

"I can put an infusion together for that," Starlight said, keeping a hand under Ariel's arm as they headed for the upstairs hall and the stairs beyond.

"Yeah, you mentioned vodka," Ariel said.

I looked at Mella, who shrugged. "I'll take whisky," she said.

"Sure." I waved her ahead of me, staying close in case she stumbled, but she walked easily, the bees encasing her in an affectionate, fuzzy cloud. I followed at a safe distance, not wanting to upset her escort.

We were up. We were out of limbo. And now we needed to find out what Booper's nose had sniffed out, and what we were going to do about it.

Also, I needed cake.

22. The witches are coming

I LEFT EVERYONE TAKING TURNS TO SPLASH WATER ON THEIR faces in the bathroom and ran across the road to the grocery store in an old pink coat from Norma's wardrobe and a cream bobble hat, which felt far enough from my usual attire that, with the mask, I might not be recognised. Not that it turned out to be a problem, as the only person in the shop was a young woman in a body-hugging jumpsuit and a crash helmet, making *whooshing* sounds to herself as she crouched on the counter, bending one way then another with a feather duster in each hand, evidently running down some serious slalom ski course in her mind. I chose a sticky ginger cake in a paper bag (*Made By Maple!* the handwritten label shouted. *With eggs by Jocelyn!*), added a hefty fruit cake after a moment's deliberation, since that was basically health food with all the fruit and nuts, then hurried past the countertop skier and retreated back to the Cosy Cauldron.

The kettle was on when I got in, vodka and three different bottles of whisky on the table, Mella examining the label of each carefully while her bees conferred over a dollop of honey on a side plate. Ariel had a generous dose of vodka in a glass in front of her already, and I slid the cakes onto the table as I sat down.

"Tisane?" Starlight suggested, holding up a bunch of mildly wilted mint. "I was thinking mint to wake up our senses, ginger for a bit of a kick, lemon—"

"Vodka," Ariel said, lifting the bottle.

"Ice cream," Mella said, looking expectantly at me. "I could really go for some ice cream after that."

"Coffee," I said to Starlight, and jumped up, scurrying out the door again. Why hadn't I thought of ice cream? We needed more than cake. This was a crisis situation.

The street was utterly deserted. Not just quiet, but *empty*. I stopped in the centre of the road, struck by the silence. The market was too far away for me to hear it, and nothing moved as far as I could see, the air still. The trees touched the translucent sky with bare branches, and snow shone pale and glossy in Petunia's persistent winter sun. Lights burned in the windows of the shops, but no one walked down the sidewalk, no one emerged from a door or called out to a friend.

The sudden, alien-invasion fright flashed back to me again, but this time it felt more as if everyone else had been snatched up, and we alone remained. I wondered where Ruiner was, fright and guilt making an unpleasant cocktail in my belly. I'd barely had time to think of him. Getting back into my body and out of the market, then getting everyone woken up, had taken up most of my energy. He could be anywhere, and there wasn't even anyone to ask, because they'd all been sucked up by E.T. for likely nefarious purposes.

But I'd just *left* the market. I knew there were people there. It was just that it was the *only* place they were. Other than our resident ski champion, that was. I headed for the shop again, reminding myself to note down everything so I could put it on my tab later. Two cakes I'd remember, but more than that I was going to lose track.

Five minutes later I was back in the Cosy Cauldron, offloading bread rolls, sliced ham, cheese, eggs, half a bag of mandarins, and a tub of vanilla ice cream.

"I didn't know what flavour you wanted," I said to Mella. "But I thought no one can really hate vanilla, can they?"

"Can," Ariel said. "Boring as all hell."

"It's just fine," Mella said, opening the tub and digging a spoon straight into it. "Sugar, you know?"

"I should've got some sports drinks," I said, surveying the table. "For rehydration. Does anyone want sports drinks?"

Ariel tipped her glass at me, and Mella ignored me entirely, busy tapping a spoon of ice cream onto the bees' plate. Starlight handed me a mug of black coffee.

"Sit," she said, and I sat, my legs suddenly weary. *Every-thing* suddenly weary, in fact, as if my consciousness was remembering what it was to be weightless, and rather wanted another go. I took a sip of coffee, then opened the bread rolls. Cake could wait. I needed actual food. Out of body experiences apparently really took their toll on you.

We sat there for a little without talking, four recently comatose witches in varying degrees of befuddlement, accompanied by a rat, a ferret, a ghost dog, and a swarm of bees. Starlight peeled about four mandarins, muttering vaguely about imported foods and how we should be eating the apples from the valley, then ate them segment by segment while I scoffed my roll. Mella dug steadily through the vanilla ice cream, and Ariel simply topped up her glass again and petted Ghost Dog — Booper — restlessly.

Starlight was the first to speak, taking a sip of her mint

tea to wash the mandarins down. "Where's Ruiner?" she asked me, and I shook my head wordlessly.

Mella looked at me. "Your brother? The cat?"

"You knew?" I asked, carving the cakes into slices.

"Any witch worth her crystals could tell he wasn't a normal cat. The whole carnival deal kind of put the rest of the pieces together."

"Your brother's a cat?" Ariel asked.

"Currently, yes."

"An actual one, or is it a personal preference thing?"

"Well, he looks like an actual cat," I said. "And it's definitely him on the inside."

"Curse?"

"Yes."

"Nice," she said approvingly.

I wrinkled my nose, helping myself to a large slab of the ginger cake. "You said before that Booper had a nose for something?"

She added a little more vodka to her glass, and Starlight started to say something. I kicked her ankle.

"*Ow,*" she mumbled, but subsided.

Ariel looked at her, her gaze level and cool through the mask. It was tattooed with vaguely Norse designs, and they bled off onto her cheeks, curling and flicking. She had other tattoos as well, visible on her bare arms, but they looked to be old and well-established, and leaned more towards cartoon ducks and darkly textured ravens. She shifted her gaze to Mella. "Any luck getting your mask off?"

"No," Mella said, touching it. It blossomed with leaves and flowers, as if someone had smashed a bridal bouquet into her face. The bees seemed to be enjoying it.

Ariel looked at Starlight and me.

"No," I said, and Starlight shook her head.

"I tried in the bathroom, but it feels like someone's superglued it on."

"You were attacked right at the start," I said to Ariel. "And you're not even from Hollowbeck. What happened?"

She drummed her fingers on the table, looking at the ceiling.

"If it's too traumatic," Starlight started, her voice soft, and Ariel threw her an irritable look, then knocked back the last of her drink, reaching for the bottle again. Starlight moved it away.

Ariel huffed. "It wasn't … actually, fine. It was a bit traumatic. Booper vanished, and I thought I'd lost him." The last words tipped up at the end, and she took one of the whisky bottles, daring Starlight with a glance to take it off her. "I mean, I didn't think that right away, he runs off and does his own thing all the time. But when he came back — it was the evening of the cocktail party — he was dragging a mask."

"The one you're wearing?" I asked. I also really wanted to ask what a ghost dog's *thing* was, but that would have to wait.

"The very one." Ariel slopped whisky into her glass, and Starlight interrupted.

"You've been unconscious for *days*. Shouldn't you have some water? Or at least some food?"

Ariel stared at her for a long moment, then, without looking away, grabbed the ice cream tub and slid it across the table towards her. She still didn't break eye contact with Starlight as she dug a spoonful out and dumped it in her whisky. Mella was left with her spoon hovering in the air, frowning faintly.

Starlight scowled, crossing her arms over her chest, and I said, "What happened with the mask, then? Why did you put it on?"

"I went to take it back," she said, looking away from Starlight finally. "Booper doesn't usually take corporeal objects — it takes a huge amount of effort for him to move anything physical — so it was a bit odd, but as far as I could tell, it was just a mask."

Booper shoved his head through the table, sniffing the ham, and I trailed my fingers over his head. I couldn't feel him, and it gave me an odd sense of loss. "He still likes corporeal food."

Ariel rolled her eyes. "He *does*. I have to feed him every night, even though he can't eat it. He howls otherwise, and ghost dog howls *suck*."

"Does he have corporeal drool?" Mella asked, eyeing the ham suspiciously, then opting for the cheese.

"What happened when you took the mask back?" I asked Ariel.

"Right, yeah. I headed over to the tent, and there was no one around, so I went inside. Bloody maze in there, and dark as anything, but I could hear someone up ahead, and I saw some light. When I got to it, it was on the other side of a tapestry, so I couldn't see who it was, but I heard something like, *it'll put the whole valley out of action*, so I listened. Doesn't do to miss out if people are cooking up a little chaos."

"*Miss out?* You wanted to join in?" Starlight demanded.

"Well, I didn't know what it was yet. Might've been a bit of fun, you know? Or profitable. Either get in on it or sell the info to the local coppers."

I wondered if she was from Darrowdale. It seemed like the sort of attitude that would fit Hollowbeck's weird, dodgy-as-discount-shrimp twin town.

Starlight sniffed and took a large slurp of tea. "That is *not* good witch behaviour."

"I never said I was a good witch," Ariel replied, giving

her a lazy grin. With the tattoos running over her face and down her neck, there was an ominous, warrior quality to her that made me check she didn't have any weapons handy. Just in case.

"Anyhow," she continued, "I didn't hear much more, because someone came through the tapestry just behind me, and I didn't want them to recognise me, so I slapped the mask on. Everything went black and white, I got a bit … well, I don't know if they attacked me or I went for them first, but there was a bit of a scrap, and the next thing I know I was in these nasty corridors. I walked them *forever*, all full of old armour and rusty swords and … and *stuff*, shouting for Booper, but I couldn't find him. Then I heard you yelling and followed it out." She tipped her head, examining me. "How did you get hold of my charms?"

"Booper," I said. "I checked your camper van the other day, and I didn't see him then, but he left the charm for me. Then when he found me in the halls, he led me to my body and I used it."

All three women looked at me, and I shoved the last bite of cake in my mouth. "What?"

"He found you?" Ariel asked. "While you were in that limbo?"

"Yes, why?"

"Witch, he didn't even find *me*."

I frowned. "That is weird. Maybe he was close by when I went in?"

"He was standing right next to me," Ariel said. "And he's been with me all my life. If he was going to be able to find anyone, it should've been me."

"Oh." I didn't know what else to say.

"And how did you use the charm on yourself?" Mella asked. "Did you somehow get back in your body first?"

"No, I was all ghosty. Jackie did most of it. I just read the charm."

"Who's Jackie?" Ariel asked, then blinked when I pointed at the rat still sleeping in my hood. "Yeah, no. That's not how familiars work. They support, but they can't do the work for you. Which means that, while disembodied, you worked a charm."

"Oh," I said again, wishing I understood what any of that meant.

Mella shook her head. "I didn't even think that was possible. I heard you weren't much of a witch, but—"

"She's a *fantastic* witch," Starlight said sharply. "But she's also a good witch, and—"

"Good in what sense?" Ariel asked, grinning.

"She's—"

"In need of help," I put in, before Starlight could defend my honour too much. It was making my skin itch. "No one can get these masks off, and the whole village's wearing them. Did you hear who was speaking, Ariel? Was it Alaric?"

"It was a woman," she said, taking a spoonful of ice cream dripping in whisky, then making a face. "This is *awful*."

A woman. Finn had been right. He had to be, because there was only one woman I knew not wearing a mask. Only one woman who'd been winning over Jackie and allowed to use the grimoire. Only one woman who probably *had* the grimoire right now, and who knew what she'd done with my brother.

"You didn't recognise the voice?" Starlight was asking, and I wasn't surprised when Ariel shook her head, taking another bite of spiked ice cream.

"Second thoughts, this isn't that bad," she said, and added another spoonful. Then she held it up, still dripping.

"Actually, other second thoughts, it sounded a bit like our mayor."

I gave up and poured myself some vodka, stomach sick with certainty. "What town?"

"Darrowdale."

"Faith?"

"That's her," Ariel said. "You know her?"

"More her twin, Grace."

"She has a twin?"

"Maybe," I said, and slugged back my drink.

"But Grace wouldn't do this," Starlight said.

I gave her a surprised look. "I didn't think you liked her."

"I don't, but she wouldn't do this. She's got no reason —" She stopped as I kicked her ankle again, and touched the empty bag at my side. Her eyes widened as she looked at it, and she frowned. It was a dubious look, but she didn't say anything else, and I turned to the others.

"Whoever it is, we have to stop them."

"Stop them doing what, though?" Mella asked. "Ghost whisperer here didn't really hear much, did she?"

Ariel raised an eyebrow, still hunched over her whisky and ice cream cocktail.

"Do you feel like yourself?" I asked. "Properly, I mean?"

Mella frowned, touching the mask and dislodging a few bees. "I mean, sort of? I'd feel better if I could get this damn thing off."

"I feel fine now," Starlight put in. "I know I was a bit…"

"Tinkerbell?" I offered.

"Yes," she admitted. "I was. But I feel okay now."

I nodded. "So do I. And, if we're lucky, maybe the masks used up all their power kicking us into limbo. But there's no knowing for sure. As long as we can't take the masks off, we're at the whim of Grace, or Alaric, or both of them. It's like being a sleeper agent, and we've no idea what they're going to make us do."

Everyone was silent for a moment, then Starlight said softly, "Or what they'll do *to* us. What if the masks are self-destruct buttons?"

We looked at each other, and Ariel was the first to speak. "Sod that. I'll be in charge of my own destruction, thanks very much."

"And I can't just leave the bees," Mella said. "They're upset enough already. They need a lot of attention."

I moved my chair slightly away from Mella and her circling cloud of striped bodyguards. "Then we need a plan."

"I'm in," Starlight said immediately, and I smiled at her. That I'd never doubted.

"Sure," Ariel said, shrugging. "Seems like a fun way to go out, anyway."

We all looked at Mella, and she sighed, then nodded. "If it's for the good of the bees. What's your idea?"

I'd been asking myself the same question for the entire last week, as far as I could tell, and I still had nothing. But necessity's quite the mother, when it comes to it.

What followed was a heated conversation that resulted at one point in Booper fleeing through the wall to get away from the bees, Ariel plucking a flower off Mella's mask and eating it with exaggerated enjoyment, Starlight confiscating all the alcohol and yelling that if anyone wanted any they were going to have come away with her and dance for a thousand years in payment, and me actually staying relatively calm until I turned around to spot Howard chewing his way through the fruit cake. I promptly threatened to turn him into chicken nuggets, and Starlight forgot about stealing dance partners and launched into a heated defence of the ferret instead, at which point Ariel observed, in between topping her glass up with the bottle she'd somehow liberated off Starlight without her noticing (I suspected Booper had a paw in things), that not only did I need to brush up on my species, but I likely wanted to stop my rat eating the bread rolls.

And somehow in there, between trying to get our living and dead familiars under control, we came up with a plan. It wasn't a fancy one, but sometimes simplicity was at the heart of the best things. We'd go to the market and find Finn, to see if he could show us where to break the masks' enchantment. If that didn't work, or we couldn't avoid Alaric, we'd just go full witch on him, whatever that was. Ariel made the statement with great satisfaction, and Mella nodded knowingly, while Starlight and I exchanged dubious glances. Whatever, we'd force him to reverse the charms if he could, and if he couldn't, and it was his mysterious female accomplice responsible (Grace, I was still sure, although Mella and Starlight were both unconvinced and Ariel kept asking if I was certain about the twin thing), we'd make him tell us how to find her.

The major advantage we had right now was that no one knew the other three witches were awake. For myself, maybe Alaric did, maybe he didn't. Presumably he thought there was no chance I was waking up, otherwise I would've been strapped to the bed, and not in a fun way. Which meant he had no reason to check on me. And it wasn't something we could fix, anyway. What we had to do was just move, before we lost that slim chance of surprise, and before the day got any later. It was one p.m. already, the solstice two hours away. Whatever was going to happen, it'd happen then. We couldn't wait for night, for Theodore, even if he emerged from the day rather less ravenous. This was on us, and we had to do it now.

It took us another half hour to get out of the shop, most of which was spent outfitting us all in Norma's clothes as a bit of disguise. The old witch had favoured everything from classic, tailored pieces that Jackie O would've given a nod of approval to, to swirling hippie gear (Starlight immediately pounced on a floor length patchwork coat, and it took a lot of persuading her that it was a bit too close to her usual style to be much of a disguise), to Eighties shoulder pads and more modern pieces I'd definitely seen in fancy magazines at the hairdressers. I didn't know how long witches lived, but evidently long enough to acquire both money and a taste for fashion.

We walked out in a selection of Norma's newer coats, sleek and well-cut in pastel pinks and pale greys, but with very un-matched, boldly knitted woollen hats from the shop stock pulled down over our hair. We paused at the edge of the street, looking at each other, and Ariel took a flask from her pocket, taking a swig and offering it to the rest of us.

"Where did you get that?" Starlight demanded. "You're not going to be able to cast a charm to save your life!"

"Witch, I can cast better charms trolleyed than you can with your knickers in such a knot," Ariel said. "Sure you don't want some? Loosen you up, like."

Starlight just scowled at her, and Mella said, "My bees are cold. Come on."

We headed off, falling into step with each other as we walked straight down the middle of the empty street side by side, the grit on the tarmac crunching under our boots and our flashy new coats swinging. Booper ranged ahead of us, and the bees offered an accompaniment of sonorous buzzing. The light was already sliding low, glittering on the windows that watched us pass, and our breath curled behind us, four dragonish trails.

The witches were coming.

23. Not exactly according to plan

I THINK, AT SOME LEVEL, I'D BEEN HOLDING ONTO A SLIVER of hope that we'd get to the market and everything would be just *fine*. Back to normal. Alaric would have realised there was a problem and recalled the masks, apologising sincerely and charmingly for any bother, and Isabella would be sweeping around in her usual, elegant way. Ruiner would be cadging oysters from the champagne bar, and when dusk came, Theodore would appear in one of his classically sharp suits, without sunburn, fangs, or bunny ears. Well, no more fangs than usual, anyway.

It hardly needs to be said that I was entirely wrong. If I *hadn't* been wrong, the streets would presumably have had more pedestrians than just us, and the shops wouldn't have been doing their best post-zombie-apocalypse impression. Minus the gore and destruction, of course. We were, so far, having a very polite and localised apocalypse.

Instead, the market was even busier than it had been the day before, the aisles heaving with masked shoppers. They bounced along in kangaroo masks, arms curved in front of them like they were imitating a T-Rex, or danced past in delicate, feathered masquerade masks, or shook jester's bells or, somewhat worryingly, tried to head-butt other shoppers with unicorn horns. I even spotted two rather elderly but distinctly spry women throwing down some pretty impressive wrestling moves, and hoped the masks supplied stronger hip joints along with their other enchantments.

Not everyone was caught up in acting out their alter-egos, though. People still meandered about, picking at stall displays and sipping on takeaway cups of hot chocolate or mulled wine, their masks smudged with icing sugar from doughnuts, or dusted with scrapings of truffles from the fancy pasta place. I'd have wondered what the stallholders were making of it, the entire village caught up in mask mania, except every one of them I spotted now had a mask on too, finally fallen victim to the decorative infection.

And I still wasn't entirely sure if they were a distraction or an attack. Although, if Grace was working with Alaric, the reason was pretty clear, and also explained why witches had been the first to go down from the masks. That had been both a nice bit of diversion, and the main play. To prove she alone was strong enough to resist the masks, and convince Jackie to hand over the grimoire. Then she could save the town and establish herself as the most powerful witch in the area, holding not just the ancient spellbook, but all the deals that were bound to it. She'd own the valley, and those were only the deals I knew about. Ruiner had come from outside to make his, after all. The book could bind half the country, for all I knew. And working with Alaric made sense too — she could clear his debt once she had the grimoire, which would be all the motivation he needed.

But there was no point musing on it all now. We needed to move quickly, before any of us were recognised. I was already starting to regret the pink coat. It might be very unlike my usual blacks and greys, but it also made me feel like a walking strawberry. I pulled my hat down a little more firmly around my ears as we headed for Alaric's tent. Ariel had some counter-curse charms that she wanted to pick up on the way, although I wasn't sure how much good they'd do. We couldn't exactly dose everyone individually, but maybe there was some master mask Alaric was using to control everything that we could tackle. The counter-curse charms couldn't hurt, anyway, especially as we had nothing else to arm ourselves with, and no time to make a better plan.

"My lady!" someone shouted, pulling me out of a slightly morbid contemplation of just how unprepared we were to go up against someone who could charm an entire village.

"Oh, no," I muttered, and sped up as Mella looked around.

"I think he's talking to you," she said.

"My lady!" Ben shouted again, and I stopped reluctantly, turning to see him marching through the stalls with his shoulders back and his head up. James slouched along next to him, his movement muscular and languid all at once, steam drifting from the nostrils of the mask and making me wonder if they were doing something irreversible to our physiology. I hoped not. I checked my fingertips again, but so far my mask was dormant. No sparks, although I still caught glimpses of swirling shapes around others, shadowy suggestions of their alter-egos.

"My lady," Ben repeated as he stopped in front of us and swept me a bow. He nodded to the others. "Ladies."

Ariel chuckled, low and throaty. "You're a bit tasty."

I ignored her and snapped, "Ben, *stop it.*"

He blinked at me, eyes unfamiliar in the shadows of the helmet, then cleared his throat and said, "Sorry. Ah … it seems to come and go in waves. One minute I'm dying for a quest, the next for a cuppa." He sounded almost like himself again.

"I can give you a quest," Ariel said, crossing her arms across her chest. She'd found a long, deep purple coat that played up her cleavage very nicely.

"Focus," Starlight snapped, and Ariel gave her that lazy grin.

I looked at James. "How about you? Are you with us?"

James burped smoke or steam or whatever it was, then said in a rough voice, "I've got terrible indigestion. Am I actually breathing flame, or is it a placebo effect? Or, you know, the opposite?"

We all looked at each other dubiously, and Starlight patted James' shoulder. "Never mind. I'll make you something for it either way."

He tipped his dragon head at her gratefully.

"We need to get on," I said, and Mella nodded, holding her hand out to me, palm up. Three bees huddled together in it.

"They really are cold," she said. "But they don't want to leave me."

"Right," I said, not entirely sure what she expected me to do with that. "We'll hurry, then."

"Good," she said, apparently satisfied, and cooed at the bees.

"Get on with what?" Ben asked. "What're you planning?"

"Witchy stuff," Ariel said, before I could answer. "Cute little knights don't need details."

"I'd like details," he said, his back even straighter, if that were possible. "I don't want you getting hurt." He said it as a general statement, but kept his gaze on me, shadowed by the visor of the helmet.

"Witchy stuff," I agreed. "We'll be fine. But can you look for Ruiner? He's gone missing."

"I'll find him," James rumbled. "Can sniff out that complaining fish-breath anywhere."

"Great." I looked at them expectantly.

Ben drew himself up, resting one hand on the hilt of his insubstantial sword, and even as I watched it firmed up, becoming something of steel rather than fancy. When he spoke, his voice had gone from his usual easy tones to theatrical and booming. "My lady, my first duty is to protect you."

"It's to protect the *town*," I said. "With Theodore out of action, you two need to look out for everyone, don't you?"

"But my lady—"

"As *your lady*, I *order* you to protect the town," I said sharply.

He hesitated. "But surely by protecting you, as the town witch, I am fulfilling my duties to the town also?"

Dammit, he really did need a quest. And the last thing I needed was a knight and a dragon under Alaric's influence trailing us around. Which gave me an idea. "Alright. In that case, I need you to clear the market. I don't want anyone in masks near us. Got it?"

"But if I were to stay with you, I could protect you from any attackers."

"No. Clear the market, alright?"

"I must object—"

"Do it, Sir Galahad," Ariel said. "It's the only way of earning the lady's favours."

I scowled at her, but Ben took an immediate step back.

"I understand," he said. "A test!" He beckoned to James. "Come, vile beast. We will lay aside our enmity and do as the lady desires!" He spun and jogged towards the centre of the market, one hand still on his sword, and I could've sworn I heard armour clanking. James roared and ran after him, taking bounding leaps as if expecting to take flight at any moment.

We looked at each other, and Ariel grinned. "Better start thinking of favours."

"It was usually a handkerchief," Starlight said.

"Sure it was." Ariel headed into the market, Booper loping ahead of her. "You go on to Alaric's and scope it out. I'll get some charms and meet you there."

I took a deep breath, straightening my coat and looking at Starlight and Mella. "Ready?"

"The bees are *really* cold," Mella said, frowning. "I think I need to take them home."

"Can't you wait just a bit?" I asked. "Maybe the bees can fly around, like a diversion. That'd warm them up, right?"

She frowned at me. "They're not a *diversion*. They're highly evolved."

"Sure, but people'll be scared of them."

"People are ridiculous. I prefer bees." She marched off towards the centre of the market, and I reluctantly gave up on the idea of a giant bee swarm descending on the market and surrounding Alaric, possibly stinging him in delicate places, until he reversed the charms. It looked like I was going to be lucky to have Mella helping, let alone the bees, and I wasn't quite sure what she could do without them.

Starlight and I hurried after her, heading for the mask tent with our heads down, trying to avoid eye contact with anyone. The crowd had a ragged, breathless air, and as we skirted the edge of the central area, the music rolled over us, frantic with excitement. Dancers waved yellow and orange capes, and beach balls bounced through the tables like it was a concert, bringing cheers from the drinkers.

Ben and James had already reached the little makeshift stage, and we paused to watch as Ben commandeered the mic from the singer. He raised his free hand like a preacher and shouted, "The solstice comes!"

"*The solstice!*" the crowd roared back, and I had the same spinning, dislocated feeling as I'd had at the cocktail night, the sense of vast things moving out of sight, of holding a flame against an endless night, rendering me abruptly breathless.

"We light its way!" Ben yelled, and suddenly his sword was in his hand, the light running off it, liquid and glowing.

"*The solstice!*" The crowd shimmered and coalesced, less a bunch of people playing dress-up, more real, actual, queens and fauns and prowling plague doctors.

I blinked. "Starlight, do you see that?"

"We call back the sun!"

"*The solstice!*"

"Starlight?" I asked again, turning to her, but she was gone. I spun and spotted her offering a man a piece of fruit cake, her head on the side and her face rendered more angular and pointed than her usual gentle features. "Starlight!"

She ignored me, and I hesitated, torn between going after her and hurrying on to the mask tent. Alaric could realise something was up at any moment, especially with Ben doing his impromptu performance. Assuming it led to getting people out of the market, of course, which it didn't seem to be yet.

"Mella," I started, turning to the bee witch, then yelped and jumped back.

"*Yes?*" she asked. Or I suppose it was her asking, but the word seemed formed by the buzzing of a mass of bees, all of them clinging to the flowers on her mask. More blooms had sprouted, turning her into a walking florist's display, the stems and blossoms waving from her head and tumbling down her back.

"Are you okay?" I demanded.

"*The bees are cold.*"

"Right. Um … are you…" I trailed off as she turned and drifted away, taking the hum of the insects with her. People heading into the market's centre gave her a wide berth, and I didn't blame them. More and more bees flocked to her, and she was turning into an ambulatory, spherical hive. "Right," I said again, and hurried towards Starlight. She had one of the man's hands in hers, while he held the fruit cake in the other, looking faintly puzzled. Wings fluttered behind her, delicate yet muscular, and running with dragonfly colours.

"Come with me," she said to the man, who was wearing a mask that was laughing on one half, crying on the other.

"Eh, I'm not sure," he said, heaving a deep sigh. "It all feels so pointless."

"You have eaten of my food. You *must*. It's your payment."

The man burst out laughing, doubling over. "Payment!" he spluttered. "*Payment!*"

Starlight frowned at him, evidently not seeing the joke, and I didn't either, but I wasn't much in the mood for it anyway. I grabbed her arm. "Starlight, *stop it.*"

She turned to me, standing too close and touching my

hair. "Will you eat of my food? Will you dance with me forever?"

"No, and no. Starlight, come *on*. I need your help."

She ran her fingers down my cheek, leaving sparks behind. "I will show you such beauty. We'll drink the moonlight and spin stories from shooting stars and—"

I stepped back, my chest too tight. One person. I needed *one person* in all this utter, utter shambles of a predicament to help me. That was all I asked. Just one. "*Starlight!*"

She held a piece of cake out to me, eyes shining an unfamiliar, icy blue under her mask. "No cares. No sorrows. Only music and magic and joy."

I retreated, shaking my head, and she watched me, the cake still held out in front of her, then her gaze shifted to a woman in a bear mask. "Would you like some cake?" she asked, offering it to the bear-woman, who slapped it out of her hand.

My eyes were stinging, making me blink hard. I touched Jackie, and she snuffled my ear gently, a small consolation now everyone else was lost. The music was so loud it had physical weight, and I checked the crowd again. I couldn't see James, but Ben had left the little stage. His raised sword led the way out of the square, and everyone seemed to be following, their cries of *the solstice!* still ringing out among the tents. That was something. I was at least two witches down, and I could only assume Ariel was out, too. My theory that the masks' influence had been used up when they'd sent us into our comatose states was evidently not holding up. Although I felt fine so far.

"Jackie," I said, lifting her out of the folds of my hood. She hung in my hands, examining me with her ears twitching. "I'm not sprouting wings or plants, am I?"

She didn't respond, so I supposed I was okay. Although

I wouldn't have said no to the witchy power-up I'd felt when the mask had been doing its thing before. I just felt entirely normal, and entirely out of my depth. Which was also normal. I sighed, tucked Jackie back into my scarf, and straightened my back. I might not be a powered-up witch, but I also wasn't climbing the side of the sausage truck, like the skinny woman in a gecko mask I'd just spotted. So it could be worse.

THERE WAS no point detouring to Ariel's camper to see if she was still on mission. She'd either meet me at Alaric's tent, or she wouldn't. So I marched straight there, my stomach sick with fright and my knees faintly wobbly, feeling desperately alone. I needed other witches — *better witches* — and I needed the grimoire, and I needed Theodore or Isabella or even my ridiculous, annoying brother, but I didn't have any of those. I had me, and I had Jackie, and I had no idea as to how I was going tackle Alaric and Grace, but I had to try. It was that or simply watch the village fall to whatever they were planning.

Everyone was slowly filtering out of the market, following Ben, and I fell into step with them for long enough to see he was taking them all out onto the green, where James and the snow monster kids were piling wood onto the bonfire at the base of the solstice creature. I had the uneasy thought it was very handy for burning witches if Alaric clicked his fingers, but I should have time to get a head start before they reached me. It was something.

I circled back to the mask tent, keeping out of the main flow of the crowd, my head down. At least Alaric's stall wasn't on the main thoroughfare from the market centre to the green, so there weren't as many people to see me. It was one-way traffic with those who were around though, and I felt desperately obvious, walking in the opposite direction. But I made it safely to a candle shop diagonally opposite the mask tent and lingered just inside, looking for Ariel without much hope. There was no sign of the candle seller either, and the scent of the waxes was soft and warm in the chilled afternoon.

I was just thinking that I should try sneaking around the back of the tent to see if I could get in the same way Booper had led me out when Alaric appeared in the entrance, peering after the crowds.

"What's going on?" he asked, and Finn emerged next to him, looking tired and pale. My heart squeezed. If I could break the masks' spell, I might be able to help him get free, too.

"Do you want me to look?" Finn asked.

"No, I'll go," Alaric said, barely looking at him. "I won't be long."

"Sure," Finn said, and as Alaric swept away the other man stayed where he was, his gaze on the crowd and a troubled look on his face.

I waited until Alaric had vanished in the direction of the green before I stepped out of hiding and hurried towards Finn. "Hey!"

He jumped, stumbling a step back, then smiled as he saw me, relief painted across his features. "Morgan! I was wondering where you were." He caught my arm. "Come on, let's get out of sight."

I went with him, his fingers hot even through my sleeve. "Everyone's masks are … I don't know, activated or whatever."

He nodded. "It's the end game now. It'll all happen in…" He checked his watch. "Half an hour."

Half an hour. That had gone horribly fast. "Right. So what do we do?"

"I'll show you." He turned to lead the way deeper into the tent, and I followed, a shiver of unease running up my spine. Even if I was firmly in my body now, the memory of those endless corridors of tapestry, and the drifting, mournful ghost masks was close and cloying. My throat clicked, and Jackie nipped my ear. I pulled my head away from her, wincing.

Finn trekked through the narrow, mask-cluttered walls, and my chest grew tighter with every step, until I was struggling to breathe at all. I stopped, unbuttoning my coat in the heat, and he looked back at me.

"Are you alright?" he asked, his form indistinct in the shadowy confines of the tapestry hall. The mask stung my face, feeling as if it were trying to melt into my flesh, and Jackie nipped me again, harder this time, making my eyes swim. It pulled the world back into focus, though, and I frowned at Finn, looming ahead of me.

"You haven't told me what we're doing."

"Breaking the masks' hold." He caught my hand, towing me forward, and his skin felt so hot it seemed it would burn me. The mask flared in response, hungry and insistent, and Finn looked back at me, his expression impossible to read. I let myself get pulled along. I could barely stay upright, let alone resist.

"I think the mask's doing something," I managed.

"Then we have to hurry." He pulled me through a final wall, into a square chamber that held a sofa, a coffee table, and a little trolley with a kettle and a couple of mugs, a washing up bowl beneath it along with a few bottles of water. Dark spots wormed across my vision, the walls reaching out to smother me. It was too much like the corridors, too much like the room I'd woken up in. I needed to be anywhere but here. My legs gave out and I sank to my knees, plucking weakly at my coat as sweat trickled down my back. I managed to lift my head to look up at Finn, and he held my gaze as he picked up a familiar, bundled scarf. He unravelled it, and held the grimoire up, heavy and hungry.

"Time to give it up, little witch," he said, and smiled, sweet and shy and treacherous.

24. Oh, THAT voice

I STARED UP AT HIM, LEGS TOO WEAK TO TRY RISING. FINN, grabbing me in the tent the first time I ventured inside. Finn, warning me of Alaric and how dangerous he was. Telling me he was *up to something* with the masks. Finn, always just behind Alaric, holding the masks, *tending* to them. Finn, quiet and gentle and trapped, in need of saving. And wasn't that always my bloody problem? I closed my eyes as if that would shut out the reality.

"*Give the book up,*" he said, and the words thundered around inside my skull, ricocheting from one side to the other. I whimpered, and Jackie nipped my ear again, hard enough that she probably drew blood. It stopped the ricochet, though, and Finn frowned at me.

"I don't know what's going on with you," he said. "Everyone said you weren't even a witch, even *you* said that, but you keep wriggling out of things. How'd you break out of the void? You should've been as trapped as the others."

I pressed my hands to my thighs, not moving. They were shaking under my grip. *The void.* It had been more of a limbo, in my mind, but the mask-creatures were certainly void-ish, as far as those things go. My fingernails bit into my legs through my jeans, competing with my stinging ear for my attention, and I savoured both. I needed to feel something other than the endless, feverish heat that had been washing over me since I arrived at the tent.

Finn bent over to examine me, like an unfamiliar animal he'd discovered in a trap, and I glared back at him as fiercely as I could. Then he reached out, the movement too fast to even flinch from, and snatched Jackie off my shoulder. I hissed in protest as he took a bunch of my hair with her, tearing it out by the roots. He held Jackie aloft, a slow smile spreading across his face.

"*There* it is. I knew that bloody cat wasn't your actual familiar."

Ruiner. What had he done with Ruiner?

Still with Jackie in a tight grip, Finn pulled a carry case out from behind the sofa and deposited it in front of me. Inside was a bunch of motionless grey fur, and I reached out towards it. Finn pushed one of my shoulders casually, and I spilled sideways to the floor, unable to keep myself upright.

"Keep your hands to yourself," he said. "I've never heard of anyone having multiple familiars of different species, but I'm not risking it." He gave me that shy little grin. "Thanks for bringing everything to me. Very helpful of you."

I lay there looking at him holding the grimoire, at Jackie trapped and my brother unconscious, and tried to think of a way out.

I couldn't. I just wanted to scream at him not to hurt Jackie, and I was terrified about what he might have already done to Ruiner, if he'd thought my brother was the one in charge of the grimoire. And then there was whatever he was going to do to the town once he had all the deals in his hands, because I had no doubt he'd figured out exactly how to take the book over. He'd planned all of this too well not to. The only small glimmer of light was that, if he hadn't known Jackie was the grimoire's keeper, it meant he wasn't working with Grace. So there was only him to deal with, not a witch as well. For all the good it did me, sprawled helpless on the floor.

At least I was remaining consistent with my poor decision-making. I could have had Grace's help the whole the time, and I'd been too fixated on what a perfect witch she was, and how terrible I was in comparison, that I'd completely missed the best chance I had to fix things. That sort of poor judgement really did prove I had no business holding onto anything as precious as the grimoire, and now Jackie was going to pay for it with her life. All three of us were, in fact.

Finn opened the crate and tipped Ruiner out. He puddled bonelessly onto the rug, not even a whisker twitching, and a little cry escaped my throat. Finn glanced at me.

"This is what happens when you play with things you don't understand," he said, and dropped Jackie into the crate, slamming the door hurriedly as she threw herself at it. "Easy, ratty. You won't have to be in there for long. Unless you're going to hand the grimoire over? Be easier for everyone."

Jackie bared her teeth at him, hissing.

"Ah, well." He looked at me. "Guess we'll do it my way."

I licked my lips, and managed, "Why do you even want it?"

He looked startled. "The fact you're even asking that shows how little you know. That book's pure power. Even Norma never used it properly."

"And you can?"

"I can do a damn sight better than her."

"It's bound to me, though."

He nodded. "Sure. Unless you give it up. Or can't hold it anymore, for one reason or another." He spoke as if it was merely a formality, a docket to be signed, and my stomach flopped over again. "The familiar's always the problem. If they can be persuaded to pass the grimoire over, then job's a good 'un. If they can't … well, they can't just be bopped off. But there are ways."

I looked at Ruiner, my heart squeezing as I wondered what the *ways* entailed. My breath caught as I met his gaze. His head was turned away from Finn, his eyes narrowed, and he winked. I had no idea what that meant, except that he wasn't dead. And that was enough. We had a chance.

There was only one thing for it.

I burst into tears.

It was surprisingly easy, weariness and fear and the sheer frustration of not being able to *do* anything making my chest so tight and my eyes so hot I had the horrified thought I was going to have trouble stopping. "Oh *noooo*," I wailed. "Oh, you *caaaaan't!* But I thought you were so *niiice!*"

"Well, I *am*," Finn said. "It's just … necessity, you know? I can't go around being a *mask-seller* forever."

I rolled over, putting my back to him and wrapping my arms around myself. "I thought you were *the one!*"

"What?"

"A fortune teller told me! She *said!* She said I'd meet the love of my life here, and I thought it was you! You only had to ask, and I'd've given you the grimoire! You've ruined it *all!*"

"Wait, you'd have *given* it to me?"

"Of course," I sobbed, my back still to him, one hand

over my face and the other in my almost empty bag. "But now it's too late, and you're going to kill me, and Jackie, and it's all just so *awful!*"

He didn't say anything at first, and I thought I'd over-played it, or he really would rather kill us all than listen to me wail, but then his feet scuffed on the rug and he rested a hand on my side, warm and gentle. "We can fix this," he said, his voice quiet. "I don't want to hurt anyone, but I never thought you'd give me the book. It'd be better if you did, though. A forced transfer is always a bit iffy."

I gave it a couple more sobs for good measure — and also because I was having trouble getting them under control — and said, "But then what? Then I'll have *nothing,* not the book or you or *anything.*" Ugh, I was exhausting myself with my own whining.

"You could come with me," he said. "You've obviously got some power, otherwise the rat wouldn't have chosen you. We could work together."

"Really?" I whimpered, still curled on my side.

"Really." He rolled me towards him, the movement soft, and I threw myself into the motion, my phone clutched in my hand. I swung at his face, putting all my weight behind the blow, trying to slam it into his nose or teeth. I was still weak and wobbly though, the mask sapping my strength, and I couldn't move as fast as I needed to. Finn lurched back, swearing and pushing me away as he fell out of his crouch.

"You—" he started, sounding more irritated than enraged, but his next word was lost to a yelp as Ruiner went from motionless to full attack mode, tearing into Finn's cheeks with his ears back and his claws out, yowling his rage.

"*Ruiner!*" I yelled, and threw myself on top of Finn, still wielding the phone as if I could stab him with it, throwing wild punches anywhere I could reach. The mask's hold was slipping. I still wasn't as much myself as I had been when we'd arrived at the market, but my body was more under my control, and I landed one hard blow on Finn's chest, just missing his throat. I'd murder him with the damn phone if I had to.

Finn stopped trying to dislodge Ruiner and threw me off, forcefully enough to send me crashing painfully into the coffee table. He came to his feet and bolted, vanishing through the tapestries, and I scrambled to my knees, panting. Ruiner had jumped free as Finn got up, and now he staggered around to face me, and we stared at each other.

"About bloody time you showed up," he said, and sat down heavily.

I shuffled up to him on my knees. "Are you okay?"

"No. Can I point out once again what bad taste you have in men?"

"Fair," I said, and reached for the crate, fumbling the door open. Jackie scrambled out before I could help her, hissing at both of us.

"Easy," Ruiner said. "You'd still be in there if not for me."

She turned her sharp gaze on me, teeth bared, and I looked around in sudden panic. "He's still got the grimoire."

"Oh, sodding *hell*," Ruiner said, and as he did everything *shifted*. The room fell away. Mist rose from the floor. The walls flattened and narrowed, becoming nothing but a corridor, and we were plunged into near-darkness.

I was back in limbo. But at least this time I wasn't alone.

～

I was still kneeling on the new floor, and Jackie bumped into my fingers. At least, I hoped it was Jackie, and not some limbo-monster. I cupped my hands, and she clambered into them, then ran to my shoulder and burrowed into my hood.

"Ruiner?" I said quietly, my words dropping into the thick silence with an awful familiarity.

"Here." He brushed against me, making me shiver.

"Want a lift?"

"No." But I had to grab him anyway when he tried to scramble to my shoulder and slipped. He hissed.

"Okay?" I asked him.

"Still no. What the hell is this place?"

"I don't know. Finn called it the void. I was here before. Well, my body wasn't, but my consciousness was, I guess."

"How do we get out?"

"No idea. A ghost dog helped me last time."

"Oh, *fun.*"

I stood up, one hand out for balance, but I was less wobbly than I had been. The corridor stretched out in either direction, the mask spirits looming above us, and I wondered if Booper would come if I called. I supposed it was unlikely, given he'd mostly got me out so I could help his mistress, who was probably mounting a Viking raid outside. But I should be able to find my own way out. I'd just rolled through the wall last time, after all.

"Ready?" I said.

"Ready for what?" Ruiner asked, and I crouched down, prodding the tapestry. It didn't want to give, so I shuffled along a little further, trying to pull it up from the bottom, or find a seam. The cloth refused any attempt to make a way through, and I squat-walked to the opposite wall to try there.

"Morgs?" Ruiner said. "What're you doing?"

"I rolled underneath it last time," I said. "There was a gap."

"You better find it quick, then."

"Why?"

"Take a look."

I turned to look down the corridor. The mask creatures were massing to our left, dozens upon dozens of them filling the narrow space, stacked one on top of the other just as the masks themselves were on the walls outside, glaring at us from shadowy eyes. I almost thought I could hear the rustle of their skirts, a desiccated whisper.

"They're harmless," I said, my voice very nearly steady. "They just pass through you."

"You mean they did when you were having an out of body experience."

"Ah." My throat clicked as I swallowed.

"Yeah."

I turned away from the creatures, walking fast, not wanting to trip over the uneven ground, and Ruiner shifted on my shoulder so he could watch behind us.

"Faster," he said, and I picked up the pace. "Faster," he repeated, and I broke into a jog, never mind the uneven floor. My heart stuttered more than the pace warranted, and I gasped for breath, as if the air had suddenly grown too thin. Was there even air in here, now that I had a body? Voids didn't have air, did they? I sucked a lungful in, and Ruiner yowled, "*Faster, Morgan!*"

I launched into a full sprint, trying to look for gaps in the walls at the same time, because they had to be there, they *had* to, but between the shadows and my panicked flight I couldn't see anything but the mottled, featureless tapestry, hostile and bare. I tripped once, twice, but recovered myself and kept going, until I realised the corridor wasn't stretching on forever anymore. A wall? A junction? A way out? A—

"*Bollocks,*" I hissed, stumbling to a halt.

"Morgan, what're you *doing?*" Ruiner hissed, scrabbling on my shoulder as he turned to face forward again. "They're closer!"

"So are they," I said, nodding ahead of us.

Ruiner said something inventive, and we both stared at the wall of mask spirits advancing steadily from the opposite direction. I checked behind, and the others hadn't stopped. We were pinned between them, and I didn't like to think what was going to happen when they reached us. They'd seemed like nothing more than chilled air before, but Ruiner was right. I hadn't had a body. Suddenly those skirts looked less floaty and more suffocating, the masks themselves less mournful and more *hungry.*

I spun to the wall, running my hands over it, the fabric moving under my touch but refusing to part. I scrabbled for seams, for tears, for *anything*, but all I could feel was the weave, intricate and unyielding. I swung around. The creatures were closing in, barely a few paces from us, and I rushed to the opposite wall, pawing at it like a panicked hamster.

"*Morgan!*" Ruiner wailed.

"I'm trying!" I clawed the tapestry desperately, but it did me no more good than scratching a sofa might have. In a rush of utter frustration and panic I stepped back and yelled, "Bloody hell, we're *alive*, let us out, you overgrown sodding playpen!"

I don't know what I thought might happen — the tent collapsing in shame, perhaps — but nothing did. So much for Miss Edna's *just use your voice* advice. Before I could try anything else, Ruiner snarled in alarm, and something brushed my other shoulder. The touch was so cold it bit to my bones, and I yelled again, "*Let us out, dammit!*"

"Stop yelling and *do* something!" Ruiner yowled, and more frigid tentacles slid along my spine, feeling as though they could wrap around my heart. I lunged for the wall in a final, frantic panic, and as I did so a blade tore through it, slashing a great gouge in the cloth and nearly disembowelling me at the same time. I squawked, but as the blade withdrew, I grabbed the tear in both hands, shouted, "Don't stab me!" and dived head-first into the hallway beyond.

Ruiner gave a squall of alarm, tumbling from my shoulder, and I caught myself on my hands before I could headbutt the floor, then rolled as fast as I could, pulling my legs through the gap. The tear bulged, full of reaching, gauzy arms, all clutching hungrily for my feet, then the tapestry snapped back together so hard it was almost audible. The cloth was as smooth as if I'd never touched it, and the floating arms sheared off, flopping to the floor. They twitched a little, clutching weakly at the rugs.

I stared at my brother, still panting, but he wasn't looking at me. He had his ears back and his teeth bared, his tail puffed out to ridiculous dimensions as Booper licked his head with a ghostly tongue.

"*Get it off,*" he hissed, retreating towards me, and I blinked from Booper to Ariel, who stood over us with her legs planted wide under her purple coat, a hefty sword resting on her shoulder. The sharp, hungry sigils of her mask spilled down her neck to her chest, and I could see them blooming on her legs, too, where they were bare under the cocktail dress she was still wearing. Somewhere she'd found some feathers and stuck them in her hair, and she glared at me with dark, gleaming eyes.

"Hi?" I said, wondering if she'd cut me out of the tent

just for a little light beheading. She bared her teeth and unshouldered the sword, levelling it at me.

"Fealty or death," she declared, and Booper whined. She blinked, shifting slightly, then scowled, and took a step forward, setting the tip of the blade under my chin. "Fealty or death, witch."

Booper barked twice, and Ruiner said, "Seconded, mate."

Ariel hesitated again, shooting the talking cat a sideways look, and I lifted my head away from the sword, took a breath, and bellowed, *"Ariel of Darrowdale, put that thing down right now and listen to your dog!"*

She staggered back a step, almost dropping the sword, and Booper shoved his head under her free hand. She grabbed hold of him, somehow steadying herself on his insubstantial frame, and blinked at me. "Right. Yes. Didn't mean it."

"I know," I said, getting up and taking a couple of steps back, just in case she got stabby again. "Thanks for the rescue."

"Sure." She looked at Ruiner. "Did he…?"

"Hi," Ruiner said.

She stared at him, her hand tightening on the sword, then nodded. "The brother."

"How did you find me?" I asked hurriedly, because she was lifting the sword again. "Everyone seems to be pretty under the influence."

"Booper heard you," she said, her voice curt. "Plus, counter-curse. Sort of working." She held her hand out to me, palm up. A fresh tattoo rendered in a few clear, sharp lines bloomed on the inside of her wrist, still bubbled with a little blood and ink. "Not entirely holding, though."

"Right," I said. "Let's sort this, then." Although how

we were going to do that without the grimoire, I still didn't know. "Have you seen Grace?"

She shook her head jerkily. "No. I've got Starlight and Mella. You need to sort this out, witch. I'll set fire to the whole place if I don't get this damn mask off soon." She turned on her heel and marched off, giving voice to a roaring battle cry that set the masks on the walls clattering in her wake, and Ruiner and I stared at each other.

"You need one of those tatts," he said, then thought about it. "Or a sword. That would do, too."

I agreed, but what I had was an ability to shout like someone's mum, apparently, and that was going to have to do. I ran after Ariel, skirting the fading remnants of the mask creatures that were left on the floor. At least we were out of limbo. That was a start.

I'd expected the tent to be booby-trapped, perhaps, for the floor to give beneath us or the masks to launch a concerted attack as we passed, but whether Finn had been too confident Ruiner and I would never find our way out of limbo, or if the entire place was too cowed into submission by Ariel and her sword, nothing leaped out at us. I could feel empty eyes watching us pass, but no gaps yawned in the walls to swallow us, and Finn didn't come back to click his treacherous fingers and set our masks off. Ariel swung her sword irritably, slashing masks from the walls and occasionally cutting us a doorway as Booper led the way, and Ruiner and I stayed well back, just in case we had to make a run for it. She didn't turn on us, though, just stopped at a final wall while Booper panted up at her, his tail wagging softly through the closest tapestry. She jammed the sword into the ground, so it stood on its own, and beckoned me towards her. I went almost timidly, and she held her hand out.

I looked at it, then at her, eyebrows raised.

She clicked her fingers irritably, then grabbed my hand in hers, pulling me towards her. She shoved my sleeve back and slapped her other hand over my wrist, clamping down so tightly I gave a squeak of protest that spiralled rapidly into a highly unimpressive screech as pain bloomed under my skin.

"*Ariel!*" I yelped, trying to pull away, but she was alarmingly strong, holding me in place. Ruiner had already leaped from my shoulder, staring up at us with his ears back. "Help me!" I shouted at him, and he took one step forward before Booper slid in front of him. Traitor of a dog, I'd thought he *liked* me.

Then Ariel let me go with a grunt, and I snatched my hand back, examining it. My wrist bore a brand, red and raw, and even as I watched it congealed into sharp lines of scar tissue, darkening and deepening, forming the same shape as the one I'd seen on her wrist.

"What the hell," I started, then took a breath. "I thought that was a tattoo."

"Usually," she said. "No time for that, though."

"You could've warned me," I complained, blowing on the swollen skin. "I could've prepared a bit better."

She shrugged. "It's done now. Come on." She turned away and poked the tapestry, and it bellied obligingly where a tear had been slashed through it. She put her head through cautiously, then climbed out. I followed, shooting Ruiner a pointed look. A lot of help he'd been.

He just narrowed his eyes at me and hissed, "*Ghost dog slobber.*"

25. The solstice

OUTSIDE, THE MARKET HAD THE SAME POST-MASS-ALIEN-abduction feel as town had earlier, the stalls empty, no one moving among the tents, the only noise coming from ahead, on the green. Ben's call and response had stopped, and instead I could hear music almost drowned out by the stomp and clap of an entire town's worth of boots and hands. It rang in the chill air, and I almost thought I could feel it trembling through the ground and up into the pit of my stomach. The low light of the fading afternoon threw long, deep shadows over everything, deep contrast to the last of the golden sun.

Starlight and Mella were waiting outside, Starlight hopping from foot to foot and making whooshing noises on every exhale. Next to her, Mella was still more hive-shaped than human shaped, but when she said, "Finally!" it was with her own voice rather than that of the bees.

"Morgan!" Starlight danced up to me and grabbed me into a hug, still *whoosh*ing away. "You're alright!" she said between breaths.

"Yes — what're you doing?"

"Mindful"—*whoosh*—"breathing. Stops me"—*whoosh*—"fairy-ing out."

"Carry on, then," I said, and looked at the bees warily. "What's the plan?"

Ariel grunted. "That's your deal, witch."

I grabbed my not-entirely-useless-after-all phone and checked the time. Two forty-five. We were almost out of chances. Finn was running about somewhere with the grimoire, ready to click his fingers and set our masks off, tatts and mindful breathing or not. And I still had no idea if Grace was involved, or if she was just another magic-worker interested in the damn book.

"We have to stop Finn," I said aloud. "I don't think he can use the grimoire, but he doesn't need to when he's got the masks. He can turn the whole town against us, to make me and Jackie give it up."

"Then we hide you," Mella said. "The effect of the masks can't last forever. He'll be tapping their existing charms to support whatever magic he's doing. It's going to weaken as soon as the solstice passes."

"We don't know that," I said. "Maybe he'll extend it somehow, or lock the masks in permanently."

"But if he can't find you," Starlight started, and Ruiner interrupted.

"Then he can use the masks to start knocking people off until Morgs gives herself up. Because she will."

The other three witches looked at me, and I crossed my arms. "Well, *obviously* I would."

"Ugh," Ariel said. "*Morals.*"

I wasn't sure if it was the mask talking, or her general disposition, but she wasn't pointing the sword at me, so that was something.

"So we stop him," Starlight said, gasped a breath, and added, "I can steal him away for a thousand — no."

"No," I agreed. "Just concentrate on your breathing."

"Not a bad idea, though," Ruiner said, and I checked the time again, as if I might've gained some minutes somewhere. I hadn't, and everyone was still looking at me. How come they'd all had mask power-ups, and I was here being as useless and unwitchy as ever? I shouldn't have let Ariel put the counter-curse on me.

The counter-curse.

I looked at Ariel. "Can you cast the counter-curse over everyone? Like in a powder of something?"

She gave me a disgusted look. "*No.* It's not bloody fairy dust."

"I have fairy dust," Starlight said, then added, "No," and focused on her breathing again.

"Yes," Ruiner said, and snagged my jeans with his claws. "Use the masks."

"What? We're trying *not* to use the masks, Ruiner."

He huffed, ears twitching. "Warrior Queen there can go riding into battle, Hive Lady can send in her minions, and Starlight can dazzle them with ditziness, whatever. *Use it.*"

"My bees aren't *minions,*" Mella said.

I ignored her, looking at Ruiner. "Maximum disruption."

"Just like we used to," Ruiner said, with a lazy purr in his voice.

I frowned. "You mean like when I set the neighbour's dogs through the house to cover for *you* breaking one of Mum's Prince Albert commemorative plates?"

"I was thinking more the time I bribed a bunch of six-year-olds to break up your fourteenth birthday party before Mum made you all take part in a re-enactment of the coronation of Queen Sophia of Sweden."

Ugh. I'd actually managed to banish that from my

memory. Aloud, I just said, "Confuse everything enough to break up whatever solstice ritual's going on, and I go for Finn while he's trying to get a hold on everyone again."

"Yes. As soon as they're not doing solstice stuff, everyone'll be going dotty with the masks again, so it shouldn't be too hard."

"It's a thought."

"We're doing it," Ariel said, swinging her sword.

I didn't fancy disagreeing with her, and it wasn't like I had any better ideas, so I just looked towards the rising and falling rumble of voices, trying to see the crowd. They were hidden from here, but I could just glimpse the green through the tents. It was hardly living up to its name, with Petunia's idyllic snow blanketing it, and someone had abandoned a snow duck not far from the tents. I frowned, then pointed at it. "Can any of you work those?"

Ariel looked from it to me, not speaking, and Mella hummed softly. Finally, Starlight said, "Well, even I can, a bit. We sell the charms at the shop."

"We do?"

"Witch, you really are bad at this," Ariel said. "I'll do it. Come on. I'm going to get stabby on someone soon." She marched off without waiting for any more discussion, which I suppose was better than her getting stabby on one of us.

"Workers, not minions," Mella mumbled, but rolled her hand in an imperious gesture. The bees rose around her in a cloud, packed in tightly humming, threatening formation, and she headed for the green. Starlight and I looked at each other, and she bounced on her toes softly.

"I can dance with them a *little*, can't I?"

"Dance as much as you damn well want," Ruiner said, and she gave a little yelp of delight, then rushed after Mella.

"Come on, witch," Ruiner said.

"Do *not* start with that," I said, and he huffed kitty laughter. I didn't miss the stiffness in his gait as he led the way toward the green, though, and the sudden heat of my anger set sparks smouldering in the corner of my vision. I was going to need to be careful with that. A little, anyway.

THE WITCHES HAD VANISHED by the time we reached the last of the market stalls, keeping to the cover while I examined the crowd stomping and chanting around the solstice effigy and its persistent torch. They surged back and forth while the bonfire burned furiously at its base, stealing the glamour of the sinking sun and leaping high above the heads of the revellers, spitting green and blue sparks into the sky. The crowd twisted and surged, one way then the other, moving to a beat led by the relentless music but kept in the thud of their feet on the frozen ground and the sharp clap of their hands. I could feel the resonance of it in my chest, as if it was searching for my heartbeat, and I paused by the bench I'd collapsed on the night before, wondering if I should have a more detailed plan than *grab Finn and get the grimoire back*.

No one was looking my way, and I scrambled onto the bench to get a better view into the heart of the crowd, scanning it quickly, looking for Finn's tangled locks. *There.* I almost ducked as soon as I saw him, but he wasn't paying me any more attention than anyone else. He had the grimoire open, tipped towards the fire as he read, and Jackie hissed in my ear. I touched her back. There was no way she could see that far, but maybe she felt her book anyway.

"We're getting it back," I told her. "I promise." We just

had to get through the pack of princesses and lizard people and courtesans and jesters. And also a knight and a dragon, flanking Finn and gazing around with the half-contained belligerence of bouncers.

Given that, more of a plan would've been nice. What I had instead was Mella already walking straight into the crowd with her arms out to her sides, trailing bees in her own personal storm cloud. Starlight meanwhile was bopping people with a shiny plastic wand she must've swiped from a stall, and even as I watched, a large man in a chicken headdress grabbed it and tried to wrestle it off her. She smashed a piece of fruitcake into his face and they both started yelling, and the smooth rhythm of the crowd fractured as the bees' sonorous tune swamped the music. Someone shrieked, *"Murder hornets!"* and a shudder of fright washed across the green.

Finn looked around finally, scowling, and I jumped off the bench before he could spot me. Someone had abandoned an umbrella nearby, a hefty, old-fashioned black thing that would've passed Mary Poppins' exacting standards. I grabbed it and gave it a couple of experimental swings, then headed for the crowd, veering to the left to circle around them. I didn't want to get in the way of Starlight and Mella's distractions. Or get stung.

The steady, mesmerised sway of the revellers had already degenerated into something rather more shambolic, everyone going in a different direction and no one quite dancing to the same tune. A handful broke away, running back towards the market with their hands waving above their heads to fend off the bees, although I couldn't see any actually following them. I dodged my way around a lumbering, bear-headed person, and bumped straight into a tall, skinny man in an ornate, chequered mask with a hooked nose.

"Dance with me," he breathed, grabbing my waist and pulling me against him.

"*No,*" I said, trying to push him off, but he was surprisingly strong for all that his arms looked like pipe cleaners.

"Dance with me *forever,* my queen," he murmured, burying his face in my hair.

"*Off,*" I snapped, and whacked him in the shins with my umbrella.

"*Ow!* Oh, you—"

"My lady." Ben pulled me away, placing one hand on the man's chest and glaring at him. "Is this knave bothering you?"

"I'll knave you, pretty boy," the man started, and Ben twisted his hand into the man's coat, bunching it into a fist. "Hey! That's expensive!"

"I'm fine," I said, tugging on Ben's arm. "Leave him."

Ben hesitated for a moment, then released the man, shoving him away. "Keep away from her."

"With pleasure," the man spat and turned back into the crowd.

"Ben," I started, but he caught my upper arm in his and propelled me towards the fire. "Ben! What're you doing?"

"He needs to see you."

"Ben, *no.*" I tried to dig my heels in, to resist him, but he pushed me on relentlessly. "*Ben!* I thought you were my knight?"

That slowed him, but he didn't stop. "I have to…" He trailed off, and Ruiner came out of the tangle of dancers at a sprint, clawing his way up Ben's leg with his claws and teeth bared. Ben yelped, letting me go and staggering away, and I turned to shove my way back through the crowd.

I made it two paces before I ran into a broad, flannel-clad chest, and Finn grabbed both my arms, twisting my right so painfully I cried out and dropped the umbrella.

"That's better," he said. "Never know what tricks you might get up to with that." He wrenched my arm behind my back and turned to propel me towards the fire. "Let's sort this out, shall we? That bloody book's trickier than I thought."

The crowd parted before us, faces turning to watch me pass, the flames reflected in sequins and glass and shining, hungry eyes. Bees bombed and dived above us, but everyone seemed to have realised they weren't going to sting, so they were mostly being ignored. The dancing had all but stopped, and Finn raised the grimoire in his free hand and roared, "Well? *Dance the solstice in, damn you!*"

A pulse of power shuddered through the crowd, physical as a punch to the chest. A collective gasp jolted out of the revellers, and they ground into movement again like clockwork dolls. The music burst into life once more, and sparks spun in my vision. Pain flared from the brand in my wrist, fighting against the wash of auras and shadows and confusion, and I hissed, "*Jackie, go!*"

Jackie unwound herself from the shelter of my hood, bolted over my shoulder and down my back, and sank her teeth into Finn's wrist. He howled, his grip loosening, and I twisted away, wrenching my arm free. Jackie released her grip and scrambled up Finn's shoulders, hissing in fury, and as Finn tried frantically to shake her off, I tried to repeat my rugby tackle approach from the day before. I had no run up, though, so I just ended up with my arms wrapped around his waist as I pushed him backwards, staggering but not falling. He stopped trying to get rid of Jackie and grabbed my hair instead, wrenching my head back.

I cried out, trying to hold on even as tears started in my eyes, and Ruiner came out of the crowd with Ben in pursuit. My brother ran straight at Finn, and the mask-seller bellowed, "*Enough! Stop these muppets!*"

The dancers swung towards us, faceless behind the masks, and hands grabbed me from every direction. Finn released my hair as I was pulled away, and Ruiner yowled, caught somewhere out of my reach. I yelled his name, and he yowled again, wordless and terrified. I twisted and thrashed, but there were too many hands on me, and as soon as I broke free of one another took its place. The music redoubled, louder and faster, and the crowd surged to its frantic rhythm, the stomping and clapping restarting. The bonfire roared higher and higher, heat building furiously as I was dragged towards it, and above the chaos Finn's voice rose clear and commanding.

"*The solstice comes!*"

"*The solstice!*" the crowd roared, and I closed my eyes for a moment, watching shooting stars racing across my vision.

"*We call back the sun!*"

"*The solstice!*"

"*You bind yourselves to me!*"

"*The* — wait, what?" one of the men holding me said, and a ripple of unease passed through the crowd. Towards the edge, someone screamed, and the rhythm faltered.

"*We call back the sun!*" Finn shouted again.

"*The solstice!*" The shouts were almost back to the previous level.

"*You gift your wills to me!*"

A little hesitation, but still the majority roared back, "*The solstice!*" and the current of power twisted through not just the crowd but the very ground, as if Hollowbeck itself was turning its attention to the man at its heart. He'd walked past me, standing near the fire with the grimoire —

my grimoire — in one upraised hand, his voice ringing loud and victorious across the green.

"*You yield this town to me!*" Finn roared, and I gathered all the shooting stars in my vision, all the sparks I could feel pulsing in my fingertips, wrapped myself around them, and flung them outwards, hard. The hands holding me vanished, accompanied with a chorus of yelps. I'd been held up by my captors, and I stumbled to the ground, catching myself on my hands. I looked up to see Finn fling his free hand out at me in a *halt* gesture, but I was already moving too fast for whatever charm he was throwing about. I didn't bother being pretty about it, and sod any witchy stuff. I was so outmatched, the points board wasn't even in the same county. I just sprinted straight at him, snatching up one of the lumps of wood waiting by the fire as I passed, and slammed it straight into his knee.

Finn went down with a howl that was as much astonishment as it was pain. I didn't even bother shifting my grip on the wood as I brought it down again on his arm, the force of the blow shocking his hand open and sending the grimoire tumbling into the snow. He shrieked, and a woman in a wicker mask grabbed my arm, wrestling me for the wood. I let it go rather than fight, far too aware that the music was still playing and the majority of the crowd were still yelling, "*The solstice! The solstice!*" Someone else grabbed my other arm, and a third person clawed my back, snagging my scarf and just about strangling me as Jackie and Ruiner pelted past me across the snow, racing for the grimoire. Finn reached for it, trying to bat them away, and Jackie latched onto his fingers, biting down so hard I heard the crunch. He shrieked, jerking away, and Ruiner went for his face as Jackie ran back to the grimoire, crouching on it with her teeth bared.

Finn threw Ruiner off and staggered to his feet,

sneering at me. "You're too late," he shouted, having to raise his voice to be heard over the roar of the crowd. "It's here. My influence holds, my——" He stopped as I grinned, and nodded over his shoulder. He whirled, just in time to meet the charge of a snow spider.

It barrelled over him, and I yelled, "*Halt!*" without thinking about it. The spider stopped so suddenly two of its stick legs shattered, and it dropped its heavy body with an audible splat, trapping Finn to the ground. His legs were still visible, kicking violently, and I looked around, held firmly in place by half a dozen hands. People were still chanting, the music was still playing, dancers were still shimmying. Nothing had *changed.*

"*The solstice!*" the crowd shouted. "*The solstice!*"

"Oh, sodding hell," I whispered, and threw myself forward, my captors still staring at the spider. I twisted out of their grip, stomped on the foot of the man who still had my arm, and ripped myself free.

"*The solstice! The solstice!*"

I dropped to my knees next to the spider, not thinking about if it would work or *how* it could work, simply *doing,* because that was all I could do. I clicked my fingers at it. "Up."

"*The solstice! The solstice!*"

The spider upped, and Finn sat upright with a strangled gasp. His head snapped towards me and he snarled, "*You——*"

"Finn of I-don't-even-bloody-care, sit down, shut up, and *behave yourself!*" I bellowed.

He stared at me, mouth hanging open, then started laughing.

"*The solstice! The solstice!*"

"You *idiot,*" he started, and my hand closed on the grimoire as Ruiner and Jackie nudged it into my hand.

"You absolute *womble*," I replied, and slammed the spine of the book straight down on his bracelet. It connected with an explosion that I felt more in my gut than in the world, the metal shattering under the blow. The grimoire *inhaled*, sucking something from him, or the bracelet, or the night, or the solstice itself, and it shocked up my arms and into my chest. It set fire to every nerve and synapse in me, and a bolt of *something* went through the world, shuddering the ground and setting the crowd staggering. The bonfire roared, the flames exploding so high that the crowd cringed away, screams ringing out across the green.

Then it was gone, and the music stopped, and silence spread around us. Finn lay motionless before me, a felled tree in the forest of the crowd. The bracelet had never been a shackle. It had been a talisman, just like the ones Grace had told me about. Luckily, because it had been a total guess on my part.

"The solstice?" someone said, and my mask flopped to my knees and slid to the ground. I gasped, the air cold on my face, and all around the fire people looked about a bit awkwardly, stragglers in the nightclub when the lights go up. Some masks slid off on their own, others stayed in place but their creeping tendrils and growths retreated, leaving them as nothing more than papier-mâché and ribbon, with their wearers poking them gingerly. I dropped the grimoire into my lap, a bone-deep shaking starting up from my belly. Jackie clambered into my lap and I cuddled her close, too exhausted to even try getting up just yet, and Ruiner slumped down next to me, leaning against my knee.

We sat there together watching the crowd ebb and flow, as the world ticked softly out of the darkest hours and on towards the light, and we waited for what would come next.

26. Dressed & unimpressed

THE CLOSING BALL HAD TO BE RESCHEDULED.

Of course it did. Half the town still weren't quite ready to make eye contact with each other, and there was a lot of unexplained bruising to cover up. Plus Isabella had broken half the glasses in the hall by pushing them off tables, and while I'm sure she could've worked around that, there was also the small matter of getting Theodore dosed up on enough of Tania's special cocktails that his fangs stopped popping out every time he saw an exposed neckline. Plus the caterers had all been too busy line dancing their souls away to actually prepare anything for the party.

The market packed up and left, the stallholders muttering about Hollowbeck getting as problematic as Darrowdale, but I think they'd done pretty well out of it, for all that. People had spent pretty wildly under the influence of the masks, and I had a sneaking suspicion that half the reason the stalls cleared out so quickly was to make sure no one had the chance to try returning things.

Now, the afternoon before the ball, only Alaric remained, his tent packed down to half its size and looking a little lost and forlorn, mired alone in the muddy green. He'd emerged from its walls shaky and disoriented two days after the solstice, having been imprisoned by Finn in the strange, haunted corridors of its limbo. Now he and I were sitting at a little table just outside the tent, huddled down in our coats and drinking black tea spiked with little blue flowers. The weather had been grey and soggy since the market showdown, Petunia too exhausted to do anything but let the more characteristic Lakes climate reassert itself, but she was obviously back on form now. The sun was bright and luminous on the thin limbs of the trees, and the sky was a polished, fragile blue. Ruiner sat in his own chair, watching Alaric with narrowed eyes. The mask-keeper looked tired, and older than he had when we'd first met, his shoulders slumped as he offered me a biscuit.

I took one, and, because we'd already dispensed with the small talk, said, "So you had no idea what Finn was doing?"

Alaric shook his head firmly. "He arrived as a boy. He always had a talent for looking after the masks, and became so good at choosing them I let him do it. I even let him handle the cleansing charms we use when we first receive them, to prepare them for the new owner." He hesitated, then added, "He created Isabella's ghost mask, and the one for Theodore, and I didn't question it. He really was excellent at them."

"But you were still the face of *Unmasked*."

"People expect it. They like a little showiness."

"And you honestly didn't think he'd mind that you got all the credit?" I asked.

"He always said he hated that side of things. I did keep saying he should branch out on his own, but he seemed so happy to remain in the shadows. I suppose I see why now."

I looked at Ruiner, who twitched his ears. I could see him just about choking on the effort of not yelling, *how did you not see any of this?* but we were back to pretending he couldn't talk. Even though Alaric had heard him when we'd been tussling with Theodore, I'd claimed it had been a voice from the crowd when he mentioned it. Alaric, to his credit, hadn't argued. He seemed quite keen to be helpful, and given how the rumours about the grimoire seemed to have travelled, we didn't need news of my cat-shaped brother out there too.

I tried to be a little more diplomatic than Ruiner. "So you really never suspected he was up to anything? I mean, he had a whole haunted dimension in your tent."

Alaric looked at his tea, sighed, and pulled a flask from his coat. He offered it to me, and I waved it away. He shrugged and splashed a generous measure into his own mug. "He was a lot more skilled than I realised. I don't even know where he got that sort of knowledge, but anyone who can create pocket dimensions under my very nose can certainly get some secret study done." He gulped his tea, shuddered, and added, "I've always been rather perceptive, though. He must've thrown some blindness charms at me."

Ruiner snorted, and Alaric gave him an offended look. I rather agreed with my brother, though. Alaric's confidence might be dented, but it certainly hadn't taken any permanent damage.

"Do you have any idea how he knew about my grimoire?" I asked. I'd have preferred to ask Finn that, of course, but things had got a little confused after our little moment of calm. The effigy had collapsed into the fire, sending an explosion of embers and shattered, burning wood into the already unnerved crowd. There had been a mild panic, not helped by Mella's bees getting very agitated and stinging half a dozen people who'd swatted their fellows. Ben had rushed to find me and pull me to my feet, apologising profusely the whole time, and the snow spider had promptly attacked him for his temerity (admittedly, I think that might've been my fault — he'd surprised me). Isabella had rushed across the green in a panic, frantic to know what had been happening and why Theodore was locked in a storeroom yelling about carrots, and in the midst of it all, Finn had simply vanished. Evidently Theodore was in no danger of being replaced by any of us.

"Norma's spell book's the stuff of legend," Alaric said now. "Magic-workers respected her or hated her for it, or both. When she died, everyone was interested in who it might go to." He gave me a smile that was almost the same flashily charming one as before he'd been through limbo. "It's not like you're a celebrity, exactly, but everyone knows there's a new town witch in Hollowbeck. And there have been rumours you're … not exactly as expected."

"That doesn't surprise me," I said with a sigh.

"Handy with a large stick, though. Or a heavy book. So I heard."

"It's something." I took a sip of tea and looked at Ruiner, who tipped his head. "What about Grace? Someone overheard her talking to you about the masks. We thought you were in it together." She'd stalked out of Alaric's tent after the solstice with her perfect hair disheveled, a large bruise on one cheek, and half a dozen masks hung around her neck like trophies, yelling for Finn to show himself. That was about the point we'd discovered he was missing, and I could still feel Grace's look of absolute disgust. It hadn't exactly been directed at me, but it had definitely *included* me.

Alaric sighed. "Well, I wasn't *in* anything, as you know."

"Sure, we know that *now*, but you did look suspicious. You were still handing out masks even after telling me you were worried about them."

"It's my duty," he protested. "I have to make sure everyone has a mask before the solstice, to protect them."

"And Grace?" I asked.

"Oh, yes. She was concerned about the masks' effects and came to talk to me about it. I was dismissive, I fear. I still believed it was just a glitch, some fluctuation in the magic I could manage. I thought they were *my* masks. I didn't realise how thoroughly they'd been corrupted." He lifted his hands, then dropped them in his lap. "I am sorry, Morgan. This was so nearly a disaster."

I examined him. It was hard to believe he'd known *nothing* about what Finn was up to, but then the man had the most spectacularly enormous ego. It could well have never occurred to him that his apprentice was far more powerful than he was.

"So what did happen with you and Finn?"

"Yes, well. He came to tell me he'd discovered the problem with the masks, and I followed him back to the tent. Then he simply shoved me straight into his *void*, as he called it." He shook his head. "I had a terrible time finding my way out. The only reason the mask-creatures didn't swallow me whole was because I was able to tame them. They still recognised me at some level."

I thought about Grace and her necklace of masks, and wondered why the other three witches had seen such different things. Maybe because they hadn't physically been in the tent. But there was no point asking Alaric. It had been Finn's void. "What're you going to do about the masks now?" I asked aloud.

He grimaced. "I can't use them. Who knows what charms still linger, and cleansing them all would be nearly impossible. Plus, they rather give me the creeps now." He shuddered, looking back into the tent. Most of the tapestries had been pulled down, turning it into a cavernous, deeply shadowed space, and the masks were all packed away somewhere, but I still didn't know how he could stand being in the place. I'd be seeing the mask spirits rushing out to greet me everywhere. "I think I may move into fashion. Elegant attire for the modern witch." He pulled his shoulders back and adjusted his scarf. "I have been told my style is rather singular."

Ruiner spluttered, and I drained my mug, getting up. "Well, that does sound better. Just keep your mannequins in line."

He laughed, a little weakly, and I shook hands with him a final time then walked off, my hands in the pockets of my familiar old puffer jacket, Jackie on my shoulder and Ruiner padding next me. I had a ball to get ready for, like it or not, and first I needed to check on Starlight. She was fine after the mask incident, other than a violent aversion to fruitcake, but she was so excited about the ball she'd set fire to her own skirt yesterday while making tinctures. I didn't fancy her burning the shop down. We'd had enough action.

Everyone was fine, really. Theodore apologised every time I saw him, of course, and kept asking me if I'd like to punish him until Ruiner had overheard and almost expired from his own laughter. Then I'd had to explain to an ancient, deeply chivalrous vampire that there were certain connotations to his question he might not be familiar with. So now he was apologising for that, too, although Isabella had arched an eyebrow at me and said, "We have had that conversation before." Ruiner had such a laughing fit over that I'd had to point out to him that cats evidently weren't designed for it.

Grace was very pointedly not talking to me. I'd seen her once at the Witching Hour since the solstice, and she'd just nodded at me tightly before walking away. I felt like a terrible disappointment as both a witch and a sort-of friend, but she *had* been far too comfortable with Jackie and the grimoire, and I still thought the gap in the shop's ceiling had been worked wider. She'd been the only person who might've known where to look for it. But, true. We might've avoided a lot of chaos if I'd just let her help me.

Booper had given me a ghostly lick, and Ariel had generously said she wouldn't charge me for any of the charms I used, then had flicked me a packet reading, *For The Dreams.* "In case the masks come back," she said, then climbed into her van and drove off, Booper with his head out the closed window watching me.

Otherwise, Hollowbeck was back to normal. Mella kept dropping off honey as thanks for getting her out of the void, so now we had a ridiculous stash of it, but we were using it to trade at the shop and Mystic Munchies, as well as at Bewitching Brews. James and Ben seemed to have not only overcome their knight versus dragon issues, but to now be inseparable, and also unbearable. They had in-jokes. It was desperately annoying.

"Alright?" Ruiner asked as we pushed through the door into the shop.

"Only me," I called automatically over the jangle of the bell, and looked at my brother. "Sure. Village saved. No one lost to the masks. Still got the grimoire. No new, creepy notes since Darrowdale. What more could we want?"

"A de-cursing spell from your Viking witch?" he suggested, looking down at himself.

"Funny, you didn't ask about that before," I said, but he wasn't the only one. I hadn't even thought of it. The issue of my brother being a cat was starting to be one of my less pressing concerns.

"I forgot," Ruiner admitted, and we were both still considering that when we walked into the kitchen, the scent of thyme and lemon with a lick of moonshine rolling out to greet us.

Starlight was already pulling her coat on. "We can't stop," she said. "It's time!"

"Time for what?" I demanded.

"Your *dress*," she said, and towed me back out the door before I could protest.

I should've taken that drink from Alaric. *Dresses.*

I HAD TO ADMIT, though, that the dress was nice. More than nice. It was *spectacular*. It was even more flattering than my borrowed one had looked when I put the mask on, a creation of deep grey-blues and silver accents. I'd never have chosen the colours myself, as they were still more blue than grey, but they did make my eyes look at least as bright as my brother's, and there were things going on with my cleavage that I was certain put a whole new meaning to the seamstress having a magic touch. I wasn't as convinced by the strappy shoes, but I hadn't had to walk far, because Ben had picked me and Ruiner up. I met him at the door and he stared at me for a moment too long, while I touched my hair and wondered if I should've done something better than stick a couple of pins in it.

Then he swept a bow and said, "My lady, your chariot awaits."

"Do you want me to hit you with the grimoire?" I demanded. "Because I will."

"Go on," Ruiner said. "I'll pay good money to see that."

"You don't have any money," Ben said, and offered me his arm. I looked at him suspiciously. "Snow," he said, pointing at the path. "No lingering mask effects, I promise."

And he seemed to be telling the truth. He still held my hand as we walked from the car to the hall, but he didn't call me *my lady* again, and he didn't offer to defend my honour when Theodore met us at the door, grabbed my hands and declared me to be ravishing. So that was something.

If I'd thought the cocktail party was Hollowbeck putting on a show, it was nothing compared to the ball. Drifting orbs of light packed the high ceiling of the hall, shedding a mellow golden glow, and lanterns flickered in sconces on the walls. There were no food tables or hot chocolate stands, and instead servers glided through the crowd, handing out champagne and sparkling cordials and local beer and spirits. Trays of canapés were offered around too, and while there were low tables and deep chairs for non-dancers to observe the festivities, they were mostly empty. Instead, the floor was packed, people dancing in groups and couples and alone, doing everything from elegant foxtrots to high energy modern dance to little head nods or some really interesting interpretive dances that looked in danger of causing twisted ankles at least.

Ben snagged a couple of glasses of champagne off a passing tray and handed me one, then nodded at the floor. "Shall we?"

"What, *dance?*"

"Why not?" he said, giving me that familiar, dimpled smile, and I found myself smiling back. If masks brought out your true self, an annoyingly chivalrous knight wasn't the worst thing.

I threw back the drink on the theory that it could only help my dancing skills, and said, "Sure. It's a ball, right?"

"Right," he said, and set both our glasses on the nearest table, then pulled me onto the floor. His hands were warm, one on my waist and the other still clasping mine, and when I stopped trying to figure out where I was meant to put my feet and just let the music wash over me, we were suddenly moving in smooth synchrony. This close I could smell the easy, familiar scent of him, books and old ink and thoughtful silence, full of their own magic, and neither of us spoke for a little, the chatter of other dancers filling the quiet.

When he finally spoke, his voice was low, and I was surprised to find we'd drifted closer to each other. He held my hand against his chest as he talked, and I could feel the vibrations of his voice. "I'm sorry about the whole knight thing," he said. "I seem to find a new way to mess things up every time, don't I?"

"You don't mess anything up," I said. "I'm the one who trusted the wrong person and almost got Hollowbeck swallowed by the solstice or whatever."

"At least you didn't dose me with calming tea," he said, giving me a half smile. His lips were very full, and close enough I could smell toothpaste on his breath still.

"You may have redeemed yourself. You know, fighting zombie hordes and tackling rogue vampires."

"I think that was more you."

"Maybe," I admitted. "But you do keep charging in to help."

"I always will," he said, his voice quiet, and I looked up, meeting his eyes finally. They were warm and deeply brown, and he didn't need saving or looking after. He was perfectly capable of doing some saving and looking after himself, and he had done, right from the first time we met. He tightened his fingers on mine, and heat bloomed in my belly, breath catching in my throat. The moment stretched, the world retreating until it was just us under the soft light of the winter ball, caught together between magic and mystery, and I could have stayed there forever, waiting to see what came next.

Except what came next was my nightmare bloody brother bounding across the floor and sliding to a stop at our feet.

"Morgan! *Morgan!*"

Ben squeezed his eyes shut, dropping his head with a slight grin as I looked at Ruiner.

"*What?*" I hissed. "What do you *want?*"

"You have to come. *Now.*"

"Ruiner, I swear to every cat god—"

"Morgan, I'm serious." And he was, damn him, his blue eyes wide and his whiskers quivering.

My belly did an altogether less pleasant flop than it had a moment ago. "What is it? Masks?"

"No." He backed up a step, then yowled as someone stood on his tail.

"Oh! Sorry!" Petunia said, looking down at Ruiner. Her dress had frogs embroidered along the hem. "Didn't see you there, Ruiner."

I picked my brother up, for once neither of us complaining about the forced proximity, and said, "Where?"

"Table by the windows," he said, his voice low, and I looked at Ben. He just nodded and fell into step with me as we walked towards the windows we'd sat at before the solstice. Before the masks and the chaos and the unconscious witches.

I saw Starlight first, her dress a glittering blue-green strapless number that turned her into a rather stunning mermaid. She was standing at the end of one of the tall tables, twisting her fingers together so tightly I could see it making hard lines in her shoulders. Isabella stood next to her, hands clasped to her chest as she spoke earnestly to someone I couldn't quite see. Theodore was there too, bending to greet whoever it was, doing his elegant if orange-tinted near-kiss of the hand. My stomach wouldn't stop churning.

"Ruiner," I whispered, stopping at the edge of the dancers. "Who is it?"

He didn't answer, his body coiled with tension in my arms.

Isabella looked around and clapped her hands in delight. "Here she is!"

Starlight turned to look at me, her eyes wide, and Theodore stepped aside. A small, neatly-dressed woman, sporting carefully curled blonde hair and a string of pearls, perched on one of the stools. She smiled at me and pressed one hand to her chest, her familiar blue eyes crinkling at the corners.

"Oh, *hello*, sweetheart," she said. "There you are!"

"*Mum?*" I said, clutching Ruiner so tightly he gave a little cough of alarm. "How— what — how did you get here?"

"I got your invitation," she said, and lifted a desperately familiar envelope from the table. Heavy white card, full of threat and promise. "Just in time for Christmas, too. It's so sweet of you!"

Ruiner and I looked at each other, and I was sure my pupils were just as wide as his.

"Drink?" Starlight suggested, her voice a little too high,

and I somehow made my legs move towards the table, aware of Ben trailing behind us.

"Please," I managed, and hugged my mother with one arm, still clinging to Ruiner with the other. He made no move to get down.

"Where's your brother?" Mum asked, looking around expectantly. "I haven't seen him for *so* long. I miss my baby boy!"

Starlight passed me a glass of wine, then offered me a shot glass as well, her eyebrows raised, but I shook my head. I can't say I wasn't tempted, though. Mum drove me to spirits at the best of times. And my brother being a cat was definitely not going to be the best of times in her book. I looked down at him and he shrugged, his eyes still wide.

"And who's this?" Mum asked, extending a hand towards Ben. He took it awkwardly. "You must tell me all about this place. Morgan never tells me *anything!*"

I gulped half my wine in one swallow, before she could see.

"I'm Ben," he said. "Welcome to Hollowbeck."

We all stood there for a moment, no one saying anything more, until Mum said, "Where *is* Rainier? And why are you carrying a cat around, Morgan? I know cat lady was always an option for you, but you don't have to be so obvious about it."

I finished my glass and took the shot from Starlight after all. This was going to make the mask fiasco look positively genteel.

The End

About the Authors

Amelia Ash likes the quiet life. During the week, she works at the tea shop inside a friend's quirky bookstore, and on the weekends, she combs the countryside for estate sales, collecting trinkets, old furniture, and, in one memorable case, a clawfoot tub. In the evenings, she likes to binge-watch HGTV with her life companion: a barely domesticated cat named Lizard, who she suspects might possibly kill her if he could double his size and operate a can opener.

~

Kim M. Watt: Originally from New Zealand, Kim (she/her) now inhabits a slightly different world, crafting funny fantasies and off-beat cosy (or cozy) mysteries in which tea-drinking dragons collude with resourceful ladies of a certain age, baking-obsessed reapers run petting cafes for baby ghouls, and cats always bring the snark.

Kim's stories blend myth and reality in small and spectacular ways, where the Apocalypse comes on a Vespa, and the healing magic of tea and a really good lemon drizzle cake is unquestioned. But most of all, her tales are about friendship, loyalty, and people of all species looking out for one another. Because these, above all things, are magic.